Only A Kiss

MARY BALOGH

piatkus

PIATKUS

First published in the US in 2015 by Signet Eclipse,
an imprint of New American Library,
a division of Penguin Group (USA) LLC
First published in Great Britain in 2015 by Piatkus

1 3 5 7 9 10 8 6 4 2

A CIP catalogue record for this book
is available from the British Library.

ISBN 978-0-349-40533-9

Printed and bound in Great Britain by
CPI Group (UK) Ltd, Croydon, CR0 4YY

Papers used by Piatkus are from well-managed forests
and other responsible sources.

MIX
Paper from
responsible sources
FSC
www.fsc.org   FSC® C104740

Piatkus
An imprint of
Little, Brown Book Group
Carmelite House
50 Victoria Embankment
London EC4Y 0DZ

An Hachette UK Company
www.hachette.co.uk

www.piatkus.co.uk

Only
A Kiss

I

*P*ercival William Henry Hayes, Earl of Hardford, Viscount Barclay, was hugely, massively, colossally bored. All of which descriptors were basically the same thing, of course, but really he was bored to the marrow of his bones. He was almost too bored to heave himself out of his chair in order to refill his glass at the sideboard across the room. No, he *was* too bored. Or perhaps just too drunk. Maybe he had even gone as far as drinking the ocean dry.

He was celebrating his thirtieth birthday, or at least he had been celebrating it. He suspected that by now it was well past midnight, which fact would mean that his birthday was over and done with, as were his careless, riotous, useless twenties.

He was lounging in his favorite soft leather chair to one side of the hearth in the library of his town house, he was pleased to observe, but he was not alone, as he really ought to be at this time of night, whatever the devil time that was. Through the fog of his inebriation he seemed to recall that there had been celebrations at White's Club with a satisfyingly largish band of cronies, considering the fact that it was very early in February and not at all a fashionable time to be in London.

The noise level, he remembered, had escalated to the point at which several of the older members had frowned in stern disapproval—old fogies and fossils, the lot of them—and the inscrutable waiters had begun to show cracks of strain and indecision. How did one chuck out a band of drunken gentlemen, some of them of noble birth, without giving permanent offense to them and to all their family members to the third and fourth generation past and future? But how did one *not* do the chucking when inaction would incur the wrath of the equally nobly born fogies?

Some amicable solution must have been found, however, for here he was in his own home with a small and faithful band of comrades. The others must have taken themselves off to other revelries, or perhaps merely to their beds.

"Sid." He turned his head on the back of the chair without taking the risk of raising it. "In your considered opinion, have I drunk the ocean dry tonight? It would be surprising if I had not. Did not someone dare me?"

The Honorable Sidney Welby was gazing into the fire—or what had been the fire before they had let it burn down without shoveling on more coal or summoning a servant to do it for them. His brow furrowed in thought before he delivered his answer. "Couldn't be done, Perce," he said. "Replenished consh—constantly by rivers and streams and all that. Brooks and rills. Fills up as fast as it empties out."

"And it gets rained upon too, cuz," Cyril Eldridge added helpfully, "just as the land does. It only *feels* as if you had drunk it dry. If it *is* dry, though, it having not rained lately, we all had a part in draining it. My head is going to feel at least three times its usual size tomorrow morning, and dash it all but I have a strong suspicion I agreed to escort m'sisters to the library or some such thing, and as you know, Percy, m'mother won't allow them to go out with just a maid for company. They always insist upon leaving at the very crack of dawn too, lest someone else arrive before them and carry off all the books worth reading. Which is not a large number, in my considered opinion. And what are they all doing in town this early, anyway? Beth is not making her come-out until after Easter, and she cannot need *that* many clothes. Can she? But what does a brother know? Nothing whatsoever if you listen to m'sisters."

Cyril was one of Percy's many cousins. There were twelve of them on the paternal side of the family, the sons and daughters of his father's four sisters, and twenty-three of them at last count on his mother's side, though he seemed to remember her mentioning that Aunt Doris, her youngest sister, was in a delicate way again for about the twelfth time. Her offspring accounted for a large proportion of those twenty-three, soon to be twenty-four. All of the cousins were amiable. All of them loved him, and he loved them all, as well as all the uncles and aunts, of course. Never had there been a closer-knit, more loving family than his, on both sides. He was, Percy reflected with deep gloom, the most fortunate of mortals.

"The bet, Perce," Arnold Biggs, Viscount Marwood, added, "was that you could drink Jonesey into a coma before midnight—no mean feat. He slid under the table at ten to twelve. It was his snoring that finally made us decide that it was time to leave White's. It was downright distracting."

"And so it was." Percy yawned hugely. That was one mystery solved. He raised his glass, remembered that it was empty, and set it down with a clunk on the table beside him. "Devil take it but life has become a crashing bore."

"You will feel better tomorrow after the shock of turning thirty today has waned," Arnold said. "Or do I mean today and yesterday? Yes, I do. The small hand of the clock on your mantel points to three, and I believe it. The sun is not shining, however, so it must be the middle of the night. Though at this time of the year it is *always* the middle of the night."

"What do you have to be bored about, Percy?" Cyril asked, sounding aggrieved. "You have everything a man could ask for. *Everything.*"

Percy turned his mind to a contemplation of his many blessings. Cyril was quite right. There was no denying it. In addition to the aforementioned loving extended family, he had grown up with two parents who adored him as their only son—their only *child* as it had turned out, though they had apparently made a valiant effort to populate the nursery with brothers and sisters for him. They had lavished everything upon him that he could possibly want or need, and they had had the means with which to do it in style.

His paternal great-grandfather, as the younger son of an earl and only the spare of his generation instead of the heir, had launched out into genteel trade and amassed something of a fortune. His son, Percy's grandfather, had made it into a *vast* fortune and had further enhanced it when he married a wealthy, frugal woman, who reputedly had counted every penny they spent. Percy's father had inherited the whole lot except for the more-than-generous dowries bestowed upon his four sisters upon their marriages. And then he had doubled and tripled his wealth through shrewd investments, and he in his turn had married a woman who had brought a healthy dowry with her.

After his father's death three years ago, Percy had become so wealthy that it would have taken half the remainder of his life just to count all the pennies his grandmother had so carefully guarded. Or even the pounds for that matter. *And* there was Castleford House, the large and prosperous home and estate in Derbyshire that his grandfather had bought, reputedly with a wad of banknotes, to demonstrate his consequence to the world.

Percy had looks too. There was no point in being over-modest about the matter. Even if his glass lied or his perception of what he saw in that glass was off, there was the fact that he turned admiring, sometimes envious, heads wherever he went—both male and female. He was, as a number of people had informed him, the quint-essential tall, dark, handsome male. He enjoyed good health and always had, knock on wood—he raised his hand and did just that with the knuckles of his right hand, banging on the table beside him and setting the empty glass and Sid to jumping. And he had all his teeth, all of them decently white and in good order.

He had brains. After being educated at home by three tutors because his parents could not bear to send him away to school, he had gone up to Oxford to study the classics and had come down three years later having achieved a double first degree in Latin and Ancient Greek. He had friends and connections. Men of all ages seemed to like him, and women ... Well, women did too, which was fortunate, as he liked them. He liked to charm them and compliment them and turn pages of music for them and dance with them and take them walking and driving. He liked to flirt with them. If they were widows and willing, he liked to sleep with them. And he had developed an expertise in avoiding all of the matrimonial traps that were laid for him at every turn.

He had had a number of mistresses—though he had none at the moment—all of them exquisitely lovely and marvelously skilled, all of them expensive actresses or courtesans much coveted by his peers.

He was strong and fit and athletic. He enjoyed riding and boxing and fencing and shooting, at all of which he excelled and all of which had left him somehow restless lately. He had taken on more than his fair share of challenges and dares over the years, the more reckless and dangerous the better. He had raced his curricle to Brighton on three separate occasions, once in both directions, and taken the ribbons of a heavily laden stagecoach on the Great North Road after bribing the coachman ... and sprung the horses. He had crossed half of Mayfair entirely upon rooftops and occasionally the empty air between them, having been challenged to accomplish the feat without touching the ground or making use of any conveyance that touched the ground. He had crossed almost every bridge across the River Thames within the vicinity of London—from underneath. He had strolled through some of the most notoriously cutthroat rookeries of London in full evening finery with no weapon more deadly than a cane—*not* a sword cane. He had got an exhilarating fistfight against three assailants out of that last exploit after his cane snapped in two, and one great black eye in addition to murder done to his finery, much to the barely contained grief of his valet.

He had dealt with irate brothers and brothers-in-law and fathers, always unjustly, because he was always careful not to compromise virtuous ladies or raise expectations he had no intention of fulfilling. Occasionally those confrontations had resulted in fisticuffs too, usually with the brothers. Brothers, in his experience, tended to be more hotheaded than fathers. He had fought one duel with a husband who had not liked the way Percy smiled at his wife. Percy had not even spoken with her or danced with her. He had smiled because she was pretty and was smiling at him. What was he to have done? *Scowled* at her? The husband had shot first on the appointed morning, missing the side of Percy's head by a quarter of a mile. Percy had shot back, missing the husband's left ear by two feet—he had intended it to be one foot, but at the last moment had erred on the side of caution.

And, if all that were not enough blessing for one man, he had the title. Titles. Plural. The old Earl of Hardford, also Viscount Barclay, had been a sort of relative of Percy's, courtesy of that great-great-grandfather of his. There had been a family quarrel and estrangement involving the sons of that ancestor, and the senior branch, which bore the title and was ensconced in a godforsaken place near the toe of Cornwall, had been ignored by the younger branch ever after. The most recent earl of that older branch had had a son and heir, apparently, but for some unfathomable reason, since there was no other son to act as a spare, that son had gone off to Portugal as a military officer to fight against old Boney's armies and had got himself killed for his pains.

All the drama of such a family catastrophe had been lost upon the junior branch, which had been blissfully unaware of it. But it had all come to light when the old earl turned up his toes a year almost to the day after Percy's father died, and it turned out that Percy was the sole heir to the titles and the crumbling heap in Cornwall. At least, he assumed it was probably crumbling, since the estate there certainly did not appear to be generating any vast income. Percy had taken the title—he had had no choice really, and actually it had rather tickled his fancy, at least at first, to be addressed as Hardford or, better still, as *my lord* instead of as plain Mr. Percival Hayes. He had accepted the title and ignored the rest—well, most of the rest.

He had been admitted to the House of Lords with due pomp and ceremony, and had delivered his maiden speech on one memorable afternoon after a great deal of writing and rewriting and rehearsing and rerehearsing and second and third and forty-third thoughts and nights of vivid dreams that had bordered upon nightmare. He had sat down at the end of it to polite applause and the relief of knowing that never again did he have to speak a word in the House unless he chose to do so. He had actually so chosen on a number of occasions without losing a wink of sleep.

He was on hailing terms with the king and all the royal dukes, and had been more sought after than ever socially. He had already patronized the best tailors and boot makers and haberdashers and barbers and such, but he was bowed and scraped to at a wholly elevated level after he became *m'lord*. He had always been popular with them all, since he was that rarity among gentlemen of the *ton*—a man who paid his bills regularly. He still did, to their evident astonishment. He spent the spring months in London for the parliamentary session and the Season, and the summer months on his own estate or at one of the spas, and the autumn and winter months at home or at one of the various house parties to which he was always being invited, shooting, fishing, hunting according to whichever was most in season, and socializing. The only reason he was in London at the start of February this year was that he had imagined the sort of thirtieth birthday party his mother would want to organize for him at Castleford. And how did one say no to the mother one loved? One did not, of course. One retreated to town instead like a naughty schoolboy hiding out from the consequences of some prank.

Yes. To summarize. He was the most fortunate man on earth. There was not a cloud in his sky and never really had been. It was one vast, cloudless, blue expanse of bliss up there. A brooding, wounded, darkly compelling hero type he was *not*. He had never done anything to brood over or anything truly heroic, which was a bit sad, really. The heroic part, that was.

Every man ought to be a hero at least once in his life.

"Yes, everything," he agreed with a sigh, referring to what his cousin had said a few moments ago. "I do have it all, Cyril. And that, dash it all, is the trouble. A man who has everything has nothing left to live for."

One of his worthy tutors would have rapped him sharply over the knuckles with his ever-present cane for ending a sentence with a preposition.

"Philosh—philosophophy at three o'clock in the morning?" Sidney said, lurching to his feet in order to cross to the sideboard. "I should go home before you tie our brains in a knot, Perce. We celebrated your birthday in style at White's. We should then have trotted home to bed. How did we get here?"

"In a hackney carriage," Arnold reminded him. "Or

did you mean *why,* Sid? Because we were about to get kicked out and Jonesey was snoring and you suggested we come here and Percy voiced no protest and we all thought it was the brightest idea you had had in a year or longer."

"I remember now," Sidney said as he filled his glass.

"How can you be bored, Percy, when you admit to having everything?" Cyril asked, sounding downright rattled now. "It seems dashed ungrateful to me."

"It *is* ungrateful," Percy agreed. "But I am mightily bored anyway. I may be reduced to running down to Hardford Hall. The wilds of Cornwall, no less. It would at least be something I have never done before."

Now what had put *that* idea into his head?

"In February?" Arnold grimaced. "Don't make any rash decisions until April, Perce. There will be more people in town by then, and the urge to run off somewhere else will vanish without a trace."

"April is two months away," Percy said.

"Hardford Hall!" Cyril said in some revulsion. "The place is in the back of beyond, is it not? There will be no action for you there, Percy. Nothing but sheep and empty moors, I can promise you. And wind and rain and sea. It would take you a week just to get there."

Percy raised his eyebrows. "Only if I were to ride a lame horse," he said. "I do not possess any lame horses, Cyril. I'll have all the cobwebs swept out of the rafters in the house when I get there, shall I, and invite you all down for a big party?"

"You are not *sherious,* are you, Perce?" Sidney asked without even correcting himself.

Was he? Percy gave the matter some thought, admittedly fuzzily. The Session and the Season would swing

into action as soon as Easter was done with, and apart
from a few new faces and a few inevitable changes in
fashion to ensure that everyone kept trotting off to tailors and modistes, there would be absolutely nothing
new to revive his spirits. He was getting a bit old for all
the dares and capers that had kept him amused through
most of his twenties. If he went home to Derbyshire instead of staying here, his mother would as like as not
decide to organize a *belated* birthday party in his honor,
heaven help him. He might attempt to involve himself in
estate business if he went there, he supposed, but he
would soon find himself, as usual, being regarded with
pained tolerance by his very competent steward. The
man quite intimidated him. He seemed a bit like an extension of those three worthy tutors of Percy's boyhood.

Why *not* go to Cornwall? Perhaps the best answer to
boredom was not to try running *from* it, but rather to
dash *toward* it, to do all in one's power to make it even
worse. Now there was a thought. Perhaps he ought not
to try thinking when he was inebriated, though. Certainly it was not wise to try planning while the rational
mind was in such an impaired condition. Or to talk about
his plans with men who would expect him to turn them
into action just because that was what he always did. He
might very well want to change his mind when morning
and sobriety came. No, better make that *afternoon*.

"Why would I not be serious?" he asked of no one in
particular. "I have owned the place for two years but
have never seen it. I ought to put in an appearance
sooner rather than later—or in this case, later rather
than sooner. Lord of the manor and all that. Going there
will pass some time, at least until things liven up a bit in
London. Perhaps after a week or two I will be happy to

dash back here, counting my blessings with every passing mile. Or—who knows? Perhaps I will fall in love with the place and remain there forever and ever, amen. Perhaps I will be happy to be Hardford of Hardford Hall. It does not have much of a ring to it, though, does it? You would think the original earl would have had the imagination to think up a better name for the heap, would you not? Heap Hall, perhaps? Hardford of Heap Hall?"

Lord, he was drunk.

Three pairs of eyes were regarding him with varying degrees of incredulity. The owners of those eyes were all also looking slightly disheveled and generally the worse for wear.

"If you will all excuse me," Percy said, pushing himself abruptly to his feet and discovering that at least he was not falling-over drunk. "I had better write to someone at Hardford and warn them to start sweeping cobwebs. The housekeeper, if there is one. The butler, if there is one. The steward, if . . . Yes, by Jove, there *is* one of those. He sends me a five-line report in microscopic handwriting regularly every month. I will write to him. Warn him to purchase a large broom and find someone who knows how to use it."

He yawned until his jaws cracked and stayed on his feet until he had seen his friends on their way through the front door and down the steps into the square beyond. He watched to make sure they all remained on their pins and found their way *out* of the square.

He sat down to write his letter before his purpose cooled, and then another to his mother to explain where he was going. She would worry about him if he simply disappeared off the face of the earth. He left both missives on the tray in the hall to be sent off in the morning and dragged himself upstairs to bed. His valet was waiting for him in his dressing room, despite having been told that he need not do so. The man enjoyed being a martyr.

"I am drunk, Watkins," Percy announced, "and I am thirty years old. I have everything, as my cousin has just reminded me, and I am so bored that getting out of bed in the mornings is starting to seem a pointless effort, for I just have to get back into it the next night. Tomorrow— or, rather, today—you may pack for the country. We are off to Cornwall. To Hardford Hall. The earl's seat. I am the earl."

"Yes, m'lord," Watkins said, the aloof dignity of his expression unchanging. He probably would have said the same and *looked* the same if Percy had announced that they were off to South America to undertake an excursion up the River Amazon in search of headhunters. *Were* there headhunters on the Amazon?

No matter. He was off to the toe of Cornwall. He must be mad. At the very least. Perhaps sobriety would bring a return of sanity.

Tomorrow.

Or did he mean later today? Yes, he did. He had just said as much to Watkins.

2

Imogen Hayes, Lady Barclay, was on her way home to Hardford Hall from the village of Porthdare two miles away. Usually she rode the distance or drove herself in the gig, but today she had decided she needed exercise. She had walked down to the village along the side of the road, but she had chosen to take the cliff path on the return. It would add an extra half mile or so to the distance, and the climb up from the river valley in which the village was situated was considerably steeper than the more gradual slope of the road. But she actually enjoyed the pull on her leg muscles and the unobstructed views out over the sea to her right and back behind her to the lower village with its fishermen's cottages clustered about the estuary and the boats bobbing on its waters.

She enjoyed the mournful cry of the seagulls, which weaved and dipped both above and below her. She loved the wildness of the gorse bushes that grew in profusion all around her. The wind was cold and cut into her even though it was at her back, but she loved the wild sound and the salt smell of it and the deepened sense of solitude it brought. She held on to the edges of her winter cloak with gloved hands. Her nose and her cheeks were probably scarlet and shining like beacons.

She had been visiting her friend Tilly Wenzel, whom she had not seen since before Christmas, which she had spent along with January at her brother's house, her childhood home, twenty miles to the northeast. There had been a new niece to admire, as well as three nephews to fuss over. She had enjoyed those weeks, but she was unaccustomed to noise and bustle and the incessant obligation to be sociable. She was used to living alone, though she had never allowed herself to be a hermit.

Mr. Wenzel, Tilly's brother, had offered to convey her home, pointing out that the return journey was all uphill, and rather steeply uphill in parts. She had declined, using as an excuse that she really ought to call in upon elderly Mrs. Park, who was confined to her house since she had recently fallen and badly bruised her hip. Making that call, of course, had meant sitting for all of forty minutes, listening to every grisly detail of the mishap. But elderly people were sometimes lonely, Imogen understood, and forty minutes of her time was not any really great sacrifice. And if she had allowed Mr. Wenzel to drive her home, he would have reminisced as he always did about his boyhood days with Dicky, Imogen's late husband, and then he would have edged his way into the usual awkward gallantries to *her*.

Imogen stopped to catch her breath when she was above the valley and the cliff path leveled off a bit along the plateau above it. It still sloped gradually upward in the direction of the stone wall that surrounded the park about Hardford Hall on three sides—the cliffs and the sea formed the fourth side. She turned to look downward while the wind whipped at the brim of her bonnet and fairly snatched her breath away. Her fingers tingled inside her gloves. Gray sky stretched overhead, and the gray, foam-flecked sea stretched below. Gray rocky cliffs fell steeply from just beyond the edge of the path. Grayness was everywhere. Even her cloak was gray.

For a moment her mood threatened to follow suit. But she shook her head firmly and continued on her way. She would *not* give in to depression. It was a battle she often fought, and she had not lost yet.

Besides, there was the annual visit to Penderris Hall, thirty-five miles away on the eastern side of Cornwall, to look forward to next month, really quite soon now. It was owned by George Crabbe, Duke of Stanbrook, a second cousin of her mother's and one of her dearest friends in this world—one of six such friends. Together, the seven of them formed the self-styled Survivors' Club. They had once spent three years together at Penderris, all of them suffering the effects of various wounds sustained during the Napoleonic Wars, though not all those wounds had been physical. Her own had not been. Her husband had been killed while in captivity and under torture in Portugal, and she had been there and witnessed his suffering. She had been released from captivity after his death, actually returned to the regiment with full pomp and courtesy by a French colonel under a flag of truce. But she had not been spared.

After the three years at Penderris, they had gone their separate ways, the seven of them, except George, of course, who had already been at home. But they had agreed to gather again each year for three weeks in the early spring. Last year they had gone to Middlebury Park in Gloucestershire, which was Vincent, Viscount

Darleigh's home, because his wife had just delivered their first child and he was unwilling to leave either of them. This year, for the fifth such reunion, they were going back to Penderris. But those weeks, wherever they were spent, were by far Imogen's favorite of the whole year. She always hated to leave, though she never showed the others quite how much. She loved them totally and unconditionally, those six men. There was no sexual component to her love, attractive as they all were, without exception. She had met them at a time when the idea of such attraction was out of the question. So instead she had grown to adore them. They were her friends, her comrades. Her brothers, her very heart and soul.

She brushed a tear from one cheek with an impatient hand as she walked on. Just a few more weeks to wait . . .

She climbed over the stile that separated the public path from its private continuation within the park. There it forked into two branches, and by sheer habit she took the one to the right, the one that led to her house rather than to the main hall. It was the dower house in the southwest corner of the park, close to the cliffs but in a dip of land and sheltered from the worst of the winds by high, jutting rocks that more than half surrounded it, like a horseshoe. She had asked if she might live there after she came back from those three years at Penderris. She had been fond of Dicky's father, the Earl of Hardford, indolent though he was, and very fond of Aunt Lavinia, his spinster sister, who had lived at Hardford all her life. But Imogen had been unable to face the prospect of living in the hall with them.

Her father-in-law had not been at all happy with her request. The dower house had been neglected for a long time, he had protested, and was barely habitable. But there was nothing wrong with it as far as Imogen could see that a good scrub and airing would not put right, though even then the roof had not been at its best. It was only after the earl was all out of excuses and gave in to her pleadings that Imogen learned the true reason for his reluctance. The cellar at the dower house had been in regular use as a storage place for smuggled goods. The earl was partial to his French brandy and presumably was kept well supplied at a very low cost, or perhaps no cost at all, by a gang of smugglers grateful to him for allowing their operations in the area.

It had been upsetting to discover that her father-in-law was still involved in that clandestine, sometimes vicious business, just as he had been when Dicky was still at home. His involvement had been a bone of serious contention between father and son and a large factor in her husband's decision to join the military rather than stay and wage war against his own father.

The earl had agreed to empty out the cellar of any remaining contraband and to have the door leading into it from the outside sealed up. He had had the lock on the front door changed and all the keys to the new one given to Imogen. He had even voluntarily assured her that he would put an end to the smuggling trade on the particular stretch of the coast that bordered the Hardford estate, though Imogen had never put much faith in his word. She had never made any mention of smuggling to anyone afterward, on the theory that what she did not know would not hurt her. It was a bit of a morally weak attitude to have, but . . . Well, she did not think much about it.

She had moved into the dower house and had been happy there ever since, or as happy as she ever could be, anyway.

She stopped now at the garden gate and looked upward. But no, no miracle had happened since yesterday. The house was still roofless.

The roof had been leaking as long as Imogen had lived in the house, but last year so many pails had had to be set out to catch the drips when it rained that moving about upstairs had begun to resemble an obstacle course. Clearly, sporadic patching would no longer suffice. The whole roof needed to be replaced, and she had fully intended to have the job done in the spring. During one particularly dreadful storm in December, however, a large portion of the roof had been ripped off despite the sheltered position of the house, and she had had no choice but to make arrangements to have the job done at the very worst time of the year. Fortunately there was a roofer in the village of Meirion, six miles upriver. He had promised to have the new roof in place before she returned from her brother's, and the weather had cooperated. January had been unusually dry.

When she had returned just a week ago, however, it was to the discovery that the work had not even begun. The roofer, when confronted, had explained that he had been waiting for her to come back so that he would know exactly what she wanted—apparently *a new roof* had not been clear enough. His workers were supposed to be here this week, but so far they had been conspicuous in their absence. She was going to have to send one of the grooms with another letter of complaint.

It was very frustrating, for she had been forced to move into Hardford Hall until the job was done. It was no particular hardship, she kept telling herself. At least she had somewhere to go. And she had always loved Aunt Lavinia. During the first year following her brother's death, however, it had occurred to Aunt Lavinia that for sheer gentility's sake she ought to have a female companion. The lady she had chosen was Mrs. Ferby, Cousin Adelaide, an elderly widow, who was fond of explaining in her deep, penetrating voice to anyone who had no choice but to listen that she had been married for seven months when she was seventeen, had been widowed before she turned eighteen, and thus made a fortunate escape from the slavery of matrimony.

For years after her bereavement, Cousin Adelaide had paid supposedly short visits to her hapless relatives, since she had been left poorly provided for, and she had stayed until someone else in the family could be prevailed upon to invite her to pay a short visit elsewhere. Aunt Lavinia had voluntarily invited her to come and live indefinitely at Hardford, and Cousin Adelaide had arrived promptly and settled in. Aunt Lavinia had collected one more stray. She collected them as other people might collect seashells or snuffboxes.

No, it was no great hardship to be forced to stay at the main house, Imogen told herself with a sigh as she turned away from the depressing sight of her roofless house. Except that now, *soon,* being there was going to become a lot worse, for the Earl of Hardford was coming to Hardford Hall.

That roofer deserved to be horsewhipped.

The new earl was coming for an indeterminate length of time. His title was really not so very new, though. He had been in possession of it since the death of Imogen's father-in-law two years ago, but he had neither written at the time nor put in an appearance since nor shown any other interest in his inheritance. There had been no letter of condolence to Aunt Lavinia, no anything. It had been easy to forget all about him, in fact, to pretend he did not exist, to hope that *he* had forgotten all about *them*.

They knew nothing about him, strange as it seemed. He might be any age from ten to ninety, though ninety seemed unlikely and so did ten, since the letter that had been delivered to Hardford's steward this morning had apparently been written by the earl himself. Imogen had seen it. It had been scrawled in a rather untidy, though unmistakably adult, hand, and it had been brief. It had informed Mr. Ratchett that his lordship intended to wander down to the tip of Cornwall since he had nothing much else to do for the moment and that he would be obliged if he could find Hardford Hall in reasonably habitable condition. And in possession of a broom.

It was an extraordinary letter. Imogen suspected that the man who had penned it, presumably the earl himself since it bore his signature in the same hand as the letter itself, was drunk when he wrote it.

It was not a reassuring prospect.

In possession of a broom?

They did not know if he was married or single, if he was coming alone or with a wife and ten children, if he would be willing to share the hall with three female relatives or would expect them to take themselves off to the dower house, roof or no roof. They did not know if he was amiable or crotchety, fat or thin, handsome or ugly. Or a drunkard. But he was coming. *Wandering* suggested a slow progress. They almost certainly had a week to prepare for his arrival, probably longer.

Wandering down to the tip of Cornwall, indeed. In February.

Nothing much else to do for the moment, indeed.

Whatever sort of man *was* he?

And what did a broom have to do with anything?

Imogen made her way toward the main house with lagging steps despite the cold. Poor Aunt Lavinia had been in a flutter when Imogen left earlier. So had Mrs. Attlee, the housekeeper, and Mrs. Evans, the cook. Cousin Adelaide, quite unruffled and firmly ensconced in her usual chair by the drawing room fire, had been firmly declaring that hell would freeze over before she would get excited about the impending arrival of a mere *man*. Though that man was unwittingly providing her with a home at that very moment. Imogen had decided it was a good time to walk to the village to pay a call upon Tilly.

But she could delay her return no longer. Oh, how she longed for the solitude of the dower house.

One of the grooms was leading a horse in the direction of the stables, she could see as she approached across the lawn. It was an unfamiliar horse, a magnificent chestnut that she would certainly have recognized if it had belonged to any of their neighbors.

Who . . . ?

Perhaps . . .

But no, it was far too soon. Perhaps it was another messenger he had sent on ahead. But . . . on *that* splendid mount? She approached the front doors with a sense of foreboding. She opened one of them and stepped inside.

The butler was there, looking his usual impassive self. And a strange gentleman was there too.

Imogen's first impression of him was of an almost overwhelming masculine energy. He was tall and well formed. He was dressed for riding in a long drab coat with at least a dozen shoulder capes and in black leather boots that looked supple and expensive despite the layer of dust with which they were coated. He wore a tall hat and tan leather gloves. In one hand he held a riding crop. His hair, she could see, was very dark, his eyes very blue. And he was absolutely, knee-weakeningly handsome.

Her second impression, following hard upon the heels of the first, was that he thought a great deal of himself and a small deal of everyone else. He looked both impatient and insufferably arrogant. He turned, looked at her, looked pointedly at the door behind her, which she had shut, and looked back at her with raised, perfectly arched eyebrows.

"And who the devil might *you* be?" he asked.

It had been a long and tedious—not to mention cold—journey, most of which Percy had undertaken on horseback. His groom was driving his racing curricle, and somewhere behind them both, in the traveling carriage, came a stoically sulking Watkins, surrounded by so many trunks and bags and cases, both inside and outside the vehicle, that its gleaming splendor must be all but lost upon the potentially admiring lesser mortals it passed on its journey. Watkins would not like that. But he was already sulking—stoically—because he had wanted to add a baggage coach, *not* in order to spread the load between the coach and the carriage, but in order to double it. Percy had refused.

They were going to be here for a week or two at the longest, for the love of God. It had felt, riding through Devon and then Cornwall, that he was leaving civilization behind and forging a path into the wilderness. The scenery was rugged and bleak, the ever-present sea a uniform gray to match the sky. Did the sun never shine in this part of the world? But was not Cornwall reputed to be *warmer* than the rest of England? He did not believe it for a moment.

By the time Hardford hove into sight, Percy was more than just bored. He was irritated. With himself. What in thunder had possessed him? The answer was obvious, of course. Liquor had possessed him. Next year he would find a different way to celebrate his birthday. He would pull up a chair to the fire at home, wrap a woolen shawl about his shoulders, prop his slippered feet upon the hearth, set his cup of tea laced with milk beside him, and read Homer—in Greek. Ah, and add in a tasseled nightcap for his head.

Hardford Hall had been built within sight of the sea, a fact that was hardly surprising. Where else could one build in Cornwall? The front-facing rooms, especially those on the uppermost story, would have a panoramic and much-prized view over the vast deep—if those rooms were habitable, that was, and what he was seeing was not just an empty facade hiding rubble. All the evidence of his eyes suggested that it was *not* a heap, though. The hall was a solid, gray stone, Palladian sort of structure, more mansion than manor, and though there was ivy on the walls, it looked as though it had been kept under control by some human hand or hands. The house had been built on a slight upward slope, presumably so that it would look impressive. But it was also sheltered from behind and partially on each side within the arms of a rock face and trees and what were probably colorful rock gardens during the summer. Its positioning thus probably saved it from being blown away by the prevailing winds and set down somewhere in Devon or Somerset. The wind did seem to be an ever-present feature of this particular corner of Merry England.

There were rugged sea cliffs well within sight, but at least the house was not teetering off the edge of them. It was some considerable distance back, in fact. And as far as he could see, the house was surrounded by a walled park, which, like the ivy, appeared to have been kept in decent order. Someone had scythed the grass before the onset of winter and trimmed the trees. There were flower beds empty of flowers, of course, but also empty of weeds. It looked as if a line of gorse bushes, instead of a wall, separated the park from the cliffs.

By the time he rode onto the terrace of the house and waited for the groom who had poked his head out of the stable block to come and lead his horse away, Percy was hopeful that at least he would not have to spend the rest of the day sweeping cobwebs. Perhaps he really did have a staff here — a housekeeper, anyway. There was, after all, at least one groom outside, and there must be a gardener or two. Perhaps — dare he hope? — there was even a cook. Perhaps there was even a *fire* in one of the rooms. And indeed, a glance upward toward the roof revealed the welcome sight of a line of smoke emerging from one of the chimneys.

He strode up the steps to the front doors. The steps had been swept recently, he could see, and the brass knocker had been polished. He disdained to make use of it, however, but turned both doorknobs, discovered that the doors were unlocked, and stepped inside — to a pleasingly proportioned hall with black-and-white tiles underfoot, heavy old furniture of dark wood that had been polished to a shine standing about, and old portraits hanging on the walls in their heavy frames, the most prominent of which depicted a gentleman in a large white wig, heavily embroidered skirted coat, knee breeches with white stockings, and shoes with rosettes and high red heels. Four sleek hunting dogs were arranged in a pleasing tableau about him.

A former earl, he assumed. Perhaps one of his own ancestors?

For a few moments the hall remained empty, and Percy found himself feeling relief that the place was obviously clean and well cared for, but also mystification as to why. For whom exactly were house and grounds being kept? Who the devil was living here?

An elderly gray-haired man creaked into the hall from the nether regions. He might as well have had the word *butler* tattooed across his forehead. He could not possibly be anything else. But—a butler for an empty house?

"I am Hardford," Percy said curtly, tapping his riding crop against the side of his boot.

"My lord," the butler said, inclining his body forward two inches or so and creaking alarmingly as he did. Corsets? Or just creaky old bones?

"And you are?" Percy made an impatient circling motion with his free hand.

"Crutchley, my lord."

Ah, a man of few words. And then a mangy-looking tabby cat darted into the hall, stopped in its tracks, arched its back, growled at Percy as though it had mistaken itself for a dog, and darted out again.

If there was one thing Percy abhorred, or rather one class of things, it was cats.

And then one of the front doors opened and closed behind his back, and he turned to see who had had the effrontery to enter the house by the main entrance without so much as a token rap upon the knocker.

It was a woman. She was youngish, though she was

not a girl. She was clad in a gray cloak and bonnet, perhaps so that she would blend into invisibility in the outdoors. She was tall and slim, though it was impossible with the cloak to know if there were some curves to make her figure interesting. Her hair was almost blond but not quite. There was not much of it visible beneath the bonnet, and not a single curl. Her face was a long oval with high cheekbones, largish eyes of a slate gray, a straight nose, and a wide mouth that looked as though it might be covering slightly protruding teeth. She looked a bit as though she had stepped out of a Norse saga. It might have been a beautiful face if there had been any expression to animate it. But she merely stared at him, as though *she* were assessing *him*. In his own home.

That was his first impression of her. The second, following swiftly upon the first, was that she looked about as sexually appealing as a marble pillar. And, strangely enough, that she was trouble. He was not used to dealing with females who resembled marble pillars—and who walked unannounced and uninvited into his own home and looked at him without admiration or blushes or any recognizable feminine wiles. Though blushes would have been hard to detect. Both cheeks plus the end of her nose were a shiny red from the cold. At least the color proved that she was not literally marble.

"And who the devil might *you* be?" he asked her.

She had provoked the rudeness by walking in without even the courtesy of a knock on the door. Nevertheless, he was unaccustomed to being rude to women.

"Imogen Hayes, Lady Barclay," she told him.

Well, that was a neat facer. If it had come at the end of a fist, it would surely have put him down on the floor.

"Am I suffering from amnesia?" he asked her. "Did I

marry you and forget all about it? I seem to recall that *I* am *Lord* Barclay. The Viscount of, to be exact."

"If you had married me," she said, "which, heaven be praised, you have not, then I would have introduced myself as the Countess of Hardford, would I not? You *are* the earl, I presume?"

He turned to face her more fully. She had a low, velvety voice—which overlay venom. And her teeth did *not* protrude. It was just that her upper lip had a very slight upward curl. It was a potentially interesting feature. It might even be a beguiling feature if *she* were beguiling. She was not, however.

He was not accustomed to feeling animosity toward any woman, especially a young one. It seemed he was making an exception in this woman's case.

Understanding dawned.

"You are the widow of my predecessor's son," he said.

She raised her eyebrows.

"I did not know he had one," he explained. "A wife, I mean. A widow now. And you live here?"

"Temporarily," she said. "Usually I live in the dower house over there." She pointed in what he thought was roughly a westerly direction. "But the roof is being replaced."

His brows snapped together. "I was not informed of the expense," he told her.

Her own brows stayed up. "It is not your expense," she informed him. "I am not a pauper."

"*You* are spending money on a property that presumably belongs to *me*?" he asked her.

"I am the daughter-in-law of the late earl," she said, "the widow of his son. I consider the dower house mine for all practical purposes."

"And what will happen when you remarry?" he asked her. "Will I then be asked to reimburse you for the cost of the roof?"

And why the *devil* was he getting into this when he had scarcely set foot over the doorstep? And why was he being so abominably ungracious? Because he found marble women offensive? No, not plural. He had never met one before now. Her eyes, potentially lovely, were absolutely without warmth.

"It will not happen," she told him. "I will not remarry and I will not ask for a return of my money."

"Will no one have you?" Now he had gone plummeting over the edge of civility. He ought to apologize abjectly and right now. He scowled at her instead. "How old are you?"

"I am not convinced," she said, "that my age is any of your concern. Neither is the list of my prospective suitors or lack thereof. Mr. Crutchley, I daresay the Earl of Hardford would like to be shown to his apartments to wash the dust of travel off his person and change his clothes. Have the tea tray brought up to the drawing room in half an hour, if you please. Lady Lavinia will be eager to meet her cousin."

"Lady Lavinia?" He drilled her with a look.

"Lady Lavinia Hayes," she explained, "is the late earl's sister. She lives here. So, at present, does Mrs. Ferby, her companion and maternal cousin."

His eyes drilled deeper into her. But there was not the smallest possibility that she was teasing him. "Not at the dower house when it sports a roof?"

"No, here," she said. "Mr. Crutchley, if you please?"

"Follow me, my lord," the butler said just as Percy heard the rumble of wheels approaching outside. His curricle, he guessed. For a brief moment he considered bolting through the door and down the steps and vaulting aboard with the command on his lips that his groom spring the horses, preferably in the direction of London. But it would be a shame to leave his favorite horse behind.

He turned instead to follow the butler's retreating back. Watkins and the baggage would be awhile, yet. Lady Barclay and Lady Lavinia Hayes and Mrs. Ferby would have to take him in all his dusty glory for tea.

Three women. Marvelous! A sure cure for boredom and all else that ailed him.

This would teach him to make impulsive decisions while he was three sheets to the wind.

3

"I felt the sheets with my own hands," Aunt Lavinia said. "I am quite sure they were well aired. I do hope he will not get the ague from sleeping between them."

"Of course he will not," Imogen assured her. All the linens at Hardford were well aired, since they were stored in the airing cupboard when not in use.

"Unless he is an elderly man and already has it," Aunt Lavinia added. "Or the rheumatics. *Is* he elderly, Imogen?"

"He is not," Imogen told her.

"And is he married? Are there children? And will they and his wife be following him here? Oh, it is very sad indeed that we know so little about him. I do not hold with family quarrels. I never have. If there cannot be peace and harmony and love within families, then what are families for?"

"Show me a family that claims to live in peace, harmony, and love, Lavinia," Cousin Adelaide said, "and I will lead the hunt for all the skeletons in the cupboards. Such a fuss over a man."

"I cannot believe," Aunt Lavinia said, "that I was so busy seeing that everything was ready for him that I did not hear him arrive. But we could not have known he would come so soon, could we? Whatever will he think of me?"

"You need to be more like me, Lavinia," Cousin Adelaide said, "and not care what *anyone* thinks of you. Least of all a man."

Aunt Lavinia had indeed been horrified to learn that she had missed the arrival of the earl and her duty to make her curtsy to him in the hall. She was seated now in the drawing room, looking a bit like a coiled spring, awaiting the appearance of his lordship for tea.

"I did not think to ask if he is married," Imogen said. If he was, she pitied the countess from the bottom of her heart. She did not often take people in dislike, at least not on first acquaintance. But the Earl of Hardford was everything she most abhorred in a man. He was rude and arrogant and overbearing. And no doubt there had never been anyone to call him to account. He was the type who would be admired and followed slavishly by men and fawned upon and swooned over by women. She *knew* the type. The officers' messes with which she had been acquainted had abounded with such. Fortunately—*very* fortunately—her husband had not been one of them. But then she would not have married him if he had been.

"You have not seen Prudence, by any chance, Imogen?" Aunt Lavinia asked. "All the others are accounted for and shut safely inside the second housekeeper's room, even though Bruce did not like it one little bit. But Prudence was nowhere to be found. I do hope she is not hiding somewhere, waiting to put in an appearance at an awkward moment."

"I have not," Imogen said. "The Earl of Hardford was unaware of my existence, you know. And of yours. And of Cousin Adelaide's."

"Oh, dear," Aunt Lavinia said. "That *is* awkward. But he really ought to have made inquiries. Or perhaps we ought to have sent a letter of congratulation when he succeeded to the title and then he would have known. But at the time I was just too upset over poor Brandon's passing. Dicky's papa," she added, lest Imogen or her cousin not understand who Brandon was.

The drawing room door opened abruptly and without even a tap upon the outer panel or Mr. Crutchley to step ahead to announce the new arrival.

The Earl of Hardford had not changed his clothes. Imogen doubted his baggage had arrived yet, since he had come on horseback. There was no doubt a coach on its way. Or two. Or three, she thought nastily. His drab riding coat and hat had been discarded, but the riding clothes he still wore were very obviously expensive and well tailored. His coat and breeches molded his tall, powerful frame, in which there was no discernible imperfection. His linen was admirably white and crisp, considering the fact that he had traveled in it. He had found something with which to restore the shine to his boots. Either he was a very wealthy man, Imogen concluded—but the estate of Hardford was not particularly prosperous, was it?—or his unpaid bills with his tailor and boot maker were staggeringly high. Probably the latter, she thought purely because she wanted to think the worst of him. His hair had been combed. It was dark and thick and glossy and expertly styled.

He was *smiling*—and even his teeth were perfect and perfectly white.

He bowed with practiced elegance while Aunt Lavinia scrambled to her feet and dipped into her most formal curtsy. Cousin Adelaide stayed where she was. Imogen stood because she did not want his earlier rudeness to provoke her to retaliate with rudeness of her own.

"Ma'am," he said, turning the full force of a devastating charm upon Aunt Lavinia. "Lady Lavinia Hayes, I presume? I am delighted to make your acquaintance at last and must apologize for descending upon you with so little notice. I must apologize too for riding so far ahead of my baggage and my valet that I am compelled to appear in the drawing room so inappropriately dressed. Hardford, ma'am, at your service."

Well!

"You must never apologize for coming to your own home, cousin," Aunt Lavinia assured him, her hands clasped to her bosom, two spots of color blossoming in her cheeks, "or for dressing informally when you are in it. And you must call me *cousin*, not *Lady Lavinia* as though we were strangers."

"I shall be honored, Cousin Lavinia," he said. He turned his smile upon Imogen, and his very blue eyes became instantly mocking. "And, if I may make so free . . . Cousin Imogen? I must be Cousin Percy, then. We will be one happy family."

He turned his charm upon Cousin Adelaide.

"And may I present Mrs. Ferby to you, Cousin Percy?" Aunt Lavinia said, sounding anxious. "She is a cousin on my mother's side and therefore no relation to you. However—"

"Mrs. Ferby," he said with a bow. "Perhaps we may consider ourselves honorary cousins."

"*You* may consider whatever you wish, young man," she told him.

But instead of throwing him off balance, her implication that *she* would consider no such thing merely turned his smile to one of genuine amusement, and he looked even more handsome.

"I thank you, ma'am," he said.

Aunt Lavinia proceeded to fuss him into the large chair to the left of the fire that had always been her brother's and in which no one else had ever been allowed to sit, even after his death. The tea tray arrived almost immediately with a large plate of scones and bowls of clotted cream and strawberry preserves.

Unfortunately, the maids left the drawing room door open behind them when they came in. Equally unfortunately, someone must have opened the door of the second housekeeper's room—so called for no reason Imogen had ever been able to fathom, since there had never been any such person on the household staff. Almost before the tea tray had been set down and Imogen had seated herself behind it to pour the tea, the room was invaded. Dogs barked and yipped and panted and chased their tails and regarded the scones with covetous eyes. Cats mewed and scratched and growled—that was Prudence, who was apparently no longer lost—and leaped onto laps and furniture and eyed the milk jug.

There was not a truly pretty or handsome animal among the lot of them. Some were downright ugly.

Imogen closed her eyes briefly and then opened them in order to observe the earl's reaction. *This* would wipe the smile from his face and put an end to the charm that oozed from his every pore. Blossom, the furriest of the cats and also the one that shed the most, had jumped onto his lap, glared balefully at him, and then curled up into a shaggy ball.

"Oh, dear," Aunt Lavinia said, on her feet again and wringing her hands. "Someone must have opened the second housekeeper's door. Out of here, all of you. Shoo! I am so sorry, Cousin Percy. There will be hair all over your ... breeches." Her cheeks flamed scarlet again. "Blossom, do get down. That is her favorite chair, you see, because it is close to the fire. Perhaps she did not notice ... Oh, dear."

Imogen picked up the teapot.

Bruce, the bulldog, had taken possession of the mat before the hearth with a great deal of noisy snuffling before addressing himself to sleep. Fluff, who was not fluffy, and Tiger, who was not fierce, settled on either side of him. They were cats. Benny and Biddy, both dogs, one of them tall and gangly with hangdog eyes and ears and jowls, the other short and long, almost like a sausage, with legs so short that they were invisible from above, circled about each other, sniffing rear ends—it was a considerable stretch for Biddy—until they were satisfied that they had met before, and then plopped down together over by the window. Prudence, the tabby, stood close to the tea tray, her back arched, growling at Hector. Hector, the newest addition to their household—if one discounted the earl—was a smallish dog of *very* mixed breed, his thin legs alarmingly spindly, his ribs clearly visible through his dull, patchy coat, his one and a half ears erect, his three-quarters of a tail slightly waving. He stood beside the earl's chair and gazed up at him with eyes that bulged from a peaked, ugly face, begging silently for something. Mercy, perhaps? Love, maybe?

Aunt Lavinia was flapping her arms in a shooing gesture. None of the animals took the least notice.

"Pray be seated, Cousin Lavinia," the earl said, a quizzing glass materializing in his right hand from somewhere about his person. "I suppose I was bound to encounter the menagerie sooner or later, and it might as well be sooner. Indeed, I believe I already have a passing acquaintance with the growling tabby. She—he?—ran through the hall while I was in it earlier and expressed displeasure at my arrival."

"She does not know," Imogen said, setting down his cup and saucer beside him, "that cats hiss and dogs growl."

She looked into his face, a foot or so from her own. He was no longer smiling. But he had not, to give him credit, lost any of his poise. Neither had he raised his glass all the way to his eye. She reached down and scooped Blossom off his lap, inadvertently brushing his thigh with the backs of her fingers as she did so. He lofted one eyebrow and looked back at her. She stooped and deposited the cat on the floor.

"Perhaps," the earl said with ominous civility while Imogen prepared to take him a scone, "someone would care to explain to me why my home appears to be overrun with what I would guess is a pack of strays."

"No one, certainly," Cousin Adelaide said, "would have chosen any one of them for a pet. They are a singularly unappealing lot."

"There are always animals roaming the countryside without a home," Aunt Lavinia said. "Most people shoo them away or go after them with sticks and brooms and even guns. They always seem to end up here."

"Perhaps, ma'am," he said, his voice silky, "that is because you take pity on them."

He seemed to have forgotten that she was *Cousin La-vinia* and that they were one happy family.

"I *always* wanted a pet when I was a child," she explained with a sigh. "My papa would never allow it. I still wanted one after I grew up and Papa died, but Brandon would not hear of it either. Brandon was my brother, the late earl, your predecessor."

"Indeed," he said as he bit into his scone without loading it down with cream and preserves.

"He scolded me when he caught me feeding a stray cat one day," she said. "Poor little thing. The leftover food would just have gone into the bin. After Brandon died, another cat came. Blossom. She was terribly thin and weak and had almost no coat. I fed her and took her in and gave her a bit of love, and look at her now. And then there was another one—Tiger. And then Benny came—the tall dog—looking as if he was one day away from dying of starvation. What was I to do?"

The earl set his empty plate aside, propped his elbows on the arms of the chair, and steepled his fingers.

"Four cats and four dogs," he said. "These are all, ma'am?"

"Yes," she said. "Eight since Hector came last week. He is the dog standing beside you. He is still dreadfully thin and timid. He must have suffered abuse and rejection all his life."

The earl looked down at the dog, and the dog looked up at him. Disdain—or what Imogen imagined was disdain—gazed steadily back at wavering hope. Hector's tail flicked once and then again.

The earl's eyes narrowed.

"I have no love whatsoever for cats," he said, "unless they earn their living as mousers and stay in parts of houses where they belong. And dogs are to be tolerated if they are good hunters." He raised his eyes to direct a hard look at Imogen. "It is to be expected, I suppose, that women left to themselves would wax sentimental and quite impractical. What is to be the upper limit of . . . strays allowed to overrun my home?"

Cousin Adelaide snorted.

Imogen sipped her tea. He was behaving quite true to the character she had assigned him. Women needed men to keep them in line. She did not answer him. Neither did Aunt Lavinia.

"As I thought," he said curtly. "No upper limit has been set. No plan has been made. And so I must learn to share my drawing room and perhaps my dining room and library and private apartments with a growing number of unappealing felines and canines, mustn't I?"

"The second housekeeper's room has been set up for them, Cousin Percy," Aunt Lavinia said.

"With bars on the windows and doors?" he asked. "And are they always kept there? When they do not escape in a body, that is, and find more comfortable accommodation here? And how does the second housekeeper like sharing her room with them?"

"There is no second housekeeper," she said. "I am not sure there ever has been. I certainly do not remember any such person. There are no bars on the windows. And they cannot stay there all the time. They need exercise. And affection."

He looked back down at Hector.

"Affection," he said, disgust clear in his tone. But the dog took one step forward and rested his chin on the earl's thigh. It was the first time to Imogen's knowledge that Hector had voluntarily touched any human. He obviously was not a very discerning dog. The earl addressed him sternly. "You are not planning to become attached to me, are you? You may forget it without further ado if you are. You would get nothing whatsoever in return. Pleading looks do nothing for me. I do not have a soft female heart."

"Now there is a surprise," Cousin Adelaide rumbled into her teacup.

The earl removed Hector's chin from his leg after rubbing his fingers over the dog's one whole ear for a few moments, and got to his feet.

"We will discuss the matter further, ma'am," he said, looking down upon Aunt Lavinia. "I will not have Hardford Hall turned into an animal refuge, even in my absence. And if there is some other chair lurking in a little-used room or tucked away somewhere in an attic that is more comfortable than the one on which I have been sitting, almost *any* other chair, in fact, I would be much obliged to you if it could be fetched to replace this one before I am required to sit here again. Perhaps you would pass on my compliments to the cook on the superior quality of the scones. I shall see you all again at dinner. Cousin Lavinia? Cousin Imogen? Mrs. Ferby?"

He bowed to each of them and left the room.

Hector whined once and lay down close to the vacated chair.

"God's gift to the female half of the species," Cousin Adelaide said.

"I suppose he is right, though," Aunt Lavinia said with a heavy sigh. "We women *are* impractical because we have *hearts*. Not that men do not, but they feel things differently. They do not feel the suffering around them, or, if they do, they know how to harden their hearts when it has nothing to do with them."

"The Earl of Hardford," Imogen said, "is definitely a man without a heart, Aunt Lavinia. I would be willing to take an oath on it. He is an ill-humored man who thinks no one will notice his nastiness if he turns on a bit of charm when it suits him."

She hated to find herself in agreement with Cousin Adelaide, but that man had severely ruffled her feathers. His charm was skin-deep at best, and it was a thin skin.

"Oh, dear," Aunt Lavinia said, taking another scone. "I would not say that, Imogen."

"I *would*," her cousin said.

4

The earl's apartments, as might have been expected, had the place of honor at the center front of the upper story of the house. They afforded the best view of any room—a panoramic prospect across lawns and flower beds to a band of gorse bushes and cliffs and the sea below stretching to infinity. It was a truly magnificent sight.

It turned Percy's knees weak with sheer terror.

His bedchamber was also damp, he discovered the first night when he lay down upon noticeably soggy sheets. The housekeeper was horrified and mystified and apologetic. She had checked the sheets *with her own hands* before they were put upon his bed, she assured his lordship, and so had her ladyship. But damp they now were, and she could not deny the evidence when confronted with it.

"Perhaps," Percy suggested, "it is the mattress itself that is damp."

Mattress and sheets and blankets were changed by one hefty footman and an army of maids, all of whom had no doubt been rousted out of their beds so that their master might sleep without drowning.

And there was also, Percy discovered when he threw back the curtains from the windows before lying down upon his newly made-up bed, a great V of soggy dampness on the wallpaper below the windowsill. A bit mysterious, he thought, since he had not encountered any rain during his journey and had not noticed that patch earlier.

The sun was sparkling off the sea the next morning when Percy got out of bed and gingerly looked out. The water was calm. Both sea and sky were a clear blue—at last. It all appeared very benevolent, in fact, and the expanse of the park between the house and the cliffs looked reassuringly broad. It would surely take all of five minutes to walk from the house to those gorse bushes. Nevertheless, he wished his rooms were at the back of the house, facing those solid rocks.

The damp patch below the windowsill appeared considerably less damp this morning, he noticed.

He could hear Watkins pottering in his dressing room and ran a hand over the rough stubble on his jaw. It was time to face the day. He grimaced slightly, though, at the prospect. One would have thought that at some time during the past two years *someone* would have thought of mentioning that the late earl had died in possession of a resident spinster sister and a widowed daughter-in-law. And there was the sharp-tongued cousin, mercifully unrelated to him, who spoke in a baritone voice that might cause one to mistake her for a man if one could not see her. And there were the animals . . .

He longed suddenly for the sanity of his London home and White's Club and his familiar friends and . . . boredom. But he had no one but himself to blame.

He had breakfast with Lady Lavinia and Mrs. Ferby.

The former explained what she thought must be the exact relationship between them from what he had told them last evening. They had clearly shared a great-great-grandfather, even though their relative ages would lead anyone to assume they were a generation apart. Cousin Percy was Lady Lavinia's third cousin. Dicky, her late brother's son, would have been his third cousin once removed. Therefore, Imogen was his third cousin-in-law once removed.

The lady in question did not put in an appearance. She was, Percy assumed, a late riser.

"Dicky!" Mrs. Ferby said, addressing the food on her plate. "He was *Richard*, was he not, Lavinia? I am surprised he did not rebel against such an infantile name." She paused in her eating and fixed Percy with a glare. "I suppose you are Percival?"

"I am, ma'am," he agreed.

"The only time my husband addressed me as *Addy*," she said, "was also the last time. He died seven months after I married him."

Percy did not ask if there was a connection between the two incidents.

"I was seventeen," she added, "and he was fifty-three. It was not a May/September match. It was more like a January/December *mis*match."

Her brief marriage, Percy concluded, had not been of the variety made in heaven, though he guessed Mr. Ferby might well have been quite happy to retire there after seven months with his young bride.

Lady Lavinia offered to show him to the morning room after breakfast, on the assumption, he supposed, that he might wish to put his feet up there and enjoy his existence before a roaring fire. It was a large chamber and was what he would call the library, though it did admittedly face east and therefore caught the morning sun. There was an impressive array of books shelved there. He would enjoy browsing through them at another time.

Two cats were lying at their ease before the windows, each in a shaft of warm sunlight. Wise cats. The great lump of a bulldog had taken ownership of the rug before the fire and was stretched out there, apparently asleep. The spindly dog of the bulging eyes was cowering under an oak desk but scrambled out when he saw Percy to wave his tail and gaze upward with abject hope. Percy trained his quizzing glass upon it and ordered it to sit. He might as well have asked it to perform a pirouette on the pointed toes of one paw.

He was going to have to *do* something about those strays, Percy thought for at least the dozenth time since yesterday afternoon.

He did not stay. At his request, Lady Lavinia took him to the steward's office at the back of the house and left him in the hands of Ratchett, who looked to be eighty if he was a day and every bit as dusty as the mountain of estate and account books that were piled everywhere, including on the top of his desk.

The man bobbed his bald head several times—or was it merely that he had the shakes?—and squinted in the general direction of Percy's left ear. He indicated the dusty piles and expressed himself of the opinion that his lordship must be desirous of spending the day going through them. His lordship desired no such thing. But looking thoughtfully at his good and faithful servant, who had not once looked directly into his face, he made the instant decision *not* to ask the man to take him about the estate in person.

He needed to do something about the strays *and* the ancient steward, he thought. And the butler was a bit on the creaky side too.

"Some other time, perhaps," he said. "I plan to spend the rest of the morning wandering about outside, seeing what is what." Which was admittedly a vague sort of plan.

And then, just as he was about to sally forth into the outdoors, he was waylaid by the butler, who informed him mournfully that the earl's bedchamber had always been more subject to damp than any other room in the house, though it was worse now than it had been in his late lordship's day. He would see to it personally that his lordship was moved to the roomiest of the guest rooms at the rear of the house.

It was exactly what Percy had wanted. Had the offer been made yesterday, before he retired to bed for the night, he might have accepted it gladly. But . . . well, his servants could jolly well make the room habitable. He had not made many demands upon them for two full years, had he?

"No need to bother," he said. "But see that a fire is lit in there and kept burning."

The butler inclined his head and creaked forward to open the front doors.

Percy stepped out and took a few deep breaths of the sea air, which was brisk to say the least. He went down the steps and strode out across the lawn in a roughly westerly direction. But leaving doors open in the house must be a habit, he concluded a minute later when he realized that the dog was following him—the spindly one, which must have been very close to the point of terminal starvation when Lady Lavinia took pity on it. It did not look firmly established in the land of the living even now.

"It is like this," Percy said, stopping and speaking with some exasperation. "Hector, is it? I have never heard a more unsuitable name in all my life. It is like this, Hector. I intend to walk, to *stride*, to cover distance. If you are foolish enough to follow, I shall not waste energy trying to prevent you. I shall *not* stop to wait for you if you should falter, nor will I carry you if you should find yourself exhausted and stranded far from the house and your feeding bowl. And, while on the subject of feeding, I have *no* doggie treats about my person. Not a one. Is that clearly understood?"

The pathetic apology for a doggie tail waved halfheartedly and, when Percy turned to stride onward, Hector trotted after him.

Perhaps he understood ancient Greek.

The park was pleasantly set up and probably made an impressive enough foreground for the house itself during the summer, when the grass would be greener and the trees would have leaves and flowers would be blooming in the beds. Its chief attraction for most people, of course, would be its position high on a cliff top with unobstructed views of endless expanses of sea. Some people—*most* people, actually—were funny that way. A couple of the flower beds here had been artfully situated in hollows, where they would be sheltered from the winds. Wrought-iron seats had been placed in them, presumably so that the beholder could enjoy the flowers without having either his hat or his head blown off.

The wall that surrounded the park on three sides was built of stones of all sizes and shapes and no mortar or anything else to bind them together, he noticed with interest. It was all held in place by the skill of the builder in matching one stone to another and . . . But he did not understand how it was done so that the whole thing did not simply collapse as soon as the builder's back was turned. He must ask someone.

Over the west wall he could see the beginnings of a valley, though he could not see what was down there. Farmland, presumably his own, stretched away to the north. Most of the fields he could see were dotted with sheep and lots of them, but there was nothing that looked like a cultivated field. It *was* only February, of course.

He wondered why the estate apparently prospered so little. Perhaps he would try to find out. Or perhaps he would not bother. How could anyone stand to *live* here? He would expire of boredom in no time at all—which, come to think of it, was exactly what he had been doing in London too. Perhaps boredom had less to do with a place than with the person who felt it. Now there was a lowering thought.

He considered following the wall around to the north, behind the outcropping of rock at the back of the house, so that he could see more of his land. But the going looked rugged, and he turned instead to follow a footpath leading southward along the inside of the wall, even though he realized that every step was bringing him closer to the edge of the cliffs. Before he reached them, however, he came to a house in the southwest corner of the park, nestled cozily in a hollow and surrounded on three sides, like the main house itself on a smaller scale, by high rocks and bushes. It was a house without a roof. Or, at least, it had the frame of a roof, but not the covering that would keep the elements out. It did not take much power of deduction to conclude that this must be the dower house, Lady Barclay's home — his third cousin-in-law once removed. There were two men up on the rafters. One of them was hammering while the other stood and watched.

Percy strode forward. The house looked square and solid and reasonably well sized. He guessed there were at least four bedchambers, perhaps six, upstairs, and several rooms downstairs. There was a neat garden, bordered on the east, the unsheltered side, by a low box hedge. A rustic wooden gate in the middle of it opened onto a straight path leading to the front door.

Percy stopped outside the gate. The two men had seen him approach. The hammering had stopped.

"How is the work progressing?" he called up.

Both men pulled at their forelocks, bobbed their heads, and said nothing. Perhaps *they* understood ancient Greek?

"It is progressing," a cool, velvet voice said, and its owner stepped into sight from beside the house, a basket of what looked like weeds over one arm, a small trowel in her other hand. Presumably weeds grew in February, even if flowers did not.

She was wearing the gray cloak and bonnet again, though the cloak had been pushed back over her shoulders to reveal a plain blue dress. Plain suited her. He had discovered yesterday that she had an excellent figure. It was not voluptuous, but there were curves in all the right places, and everything was in perfect proportion to her height. She had long legs, which he might have considered interesting if she had held any sexual appeal for him. He had never fancied the idea of making love to marble. It sounded chilly.

Her hair too was more appealing without the bonnet. It was thick and shiny and smooth and simply styled. He guessed that it was straight—and long. But he did *not* entertain any fantasies of running his fingers through it.

"It would proceed much faster if there were more men up there," he said. "Or if the two of them worked in tandem rather than one at a time. I will have a word with Ratchett. That roof needs to be on before the weather produces something nasty."

"You will do no such thing," she told him, her eyebrows halfway up her forehead. "My cottage has nothing to do with Mr. Ratchett. Or you."

He looked deliberately about him as he clasped his hands behind his back. The dog, he noticed, was still with him, and was now sitting at his feet like a faithful hound.

"Is this or is it not my land?" he asked her. He looked at the building. "And my house? Are not repairs to my property my concern and my expense? Is Ratchett or is he not my steward?"

That last point, actually, might be questionable.

"By law," she said, "it is yours, of course. In reality it is mine. I am entitled to live here as the daughter-in-law of the late earl and the widow of his only son. Its upkeep is *my* responsibility and *my* expense."

He looked steadily at her, and she looked steadily back.

An impasse.

Were not such arguments usually the reverse of this one? Ought they not to be scrapping over who should *not* pay for the repairs?

"We will see," he said.

"Yes, we will," she agreed.

They certainly were rubbing each other the wrong

way. He was quite unaccustomed to having adversarial relationships with women. Or with anyone, in fact. He was usually the most amiable of mortals. Perhaps she resented the fact that he had inherited from her father-in-law. She must have married the late Dicky in the full expectation that she would be Lady Hardford of Hard-ford Hall one day. It must be a nasty comedown to be a dependent widow instead, with only the less illustrious courtesy title to call her own, and to be living in a modest house in one obscure corner of the park.

"Back to work," he said, raising his eyes to the roof, where the two men were gawking downward, interested spectators of the altercation going on below. "Lady Barclay, can I persuade you to abandon your weeding in order to walk with me?"

Perhaps they could take a step back and start over again. He regretted the way he had greeted her yesterday—*and who the devil might you be?* It was not surprising that she resented him, especially when her husband ought to have owned the property he himself had ignored for all of two years. But what could she expect when the man had abandoned her in order to go dashing off to Portugal and Spain to play at war?

She considered his offer, looking at him the whole while. Then she pulled off her gloves, which apparently had been donned for her gardening, set them on top of the weeds in her basket with the trowel, set the basket beside the front steps of the house, and pulled her cloak back over her shoulders. Another pair of gloves appeared from a pocket.

"Yes," she said.

"You must resent me," he told her as they set off east along the cliff path, which, he realized too late, was uncomfortably close to the edge of the cliffs themselves, cut off from the park by the thick hedge of gorse bushes. And, being a gentleman, he was forced to walk on the outside.

"Must I?"

"You expected your husband to be in my place," he said. "You expected to be the countess."

"If I did," she said, "I have had plenty of time in which to adjust my expectations. My husband has been dead for longer than eight years."

"Eight?" he said. "Yet you have not remarried?"

"And you have not *married*?" she asked in return. At first it seemed like a non sequitur, but then he understood the point she was making.

"It is surely different for a woman," he said.

"Why?" she asked. "Because a woman cannot function in life without a man to protect her and order her life for her?"

"Is that what your husband did?" he asked. "Order your life? Did he leave you to go off to war and order you to stay behind, playing the part of patient, dutiful wife while you awaited his return?"

"Dicky was my friend," she told him. "My dearest friend. We were equal companions. He did not leave me behind when he went to war. He took me with him. No, correction. I went with him. I was with him to the end."

"Ah, a woman who followed the drum," he said, turning his head to look at her. Yes, he could imagine it. This was a woman who would not wilt under harsh conditions or flinch in the face of danger. "Admirable. He died in battle, did he?"

She was staring straight ahead, her chin raised. Gulls were screeching about somewhere below the level of his feet. He found it a mite disturbing.

"He died in captivity," she said. "He was a reconnaissance officer. A spy."

Ah, poor devil. But were not captured officers treated with dignity and honor and courtesy, provided they gave their parole—that is, their promise as gentlemen not to try to escape? Unless, that was, they were out of uniform when caught, as a reconnaissance officer might well have been. He would not ask. He did not want to know. But—

"You were with him *to the end*?" He frowned.

"I went partway into the hills with him at the start of that particular mission," she said, "as I often did when it was deemed safe enough. His batman would have escorted me back. We were still well behind our own lines. We were both captured."

"And the batman?"

"He was foraging for firewood at the time," she said, "and was able to make his escape."

One captive had survived and one had not. Suddenly he saw her marble demeanor in a wholly new light. What had happened to her during her captivity? Especially if her husband had not been in uniform? It was really too ghastly to think about and he was not going to do it. He certainly was not going to ask any more questions. He did not want to know.

"And so you returned to England alone," he said. "Did you move immediately to the dower house?"

"I went home," she said, "to my father's house twenty miles from here. But I would not speak or sleep or leave my room. Or eat. My mother is a cousin of the Duke of Stanbrook. He lives at Penderris Hall on the eastern side of Cornwall. He had opened his home to military officers who had returned from the wars severely wounded in one way or another, and he had hired a skilled physician and other people to nurse them. My mother wrote to him out of despair, and he came to fetch me. I was there for three years. There were six of us who stayed that long, seven counting George — the duke, that is. We called ourselves the Survivors' Club. We still do. We still get together for three weeks of every year during March."

They had stopped walking. There was a break in the cliff face here, he noticed, and what appeared to be a zigzagging path down to the beach below — a rather steep and surely dangerous descent. The dog sat down beside him, its head against the side of Percy's boot.

"When one imagines oneself striding about one's land, faithful hound at heel," he said, "one tends to picture a robust and intelligent sheepdog or some such."

She looked at Hector. "Perhaps," she said, "when a dog imagines following upon the heels of its master, it pictures kind words and a gentle touch."

Touché. She had a wicked tongue.

"I am not its master," he said.

"Ah," she said, "but who gets to choose?"

"Three years," he said. "You were at Penderris for *three years*?"

Good God! How damaged had she been? And why was he pursuing this line of questioning? He did not deal in darkness. He hoped she would answer with a simple monosyllable or not at all.

"Ben — Sir Benedict Harper — had his legs shattered and refused to have them amputated," she said. "Vincent, Viscount Darleigh, was blinded in his first battle at the age of seventeen, and deafened too at first. Ralph, Duke of Worthingham, was hacked almost to ribbons with a saber when he was unseated from his horse in a cavalry charge. Flavian, Viscount Ponsonby, was shot in the head and then fell on it from his horse. Hugo, Lord Trentham, was not wounded at all. He sustained not even a scratch, though he had led a Forlorn Hope that killed almost all his men and severely wounded those few who survived. He went out of his mind. George did not even go to war, but his only son did and died, and then his wife jumped to her death over the cliffs at the edge of his estate. And I . . . ? I was present when my husband died, but they did not kill me. Yes, three years. And those men are my very dearest friends in this world."

Percy found himself fondling Hector's damaged ear and wishing again that he had not started this. *Shattered legs. Blind at the age of seventeen—and deaf too. Sons dying and wives committing suicide—over the edge of a cliff.* And what the devil had happened to Lady Barclay while her husband was in captivity, presumably being tortured? It was something ghastly enough that she had spent three years at Penderris Hall. He felt a trickle of sweat snake down his spine. *He did not want to know.*

"When I left Penderris," she said, "I came here. My father had died during those three years, my mother had gone to live with her sister, my aunt, in Cumberland, my brother had taken my father's place with his wife and children, and I did not think it fair to go there, though my sister-in-law very graciously invited me. I could not bear to live in the hall here with my father-in-law and Aunt Lavinia, even though more than three years had gone by. I asked for the dower house, and my father-in-law reluctantly allowed me to go there. That is my story, Lord Hardford. You were entitled to hear it since you have come here for however short a time to find me living on your land. Shall we go down onto the beach?"

"Down *there?*" he asked sharply. "No."

She turned her head to look steadily at him.

"I have never seen the attraction of beaches," he said—well, not for a long time, anyway. "They are just a lot of sand and water. Why is Hardford not more prosperous than it is? Or do you not know?"

"It pays its way," she said. "At least, that is what my father-in-law was always fond of saying."

"It does," he agreed. "And he was content with that?"

She turned her face away and did not answer immediately.

"He was never a particularly ambitious man," she said. "Dicky used to get impatient with him. He had all sorts of ideas and plans, but they were never implemented. He decided that the military life would be a better outlet for his energy. I believe his father lost all heart after Dicky died."

"And Ratchett?" he asked. "Was he ever an efficient steward?"

"Maybe once upon a time," she said. "My father-in-law inherited him."

"And he never considered that it might be time to put the man out to pasture and hire someone more . . . vigorous?" Percy was frowning. And he was wishing with all his heart that he could go back to the night of his birthday and erase the sudden drunken impulse to come to Cornwall. Sometimes what one did not know was best left that way.

"I doubt he ever considered it," she said. "Mr. Ratchett keeps very neat and orderly books. He spends his days surrounded by them and makes new entries in them as needed. If you wish to know anything concerning rents and crops and flocks or anything else on the estate for the past forty or fifty years, you will surely find the answer in meticulous detail within those pages."

"I feel rather, Lady Barclay," he said impatiently, "as though I had stepped into a different universe."

"I suppose," she said, "the situation is reversible. You could go back to where you—" She stopped abruptly.

. . . where you came from?

. . . where you belong?

"And leave that house, *my* house, to be turned into a menagerie?" he asked. "Do you realize that eventually, if Lady Lavinia continues to add every stray who is canny enough to wander up to the doors—and word must be spreading fast in the animal kingdom—eventually the house is going to become uninhabitable by humans? That it will be hopelessly coated with dog and cat hair? That it will *smell*?"

"You would have them turned away to starve, then?" she asked.

"It is not possible to feed all the hungry of this world," he said.

"Aunt Lavinia does not even try to take on the world's woes," she told him. "She merely feeds the hungry who come to her door—to *your* door."

He felt a sudden suspicion. "Are we talking *just* about dogs and cats?" he asked.

"There are people," she said, "who cannot find work for one reason or another."

He stopped in his tracks again and looked at her, appalled. "If I were to wander into the nether regions of the house," he said, "or into the stables, I would find all the maimed and criminally inclined vagabonds of the world eating me out of house and home, would I?"

One of the maids who had come to make up his bed

last night had been lame and looked as if she might be a bit simpleminded too.

"Not *all*," she said. "And those you would find are usefully employed and earning the food for which you pay. More gardeners and stable hands were needed by the time my father-in-law died, and the indoor staff had grown rather sparse. Aunt Lavinia has a tender heart, but she was never able to give it room while her brother lived. He was content with life as it had always been. He disliked change more and more as he grew older and after he lost Dicky."

"One of these strays is, I suppose, Mrs. Ferby," he said. "Cousin Adelaide, who is not under any circumstances to be called Addie."

"I suppose you were given an account at breakfast of the seven-month marriage, were you?" she said. "She has to live upon the charity of her relatives since she has almost no private means, and Aunt Lavinia convinced herself that bringing a companion to the house was the respectable thing to do after she was left alone. Perhaps she was even right. And her chosen companion *is* a relative."

"Not of mine," he said testily. "I can understand why you would rather I went back to where I came from, Lady Barclay."

"Well, you do seem to have managed very well without Hardford Hall for the past two years," she said. "Now, having come here on what seems to be some sort of whim, you have whipped yourself into a thoroughly bad temper. Why not go away and forget about our peculiar ways and be sweet-tempered again?"

"A thoroughly bad temper?" The dog whimpered and cowered at his feet. "You have not *seen* me in a bad temper, ma'am."

"It must be a very disagreeable sight, then," she said. "And like all bad-tempered men, you have a tendency to turn your wrath upon the wrong person. I am not the one who has neglected Hardford and the farms belonging to it. I am not the one who has filled the house with strays without a clear plan for what to do with them. I am not the one who brought Cousin Adelaide here as a companion, with the full knowledge that she will remain here for the rest of her life. Under normal circumstances, I mind my own business in my own house and make no demands upon the estate or anyone on it."

"The most abhorrent type of person on this earth," he said, narrow eyed, "is the one who remains cool and reasonable when being quarreled with. Are you *always* cool, Lady Barclay? Are you always like a block of marble?"

She raised her eyebrows.

"And *now* see what you have done," he told her. "You have provoked me into unpardonable rudeness. Again. I am *never* rude. I am usually all sweetness and charm."

"That is because you are usually in a different universe," she said, "one that revolves about you. The Peninsula was full of rude, blustering officers who believed other people had been created to pay them homage. I always thought they were merely silly and best ignored."

And she turned, the baggage, and began walking back the way they had come. She did not look behind her to see if he was following. He was not. He stood where he was, his arms folded over his chest, until she was out of earshot. Then he looked down at the dog.

"If there is a type of woman that grates upon my every nerve more than any other," Percy said, "it is the type that always has to have the last word. *Rude* and *blustering. Silly. SILLY!* '*I always thought they were best ig-*

nored.' For two pins I would go straight to the stables, mount my horse, and set its head for London. Forget about this ungodly place. Let you and all your playmates overrun the house until it is derelict. Let the earl's apartments turn to mildew. Let that steward turn into a fossil in his dusty office. Leave Lady Lavinia Hayes alone with her cousin and her bleeding heart. Let that marble pillar beggar herself with the bill for her roof and all the other repairs that are bound to be needed. Let the tide ebb and flow against the cliffs until eternity wears them away and both houses fall off."

Hector had no opinion to offer, and there was no point in Percy's standing here, pointlessly venting his frustration as he watched the cause of it recede into the distance.

"At least then I would not find myself babbling nonsense to a *dog*," he said. "I suppose you have exhausted yourself, though if you have it is entirely your own fault. You cannot say I did not warn you. And I suppose you are ready for your dinner so that you can build up some fat to hide those bones from sight. Come, then. What are you waiting for?"

He looked for a gap in the gorse bushes and found one that would leave only a few surface scratches on his boots as he pushed through it—Watkins would look tragically stoic. But as he stepped into the gap, he looked back at the dog, scowled at it, and stooped to lift it over the prickly barrier, hoping as he did so that no one could see him. He set off grimly across the lawn in the direction of the house.

At least, he thought—*at least* he was not feeling bored. Though it did occur to him that boredom was perhaps not such a sad state after all.

5

The afternoon brought visitors.

Somehow word had spread that the Earl of Hardford was in residence, and since the correct thing to do was to call upon him, people called. Besides, everyone was agog with curiosity to make his acquaintance at last.

Imogen had been planning to spend the afternoon at the dower house, although its roofless state made even the downstairs rooms almost unbearably chilly. She had missed luncheon because she could not bear the thought of making polite conversation with *that man,* who had provoked her to rudeness but who would no doubt be all smooth charm with the older ladies. She had also been feeling agitated after telling him her story, brief and un-detailed though she had made it. She almost never spoke of the past or thought of it when she could help it. Even her dreams were only rarely nightmares now.

Before she could set out for her own home, however, the first of the visitors arrived, and it would have been ill-mannered to leave even though they had not come, strictly speaking, to see her. She just wished she did not have to be sociable on this particular afternoon, though.

For everyone was enamored of the Earl of Hardford as soon as they met him. His very presence here was sufficient to please them, of course. But his youth and extraordinary good looks, coupled with the excellence of his tailoring, dazzled the ladies and impressed the gentlemen. His charm, his smile, and his ready conversation completed the process of bowling them over. He assured everyone that he was delighted to be here at last, that there was surely nowhere else on earth to compare with Hardford and its environs for beauty, natural and otherwise.

Those words *and otherwise* were spoken, as if by chance, while his eyes rested upon Mrs. Payne, wife of the retired Admiral Payne. Mrs. Payne, whose mood usually hovered on the edge of sourness, when it did not spill quite over into it, inclined her head in gracious acceptance of the implied compliment.

The Reverend Boodle, though, was the first to arrive with Mrs. Boodle and their elder two daughters. The admiral and his wife came next, and they were soon followed by the Misses Kramer, middle-aged daughters of a deceased former vicar, with their elderly mother. Those three ladies could not admit to the social faux pas of calling upon a single gentleman, of course. They had come, the elder Miss Kramer explained, to visit dear Lady Lavinia and Lady Barclay and Mrs. Ferby, and what a surprise it was to discover that his lordship was in residence. They could only hope he did not think them very forward indeed to have intruded all unwittingly thus upon him. His lordship, of course, responded with the predictable reassurances and soon had the three ladies quite forgetting that they had come to see Aunt Lavinia.

Imogen would undoubtedly have been amused by it

all if she had not taken the man so much in dislike. Though actually, she thought, these visits were probably akin to excruciating torture for him and were therefore no less than he deserved. She met his glance as the malicious thought flashed through her mind and knew from the infinitesimal lift of his eyebrows that she was right.

As the Reverend Boodle and his female entourage were leaving after a correct half hour, Mr. Wenzel drove up in the gig with Tilly. Imogen greeted the latter with a brief hug and sat beside her in the drawing room. But even Tilly was not immune to the earl's charm. She leaned toward Imogen after a few minutes and murmured beneath the sound of the general conversation.

"One has to admit, Imogen," she said, "that he is a perfectly gorgeous specimen of manhood."

But her eyes were twinkling as she said it, and the two of them exchanged a brief smirk.

Mr. Soames, the elderly physician, came with his much younger second wife and his three daughters and one son of that second marriage. Mr. Alton arrived last with his son, a gangly youth who had been wrestling with facial pimples for the last year or so, poor boy. He was soon in the throes of a serious case of hero worship, having been complimented by his lordship on the knot of his cravat, which looked like a perfectly ordinary knot to Imogen.

She gave the earl a penetrating look. She really did not want to believe that he was *kind*. He had not paid any compliment to Mr. Edward Soames, a good-looking young man who had been affecting the appearance and manners of a dandy since making a brief visit to London last spring to stay with one of his older half sisters.

By the time the last of the visitors had taken their

leave, the four residents were left in possession of a number of invitations—to a dinner party, to an evening of cards, to an informal musical evening, to a picnic on the beach, weather permitting, of course, for the eighteenth birthday of Miss Ruth Boodle, though that would not be until the end of May. They had also been informed by each wave of callers that the next dance in the assembly rooms above the village inn was to be held five evenings hence, and it was to be hoped the Earl of Hardford would condescend to grace it with his presence—as well as the ladies, of course.

Wild horses could not keep him away, the earl had assured everyone. He had solicited a set with the eldest Boodle daughter, the eldest Miss Soames, and Mrs. Payne. The elder Miss Kramer meanwhile had promised herself a comfortable coze with Aunt Lavinia and Cousin Adelaide while the young people danced. And Mr. Wenzel and Mr. Alton had each reserved a set of dances with Imogen.

"Well," Aunt Lavinia said when everyone had left, "that was all very gratifying, was it not? As you have seen, Cousin Percy, we are not without genteel neighbors and genteel entertainments in the country here. There is little chance you will find time hanging heavily on your hands."

"That Kramer woman who does all the talking for her mother and sister is a bore," Cousin Adelaide remarked. "*You* may have a comfortable coze with her during the assembly, Lavinia. *I* shall choose more congenial company."

"It would seem," Imogen said, "that you are doomed to remain here for at least the next two weeks, *Cousin* Percy, since you have accepted invitations extending that far into the future. Not to mention Ruth Boodle's birthday party more than three months from now."

"Doomed?" He smiled with what she recognized as his most practiced, most devastatingly charming smile at her. "But what a happy doom it is sure to be, Cousin Imogen."

God's gift to womankind, Cousin Adelaide had said. And to mankind too. That was what he thought he was, and it seemed that everyone who had called here today was only too eager to confirm him in that opinion. He was in reality an empty shell of vanity and artificiality and arrogance and peevish temper when he was thwarted. He was in sore need of a good setdown.

But it really would not do to allow herself to continue being ruffled by someone who had done nothing more lethal to harm her than to demand of her *and who the devil might you be*? She was not usually one to bear a grudge.

His smile had become more genuinely amused, and she realized that she had been holding his gaze. She got to her feet and pulled on the bell rope to summon a maid to remove the tea tray.

Had he been right earlier when he had suggested that she resented him because he was in the place Dicky should have been? She hated to think it might be so.

Her eyes rested fondly on Aunt Lavinia for a moment. Imogen's mother and Aunt Lavinia had been at a girls' school together in Bath for several years and had remained fast friends afterward. Imogen had come here often as a girl, sometimes with her mother, sometimes alone for extended periods. Aunt Lavinia had always declared that Imogen was the daughter she had never had. Being rather on the tomboyish side, Imogen had played with the son of the house from the start. They had become fast friends and comrades. They had never really fallen in love. The very idea seemed a little absurd. But at some point after they grew up they had made the mutual decision to continue their friendship into marriage so that they could remain together. Imogen could not even remember if there had been a marriage proposal and, if so, which of them had made it. Everything had always been mutual with them.

She had loved him dearly. There had, of course, been the sexual component too after they married. That had always been vigorous and satisfying, though it had never been central to their relationship. Perhaps she was incapable of that emotional condition people called "being in love." Which was just as well under the circumstances.

"Who, with the name of Alton," the earl asked of no one in particular, "would name his son Alden?"

It was clearly a rhetorical question.

He shook his head as though to clear it and fixed his gaze upon Aunt Lavinia.

"About the strays," he said.

"Oh, dear," she said. "But they have remained in the second housekeeper's room all afternoon, Cousin Percy. Please do not make me send them away. It would be worse than ever for them to become strays again now that they have experienced a roof over their heads and regular feedings. And a little love. *Please* do not make me send them away."

"I will not," he assured her. "Those that are here now may remain, though I will doubtless live to regret that decision. But there must be no more."

"It is so hard to turn any away," she said, clasping her hands to her bosom, "when they are starving and look at one with such hopeless pleading in their eyes."

"Might I make a suggestion?" Imogen said.

Those blue eyes turned on her, dark eyebrows arched above them.

"Please do."

"The strays always look far more attractive," she said, "after they have been tended and fed for a while. They gain weight, and their coats become thicker and shinier. There are surely a number of people who would be more willing to take in an attractive pet that needs a home than a mere stray which has never had one."

"Oh, dear Imogen," Aunt Lavinia said, "I am sure you must be right. All little girls want a cat or a dog. *I* did. Little boys too, I daresay. And perhaps the Misses Kramer or ..."

"*I* never wanted an animal," Cousin Adelaide said, winning for herself a look of acute distress from Aunt Lavinia and one of fleeting amusement from the earl.

He had stepped away from the door to allow two maids to enter and pick up the trays. Imogen noticed that his eyes rested thoughtfully upon one of them, a thin girl with stooped shoulders who was a deaf-mute, though he had no way of knowing that yet since he had not spoken to her. Mr. Soames, the physician, had been in the process of finding an insane asylum for her after her father, a farm laborer, died. But Aunt Lavinia had stepped in with a solution of her own.

"You are suggesting, Cousin Imogen," the earl said when the trays had been borne away, "that we run a sort of pet-grooming business here, free of charge, to supply our neighbors with pretty cats and handsome dogs over which their children and womenfolk may coo with tenderness?"

Aunt Lavinia looked as if she was holding her breath.

"In a word, yes," Imogen said. "Though I believe you used the wrong pronoun. I do not suppose for a moment that *we* would do any such thing. I cannot imagine you feeding or petting stray animals, Cousin Percy, especially ugly ones. Or loving them."

"Oh, Imogen, dear," Aunt Lavinia said reproachfully.

The earl pursed his lips. "My contribution would be the house and the food, I suppose," he said.

"Yes," she told him, "though I do think perhaps a corner of the stables could be prepared for Fluff, who will be birthing her kittens soon."

"What?" His eyebrows snapped together.

"Oh, the whole world loves a kitten," Imogen said. "They will be easy to place once they are ready to leave their mother."

He gazed at her narrow-eyed and then transferred his attention to Aunt Lavinia.

"No more strays in the house, ma'am," he said gently enough. "Besides, it is to be hoped that you have denuded the neighborhood of the lot of them by now. I will give directions for a nest to be prepared in the stables. Perhaps . . . *Fluff* will prove to be a decent mouser and can earn her living out there after delivering herself of her kittens. I shall talk to you some other time about the human strays. I believe I have just seen one of them in the guise of a maid."

"Annie Prewett?" Aunt Lavinia said. "She is a good girl. She does exactly as she is told once she understands what that is. Provided she can see your lips as you speak and you speak slowly, she understands."

He continued gazing at her for a few moments before looking back at Imogen.

"Has the waltz penetrated this far into the wilderness?" he asked her. "If so, you will reserve the first of them for me at the village assembly. *If you please.* I will not hoof it around the floor with someone who does not know how it is done, and I daresay you do."

It sounded like a command to Imogen, though he had added the words *if you please.*

Mr. Alton was the one who usually waltzed with her, his plump, always somewhat moist hands at her waist and clasped about her own. Waltzing with the Earl of Hardford would surely be an improvement upon that severe trial. She felt an unexpected frisson of pleasurable anticipation.

"Thank you," she said. "I shall consult my dancing card."

He grinned at her suddenly, and that frisson leaped up into something that quite unsettled her stomach. For that grin was not his usual smile of practiced charm, but seemed to be one of genuine appreciation.

"I shall challenge to pistols at dawn any man other than myself who dares write his name next to the first waltz in your card," he said, making her a slight bow.

Good heavens, was he flirting with her? Was his arrogance such that he thought he could draw even her within the orbit of his charm?

She raised her eyebrows and looked coolly back at him while Aunt Lavinia laughed and Cousin Adelaide snorted.

There was an image of the country gentleman that had always been singularly unappealing to Percy. It was that of the landowner who tramped about his land in ill-fitting coat and breeches and shapeless boots, sturdy staff in hand, faithful dog at heel, discussing crops and livestock and the weather with his foremen and laborers, and crop rotations and markets and the weather with his steward, horseflesh and bonnets and the weather with his neighbors, and the weather and the Lord knew what else with all and sundry while kicking up his heels at their various entertainments and admiring their hopeful, fresh-faced daughters.

Heaven help him, he thought during the following days, but he was in sore danger of becoming that country gentleman himself. He could be in London, he thought the afternoon following the first wave of visits—there were others—enjoying himself even if the Season had not yet begun and town was thin of company. He could be at Tattersall's or Jackson's boxing saloon or calling upon his tailor or his boot maker or be in his bed sleeping off the effects of last night's carousing with friends—or enjoying the favors of a new mistress. Instead, he was looking about Ratchett's dusty office and suggesting that with his superior skills the head steward—at that point Ratchett was the *only* steward, but that was a minor point—ought to be able to spend all his time in the office, engaged in the invaluable task of keeping the books in order, while a younger, less skilled and experienced man, an underling, in fact, undertook the mundane day-to-day task of running the farms and suggesting ideas for change and improvement. A second steward, that was, who could benefit from the advice and guidance of the head man. A subordinate, of course. A sort of disciple, in fact.

Ratchett squinted at Percy's left ear and muttered something about making inquiries in the neighborhood, though he did not know what a new man could do that was not already being done. But Percy had already written to Higgins, his man of business in London, directing him to find an experienced steward, a man who would be willing to be known officially as the understeward, though in reality he would be no such thing, and who would also be willing to incarcerate himself in the depths of nowhere for a somewhat better-than-average salary. The sooner such a paragon was found, Percy had added, the better he would be pleased. Soonest would be even better than sooner.

He had written the letter last night while his bedchamber was being cleaned up. He had discovered upon retiring that the fire was out and that a whole chimneyful of soot had descended into the room with a slightly charred, very dead bird. Crutchley, who had arrived in answer to his summons only moments after a distraught Mrs. Attlee, had given it as his opinion that the front rooms, especially *this* front room, were more likely to have such things happen than the back rooms, given that they got the brunt of any wind that happened to be blowing. Yet again he had advised Percy to move into the best guest chamber at the back. Yet again Percy, for no reason that was apparent to himself, had chosen to be stubborn. The earl's apartments *would* be made habitable for the earl, and he was the earl. At least his bed, when he had finally climbed into it, was dry, as was the wallpaper, slightly water stained, beneath the window.

Percy had discovered during the morning that almost none of his land had been cultivated for a number of years and would not be this year either if plans to the contrary were not made soon. Ratchett and the old earl had apparently not held with crops, which required too many workers to seed them, then to tend them, and then to harvest them, and which were too much at the mercy of the weather at all three stages. There were sheep galore, however, and some of the new lambs had already put in an appearance, no one having warned them that it was still winter and they might be well advised to remain inside their mothers where it was warm and out of the wind for a little longer.

Most of the income of the estate came, in fact, from wool. But the sheep were reproducing at far too exuberant a rate for them all to remain comfortably on the land until old age took them off. Someone needed to *manage* the flock just as someone needed to manage the land. Percy was not a manager, nor did he have the slightest ambition to become one. The very idea! But he did recognize need when he saw it, as well as poor management or pretty much no management at all.

The farmyard, just beyond the confines of the park to the north, was looking considerably down-at-the-heels. It sported a few milk cows and would soon sport some calves too—Percy did not ask where the bull was that had made the latter possible. There were a few goats, which appeared to have no particular function, and so many chickens that it was hard not to trip over them at every turn as they pecked about the yard. It was also quite impossible not to step in their droppings. A duck pond had some ducks to complement it. There were a few sheep pens for the lambing and, presumably, to house the flock during shearing season and in particularly bad weather. The pens looked as if they would be perfectly happy to give up the ghost any day now.

The hay in the sagging barn looked somewhat gray, as though it might have been there as long as the barn itself. The mice within it probably lived in comfort and died at a ripe old age.

The farm laborers seemed to be mostly gnarled old men, their sons presumably having departed long ago for pastures that were literally greener. The stable hands and gardeners within the confines of the park showed somewhat more youth and vigor, though they did appear to include more than their fair share of the lame and decrepit, further evidence of Lady Lavinia's tender sensibilities.

Percy hoped a new steward would be found sooner than soon and that he would gallop out here without stopping for food or rest along the way. He hoped the man would not take one look when he arrived and turn tail and flee.

Percy had worn his oldest clothes as he tramped about, though the fact was he did not possess anything that was much older than a year. Watkins would not have stood for it. The same applied to his riding boots, which were quite undeserving of the punishment they suffered in the farmyard. He did not carry a staff, but he did have a faithful dog at heel, that embarrassment of a skinny mutt with the grandiose name of Hector. The great Trojan hero Hector had shot the mighty and seemingly immortal Achilles in the heel and killed him. At least Hector the dog did not try to bite *his* heel. It had attached itself to him, Percy believed, only because the other dogs at the house, including that massive and lethargic bulldog and the sausage dog, shunned it and would not share their feeding bowls with it or allow it uncontested access to its own—and because the cats, especially the growling Prudence, intimidated it. Hector was, in fact, a sniveling coward and did nothing to enhance Percy's manly image as he strode about his neglected land.

It was enough to make any self-respecting gentleman farmer weep. Not that he *wanted* to be a gentleman farmer, at least not a gentleman farmer who behaved like one. Heaven forbid.

The following morning, after an uneventful night in his bedchamber, Percy walked purposefully across the lawn toward the dower house and found exactly what he had suspected he would find, namely a roofless edifice barren of any workers at all or any other discernible sign of life. He returned to the hall and changed his clothes. By the time Watkins had finished with him, he would have turned startled heads even on Bond Street— *especially* on Bond Street, in fact.

"My ebony cane, Watkins," he said. "We did bring the ebony, I suppose?"

"We did, m'lord." Watkins produced it.

"And my jeweled quizzing glass."

"The *jeweled* one, m'lord?"

Percy fixed him with a look, and the jeweled glass was produced without further comment.

"And a lace-edged handkerchief," Percy said. "And my ruby snuff box, I believe. Yes, the ruby snuffbox."

Watkins was too well bred to comment on these ostentatious additions to a morning outfit, but the wooden expression with which he always demonstrated disapproval became almost fossilized.

"Be so good as to look through the window to see if my traveling carriage is at the door," Percy instructed him.

It was. And a grandiose piece of workmanship it was too. He had inherited it from his father and seldom used it. He had brought it here only because Watkins would have been stoically disappointed if he had been forced to travel in a lesser specimen of coach.

Percy had ascertained upon his return to the house that Lady Barclay had taken the gig into Porthdare, as she had said at breakfast she intended to do. There was apparently an elderly lady with a sore hip who needed visiting. Women really could be angels on occasion, though it took a stretch of the imagination to consider his third cousin-in-law once removed and angels in the same thought.

Sometime later, having discovered the name and place of business of the roofer from his butler, Percy stepped unhurriedly down from his carriage outside the man's shop, which was situated in Meirion, a village six miles up the river valley. He looked languidly about him, ignoring the smattering of gawkers who had stopped to watch the show — or, that is, him.

He nodded to his coachman, who had been surprised earlier by the instruction to wear his livery.

"His lordship, the Earl of Hardford," the coachman now announced with clear enjoyment after flinging open the door of the shop.

His lordship stepped inside, shook out his handkerchief, flicked open the lid of his snuffbox with the edge of one thumb, paused, changed his mind — he did not enjoy taking snuff anyway — and snapped it shut again, put it away, and raised his quizzing glass to his eye.

"It has occurred to me to wonder why it is," he said with a sigh as he regarded three saucer-eyed men through his glass, "that the dower house at Hardford Hall lost its roof in December and is still without a roof in February. I have wondered too why there are occasionally two men to be seen on the rafters, one hammering nails while the other watches. And yet, no sign of progress. It has been brought to my attention that it is altogether possible I may discover the answers here. Indeed, I must insist upon doing so."

Less than fifteen minutes later his carriage was moving back along the village street, watched by far more than a smattering of spectators lined up on either side as though he were a parade. All the roofer's workers had apparently been indisposed or busy with other jobs, but all had miraculously recovered their health or completed those jobs that very morning and had been about to proceed to the dower house at Hardford Hall when his lordship arrived and delayed them. The sly suggestion, though, that the presence of all those workers on one job would raise the price of the repairs had met with his lordship's quizzing glass again, sparkling with blinding splendor in a shaft of light from the doorway, and the price had been instantly lowered below the original quote to an amount Percy guessed was only slightly inflated.

The Earl of Hardford had signaled his coachman, who had opened a fat leather purse and paid the roofer half the amount in advance. The other half would be paid upon the satisfactory completion of the job by Lady Barclay, his lordship's cousin—there was no point in confusing the issue by talking about thirds and removes and in-laws. Her ladyship was to be informed that the price had been dropped in compensation for the unconscionable delay.

Sometimes, Percy reflected during the seemingly interminable journey home, being a titled aristocrat could be a distinct advantage to a man. Not that he would have been incapable of making mincemeat out of that particular tradesman even as plain Percival Hayes.

6

Imogen was feeling almost cheerful as they sat down to an early dinner later that same day. They were to attend a musical evening at the Kramers' house afterward, and it was a welcome prospect, since she was still unable to spend the evening alone in her own home with a book, something she was longing to do again. The anticipation of an evening spent with neighbors was not what had lifted her spirits, however.

"A very welcome sight awaited me when I walked over to the dower house this afternoon, expecting it to be deserted as usual," she told the other three gathered about the table. "Mr. Tidmouth, the roofer, was there in person, supervising the work of no fewer than *six* workers, who were all busy up on the rafters."

"Six?" Aunt Lavinia said, her soup spoon pausing halfway to her mouth. "They should be finished in no time at all, then."

"*If* they come again tomorrow," Cousin Adelaide added.

"Oh, but I believe they will," Imogen assured her. "Mr. Tidmouth was most apologetic for all the delays.

He told me that he has been unwell since Christmas and that his second-in-command has been sending out the men to other, less important jobs without his knowledge. He will see to it personally that every one of his men comes to Hardford every day until the work is finished. He even assured me that having now seen the house for himself, he realizes that he overestimated the cost of the repairs and will lower the new, reduced estimate even further as an apology for the long delay."

"Never trust a man who apologizes to a lady," Cousin Adelaide said, "or a businessman who reduces his price."

"I am very happy for you, Imogen," Aunt Lavinia said, "though the repair to the roof will mean your removal back to the dower house, I suppose. I shall miss you."

"But I will be close by," Imogen said, "and will call on you almost every day, as I always have."

She would be *so* happy to be back home with just herself for company except when she chose to go out. She would be *very* happy to be away from the disturbing presence of the earl.

He had not contributed to the conversation about her roof. He had concentrated instead upon his food and his wine and merely regarded her somewhat sleepily once in a while from below half-lowered eyelids. It was a new expression, an annoying affectation.

"I daresay," she said, addressing him directly, "it was the letter I wrote yesterday that brought Mr. Tidmouth here today with his apology and his men. The *polite* letter. Good manners are often more effective than bluster. If I had gone all the way to Meirion merely to fume at him, as you advised yesterday, Cousin Percy, I would probably have been kept waiting another week or so as punishment."

"Quite so, Cousin Imogen," he said agreeably, raising his glass to her. "My hat is off to you."

But as she cut into her roast beef, she suddenly felt a horrid, ghastly suspicion. *Never trust a man who apologizes to a lady, or a businessman who reduces his price.* She looked up sharply at the earl, but his attention was upon his own roast beef, and suspicion gave way to irritation over the fact that he looked simply splendid in his dark blue evening coat with paler blue satin waistcoat and snowy white cravat and a neckcloth so intricately arranged that poor Alden Alton, if he was at the Kramers' house tonight, would surely die of envy and despair.

What was the *real* explanation, though, for the sudden appearance of so many workers, all diligently occupied, this afternoon? And for the oily apologies Mr. Tidmouth had uttered? And for the strangely drastic drop in price? Had she been very naive to be delighted by it all?

She had no chance to confront her suspicions or the man who had aroused them. They all rode to the village together in the earl's opulent traveling carriage. He must, Imogen concluded, have other sources of income than just Hardford. Perhaps the younger branch of the Hayes family had been somewhat more ambitious than the elder. Imogen sat with her back to the horses, as did the earl, so that the older ladies might have the more desirable forward-facing ones. But the carriage, she discovered, though luxurious, was no wider than the more humble one that sat idle in the carriage house. She could feel his body heat along one side, a fact that would have been comforting on this chill February evening if the heat had not carried with it the faint odor of an expensive, musky cologne and a powerful aura of masculinity. That latter fact annoyed her intensely. She could not remember ever being suffocated by any other man's masculinity, though she had known many virile, attractive men.

Oh, she would be *very* happy when she was back home in her own house.

And it was for this that he had dashed down to Cornwall to escape his boredom, Percy was thinking. Though that was not strictly accurate, was it? He had not expected to escape boredom, but had decided quite consciously to travel deeper into it just to see what happened. Well, *this* was what happened.

He was sitting in his traveling carriage with three ladies, one of whom suffered from tender sensibilities and had filled his house and park with strays; another of whom spoke in a baritone voice and had not uttered a single complimentary word about the male half of the species since his arrival, but had spoken plenty of derogatory ones; and a third of whom was made of marble. And if this journey was not enough to plunge him into the deepest gloom, there was the fact that their destination was the Kramer house, where they were to be entertained by the musical talents of the Kramer ladies and the neighbors at large.

The Misses Kramer, he discovered after their arrival, fancied themselves as pianists and vocalists, and proceeded over the couple of hours following the arrival of all their other invited guests to demonstrate the truth or falsity of that fancy. To be fair, however, they did not monopolize the evening's entertainment. A few other ladies sang and played the pianoforte. Alton had brought his violin, and his son, looking as though he would rather be cast into the fiery furnace with the lions thrown in for good measure, played along with him on a flute. The Reverend Boodle sang to his wife's accompaniment in a bass voice that might have set the liquor decanters to rattling if there had been any in the room.

Lady Barclay conversed with Lady Quentin, wife of Sir Matthew Quentin, and with Miss Wenzel before the recital began. When everyone took a seat for the entertainment, it was Wenzel, gentleman farmer, who seated himself beside her, drawing his chair a little closer to hers as he did so. He proceeded to engage her in conversation — or, rather, to deliver a monologue — while ignoring the music. It was ill-mannered of him, to say the least, though he did keep his voice low enough not to disturb those around them who chose to be polite and listen, among which virtuous number Percy included himself. Wenzel did not even pretend to listen. His eyes and his whole attention were fixed upon the lady, who admittedly was looking fetching enough in a blue gown that complemented every curve of her body to perfection — as well as complementing his own waistcoat, Percy had noticed at dinner. Wenzel did not applaud any of the entertainers. The man must not have visited a tailor for the past five years, and he was more than half bald — for which uncharacteristically uncharitable thoughts Percy did not pause to berate himself.

Lady Barclay herself *did* listen to, or at least keep her eyes upon, the performers. And she applauded. Only twice did Percy see her make a brief answering remark to Wenzel, and only one of those times did she turn her head to look at him.

The man irritated Percy. The *really* annoying thing, though, was that he was noticing such things. Wenzel was trying to fix his interest with Lady Barclay, as he had every right to do. He was a single gentleman of roughly her own age, and she was a widow. Good luck to him if he aspired to marry her. He would need luck, though. She was giving him no encouragement. Nor, it was true, was she giving any sign that she felt harassed by his attentions. She was being her usual marble self. Percy had no excuse whatsoever for wanting to express his displeasure.

But why should he feel irritated? Had he become all proprietary just because the woman lived beneath his roof? The very idea threatened to bring him out in a cold sweat.

Mrs. Payne, the admiral's wife, had a soprano voice with a pronounced vibrato and more than lived up to her name during the Handel aria she had chosen. Percy dutifully clapped when she was finished and agreed with Mrs. Kramer in a slightly raised voice because the latter was deaf that yes, indeed, it had been a fortunate day for the neighborhood when Admiral Payne decided to settle among them upon his retirement.

The grand finale of the entertainment portion of the evening was a Bach piece with some clever finger work performed by Miss Gertrude Kramer, the younger sister. It was clearly the signal to the servants to bring in the refreshments, which were set out along a large sideboard at one side of the room, while tea and coffee trays were placed on a table for the elder Miss Kramer to pour. There was no sign of anything alcoholic making its appearance.

Wenzel leaned closer to Lady Barclay before getting to his feet and making his way over to the sideboard. Percy stood unhurriedly, congratulated two or three of the evening's performers who were within his orbit, including a stammering, blushing Alden Alton, strolled across the room away from the sideboard, and took the empty seat beside his third cousin-in-law once removed.

She looked up at him in some surprise and what he would have interpreted as relief if it had not been highly unlikely.

"I hope," he said, "you enjoyed the musical entertainment, ma'am?"

"I did," she said. "Everyone means well and tries very hard."

Which was damning the artistes with faint praise, he thought appreciatively. "Quite so," he agreed. "And did you also enjoy the conversation?"

She raised her eyebrows. "I would have preferred to concentrate all my attention upon the music."

"Why did you not instruct him to stuff it, then?" he asked her.

"Perhaps, Lord Hardford," she said, "because I try at all times to observe good manners."

"Perhaps you were enjoying the gentleman's attentions," he said, "even if you would have preferred to listen to the music first. Shall I give him back his chair when he returns with a plate for you? I take it that is what he has gone to fetch."

"I believe it is not your concern whose attentions I enjoy or do not enjoy," she told him. "But, no. Please stay where you are."

At almost the same moment Wenzel was back, a loaded plate in each hand. He looked pointedly at Percy, his eyebrows raised.

"Ah," Percy said, "how very good of you, Wenzel." And he took one of the plates and handed it to Lady Barclay with a smile before taking the other for himself.

Wenzel was left with empty hands and an unfathomable expression on his face.

"But you must go back and fill a plate for yourself," Percy said kindly, "before all the food is gone. Though there does seem to be an abundance of it. Mrs. Kramer and her daughters have done us proud. I trust you enjoyed the recitals?"

Wenzel looked speakingly at the lady before murmuring something indecipherable, bowing, and moving off.

"Thank you," Lady Barclay said.

"Oh, it was nothing, ma'am," Percy assured her. "Procuring you a plate took no effort at all."

And she laughed.

It was a ghastly shock. It almost knocked him off his chair and onto the floor.

It was a brief laugh that lit up her whole face with amusement, gave an impression of dazzling, vibrant beauty, and was gone without a trace.

And it left him with the shocking realization that he wanted to make love to her.

It was fortunate—*very* fortunate—that conversation had become general and that Sir Matthew Quentin was asking his opinion on what appeared to be a matter of interest to everyone.

"And you, Hardford," he said, "what is *your* opinion on smuggled brandy?"

Since there was no liquor in sight, Percy assumed it was an academic question. "Undoubtedly it is usually of a superior quality," he said. "However, the fact that it has been brought into the country illegally makes it a forbidden delight."

It seemed to him that almost everyone smirked as

though he had just uttered something witty, and by doing so had been admitted to membership of a secret club.

"Ah, but are not forbidden fruits always the sweetest?" the dandyish young Mr. Soames asked.

His father frowned at him, two of his sisters tittered, and the Misses Kramer looked shocked. The third Soames sister and one of the Boodle girls put their ringleted heads together over by the pianoforte and giggled behind the fan one of them held open.

"Quite so," Percy said, nodding genially in the direction of the young man, who would undoubtedly be on the receiving end of his father's wrath later tonight.

Lady Quentin began a determined discussion of the varying merits of Chinese and Indian tea.

Percy, listening with half an ear, was making connections. Smuggled brandy. Smugglers. Cornwall, specifically the southern *coast* of Cornwall.

"*Is* there any smuggling activity hereabouts?" he asked the ladies on the way home.

"Not much now," Lady Lavinia said into a silence that lasted a beat too long. "There used to be, I believe, during the wars."

"But there still is *some*?"

"Oh, it is possible, I suppose," she said, "though I have not heard of any."

"And there is nothing even vaguely romantic about it," Lady Barclay added.

"Romantic?" He turned to face her as far as he was able given the narrow confines of the carriage seat. Not that he could see her clearly even then. It was a dark night and the carriage lamp was throwing its light forward rather than back.

"Smugglers, pirates, highwaymen," she said. "They are often glamorized as rather dashing heroes."

"Carrying off the swooning heroine lashed to the mast of the ship or thrown over the back of the horse or tossed over a man's shoulder and carried by superhuman strength to the top of a sheer cliff?" he said. "You are not a romantic, Cousin Imogen?"

Mrs. Ferby snorted.

"Not on the subject of bullies and criminals and cut-throats," Lady Barclay said.

He continued to look her way in the darkness. There had been real bitterness in her voice.

"But is he not always the wronged son of a duke?" he asked her. "The *eldest* son, that is, and is he not, through seemingly suicidal acts of great derring-do, setting the world to rights and clearing his name and winning the undying love of the sweet damsel in distress, who is quite possibly a princess, and, as a final reward, being restored to his inheritance and his father's bosom and marrying the princess and living happily ever after?"

Mrs. Ferby snorted again. "One must give the man his due, Lavinia," she said. "He has a sense of humor."

"You ought to be writing for the Minerva Press," Lady Barclay said.

He wondered if she was smiling, even if only inwardly. It would be a worthy, heroic thing to do, he thought, to make this woman laugh again as she had laughed at the Kramer house, and to make her do it again and again. Perhaps he ought to make it his life's mission. Would it be an achievable goal, though? He half smiled in the darkness. Sometimes one wondered where such absurd fancies came from. He must still be horribly bored.

According to the older ladies, it was dreadfully late

when they arrived home. According to the grandfather clock in its splendid old case in the hall, it was not quite eleven o'clock. Percy bade the ladies good night, ascertained from Crutchley that a fire had been lit in the library, and took himself off there for a read and a drink before going to bed for sheer lack of anything more interesting to do.

Inevitably there were animals in the room—two cats on the hearth and Hector under the desk. Percy ignored them.

He was pouring himself some port at the sideboard when the door opened and Lady Barclay stepped inside. She had shed her cloak and bonnet and donned a woolen shawl over that fetching blue evening dress of hers. It was not elaborately styled. None of her dresses was that he had seen. They did not need to be, though. She had the most perfect figure he had ever seen. Not that anything could be *most* perfect or even *more* perfect, since *perfect* was an absolute in itself. He could hear that explanation in the voice of one of his tutors.

"Wine?" he asked her.

"Why was Mr. Tidmouth at my house this afternoon?" she asked him. "And why were there *six* workmen with him? Why has the cost of the new roof dropped in half?"

Ah.

"Wine?" he asked again.

She took a few steps in his direction. She had come to do battle, he could see. She did not answer his question.

"*My* house?" he said. "As in *yours*? I still maintain that it is mine, Lady Barclay, though you may live in it with my blessing until your eightieth year if you so choose, or your ninetieth should you live so long. After that we will renegotiate."

"You went to see him." She took another step closer. "You ranted at him. You threatened him."

He raised his eyebrows. She looked rather magnificent when she was angry. Anger put some color in her cheeks and a sparkle in her eyes.

"Ranted?" he said faintly, closing one hand about the handle of his quizzing glass—*not* the jeweled one—and raising it halfway to his eye. "Threatened? You wrong me, ma'am, I do assure you."

"Oh." Her eyes narrowed. "I suppose you just played haughty aristocrat."

"Played?" Briefly he raised the glass all the way to his eye. "But what is the point of being an aristocrat, ma'am, if one cannot also play at being what one is? I do assure you, it renders rants and threats quite unnecessary. Underlings, in which category I number roofers, quite wilt in the presence of hauteur and a jeweled quizzing glass and a lace-edged handkerchief."

"You had no *right*." She had taken yet more steps closer.

"On the contrary, ma'am," he said, "I had every right."

He was rather enjoying himself, he realized. This was better than reading his book, which was the poetry of Alexander Pope of all things.

"It was *my* battle to fight," she told him. "I resent your interference."

"Despite your title, ma'am," he said, "and the impressive fact that you are the third cousin-in-law once removed of the Earl of Hardford, you seem not to have overcome what must be Tidmouth's total disregard for women. He undoubtedly belongs to an inferior subspecies of the human race, and one must pity his wife and daughters, if there are such persons. But the fact remains that you need his services, since he appears to have no competition for at least fifty miles around. *I* need his services too. Without them I might be doomed to having to offer you my continued hospitality here at Hardford Hall for another year or more."

That took the wind out of her sails. His too, actually. He was never rude to women. Well, almost never. Only to this one woman, it seemed.

"You are no gentleman, Lord Hardford," she said.

He might not have proved her right if she had not been close—entirely her own doing, since he had not moved an inch away from the sideboard. But she *was* close, and he did not even have to stretch his arm to the full in order to curl his hand about the nape of her neck. He did not have to bend very far forward in order to set his mouth to hers.

He kissed her.

And he did not need even the fraction of one second to know that he had made a *big mistake*.

From her point of view it was certainly that. She broke off the kiss after perhaps two seconds and cracked him across one cheek with an open palm.

And from his point of view—he wanted her. But she was the most inappropriate woman to want he could possibly have chosen—except that he had not chosen. That would be preposterous. She was the marble lady.

His cheek stung and his eye watered. It was a new experience. He had never before been slapped across the face.

"How *dare* you."

He owed her a groveling apology—at the very least.

"It was only a kiss," he said instead.

"Only—" Her eyes widened. "That was no kiss, *Lord*

Hardford. *That* was an insult. It was insufferable. *You* are insufferable. And I suppose you paid Mr. Tidmouth for half of my roof?"

"In my experience," he said, "half a roof is more or less useless."

"I can well afford the whole thing," she told him.

"So can I," he assured her. "You will note, ma'am, that I pandered to your pride sufficiently to leave half the bill unpaid."

She stared at him. She was probably admiring her handiwork. He did not doubt that his cheek bore the scarlet imprint of her palm and all five fingers. It was still stinging like the devil. He would be wise not to provoke her in the future.

"Shall we agree to the compromise?" he asked her.

"It will be the greatest of pleasures," she said, "to move back into my own house. For me as well as for you."

"You see?" he said. "When we try hard enough, we can come to mutual agreement on more than one theme. How bad is smuggling in this part of the world? *Would* you like some wine?"

"Yes," she said after a small hesitation.

She took her glass from him after he had poured the wine, but she did not move away toward a chair.

"My father-in-law liked his brandy," she told him, "as do most of the gentlemen in this part of the world. He saw no wrong in defrauding the government of some taxes and tariffs. He saw customs officials and riding officers as the natural enemy of freedom and luxury, while the smugglers were heroes upholding the right of a gentleman to the best brandy his money could buy."

"This house is close to the sea," he said. "Its cellars were used to store smuggled goods, I suppose?"

"Close, but not close enough," she said, swirling the wine in her glass for a moment before lifting it to her lips.

"The dower house?"

She raised her eyes to his. "You may have noticed," she said, "that it is not far from that precipitous path to the beach. There are steps and a doorway on the side of the house facing the sea that lead directly to the cellar. I insisted upon having every item of contraband removed and the door blocked up from inside and out before I went to live there. Father-in-Law saw to it. He was fond enough of me to want me to be safe and not endangered in any way by all that viciousness. And he knew that Dicky had always been vehemently opposed to allowing smuggling on Hardford land and the products of smuggling in the dower house."

Well. Interesting.

"Viciousness?"

"It is *not* a romantic business," she said, "despite all the stories to the contrary that you parodied on the way home." She drained her glass and set it down on the sideboard. "Good night, Lord Hardford. And if you ever try to kiss me again, I will reply with my fist rather than my open hand."

He grinned at her. "A tactical error, Lady Barclay," he said. "One never forewarns an adversary. To forewarn is to forearm."

She turned and left him. She closed the door quietly behind her. Not for Lady Barclay any unbridled passion or slammed doors.

His cheek was *still* stinging.

What the devil had possessed him? But if that kiss had lasted for two seconds, and he believed it had, then for at least one of those seconds she had kissed him back. It was like that laugh at the Kramer ladies' house—blink and you missed it.

He had not blinked on either occasion.

When was marble not marble? And why was marble marble? Especially when it was not actual marble but a woman. *Why* was she marble? There must be thousands of women who had been widowed by the Napoleonic Wars. If they had all turned to marble forever after, England would be a marble nation, or half marble anyway. There would still be human men, he supposed. Pretty frustrated human men.

He considered his book. Perhaps poetry—blank verse, no less—was just what his mind needed to compose itself for sleep.

He strode back into the hall instead and donned his greatcoat and hat and gloves. He ought to go upstairs to change his footwear, but evening shoes would have to do. He let himself out through the front doors and strode directly across the lawn toward the cliffs. The clouds had moved off sufficiently to allow some moonlight and starlight through to light his way and ensure that he did not stride right off the edge. An alarming thought—but he would be pricked to death first by the gorse bushes.

Hector, he noticed suddenly, was at his heels. Lord, that dog would be sleeping at the end of his bed next.

"Protecting me from ghosts and smugglers and other assorted villains, are you?" Percy asked him. "That's my boy."

7

Imogen's palm was still stinging. It was still red too, she saw in the light of the candle on her dressing table.

She hated him. Worse, she hated herself. *Hated* herself.

She could have avoided that kiss. She could have kept her distance from him. But even apart from that, there had been time to realize his intent and turn away. There had been a look in his eyes to warn her, the lifting of his hand to set at the back of her neck, the bending of his head toward hers. Oh, yes, there had been time.

She had not turned away.

And though for the first moment after his mouth touched hers—*mouth,* not just lips—her mind had been blank with shock, there had also been that next moment when her mind had not been blank at all, when she had wanted him with a fierce longing and had kissed him back. Just the merest moment.

But how long was a moment? Had anyone ever defined it? Set time limits upon it? Was a moment one second long? Half a second? Ten minutes? She had no idea how long her moment of weakness had lasted. It did not matter, though. It had happened, and she would never forgive herself.

Only a kiss, indeed.

Only a kiss!

He had *no* idea. But could she expect him to? He was a mere man—a handsome, virile, arrogant man who had probably always had just what he wanted of life, including any woman he desired. She had seen the way all the women, regardless of age and marital status, had looked at him tonight. Oh, no, he certainly could have had no idea. They had been alone together in the library late at night, they had been standing close to each other, and they had been quarreling. *Of course* his thoughts had turned to lust. It would have been surprising if they had not.

Imogen sat on the stool before the dressing table, her back to the mirror. Her life was suddenly in tatters again, and there were still several weeks to go before the annual gathering of the Survivors' Club at Penderris Hall. Her longing for the company and comfort of those six men was suddenly so acute that it bent her in two from the waist until her forehead almost touched her knees. George, Duke of Stanbrook, was probably at home. If she went early . . .

If she went early, he would welcome her warmly and without question. She would find herself enveloped in peace and safety and . . .

But she had to learn to cope alone with her living. That was what she thought she *had* done by the end of those three years at Penderris. She had made a pact with life. She would go through the motions of living it, return to Hardford, be an attentive daughter-in-law and niece, a cheerful and sociable neighbor, a fond daughter and sister and aunt. She would live alone without allowing herself to become a recluse. She would be kind—above all else she would be kind. And she would breathe one breath after another until there were no more, until her heart stopped and brought her final, blessed oblivion.

She would go on, she had decided, but she would not *live*. She was not entitled to do that. The physician at Penderris had tried to lead her out of it, but she had remained adamant. Her six friends had offered comfort and encouragement and love, abundant and unconditional. They would have offered advice too if she had solicited it, but she had never asked them to talk her out of the future she had set herself.

She spread her hands over her face and ached with longing to see them all again, to hear their voices, to know herself accepted for who she was, *known* for who she was and loved anyway. Ah, yes, for three weeks out of each year she allowed herself to be loved.

Now her fragile peace had been shattered—by one moment and what the Earl of Hardford had carelessly dubbed *only a kiss*.

Imogen undressed for bed though she had no expectation that she would sleep.

Percy absented himself from home for most of the next day. Assaulting a lady who was living under the protection of his own roof was decidedly *not* the thing, and he certainly owed her an apology, which he would get to in good time. First, though, he needed to take himself off and out of her sight for a while.

He checked that the roofers were working at the dower house again—they were, all six of them, as well as

Tidmouth, who was inside the garden gate, leaning back against it, arms folded, looking masterful. Percy did not linger in case Lady Barclay should come on the same errand.

He paid calls upon Alton and Sir Matthew Quentin, both of whom owned land and farmed it even if they had never actually wielded a hoe or sheared a sheep. He felt woefully ignorant. No, he *was* woefully ignorant, and he needed to do something about it. He found himself tramping about the land of each in turn for the whole day and talking about virtually nothing other than farming—even with Lady Quentin at luncheon, since she set the topics of conversation. Alarmingly, he realized as he rode homeward in the late afternoon, he had enjoyed himself enormously and had felt not one jot of boredom. He had begun to conceive ideas for his own land. He was even excited at the prospect of conferring with his new steward when that as-yet-unknown individual arrived.

Excited?

He was going to be a candidate for Bedlam if he did not leave Cornwall soon and return to civilization and his familiar idle existence.

He spent the evening in the library reading Pope, while the ladies presumably conversed and drank tea and busied themselves with whatever worthy and productive projects ladies *did* busy themselves with in the drawing room above. Lady Barclay had been almost silent during dinner and more like granite than marble. He obviously owed her a *serious* apology.

He took the path toward the dower house again the following morning, Hector trotting inevitably in his wake, though it was not his intended destination. That was something altogether different, something for which he had steeled his nerve last night after Pope had lost his appeal—twenty pages of blank verse could do that.

She was at her house before him today. She was standing at the gate—a popular place, that—talking with Tidmouth, who was oozing oily obsequiousness, especially after he spotted Percy approaching. And good God, there was actually a roof on the house, six workers swarming over it, looking diligent.

Percy considered turning away and proceeding with his main plan for the morning, but sooner or later she was going to have to be confronted at more than a dining room table with her aunt and the female baritone to stand between him and embarrassment and humble pie.

"Ah, Tidmouth," he said after bidding Lady Barclay a good morning, "you are gracing us with your presence and your expertise again today, are you? Cracking the whip?"

"Anything and everything to oblige a lady, Your Lordship," the man said with a leer, revealing a mouthful of square, yellow teeth. "Cold as the weather is, it being only February and not normally the time of year for such bitter outdoor work, I will put myself and my men to any trouble and inconvenience necessary for the lady to have a roof over her head. No whipping required."

"Quite so," Percy said. "I will leave you to it, then. Cousin, may I interest you in a walk?"

She looked at him as though walking with him was the very last thing she wished to do. But perhaps she recognized the inevitability of a tête-à-tête encounter with him sooner or later.

"You may," she said.

He did not offer his arm, and she did not show any sign that she either needed or expected to take it as she fell into step beside him.

"I believe," she said stiffly as they moved out of ear-shot of the man at the gate, "I ought to thank you for intervening on my behalf with Mr. Tidmouth. I was despairing of getting back into my house this year, but he has promised that I will be in next week."

"You are thanking me, then," he said, "for making it possible for you to leave me so soon?"

"That would sound ungracious."

"But true?"

"May I remind you," she said, "that it was you two evenings ago who lamented the fact that the longer my house was uninhabitable, the longer you were obliged to offer me hospitality in yours."

"I am sorry about that kiss," he said. "It ought never to have happened, especially beneath my own roof, where I should be protecting you from insult, not offering it myself."

"But as you observed at the time," she said, turning her head away so that he could not see her face around the brim of her bonnet, "it was *only* a kiss."

It sounded as if he was not to be forgiven.

They stopped at the top of the broken cliff face with its zigzagging path downward. He had stopped a little farther back two nights ago, on the other side of the gorse bushes, when he had come to see if any smugglers were swarming the beach, cutlasses at the ready—at least, that was what he assumed he had come to see. He had been a bit agitated at the time. His knees felt decidedly weak now, and his breathing quickened.

It was not a windy day, but there was enough of a breeze to make the air nippy. The tide looked halfway in—or halfway out. He had no idea which. Waves were breaking in a line of foam along the beach. The sea beyond them was foam-flecked too. Apart from that, it was steely gray.

"Would you care to go down?" he asked her.

Please say no. *Please say no.*

"I thought you were afraid of the sea and the cliffs," she said.

"Afraid?" He raised his eyebrows, all incredulity. "I? Whatever gave you that idea?"

Her eyes searched his face for a disconcerting moment, and then she turned and disappeared over the edge. Oh, nothing quite as drastic as that. She stepped off the cliff-top path and onto the track down and then she kept on going. She did not look back.

He looked down at Hector. "Stay here or trot back home," he advised. "No one, least of all I, will call you a coward."

And no one would call him a coward either, by thunder. No one ever had. No one had ever had cause — well, except once. He just happened to be terrified witless of the sea. Ditto of sheer cliffs. Not too fond of golden sands either, mainly because they had a nasty habit of widening and narrowing with the tide — sometimes narrowing to a point at which sea and cliffs joined forces.

Why the devil did he need to prove anything to himself? But it was too late now to change his plan. He could hardly stand up here and wait to wave down at her when she reached the beach.

He launched out into space.

It was not even a particularly dangerous track, of course. Indeed, it was a well-used thoroughfare. It had been climbed numerous times, had it not, by bands of smugglers as they hauled casks of brandy and Lord knew what other contraband, to be stored in the cellar of the dower house. Lady Barclay had probably tripped up and down here a thousand times for pure pleasure—though his mind's choice of the word *tripped* caused his stomach a moment of distress.

There were just a couple of places where the path disappeared, to be replaced by rocks large and sturdy enough to provide perfectly safe footing. He was down on the beach almost before he knew it, his feeling of relief and triumph tempered only by the knowledge that somehow he was going to have to get himself back up there in the foreseeable future.

Something was bleating. There was no sign of any sheep. But Hector, he could see, was stranded on the jutting rock just above shoulder level and could not seem to find the path that would have brought him the rest of the way down.

"I believe," Lady Barclay said, "you have a friend, Lord Hardford."

"Only one?" he said. "Could I be that pathetic?"

He reached up and gathered the dog in his arms. He did it carefully. The creature's legs still looked as if they could be snapped as easily as dry twigs. Its ribs were still clearly visible, though they were beginning to acquire a thin covering of fat. He turned, the dog still in his arms, and caught a look on Lady Barclay's face that surely teetered on the brink of laughter.

"What?" he asked.

"Nothing," she said.

"Something."

"I was reminded," she said, "of a picture Aunt Lavinia has hanging in her bedchamber. It is a sentimental depiction of Jesus holding a lamb."

Good God!

He set Hector down on the sand, and the dog gamboled off to visit a pair of seagulls, which did not wait to be greeted.

"It is to be hoped, ma'am," Percy said, "that you never have a chance to make that observation in the hearing of any of my acquaintances. My reputation would be in tatters."

"Your reputation for manliness, I suppose you mean," she said. "I daresay that is more important to you than anything else."

"You have a caustic tongue, ma'am," he said, clasping his hands behind his back and squinting down the beach toward the sea. Actually, everything looked a bit better from down here. The sea was still far enough away to seem unthreatening.

"I merely meant to suggest," she said, "that there is nothing particularly *unmanly* about caring for a dog that cannot care for itself."

He had no desire to pursue that particular line of conversation. "I can see," he said, "that this would be a perfect spot for smugglers."

"Yes," she agreed. "The bay is sheltered, and there are no dangerous rocks to make a landing treacherous. There is a way up the cliffs too. There is even a cave."

"Show me," he said.

It was a large one and conveniently close to the path up to the top. It stretched deep into the cliffs. Percy stood on the threshold, peering in.

"Does the tide reach this high?" he asked.

"Almost never," she said. "The high-tide mark is well below here."

Yes, he could see the dividing line between soft, powdery sand and hard, very flat beach that got watered every twelve hours by the tide.

"There is no smuggling in this particular bay any longer?" he asked.

"If there is," she said, "they do not come up onto Hardford land. Not that I would know for sure, I suppose, unless I sat at a darkened window deep into the blackest nights. They certainly do not use the cellar of the dower house any longer."

"Why did you use the word *vicious*?" he asked her as they turned from the cave to stroll along the beach, the chilly salt breeze in their faces.

She shrugged. "The leaders can be bullies and tyrants. They sometimes press men into service, I have heard. And they have been known to enforce loyalty and secrecy with threats and even violence. There was a young groom here who worshiped my husband and loved to work for him. He begged to go to the Peninsula as his batman, but he was only fourteen at the time and his father refused his permission. He remained here in safety. I do not know exactly what his transgression was—we were away from here by then—and he would not say the only time I asked him after I came back, but they broke both his legs. He still works in the stables— Aunt Lavinia saw to that. But the bones did not set well. And his spirit was broken."

Lord, he did not need this, Percy thought. His life to the age of thirty had been remarkably serene and trouble-free. He had been careful to keep it that way. And he had no wish to change things. Why should he? He liked his life just the way it was. Well, except for the boredom, perhaps, and the general feeling of uselessness and time passing him by.

"Wenzel fancies you," he said, bending to pick up a piece of driftwood to hurl for Hector's entertainment.

She turned her head sharply toward him at the sudden change of subject. "He is a good man," she said. "He was my husband's closest friend."

"But you do not fancy him?" he asked her.

"I do not believe, Lord Hardford," she said, "my personal life and fancies are any concern of yours."

"Ah," he said, grinning at her.

Her cheeks were pink—from the wind rather than from indignation, he guessed, for her nose was a bit rosy too. She looked very wholesome—neither marble nor granite. Though definitely peeved. "But you are my third cousin-in-law once removed and therefore of familial concern to me."

"I am not at all convinced Aunt Lavinia is certain of her facts," she said. "But even if she is right, it is a *very* remote connection and not one of blood. I do not *fancy* Mr. Wenzel or any other man, Lord Hardford. I have no interest in courtship or remarriage, as I believe I have told you before."

"Why?" he asked. "Oh, yes, I know we started this conversation before, but it did not progress very far. I asked your age, I recall, but you would not give it, and who can blame you? It is impolite to ask such a question of a lady. I am guessing you are about my age. I celebrated my thirtieth birthday two days before I set out for Cornwall."

"There is no shame in being thirty," she said, "even for a woman."

Which, he supposed, provided him with his answer.

"In my experience," he said, "there is a marked difference between men and women when it comes to matrimony. Women want it, full stop; men want it or at least will tolerate it in their own good time."

"And will *you* tolerate it in *your* good time?" she asked.

Hector was standing before him, panting and gazing upward with his bulging, ever-hopeful eyes. That dog was *not* going to be pretty even when it had fattened up. The stick lay on the sand between them. Percy bent to pick it up and hurl it again.

"Probably," he said. "There is the succession to secure and all that since there appears to be an alarming dearth of possible heirs at present. How long has your husband been gone?"

"More than eight years," she said, turning to walk onward.

She had probably told him that before too. "So you were about twenty-two," he said.

"According to your calculations," she said, "I suppose I was."

"And how long were you married?" he asked.

"Almost four years."

"Eight years have not been a long enough time in which to heal?" he asked. "Twice as long as you were married?" He was genuinely puzzled. He could not imagine a love quite so enduring or a pain quite so intense. He did not particularly want to imagine it either.

She stopped again and turned to look out to sea. "Some things do not heal," she said. "Ever."

He could not leave it alone. "Is there not some . . . indiscipline?" he asked. "Some self-indulgence? Have not other people suffered widowhood and got over it? Is there not a point at which continuing to suffer becomes . . . almost ostentatious? Worn like a badge of honor to set you above other, ordinary mortals whose sufferings cannot possibly match your own?"

He was being markedly offensive. And with each added word he was making things worse. He was almost angry with her. But *why*? Because he had once kissed her for all of two seconds and could not seem to put the kiss out of his mind? Because she had once laughed at something he said but had not laughed since? Because she was the one woman out of the legions he had known who was quite impervious to his charms?

He was beginning not to like himself a great deal.

He ought to have apologized, but was silent instead. Hector was panting at his feet again, and once more was sent in pursuit of the stick. Where did such a skeletal creature find the energy?

"Have you seen me on any occasion display open suffering, Lord Hardford?" she asked, her eyes on the incoming waves—they were definitely *in*coming. "If you have, I beg you to inform me so that I may make the necessary adjustments to my behavior." She waited for an answer.

"You have shown none, of course," he admitted. "But one cannot help wondering when one meets a young and beautiful woman who has clothed herself in marble what lies within. And one cannot help guessing that it must be suffering."

"Perhaps," she said, "there is nothing. Perhaps the marble is solid, or perhaps it is hollow and there is nothing but emptiness within."

"Perhaps," he conceded. "But if that is the case, where

did the laughter come from two evenings ago? And the kiss? For a moment on that evening it was not just I kissing you. We were kissing each other."

"You have the imagination of a thoroughly conceited man, Lord Hardford," she said.

"Ah, and you have a lying tongue, Lady Barclay."

Hector appeared to have tired himself out. He fetched the stick and plopped down at Percy's feet. He became instantly comatose.

"If it is any consolation to you," she said, "my total lack of interest in you has nothing to do with you personally. Without any doubt, I have never met a more handsome man than you or one more capable of charm. If I *were* interested in flirtation or courtship or remarriage, I might well consider setting my cap at you, though I am fully aware that doing so would be inviting certain disappointment and heartache. Fortunately, perhaps, I am *not* interested. Not in you and not in any other man. Not in *that* way. Ever. And if it offends your manly sensibilities to hear me say it, then comfort yourself with the thought that within a week I will be back living at the dower house."

"Total lack of interest," he said, "yet you kissed me."

"You took me by surprise," she said, and the words hung between them almost as though they had some significance beyond their surface meaning.

What *did* her self-discipline hide? Why would she not let go of it? Mourning for eight years after a four-year marriage surely *was* excessive and self-absorbed. But he would not pry further. She would not tell him, and if she did, he had the feeling he really, *really* would not want to know.

What had happened to her when she was in captivity?

"If I wear marble as an armor," she said, breaking the strange silence, which had made him very aware of the elemental roar of the sea and the harsh, lonely cry of seagulls, "then you wear charm, Lord Hardford. A careless sort of charm. One wonders what lies behind it."

"Oh, nothing, I do assure you," he told her. "Nothing whatsoever. I am pure charm through to the heart."

Although the brim of her gray bonnet half hid her face from view, he could see that she smiled.

And it somehow made his heart ache—his very charming heart.

She turned her head to look at him. The smile was gone, but her eyes were open. Well, of course they were. She would hardly look at him with closed eyes, would she, unless she was inviting another kiss, which she decidedly was not. But they were . . . open. The only trouble was that he could not interpret what he saw inside them.

She really was quite incredibly beautiful. He clasped his hands behind his back to stop himself from touching one finger to that tantalizingly curved upper lip.

"I believe," she said softly, "that after all you are almost likable, Lord Hardford. Let us leave it at that, shall we?"

Almost likable.

Foolishly, he felt that it might be the most precious compliment he had ever been paid.

"Am I forgiven, then?" he asked her. "For kissing you?"

"I am not sure you are *that* likable," she said, turning to make her way back toward the path to the top.

She had actually made a *joke,* Percy thought, looking down at Hector, who had awoken from his coma and was scrambling to his feet.

"I am not going to have to carry you up, I hope," Percy said.

Hector waved his stubby tail.

8

I believe that after all you are almost likable.

It embarrassed Imogen to recall that she had said that aloud. It puzzled her that she might have meant it, with the reservation of that *almost,* of course.

She would love to have seen him confront Mr. Tidmouth in his shop. It would have made a delicious anecdote with which to regale her friends at Penderris next month. She would wager he had neither blustered nor raised his voice. She wondered what he *did* hide behind his surface charm, if anything. He had not always been charming with her, of course. It would be a long time before she forgot his very first words to her—*and who the devil might you be*? He might be nothing but empty conceit. That poor dog was firmly attached to him, though, and dogs were often more discerning than people. Of course, Hector did nothing to enhance his chosen master's manly image. Imogen found herself smiling at the thought—and she *must* remember to tell her friends how he had resembled that very sentimental painting of Jesus cradling a lamb in his arms and how thunderstruck he had looked when she told him so.

She found herself thinking altogether too much about the Earl of Hardford during the rest of that day and the next. His very masculine presence in the house, though she did not see much of him, was altogether too suffocating. But she could not resent it or, ultimately, him. For this was his home. The hall and the park and estate belonged to him. Even the dower house belonged to him — as he had not scrupled to point out to her on more than one occasion. The *title* belonged to him.

How she longed to be back in the dower house, where she would have to see the Earl of Hardford far less frequently. She hoped he would not stay. But surely he would not. The new parliamentary session and the Season would begin in London after Easter. Surely he would not wish to absent himself from either. Perhaps by the time she returned from Penderris he would be gone. And perhaps he would never come back. He seemed not to be overfond of the sea. She would swear he had had to steel his nerve to descend the path to the beach, as though it were a challenge he had set himself. And he had stood gingerly on the threshold of the cave rather than going inside to explore it. He had eyed the incoming tide with noticeable unease.

He was not finding the house too comfortable either. He had told Aunt Lavinia that he intended giving the order to have all the chimneys cleaned and had looked surprised when she informed him that they had all been swept before Christmas. Apparently a whole shower of soot had fallen from the chimney in his bedchamber one night and blackened half his room. And he had also mentioned the damp bed linens he had had to have replaced on his first night here, a fact that was puzzling, since Aunt Lavinia had been so sure those sheets had come directly from the airing cupboard. She had even checked them herself. The dampness had probably been his imagination. Bed linens could be cold on a winter night and *seem* damp.

Imogen checked her appearance in the pier glass in her room. Fortunately, one did not have to dress with any great formality for an assembly at the village inn. Her sage green silk with its overdress of silvery gauze, always one of her favorites, would do nicely, even though it was almost two years since she had bought it in London for Hugo's wedding, and she had worn it to a number of village entertainments. She adjusted the silver ribbon about the high waist and shook out the skirt, which fell straight and loose before flaring slightly at the hem. The sleeves were short, the neckline square and low but not immodestly so. She ran her hands lightly over her smooth chignon to make sure it did not need any more hairpins, and then drew on her long silver gloves and picked up her fan.

He had asked her to reserve the first waltz for him, Imogen remembered with a slight lurching of the stomach as she left her room. It would be the *only* waltz, actually. There was always only one, since most people here had never learned the steps and a few outright disapproved of the dance because of the intimacy it forced upon the partners. Fortunately, other more liberal opinions had prevailed, thus far anyway.

Imogen liked waltzing, even though there was no gentleman here who could perform the steps with true grace.

Tonight she would waltz with the Earl of Hardford.

He was waiting in the entrance hall with Cousin Adelaide, who looked formidable in purple, her usual outfit for the assemblies. It included three tall purple plumes, which stood straight up on her head. Two circles of rouge had been painted onto her cheeks with admirable geometric precision.

The earl's eyes swept over Imogen from head to toe. She returned the compliment and saw his lips purse as he understood what she was doing.

There was nothing with which to find fault in his appearance, of course. He was dressed immaculately in black, white, and silver and looked quietly elegant as a true gentleman ought. With his looks and physique, of course, he needed no padding.

"No jewelry, Lady Barclay?" he asked. "But then, you do not need any. Or frills and flounces either."

Actually, she was wearing the small pearl ear studs her father had given her on her marriage, and her wedding ring. But . . . had she just been complimented? She thought she had. And he did it awfully well. One felt a certain warmth about the heart without realizing just what had caused it. A certain warmth toward *him*. He had, she supposed, perfected the art of gallantry—probably of seduction too.

Aunt Lavinia appeared on the stairs before she could answer him, and she turned to take her cloak from Mr. Crutchley. But another hand took it from the butler instead, and the Earl of Hardford wrapped it about her shoulders while at the same time complimenting Aunt Lavinia upon the evening gown she had had made earlier this winter.

And then they were crammed inside his traveling carriage again, with the same seating arrangement as before. They arrived at the inn just before the journey could become too uncomfortably cold. There was already a crowd in the assembly rooms upstairs. Imogen noticed the extra buzz of excitement the appearance of the Earl of Hardford caused as he stepped into the rooms, all charm and ease of manner. Fans began fluttering at a fast pace.

"You put us all to shame as usual, Imogen," Lady Quentin said, linking an arm through hers while her husband undertook to introduce the earl to some people he had not yet met. "You always make simplicity look quite exquisite. However, you have the face and figure to carry it off. The rest of us would merely look plain or worse if we tried to imitate you."

"You look perfectly wonderful, as always, Elizabeth," Imogen assured her. Lady Quentin was on the small side and on the plump side too, but she had glossy dark hair, worn in intricate curls and ringlets tonight, and she had a pretty, animated face.

"You have not, I suppose," she said, "fallen head over heels in love with Lord Hardford? You never do fall in love, do you? Sometimes I wish you would, though he would have to be the right gentleman. My guess is that the earl is definitely *not* the right one. You are not the sort to be willing to share her mate with all the rest of the female world. Am I being spiteful?"

"Dreadfully," Imogen said, turning with her friend to look at him work his charm on a blushing, tittering, already adoring circle of fan flutterers. "Though I do believe his charm is something of an armor. He will smile at all those girls and flatter them and pay them outrageous compliments. He will dance with as many of them as time will allow. But he will not marry any of them—or, more important, do anything specifically to single any out or raise her hopes or compromise her virtue either."

Her own words surprised her. Was she so sure of that—

that he would not willingly hurt any virtuous lady or girl? Oh, dear, she really must be starting to like him—or falling prey to some of his charm herself.

Tilly Wenzel arrived with her brother at that moment and came to join them, and the three of them spent an entertaining quarter of an hour before the dancing began observing their neighbors and friends as they arrived and commenting upon their looks and demeanor and an occasional new dress or trimming. There was nothing spiteful in their remarks, however. On the whole, they were a neighborhood of friends. She was fortunate in that, Imogen realized. They were all particularly pleased to see Mrs. Park make a slow entrance between her son and the vicar. She was determinedly recovering from her hip injury. Young Mr. Soames held the most comfortable chair in the room for her while she seated herself, and then he drew up a chair for Cousin Adelaide and another for Mrs. Kramer so that the three of them could converse comfortably.

For a few years after leaving Penderris Hall, Imogen had not danced. As a girl she had always enjoyed dancing—had *loved* it, in fact, and would dance long into the night whenever the chance presented itself. After—she tended to think of her life in terms of before and after—she would not allow herself any such indulgence. But eventually she had realized that her refusal to dance when she was still only in her middle twenties was a disappointment to her neighbors. For in addition to her youth, she was the Viscountess Barclay, daughter-in-law of the Earl of Hardford, widow of the young viscount of whom they had all been inordinately fond. They all genuinely hoped to see her recover from her bereavement and breakdown. They wanted to help make her happy again.

It had never been her intention to make a parade of her grief. Suffering was not attractive when put upon display.

And so she had started to dance again.

Tonight she danced the opening set of country dances with Mr. Wenzel, who hoped Mr. Alton had not yet reserved the waltz with her and that he might do so himself. And then she danced the Sir Roger de Coverley with Mr. Alton, who flattered himself that Lady Barclay must already have reserved the waltz for him. She had to explain to both that the Earl of Hardford had already spoken for that particular set. She danced with Admiral Payne and then Sir Matthew Quentin before supper.

And then, after partaking of a hearty meal, Cousin Adelaide announced that she was ready to go home. Aunt Lavinia admitted that she too was feeling somewhat weary, though the evening had been very pleasant and she was sorry to cut it short for dear Imogen's sake. Imogen quelled her disappointment—the waltz was still to come.

"I will have the carriage brought up to the door," she said, "and see if the landlord can arrange for some hot bricks for your feet."

But the Earl of Hardford had moved up behind them at the table where they had sat for supper.

"You need not concern yourself, Cousin Imogen," he said. "I will arrange it all myself. My carriage will convey Cousin Lavinia and Mrs. Ferby back to the hall and return later for you and me."

And he sauntered away even while Aunt Lavinia was still thanking him.

"I am quite delighted that you will be able to stay," she said, setting a hand on Imogen's arm while she spoke quietly beneath the hum of conversation around them. "It is far too early for young people to return home when there is so much enjoyment still to be had here. Cousin Percy is most kind and thoughtful."

Yes, he was, Imogen agreed. His leaving so early might have caused a village riot, of course, but he could have sent her home in the carriage and remained here himself, unencumbered by female relatives. Did she wish he had done just that? She could still insist upon going, she supposed. But ... there was the waltz. And he *did* dance well. She had noticed. He had danced each set so far with a different lady, and he had given each his full attention, smiling and talking whenever the figures brought him close to his partner. He danced with assurance and easy grace.

It was so *hard* to find fault with him.

But ... was there anything to his character apart from the charm? Any substance? She still had not made up her mind. But it did not matter. Soon she would be back in her own home and need have little to do with him even if he stayed at Hardford Hall, which was doubtful.

He made the arrangements for the carriage and the hot bricks and saw the two ladies on their way before leading Ruth Boodle, the second and plainest of the vicar's daughters, into a vigorous reel. He soon had her flushed and laughing and looking really quite pretty. Imogen returned her attention to her own partner.

And then it was time for the waltz and he was standing before her, one hand extended for hers, no smile on his face, no bow, no words, merely a very direct look into her eyes. His own were quite extraordinarily blue, she thought foolishly, as though she were noticing their color for the first time. Even in *them* there was no imperfection.

It was all very deliberate, she thought. And, yes, very effective too. For of course her stomach muscles clenched and her stomach fluttered and she hoped—oh, she *hoped*—her cheeks were not flushing.

She set her hand in his and allowed him to lead her onto the almost empty dance floor. It always was almost empty for the waltz. Not many people knew the steps, though they were simple enough, and even fewer had the courage to perform them before their neighbors. But nearly everyone loved to watch those who *did* have the courage. And the very sparseness of the dancers allowed for all sorts of twirls and fancy footwork, at all of which Mr. Alton, her usual waltzing partner, was adept.

On this occasion, she could see, Mr. Alton was to dance with Tilly. Young Mr. Soames was leading out Rachel Boodle, while Sir Matthew Quentin had taken to the floor with Mrs. Payne. Elizabeth was with Mr. Wenzel. And that was to be that. There was always a feeling of exposure just before a waltz began, an anticipated exhilaration, a certain fear that one would trip over one's own feet or tread upon one's partner's or otherwise make a cake of oneself.

The Earl of Hardford had not taken his eyes off her. She would swear he had not. Nor had he smiled—or spoken. It was all very different from the way he had treated his other partners. Imogen looked into his eyes again and found that they were indeed focused upon her.

"What part are you playing now?" she asked him.

"Part? As in a play?" He raised his eyebrows. "Now? As opposed to . . . when?"

"You are neither smiling nor oozing charm," she said, "as you have been with your other partners."

Oh, dear, she was never rude to people.

"But if I were doing either, Cousin," he said, "you would quite surely accuse me of playing a, er, part. Would you not? It appears I cannot win your approbation no matter what I do. Perhaps it would help if I knew what game it was we played."

Why did the music not begin? It appeared that the violinist had broken one of his strings and was still tuning the new one with the help of the pianist.

"I thought to appear sober and serious in your eyes," he said. "Even brooding. I thought to *impress* you."

"Shall we forget my rudeness?" she suggested. "I apologize for it."

"And you have been watching me, have you?" he asked her.

She frowned her incomprehension.

"You noticed that I have been smiling and oozing charm for the benefit of my other partners," he explained.

"How could I *help* but notice?" she asked curtly.

"Quite so." His head had dipped slightly closer to hers, and he . . . smiled. Oh, not the smile of practiced charm he had used upon everyone else this evening, but one that crinkled his eyes at the corners and looked warm and genuine and . . . affectionate?

The way one would smile at a valued cousin?

Imogen pressed her lips hard together and tried to curb her indignation. She was very aware that they were standing in the middle of the large assembly room, surrounded by empty space, the eyes of a largish gathering of people upon them.

The orchestra came to her rescue with a decisive chord before she could make any other sharp retort.

He set his right hand against the back of her waist and took her right hand in his left as she placed her hand on his shoulder. And . . . Oh, and he was *very* different from Mr. Alton. He was taller for one thing. His hands were firm and long-fingered and warm. His shoulder was solid muscle and broad. And he had . . . an aura? There was body heat, certainly, accentuated by a faint, enticing cologne. But it was more than body heat and more than cologne. Whatever it was, it wrapped about her even though he stood a very correct distance away. It was more than an aura too. An aura was sexless, or at least she thought it was. This was raw masculinity.

Could it be deliberate? Or was it a part of him, just as the blue eyes were and the dark hair and the handsome face?

The music began.

Imogen's first thought was that he certainly knew how to waltz. Her second thought was that he had a feel for the soul of the dance to a degree that he did not need to show off with fancy steps and exaggerated twirls. Her third thought was that dancing had never ever been so exhilarating. And then all thought ceased. She was too caught up in the moment, in pure *feeling*. And feeling involved all five senses as she saw colors and light swirl about them and heard the melody and the rhythm and smelled cologne and somehow tasted the wine she had drunk at supper and felt the warmth of hands touching her and leading her and making her feel cherished and exhilarated and happier than she had felt since . . . Well, *since*.

But inevitably thought intruded at last, just before the music ended, and with it came a tidal wave of resentment. Against him, for it was all deliberate with him, all artifice. And against herself. Oh, overwhelmingly against herself. For she had allowed herself to be beguiled, to be swept beyond simple enjoyment into mindless euphoria. She could not even blame him entirely or perhaps at all. She had acquiesced without a struggle.

"Thank you," she said when the dance ended and everyone applauded, as they always did after the waltz.

She dropped her hand from his shoulder, but his arm was still about her waist, and his clasp on her other hand was still firm. His eyes, she saw when she looked into them, were regarding her keenly. And then he stepped back, bowed, and smiled.

"Ah, no," he said. "Thank *you,* Cousin Imogen."

He was using his polished, charming manner again. His shield of unknowing.

He took her hand once more and set it on his sleeve before leading her off the floor to join Elizabeth and Sir Matthew. He stayed to converse for a few minutes before strolling off to solicit the hand of Louise Soames, who looked in danger of being a wallflower for the final set of the evening. Mr. Wenzel claimed Imogen for the second time that evening.

She wished—oh, she wished, wished, *wished*—she had gone home with Aunt Lavinia.

And she had to share a carriage with him on the way back. Just the two of them.

He had been here exactly a week, Percy thought, and it seemed like a year. It amazed him that he was still here, when it would be the easiest thing in the world to leave. Hardford was not the epitome of comfort—he had found when he went to bed last night that the window curtains, a tasteful match for his bedcover, had been replaced by draperies of a heavy dark brocade, and they were somehow stuck on their rod and would not open unless held back by hand. They had been put there to hold out some of the draft, Crutchley had explained when summoned. His lordship had been fortunate so far that there had not been much wind. When there was, he would soon discover that it blew through his bedchamber window almost as though it was not there. He would be far more comfortable in the guest room at the back.

Percy was beginning to wonder half seriously if someone was deliberately trying to nudge him out of his own room—and perhaps out of his own house?

He should not need nudging. There was almost nothing here with which to alleviate his boredom. And no one with whom to strike up a close friendship. No one like his usual friends, anyway, though he found himself feeling kindly disposed toward Sir Matthew Quentin and even Wenzel when the man was not foisting his attentions upon Lady Barclay. He was forced to share his home with three women and a menagerie of animals, one of which stuck to him like glue. It was a wonder Hector had not turned up at the assembly rooms tonight. There were the other strays too, the ones of the human variety. And there was a steward who appeared to be gathering dust along with the estate books and must somehow be persuaded to retire. There was an estate going to ruin. There was . . .

Well, there was the woman beside him in the carriage, silent, stiff, as cold as marble again. He had no idea what he had done to offend her this time. If they had quarreled, she had started it—*What part are you playing now? . . . You are neither smiling nor oozing charm.* She had seemed to thaw a bit after that, though. She had even apologized for her rudeness. But now . . .

He had *no idea* why she was so prickly. What was

more, he did not care—or should not care. She irritated him beyond endurance. She alone was enough to drive him back to his own world, except that he had discovered a stubborn streak in himself this week. Had it always been there? He was almost sure he did not like her. And there was nothing particularly attractive about her. Or beautiful—despite an earlier thought to the contrary.

There was that curled lip, though.

A curled upper lip did not an attractive woman make.

He kept to his own side of the carriage seat and looked out onto darkness. *She* kept to *her* side and did the same. Not that it was possible to put much distance between oneself and another on a carriage seat or prevent the occasional touch when the carriage turned the slightest of bends or hit a rut, which was a lamentably frequent occurrence on English roads. The air was cold. They could have seen their breath if there had been any light to see by.

Percy had always enjoyed waltzing, provided he could choose his own partner. For some totally unfathomable reason, considering the surroundings and the quality of the music, he had found this evening's waltz more than usually enchanting. And *so had she,* by thunder. That was the most irritatingly annoying thing about Lady Barclay. It was as if she had set herself quite deliberately never to be finished with her mourning, never to allow herself a fleeting moment of happiness, even on the dance floor.

Let her wallow in her own self-pity, then. It did not matter to him. He would remain silent in her presence forever after. Lips locked shut. Throw away the key.

"I suppose," he said, "you were raped."

Good God! Oh, devil take it and a thousand thunderbolts fall on his head. Good Lord! Had he spoken those words aloud? But of course he had. He could hear the echo of them, almost as if they were rattling about the interior of the carriage like bullets from a gun and could find no escape. And if there was any vestige of doubt to be clung to, there was the fact that she had swung about to face him and drawn in a sharp, very audible breath.

"Wh-a-a-t?"

"I suppose you were," he said more softly, closing his eyes and willing himself to be anywhere else but where he was. Preferably tucked up in his own bed coming to the end of a nightmare.

"In *Portugal,* do you mean?" she said. "In *captivity*?"

He kept his eyes and his mouth shut, a bit too late. *Please don't answer. Please don't.* For someone who had become a great expert at avoiding all that was unpleasant in life, he had developed a huge capacity during the past week to invite calamity.

He *did not want to know*.

"You suppose wrongly," she said, her voice quiet and flat. He would have been far happier if she had raged at him, even come at him with her fists.

He ought not to believe her. What could she be expected to do, after all, but deny it? What woman would wish to admit to having been raped while held captive? Especially to a near stranger.

But he did believe her. Or perhaps he just wanted to. Desperately.

"You suppose wrongly," she said again and even more quietly.

He turned his head. He could not see her clearly in the darkness, but of course they were very close to each other, and his mouth did not need eyes. It found hers very accurately without their aid.

He drew back after no more than a few seconds and waited for the sting of her slap on his cheek—or a punch to the chin. Neither one came. Instead she sighed, a mere breath of sound, and when his arms went about her to draw her closer, *hers* wrapped about *him,* and her lips parted when his own touched them again, and she made no protest when his tongue pressed into her mouth.

It was a good thing he was sitting. When she sucked inward on his tongue, he felt his knees going, and in sheer self-defense he curled the tip of his tongue to draw along the ridge of bone at the roof of her mouth until she moaned softly and he realized what he was up to.

Willing, warm widow.

Whom he wanted with a fierceness that seemed to go beyond the mere lust for sex.

Who could turn to marble at the mere drop of his hat.

Whom he did not very much like.

Who was going to hate him more than she already did when she remembered her dead husband once more.

A thousand damnations, and another one thrown in for good measure!

It was he who moved back, releasing her and folding his arms over his chest as he settled his shoulders across the corner of the seat. Was this February or July?

"This time, Lady Barclay," he said ungallantly, "a slap across the face would be hardly justified. For all of two minutes you were a willing participant."

"You are no gentleman," she said.

Whatever *that* meant. It was not the first time she had said it either.

She had not been raped. Then *what*?

He reminded himself of a schoolboy worrying a scab on his knee instead of leaving it alone to heal, knowing that he would only make it bleed again.

9

*I*mogen moved back to the dower house the following morning. The work on the roof was not quite finished and the upper floor was a mess—the furniture that had been left up there was draped with Holland covers and coated with dust and debris. The lower floor was crowded with much of the upstairs furniture. The house had not been heated or cleaned for two months. There was no food in the larders or coal in the coal bin.

She did not care. She moved back anyway.

An army of servants arrived within an hour of her return, though *not* by her instructions. They brought her personal belongings, all neatly packed, and food and candles and coal, as well as pails and mops and brooms and other cleaning paraphernalia—as though she had none of her own. They did not look to her for instructions, but set about lighting fires in all the downstairs rooms and cleaning everywhere and getting the kitchen orderly and functional and doing a hundred and one other tasks. They were supervised everywhere by a ferociously energetic Mrs. Primrose, Imogen's housekeeper and cook, who had been staying with her sister in the lower part of the village during the latter's confinement, but had come almost at a run when a footman from the hall brought her the news that my lady was back in residence.

She soon had a cup of tea to set at Imogen's elbow in the sitting room and some raisin scones fresh out of the oven, and professed herself to be in her seventh heaven at being back working where she belonged. Those last words were said with a note of reproach. Imogen had chosen to live alone when she first came here, much to the consternation of her father-in-law and the disappointment of Mrs. Primrose — it was a courtesy title since she had never been married — who had been promoted from senior chambermaid at the hall and still lived there in her room in the attic.

Blossom had been brought to the dower house in a housemaid's basket. She had expressed no particular objection, having never quite recovered from having had her chair by the drawing room fire taken away and replaced with one she did not find nearly as comfortable, and one she was moreover expected to relinquish every time a certain man was in the room to claim it for himself. She prowled about the new environment, upstairs and down, before selecting a chair on one side of the fireplace in the sitting room. No one ordered her to get down. She was fed tasty victuals in the kitchen and assigned a comfortable bed for the nights in one corner beside the oven. She promptly forgot the old home and adopted the new.

The sound of hammers from the direction of the roof was close to being deafening all day, but Imogen did not mind. At least the noise gave indication that the job was being done. And living in a noisy, chilly, slightly damp, very dusty house—at least for the first hour or two—was certainly preferable to the alternative.

She did not set foot outside the house for the entire first day, even to check her garden to see if an early snowdrop had made its appearance yet. She had hardly left the sitting room since it had been cleaned and all was bustle and activity elsewhere. She even ate there, as Mrs. Primrose declared the dining room still unfit for her ladyship.

Imogen felt she was in heaven. She sat during the evening, as she had all afternoon, with her workbag beside her and a book open on her lap. Mostly, though, she enjoyed the silence and solitude. Her housekeeper and the roof workers were gone for the day, and all the extra servants had returned to the hall.

He read Alexander Pope, she thought as she turned a page of her own book. At least, that was the volume that had been on the table beside his chair in the library when she had looked one morning. Perhaps he had taken one glance inside it and closed it and neglected to return it to the shelf. Perhaps he had not even taken a glance.

And perhaps he had read it.

Why did she always want to believe the worst of him?

She set a hand flat on her book to hold it open, closed her eyes, and rested her head against the back of her chair. If only last night could be erased from memory. No, not just from memory—from fact. If only none of it had happened. If only she had returned home with Aunt Lavinia and Cousin Adelaide.

But *if only*s were pointless. She had spent three years learning that lesson.

Could she not simply have enjoyed that waltz without ... Well, she could not even complete the thought.

She did not know what else she had felt *but* enjoyment. Enchantment, perhaps?

He had asked *the question* on the way home. Very few people ever had, even her own family, though she suspected many had wondered. Only her fellow Survivors and the physician at Penderris knew the truth—the *full* truth, and she had volunteered the information to them.

How had he dared to ask? He was a near stranger. *I suppose you were raped.* But she guessed he was the sort of man who dared ask anything, who believed it was his God-given right to pry into other people's secrets.

She hated him with a passion.

She wondered if he had believed her answer.

She had hated him for asking. Yet she had kissed him immediately after. Oh, yes, she had. There was no denying it this time. *He* had kissed *her* for a few seconds, it was true. But after that she had kissed with as much passionate abandon as he had kissed her. Probably more, for she doubted his passion had been anything more than lust, while hers . . . She did not know what hers had been. And if it had been pure lust on his part, why had he put such an abrupt end to their embrace? Why had he not taken more liberties while he could? It must have been obvious that she was not resisting him, and there had been several minutes left of the journey and its enforced closeness and privacy.

She did not understand him or know him. She liked to believe she did both. She disliked him and wanted to despise him. And he made it easy for her to believe that he was empty of everything but arrogance and conceit— and charm.

She liked to *believe* she disliked him. Yet down on the

beach she had said he was almost likable. Oh, this was all very confusing and very upsetting.

He was the one who had sent the army of servants after her to the dower house this morning. One of them had admitted it when she was still hoping it had been Aunt Lavinia. He might have done it, of course, out of sheer delight to be rid of her and determination to give her no possible excuse to return. But it would be spiteful to believe that.

She really did not know him at all. And sometimes, she thought, extraordinary beauty, even male beauty, must be a disadvantage to the person who possessed it, for it was easy to look only at the outer package and assume that there was nothing of any corresponding worth within.

When confronted, he had assured her that there was nothing inside him but charm. Despite herself, Imogen smiled at the memory. He had a gift for absurdity—a fact that suggested a certain wit, a certain intelligence, even a certain attractive willingness to laugh at himself. She did not want to believe it of him.

She went to bed early after an exhausting day of doing nothing and lay awake until sometime after four o'clock.

The first thing Percy did when he got out of bed the morning following the assembly was tear down the offending curtains at his window, rods and all. They had made his room so dark through the night that when he awoke at some unknown hour he had been unable to see so much as his hand before his face. If he had got out of his bed and taken a few steps away from it, it might have taken him an hour to find it again. Had Lady Barclay told him that one of her Survivor friends was blind? It did not bear thinking of. Neither did she. Last night . . . Well, *that* did not bear thinking of either.

A whole lot of things in the past week did not bear thinking of.

He instructed Crutchley to have the old curtains restored to his bedchamber, winds and gales be damned, and to see to it that there were no more uncomfortable surprises awaiting him when he went to bed at night. His heart might well not stand the strain. And he intended to stay in the earl's chambers, he added, even if he found eels or frogs or both in his bed tonight.

He steeled himself for the ordeal of stepping into the dining room for breakfast. He was still not sure if he owed Lady Barclay an apology, though he was rather inclined to believe he did not. If she did not like being kissed, then she could jolly well keep herself out of his reach. Which was, as it quickly became apparent, exactly what she had decided to do. Lady Lavinia almost fell over her tongue in her eagerness to impart the dreadful tidings that dear Imogen was *gone*. But before Percy could conceive more than a flashing image of her fleeing up over the bleak moors in the general direction of the even bleaker Dartmoor, he was informed that she had returned to the dower house to stay even though all those *men* were still swarming all over the roof. Lady Lavinia made it sound as though each of them had a peephole up there and had nothing better to do with his time than peep through it.

Lady Barclay had taken nothing with her, of course, impractical woman as she was. Presumably she would prefer to freeze and starve and live forever in the same clothes and be deafened by hammer blows rather than spend another day beneath a roof with him.

Well, he preferred it too—that last part, anyway.

He left the dining room without further ado and gave orders to pack up her clothes and other personal belongings and send them after her, together with any and all supplies she would need, including her own housekeeper. He gave instructions that the servants who conveyed everything remain to make the house fully habitable even if it took all day, as it probably would. The roof, he believed, would not let any of the elements in, even if it was not quite finished. When he stepped into the drawing room for a moment, the cat that always kept his chair warm for him glared balefully at him and dared him to banish her, and he gave the order to send her over to the dower house to glare at Lady Barclay and perhaps give her some company. That would get rid of *one* stray.

She was *not* going to make a martyr of herself for the pleasure of sitting heavily on his conscience. It would be just like her—a conclusion that was without any solid evidence and doubtless unworthy of him.

He needed to get away from the hall and the park. He needed to blow away some cobwebs.

He spent much of the day in Porthmare, therefore, though not the part of it in which most of his new acquaintances had their homes, the genteel part in the river valley, sheltered from the sea and the rawest of the elements, their houses arrayed on the slopes to either side of the river with pleasant views over it and the picturesque pair of arched stone bridges that spanned it. He decided instead to see the fishing village below, its whitewashed cottages built about the broad estuary that connected river and sea and was fully exposed to the latter. The people down there, mostly fisherfolk, did not belong to him and did not work for him, except perhaps at some seasonal jobs when extra hands were needed. But they were a part of the neighborhood in which he had his principal seat, and while he was here he might as well acquaint himself with some of them if he could. He might even be able to think of some intelligent questions to ask.

He left his horse at the inn where the assembly had been held the night before and walked down to the lower village. There was much open space here, he found, the steep cliffs at some distance on either side of the wide estuary. Fishing boats bobbed on its sheltered channels. Gulls wheeled and cried overhead. It seemed a little warmer down here than it did up on Hardford land. The scenery was definitely more stark, though. The air was saltier. The tide was out.

He spent several idle hours simply wandering about and exchanging greetings with villagers who happened to be outdoors, working on an upturned boat or a net, or standing in groups gossiping while children darted about in exuberant pursuit of one another. He ended up in the taproom of an inn less grand in appearance than the one in the upper village, but reasonably clean and serviceable nonetheless. There were several men there, hunched over their ale, and Percy drew a few of them into conversation

He did not have a perfectly easy time of it, of course. It was impossible to blend into near invisibility among these villagers, who probably all knew one another anyway. They tended to be either awed speechless by the sight of him or clearly suspicious, even resentful, of his appearance thus among them in their own domain instead of remaining in his own, where he belonged. Well, he could not blame them, he supposed. He might resent it too if they took to wandering uninvited about his park and expected him not only to bob his head and pull on his forelock at the sight of them but also to exchange respectful greetings. And when a few men at the inn did respond to his conversational overtures, it seemed at first almost as if they were speaking a foreign language, so thick was their Cornish accent. He had to listen carefully just to get the gist of what they were saying.

He did not begin the conversation with any agenda in mind beyond getting better acquainted with this particular remote corner of England. But after a while he found himself tilting his apparently aimless chatter in a certain direction and gathering a few snippets of interesting information, even if doing so involved sifting through the barefaced lies he was told to get at the truth.

Smuggling in this area? *This* area? Puzzled looks and slowly shaking heads. Scratched heads. No, never. Not in a hundred years or more, anyway. Not like in the days of their long-ago forebears. The old-timers, now, would be able to tell him a tale or two, but even they could only tell the tales *they* had been told around a winter fire when they were nippers. Smuggling wouldn't pay these days, even supposing anyone was interested in starting it up. Not with the revenue men breathing down their necks and the riding officers wasting their time out and about on the headlands looking for what was just not there. The government was wasting its money on their wages, it was. There was nothing for them to find hereabouts. Why should they use their boats for smuggling, anyway, when they could get a good catch of fish far more easily and make a lawful and decent living that way?

Gangs? Violence? Enforcement? In the olden days,

maybe. The old-timers did tell some tall tales that would lift the hairs on the back of your neck, but no doubt they were just that—*tall* tales with no real truth to them. All they were good for was to make the nippers' eyes grow big as saucers and get them calling out for their mams in the middle of the night. These days they were a law-abiding lot, they were.

There was definitely smuggling in the area, then, Percy concluded as he walked back to his horse and rode home. And it was clearly organized for maximum efficiency, with a leader and rules and a sure way of enforcing secrecy.

He did not particularly care if there was smuggling or not. It was a fact of life and was never going to end. There was no point in getting all excited and righteous about it unless one were a revenue man or a riding officer—or unless one's own property was sometimes used as a transportation route or even for storage, as the cellar of the dower house had once been. And unless the servants in one's employ were being terrorized and even harmed, presumably so that they would keep their mouths shut.

And, he wondered suddenly, arrested by the thought, unless the room one occupied at night were facing full-on to the sea so that on some dark and moonless night one might, if one happened to be awake, have a panoramic view of a fleet of small boats rowing into the bay below from a larger ship anchored some distance out and of a band of smugglers appearing through the break in the headland loaded to the gills with boxes and casks?

Was *that* the explanation for damp beds and walls and soot and thick, opaque curtains?

He tried to picture Crutchley with a cutlass between his teeth and a patch over one eye. He found himself smiling at the mental image his mind created. But he had thoroughly aroused his own curiosity.

He rode back home and tethered his horse in the paddock behind the stables rather than leading it straight inside to be tended. He instructed Mimms, his own groom, to make himself scarce for at least the next half hour, and went in search of the limping stable hand he had seen a few times.

He was a thin, ginger-haired man who must be in his middle twenties if he had been fourteen when Lady Barclay went off to war with her husband, though he could easily have passed for thirty or forty or more. His legs were noticeably crooked. His face was pale and curiously dead looking. He was mucking out a stall when Percy hailed him.

"Bains?"

"M'lord?" He stopped what he was doing and looked in the general direction of Percy, round-shouldered and shifty-eyed.

"Walk out to the paddock with me," Percy said. "I am a bit concerned about the right foreleg of my mount."

The man looked surprised. "Shall I fetch Mr. Mimms?" he asked.

"I have just sent Mimms on an important errand," Percy said. "I want *you* to take a look. You were personal groom to the late Viscount Barclay once upon a time, were you not?"

Bains looked further surprised. But he set aside his fork, brushed straw from his coat and breeches, and stepped outside. Percy waited until he had gentled the horse with skilled hands and crooning voice and was bent over its foreleg. They were out of earshot from the stables.

"Who did it to you?" he asked.

He did not expect an answer, of course, and he got none. Well, almost none. Bains did straighten up sharply.

"Who did *what,* m'lord?"

"Keep working," Percy said, leaning his arms along the fence. "In all fairness, I did not expect you to come out with a name. Will you answer a few questions with *yes* or *no,* though? Viscount Barclay was opposed to the smuggling that was going on in this area, was he not?"

Bains was carefully examining the horse's leg.

"I was just a lad," he said. "I was not his lordship's *personal* groom."

"He opposed smuggling?"

"I knew his opinions on horses," the man said. "That was all."

"Did you too voice an objection to smuggling after he had gone?" Percy asked. "Because you admired him so much?"

"I wanted to go with him," Bains told him. "I wanted to be his batman, to look after his things and him. My dad wouldn't let me go. He was afraid I would get hurt."

"Ironic, that," Percy said. "You liked Viscount Barclay?"

"*Everyone* liked him," Bains said.

"And admired him?"

"He was a fine gentleman. He ought to have been—"

"—the earl after his father's passing?" Percy said. "Yes, indeed he ought. But he died instead."

"That Mawgan went with him instead," Bains said. "Just because he was Mr. Ratchett's niece's boy and had pull and was eighteen years old. But he was no good. He ran away in the end. Said he was foraging for firewood up in them foreign hills when the frogs came and took his lordship and her ladyship. But I would bet anything he was hiding among the rocks scared as anything and then ran away. I would have saved them if I had been there. But I wasn't. There is nothing wrong with this horse's leg, m'lord."

"I must have just imagined that he was favoring it on the way back up from the village, then," Percy said. "It is always as well to check, though, is it not? Did you try to stop the smuggling here so that Lord Barclay would be proud of you?"

"There is some smuggling going on up the Bristol Channel way, or so they say," Bains said, straightening up again. "And some over Devon way. But I never been farther from home than ten miles, if that, so I wouldn't know for sure."

"Or did you flatly refuse to join the gang?" Percy asked. "Or threaten to expose them to the revenue men? No, don't answer. There is no need. Take one last look down at that leg. I will do so as well. One never knows who is watching, does one, even if we cannot be heard. Nothing? I am glad to hear it. Off with you, then. You might as well take the horse with you."

Bains made his way back to the stables, leading the horse. It was obvious that every step was painful to him. Percy wondered if the old earl had hired a reputable physician to set his broken legs. Soames? He wondered too just how badly they had been broken.

He was going to have to stop all this, he thought as he made his way back to the house. He must be very bored indeed if he was starting to fancy himself as some sort of Bow Street Runner. He was going to be getting himself into trouble if he was not careful. And he really did not want to be thinking about smashed legs and dark coves on moonless nights and weighty kegs being carried up that cliff path and shady characters breaking into the cellar of the dower house beneath the very feet of the marble lady.

Or of himself dashing to her rescue, sword flashing in one hand, pistol brandished in the other.

Did he owe her an apology? She had been a full participant in that kiss last night. But what gentleman asked a lady with barefaced cheek if she had been raped? The very thought that he had done just that was enough to make him break out in a cold sweat.

Imogen was kneeling in the grass the following morning, looking at what was definitely a snowdrop, though there was no blossom yet. Even the frail shoot, though, was a welcome harbinger of spring. And surely the air was marginally warmer today. The sun was shining.

The work on her roof was finished. Mr. Tidmouth had been paid, and he and his men had gone away. He had assured her that the roof was good for the next two hundred years at the very least. She hoped it would not leak the next time there was rain.

She ought to walk down into the village and call upon Mrs. Park to see if she had taken any harm from her outing to the assembly. She ought to call at the vicarage and let the girls twitter at her about the dance and their conquests there—their parents always discouraged frivolous talk, but girls sometimes needed someone to whom they could twitter to their hearts' content. She ought to go up to the hall to assure Aunt Lavinia that the dower house was perfectly comfortable again. She ought to write an answering letter to Gwen, Lady Trentham, Hugo's wife, who had written to inform her that young

Melody, their new daughter, appeared to have recovered from her colicky, crotchety start to life before Christmas and was eagerly anticipating her journey to Penderris Hall with her mama and papa in March. She ought to . . .

Well, there were numerous things she ought to do. But she could settle to nothing even though she kept telling herself that it was sheer heaven to be back in her own home. Alone.

And lonely.

She *must* be feeling depressed. She never admitted to loneliness—simply because there was no loneliness to admit to.

And then she was alone no longer. A shadow fell across her from the direction of the garden gate, and she looked up, desperately hoping it was Aunt Lavinia or Tilly or even Mr. Wenzel or Mr. Alton. Anyone but . . .

"Saying your prayers in the brisk outdoors, Cousin Imogen?" the Earl of Hardford asked.

She got to her feet and shook out her skirts and her cloak.

"There is a snowdrop here," she said, "though it has not bloomed yet. I always look for the first one."

"You believe in springtime, then?" he asked.

"Believe in?" She looked inquiringly at him.

"New life, new beginnings, new hope," he suggested, circling one gloved hand in the air. "Off with the old, on with the new, and all that rally-the-old-and-tired-spirits stuff?"

"I want only an end to the cold," she said, "and the sight of flowers and leaves on the trees."

If he asked her to walk with him today, she would say no. But even as she thought it, he opened the gate and stepped inside, Hector at his heels.

"It is a lovely day," she said.

He looked up at the blue sky above and then back down at her.

"Must we talk about the weather?" he asked. "It lacks a certain ... originality as a topic of conversation, would you not agree? But it *is* a lovely day, I must concede. I came to bring the joyful tidings that dearest Fluff has presented the world with kittens—six of them, all apparently as healthy as horses. No runts. And I have it on the most reliable authority that they are the sweetest things in the world."

"Aunt Lavinia?"

"And a few assorted maids and one footman, who ought to have been on duty in the hall but had inexplicably taken a wrong turn and ended up in the stables instead," he said. "Mrs. Ferby is as usual unimpressed with such sentimental stuff. I may even have heard a rumble of *drown 'em* spoken in her voice as I left the dining room after breakfast, but it may have been merely the rumble of a bit of dyspepsia coming from her, ah, stomach."

She had no choice, Imogen thought. She could not be openly rude, even to him. Especially when he was spouting absurdities again.

"Would you care to step inside, Lord Hardford?" she asked him. "Would you care for a cup of tea, perhaps?"

"Both, thank you." He smiled at her, his spontaneous, genuine smile—which somehow did not look either spontaneous or genuine.

If she did not know better, Imogen thought as she led the way inside, she would say he was ill at ease. She did not want him here. Did he not realize that? Did he not understand that she had come back here yesterday, even before the house was ready for her, in order to escape from him? Though that was perhaps a little unfair. She had come back to escape from herself, or, rather, from the effect she had allowed him to have on her. She did not *want* to feel the pull of his masculinity and the corresponding stirring of her femininity.

He and Blossom eyed each other in the sitting room. Blossom won the confrontation. He took the chair on the other side of the fireplace after Imogen had seated herself firmly in the middle of a love seat. Hector plopped down at his feet, ignored by the cat. Mrs. Primrose had seen them come in and would bring the tea tray without waiting for instructions. Visitors were always plied with her tea and whatever sweet delight she had baked that day.

He talked with great enthusiasm about the weather until the tray had arrived and Imogen had poured their tea and set his beside him with two oatmeal biscuits propped in the saucer. He made dire predictions for the future based upon the fact that they had been enjoying a string of fine days and must surely suffer as a consequence. He almost had her laughing with his monologue, and once again she was forced to admit to herself that she *almost* liked him. She might even withdraw the qualification of the *almost* if he did not fill her sitting room to such an extent that there seemed to be almost no air left to breathe.

She resented that charisma he seemed to carry about with him wherever he went. It seemed undeserved.

He picked up one of his biscuits and bit into it. He chewed and swallowed.

"If not *that,* then *what*?" he asked abruptly, and curiously she knew exactly what he was talking about. His whole manner had changed, and so had the atmosphere in the room. If not rape, he was asking her, then what?

She ought to refuse to answer. He had *no right*. No one else had *ever* asked her outright. At Penderris, every-one—even the physician, even *George*—had waited un-til she was ready to volunteer the information. It had taken two years for it all to come out. *Two years.* She had known him . . . how many days? Eight? Nine?

"Nothing," she said. "You were mistaken in your as-sumption."

"Oh," he said, "I believe you. But *something* hap-pened."

"My husband died," she said.

"But you not only mourn," he said, looking at the bis-cuit in his hand as though he had only just realized it was there, and taking another bite. "You also refuse to con-tinue to live."

He was too perceptive.

"I breathe air into my lungs," she told him, "and breathe it out again."

"That," he said, "is not living."

"What do you call it, then?" she asked, annoyed. Could he not take a hint and talk about the weather again?

"Surviving," he said. "Barely. Living is not merely a matter of staying alive, is it? It is what you *do* with your life and the fact of your survival that counts."

"Spoken by an authority?" she asked him.

But she thought unwillingly of her fellow Survivors who had done a great deal with their lives and their sur-vival in the years since Penderris. Ben, though he still struggled to walk, had acquired a great deal of mobility since taking to a wheeled chair and was the very busy manager of prosperous coal mines and ironworks in Wales. He was also happily married. Vincent, despite his blindness, walked and rode and exercised, even boxed, and composed children's stories with his wife, stories that she then illustrated before they were published. They had a son. Flavian, Hugo, Ralph—they were all married too and living active, presumably happy lives. Yet she could remember them all when they were so broken that even drawing in another lungful of air had been a burden. Ralph in particular had been suicidal for a long time.

But none of them carried her particular burden. Just as she carried none of theirs. What if she could not see the first snowdrop, not this year or ever? What if she could never stride along the cliff path or the beach below?

He had not answered her question. He was chewing the last mouthful of his first biscuit.

"What happened?" he asked.

"Oh, confession is a two-way business, Lord Hardford," she said sharply. "Unless one is a priest, perhaps. You also have stories you would rather not tell."

The progress of his second biscuit was arrested two inches from his mouth. "But one would not wish to scandalize a lady," he said, lowering it, "or scorch her ears with unsavory stories."

She tutted. "You are terrified of the sea," she said, "and of the cliffs. I daresay it was only your pride because I, a mere woman, was there that got you down the path onto the beach a few days ago."

He set the biscuit back in his saucer.

"Are we bartering here, Cousin Imogen?" he asked. "Your story for mine?"

Oh.

Oh. No.

She ought to have thought before she spoke. She ought not to have started any of this.

"Shall I go first?" he asked.

IO

*H*e did not wait for her answer.

"I was ten or eleven," he said. "I was at that obnoxious age, which all boys go through and perhaps girls too, when I knew nothing and thought I knew everything. We were spending a few weeks by the sea. I have no memory of quite where, though it was somewhere on the east coast. There were golden beaches, high, rugged cliffs, a jetty and boats, the sea to splash around in and foaming waves to hurl myself beneath. A boy's paradise, in fact. But—the blight of a boy's existence—there was an army of adults with me, united in its determination to see that I did not enjoy a single moment of my time there—my parents, one of my tutors, various servants, even my old nurse. The sea was dangerous and drowned little boys; the boats were dangerous and tipped little boys into the water before drowning them; the cliffs were dangerous and dashed little boys to their death on jagged rocks below—*everything* was dangerous. The only thing that could keep me safe was constant adult supervision, preferably of the hold-my-hand-don't-do-that variety. I resented every *little* that was uttered and every hand that was held out for mine."

"I suppose," Imogen said, "you found a way to come to grief."

"In a spectacular way," he agreed. "I escaped one evening, Lord knows how, and went down onto the beach alone. It was deserted. The sea was calm, the boats were bobbing invitingly by the jetty, and I decided to try my hand at the oars of one of them, something I had not been allowed to do despite my pleas that I knew how to use them. I did too. I even discovered the art of holding a course parallel to the beach rather than one that would take me across it in the general direction of Denmark. After a while I spotted a cove that looked like a perfect pirates' lair and decided to land and play awhile. I dragged the boat up onto the beach and became a pirate king. I climbed the cliff until I came to a flat ledge that made a perfect lookout and continued with my game until I noticed several things all at once. I believe the first was that I was a bit chilly. I was chilly because the sun had gone down and dusk was coming on. Then, in quick succession, I noticed that while I had been searching the horizon for treasure ships to plunder, the tide had come in and claimed almost all the beach below me, that the boat had been lifted from its resting place and had floated away, and that the cliffs behind me and to either side of me were all very high and very sheer and very menacing."

"Oh," Imogen said, "your poor mother."

"Well, yes," he agreed, "though it was only poor me I could think of at the time. I spent the night there and a good part of the next day. It seemed like a week or a year. The tide went out and came in again, but even low tide did not help me. There was no way around the end of the rocks to the main beach. And even if there had been, I was so paralyzed by terror that I could not move an eyelash or an inch from where I was, perched precariously upon a ledge that seemed to become narrower and higher off the beach with every passing hour. And then the wind got up and tried to snatch me off my perch and the sky turned leaden gray and the sea heaved and foamed and I got seasick even though I was not on it. When a boat finally hove into sight, tossing and pitching quite alarmingly, and the boatman and my tutor spotted me from within it, they had the devil's own time landing. And then they were compelled to virtually scrape me off the face of the cliff. The boatman had to toss me over his shoulder and order me to shut my eyes before carrying me down and lifting me into the boat. I daresay my eyes were rolling in my head and I was foaming at the mouth. I was sick again on the way home."

He eyed his cup and the biscuit but did not move a hand toward them. Perhaps, Imogen thought, he was afraid his hand might be shaking.

"They had thought I was dead, of course," he said, "especially when a boat was discovered bobbing on the open sea soon after dawn, empty and mysteriously minus one oar. My father celebrated my resurrection from the dead when I was ushered into our lodgings first by hugging me so tightly it was amazing he did not suffocate me and break every bone in my body, and then by bending me over the back of the nearest chair, hauling down my breeches, and spanking the living daylights out of me with his bare hand—the *only* time I can ever remember his hitting me. Then he sent me to apologize to my mother, who had taken to her bed with smelling salts and other restoratives, but leapt out of it in order to crush my bones again and half drown me in her tears. After I had eaten—standing—from a tray the cook had sent up, laden with enough food to feed a regiment, I crept off to my room, where my tutor was awaiting me with his cane in hand. He had me bend myself over, hands on knees, before giving me twelve of the best. Then he sent me off to bed, where I remained until we set off for home next morning. I slept on my front, a position I have always found uncomfortable."

"And you have been terrified of all things connected with the sea and cliffs since," Imogen said.

He turned his head and grinned at her—an expression so totally without any of his usual artifice that it caught at her breath.

"A fate I thoroughly deserved," he said. "It must have been a night and morning of sheer hell for them. I *was* loved, you know, worthless cub though I could sometimes be. It was *only* sometimes, however, to be fair."

Yes, she imagined he had been loved.

"I was proud of myself a few mornings ago," he said. "It was unkind of you to notice my discomfort and remark upon it."

"Well," she said, "it takes courage to confront one's worst fear and move into it and through it. Perhaps it was your courage I was remarking upon."

He laughed outright and she realized something she would really rather not know. She *did* like him. Or, rather, she had to admit that he was a likable man who disturbed an inner calm she had spent years establishing. She did not like what he did to that hard-won discipline.

"Your turn," he said so softly that she almost missed the words.

But their echo remained.

Imogen swallowed. Her throat was dry. Her tea was untouched, as was the single biscuit she had taken. The tea was probably cold by now, though, and she hated cold tea. And if he had feared that his hand might be shaking, she *knew* hers was.

"There is not much to tell," she said. "They knew my husband was a British officer, though the fact that he was not in uniform gave them all the excuse they needed to pretend they did not believe him and to use every means at their disposal to force information from him."

"Torture," he said.

She spread her hands across her lap and looked down at them.

"They treated *me* with the utmost respect," she said. "I was given a private room in their temporary head-quarters and the services of a maid, the wife of a foot soldier. I dined each day with the most senior of the French officers, and they made an effort to converse with me in English though I speak French reasonably well. I had not been so well treated since leaving England."

"But you did not see your husband," he said.

"No." She drew a slow breath and licked dry lips with a dry tongue. "But sometimes, seemingly quite by acci-dent, for which they always apologized profusely after-ward, they let me hear him scream."

Her skirt was pleated between her fingers.

"He did not divulge his secrets?" he asked her after what seemed like a lengthy pause.

"Never." She smoothed out the creases. "No, never."

"They did not try to get information from you?" he asked.

"I knew nothing," she told him. "They understood that. It would have been a waste of their time."

"And they did not use you to pry information out of him?"

And *he* understood too much. Her skirt pleated itself between her fingers again.

"He never told them anything," she said again, raising her eyes to look at him. He was looking a bit pale and grim about the mouth. "And they never . . . did anything to me. They never hurt me. After his . . . death, a French colonel escorted me back to British headquarters under a flag of truce. He even had the soldier's wife accompany us for propriety's sake. He was gracious and courteous. And of course he was all surprise and regret when he was informed that I was indeed the wife—the widow— of a British officer."

"You were present when your husband died?" he asked.

Her eyes were locked with his, it seemed. She could not look away.

"Yes." She spread her fingers, releasing the creased fabric.

He stared a moment longer and then got abruptly to his feet. The dog scrambled to *his,* and Blossom eyed them both without raising her head, saw that her ownership of the chair was not about to be disputed, and closed her eyes again. Lord Hardford set one forearm along the mantel and one booted foot on the hearth and gazed into the fire.

"He was a brave man," he said.

"Yes."

"And you loved him."

"Yes."

She closed her eyes and kept them closed.

She opened them with a start of alarm when he spoke

again. He had crossed the room to the love seat without her realizing it and was leaning over her. His face was not many inches from her own. But his intent was not sexual. She realized that immediately.

"War is the damnedest thing, is it not?" he said without either apologizing for his language or waiting for her answer. "One hears about those who were killed and feels sorrow for their relatives. One hears about those who were wounded and winces in sympathy while believing they were the lucky ones. One imagines that once they heal as far as is possible, they continue with their lives where they had left them off before they went to war. One scarcely thinks of the women at all, except with a little sorrow for their loss of loved ones. But for everyone concerned, dead or alive, it is the damnedest, *damnedest* thing. Is it not?"

This time he waited for her answer, his face pale and grim and almost unrecognizable.

"It is," she agreed softly. "It is the *damnedest* thing."

"How did they know you were there?" he asked.

She raised her eyebrows.

"The French," he explained. "They were behind enemy lines when they took you, were they not? Your husband thought it safe enough to take you that far. How did they know you were there? And how did they know he was important enough to take? He was not in uniform."

"It was a scouting party," she said. "The hills were full of them, theirs and ours, on both sides of the line. The line was not a physical thing, like the wall between the park here and the land beyond, and it changed daily. There is nothing tidy about war. Even so, he was assured that that particular part of the hills was safe for me."

He straightened up and turned, all impatience and arrogance once more.

"There is that evening of cards with the Quentins tonight," he said. "Shall I have the carriage wait for you? I will take my curricle. Or would you prefer that I make some excuse for you?"

"The carriage, please," she said. "I may choose to live alone, Lord Hardford, but I am not a recluse."

He looked at her over his shoulder. "Are you ever tempted to be?"

"Yes."

He regarded her in silence for a few seconds. "One *ought* to consider the women," he said. "Your husband was not the only brave one in your marriage, Lady Barclay. Good day to you."

And he strode from the room, the dog trotting at his heels. A few moments after the sitting room door closed behind him, Imogen heard the outer door open and close too.

Your husband was not the only brave one in your marriage. . . .

If only she had died when Dicky had, the two of them together, just seconds apart. If only they had killed her, as she had fully expected they would—as Dicky had fully expected they would. *Courage,* that last look of his had said to her as clearly as if he had spoken the word aloud.

Courage.

She sometimes forgot that that was the *last* word his eyes had spoken. *Me* had come a few second before it. *Me, Imogen.* And even those unspoken words she sometimes forgot—or did not trust because they had not been spoken aloud. Though she and Dicky had always known what was in the other's mind. They had been that close—husband and wife, brother and sister, comrades, best friends.

Me. And then, *Courage.*

She sat where she was while a grayish film formed over the cold tea in her cup—and the Earl of Hardford's.

He pretty much hated himself, Percy decided as he shut the garden gate behind him and, without conscious thought, took the cliff path until he came to the gap. He scrambled down the steep track to the beach, heedless of possible danger, and strode the short distance to the cave. He went inside without stopping, daring the tide to come galloping up over the sand to trap him in there and drown him. The cave was much larger than he had expected.

Yes, he did, he decided as he placed one hand on a protruding rock and gazed out into daylight. He hated himself.

"You came all the way down this time without help, did you?" he asked Hector, who was lying across the mouth of the cave, his head on his paws, his bulging eyes looking inside. "Well done."

Why was the dog so attached to him when he was a worthless lump of humanity? Dogs were supposed to be discriminating.

He had just confessed to the big dark blot on the otherwise relatively serene progress of his life—the great terror from which he had never recovered. A boy's disobedient folly gone wrong. The ghastly humiliation that had dogged him into adulthood, though he had always hidden it well by the simple expedient of staying far from the sea and confronting every other challenge that came his way, the more dangerous the better, with a reckless disregard for his own life. It was mildly ironic, he supposed, that when he had inherited the title totally unexpectedly two years ago, it had come with a house and park that not only were in Cornwall but also were perched spectacularly upon a high cliff top.

.That boyhood episode had been virtually the *only* dark blot on his life. Well, there had been his father's death three years ago, and that had been excruciatingly painful. But such losses occurred in the natural course of one's life, and one did recover over time. It seemed to him that he had spent all the rest of his life studiously *avoiding* pain and really doing quite a good job of it. But who would not do likewise, given the choice? Who would deliberately court pain and suffering?

He was not in the mood for making excuses for himself, though. His adult life had been one escapade piled upon another. Since coming down from Oxford almost ten years ago, he had taken care to remain uninvolved in all except shallow, meaningless, often downright stupid frivolity. He was thirty years old and had done *nothing* in his life of which he could feel proud. Well, except his double first degree with which he had done *nothing* since getting it.

Was it *normal*?

It certainly was not admirable.

He had said something—this very morning. He frowned in thought for a moment.

Living is not merely a matter of staying alive, is it? It is what you do with your life and the fact of your survival that counts.

And he had said it in criticism of *her,* pompous ass that he was.

He was a survivor too, was he not? He had survived his own birth, no mean feat when so many newborns did not. He had survived all the perils and illnesses of early childhood. He had survived that ordeal on the cliff face. He had survived reckless horse and curricle races and a duel with pistols and the jumping of broad gaps between houses from four stories up, once during a heavy rainstorm. He had done a lot of surviving. He had got to the age of thirty more or less intact physically and mentally and emotionally.

It is what you do with your life and the fact of your survival that counts.

What the devil had he ever done with his? What real use had he made of the precious gift of breath?

He left the cave and walked down the beach until he was at the water's edge. The salt of the air was more pronounced here. He felt exposed, surrounded by vastness, half deafened by the elemental roar of the sea and the breaking of the waves. The sun was sparkling across the water, half blinding him. Hector was gamboling along in the shallows, knee-deep in water, sending up cascades of it behind him. He was going to be caked with sand to take back to the house.

What was it exactly he feared about the sea? Percy asked himself. Was it that all that water could trap him and drown him? Or was it something more fundamental than that? Was it the fear of vanishing into nothing in such vastness? Or the fear of coming face-to-face with the vast unknown? Was it just that it was easier to cling to his own trivial little inland world?

But he was not used to introspection and turned his attention back to his dog, which was obviously enjoying itself.

His dog?

"Damn your eyes, Hector," he murmured. "Could you not have been a proud, handsome mastiff? Or taken a fancy to Mrs. Ferby instead of me?"

She had not played fair—Lady Barclay, that was, not Mrs. Ferby. He had told her the whole of his story, even to the pulling down of his breeches for his spanking. She had told him only part of hers. A chunk of it, the key part of it, had been omitted. And it was the very part that he suspected would explain everything.

He had no right to know. He had had no right to ask in the first place. He had only more or less tricked her into telling her story by offering his own in exchange. And he did not *want* to know what she had withheld. He had cringed even from what she had told him. He had the feeling—no, he *knew*—that the missing details would be unbearable.

He always avoided what was unbearable.

She had spent *three years* at Penderris Hall. And she was not mended even now. Far from it. It was not simple grieving that kept her broken.

He did not want to know.

He did not usually pry into other people's lives. He was not usually curious about what was of no personal concern to him, especially if it promised something painful.

Lady Barclay was not of any personal concern to him. She was not in any way at all the type of woman to attract him. Indeed, she was all that would normally repel him.

What was *abnormal* about his dealings with her, then?

Devil take it, he thought abruptly, he needed to leave. Not just the beach, though he turned to stride back up it anyway, leaving Hector to catch up to him. Hardford Hall. Cornwall. He needed to put them behind him, forget about them, send a decent steward down to manage the estate and content himself with the knowledge that he had done his duty by coming and setting things in order. He needed to get back to his own life, to his friends and his family.

He needed to forget Imogen Hayes, Lady Barclay— and she would surely be only too delighted to be forgotten. She would not have to hide out so much in the dower house with him gone.

He would definitely leave, he decided as he scrambled up the path to the top, out of breath but unwilling to slow down. Today. Or at worst first thing in the morning. He would get Watkins to pack his belongings and would send word to Mimms in the stables. But he would not have to wait for either of them. He could ride his horse home as he had ridden it here.

He would leave today.

He would send an excuse to the Quentins.

He was feeling purposeful, even cheerful, as he pushed through a gap in the gorse bushes without quite murdering his boots, and then strode across the lawn toward the house. The only decision that remained was whether he would take Hector with him—not running beside his horse, of course, but in the carriage. Watkins might well abandon stoicism and hand in his notice. And Percy would be the laughingstock of London. But who cared?

He would be many miles on his way before darkness. His spirits were buoyed by the thought and his stride lengthened at the pleasant prospect of going home—and never coming back.

There was no one in the hall when he let himself into the house. But there were two letters on a silver tray on the table facing him. Percy looked down at them, hoping they were for anyone but him, as they probably were. No one had written since he came here.

He recognized the writing on both—that of Higgins, his man of business in London, on the one and ... his mother's on the other.

II

*P*ercy frowned at the letters. He could have done without this distraction when he was all set to march upstairs and ring for Watkins before his purpose cooled.

Perhaps Higgins had found someone to take on the job of steward. Now *that* would be well-timed news—and fast too. But how the devil did his mother know he was here? He had been very neglectful and not written since he came here. Perhaps Cousin Cyril had passed the word on. And then his frown deepened as he cast his mind back. Had he written to her himself? That night before he set off for Cornwall after writing to warn Ratchett that he was coming here and to suggest that the cobwebs be swept off the rafters before he arrived? Devil take it, had he really added *that* to the letter? That was what came of setting pen to paper when one was inebriated. *Had* he written to his mother too? And if so, what the deuce had he said?

He broke the seal and opened the single sheet. His eyes scanned the closely spaced lines of her small, neat handwriting.

Yes, she had indeed received his letter from London, and she was delighted that he was at last doing his duty by going down to his Cornish estate. However, she was deeply disturbed to learn how unhappy he was with his life and how lonely . . .

He would swear off liquor from this moment on. Not a single drop would ever again pass his lips. What sort of sentimental, self-pitying drivel had he written in that letter? *To his mother?*

He read on.

Perhaps taking up his responsibilities at Hardford Hall would be the making of him, and it would not surprise her at all if his neighbors were welcoming him with open arms after two long years of waiting. He would surely discover purpose and friendship there — and perhaps even a special someone?

Percy grimaced. His mother was ever hopeful and ever the hopeless romantic. He must write to reassure her — and squash her expectations — before he rode off in the direction of London. Dash it all, that was going to delay his departure by at least half an hour.

And double dash it all, he was going to be letting her down.

Again.

And disappointing her.

Again.

She never said as much, but he knew she was still hoping that one day he would make her truly proud of him. She was forever declaring her love and her pride, but he knew he had disappointed her from the moment he left Oxford after scaling such heady academic heights there and slid into a life of idleness and frivolity.

His eyes had become unfocused and gazed through

the page rather than at it. There was only a sentence or two left, though, probably just the courtesies with which one always felt obliged to end a letter. He focused his eyes upon them.

"I will do all in my power to lift your spirits, Percy," she had written. "I and perhaps a few of your aunts and uncles and cousins. We never did have a chance to celebrate your birthday together as a family. We will do it belatedly. I will be leaving for Cornwall tomorrow morning."

He stared at the last sentence in the hope that somehow, by some wizardry, the words would change before his eyes, dissolve and evaporate, become something else or nothing at all.

His mother was coming.

Here.

With other assorted and unidentified relatives.

To stay. To celebrate his birthday belatedly. To lift his spirits.

By now she was already on her way. Given his mother's usual manner of moving herself with her baggage and entourage from one geographical location to another, it would take her forever to get here, since she was coming all the way from Derbyshire. But even so . . . *She was on the way.* That meant there was no chance of stopping her. And maybe there were hordes of aunts and uncles and cousins all gradually converging upon this particular spot on the globe too. There was no way of stopping *them*—assuming any of them had heeded his mother's rallying cry, that was.

It was a pretty safe assumption that some of them had.

All would be hearty jollification at Hardford. A family party. A grand one. It would not be just about his birthday either, or just about family, he suspected. It would be about his homecoming as Earl of Hardford too. There was a ballroom at the back of the house, a largish room, gloomy, shabby, and sadly neglected. He would be willing to wager half his fortune that his mother would take it on in a great burst of energy as her special project. The birthday-cum-family-cum-welcome party would become a grand ball the likes of which Cornwall had never seen before—and throw in Devon and Somerset for good measure. He would wager the other half of his fortune on it.

One thing was crystal clear. He was not going to be galloping off anywhere today after all. Or tomorrow.

Crutchley creaked his way into the hall. Prudence came darting after him and growled at Percy before darting away again. It was like déjà vu.

"Crutchley," Percy said, "give the order to turn the house upside down and inside out, if you please. My mother is expected within the next couple of weeks, with the possibility of an indeterminate number of other guests ambling in either before or after her. Or even *with* her, I suppose."

If his butler was taken aback, he did not show it. "Yes, m'lord," he said, and creaked away back whence he had come.

Percy proceeded upstairs with lagging steps to see if Lady Lavinia was anywhere to be found. He would be willing to wager another half of his fortune—no, that would make three and there were not three halves in a whole, were there? Anyway, he would wager *something* that she would be ecstatic when he told her the news.

So he was fated to see her again, then. He did not *want* to see her. She bothered him.

He wished he had not pressed her to tell any of her story. The gap in it made his stomach churn even more than the whole thing had before she told him.

Two days later Imogen admitted to herself that she was restless and unhappy. And lonely. And very, very depressed.

She had hit bottom, it seemed, a dreaded place to be. It had not happened since she left Penderris five years ago. Not that she had ever been happy during the intervening years. She had never wanted to be. It would be wrong. And she had certainly felt moments of loneliness and depression. But she had never allowed herself to be engulfed in near despair without any discernible way of dragging herself free.

She had held her life to an even keel by killing all deep feeling, by living upon the surface of life. The only times she had allowed her spirits to come close to soaring were those three weeks of each year when she was reunited with her fellow Survivors. But that was a controlled sort of euphoria. Although she adored those friends, sympathized with their continued sufferings, rejoiced in their triumphs, she was not intimately involved in their lives.

Now her life felt frighteningly empty.

Perhaps it was because almost a year had passed since the last reunion and she had not seen any of them in the interim. She would be with them again soon. But even that prospect could not significantly cheer her.

She had kept herself busy. Her flower beds were bare of weeds and she had clipped the box hedge on either side of the gate, though it was too early in the year for there to have been any real growth. She had worked at some fine crochet she had started at her brother's house over Christmas and read a whole book, though she was not sure she remembered its contents. She had written letters to her mother and her sister-in-law; to Lady Trentham and Hugo; to Lady Darleigh, who would read it to Vincent; to George. She had walked into Porthmare to make a few purchases and to make a few calls. She had baked a cake earlier to take to Mrs. Primrose's sister in the lower village—she had recently given birth to her fourth child. She had checked every room upstairs and every cupboard and wardrobe and drawer to make sure everything was back in order.

There was nothing left to do except more reading or crocheting. She was alone and there was no social event planned for the evening.

Self-pity was a horrible thing.

She had last seen him the evening before last at the Quentins' card party. He had been his usual charming self, and had behaved toward her just as if she did not even exist. She did not believe their eyes had met even once during the evening. They had spoken not one word to each other and had sat at different tables for cards.

It had all been an enormous relief. She had still been feeling raw from the telling of her story. Why *on earth* had she allowed him to maneuver her into doing it?

But could he not have *looked* at her even just once? Or said good evening to her at the start or good night at the end? Or *both*?

The confusion of her feelings puzzled and alarmed her. It was so unlike her to allow anyone to dominate her thoughts or control her moods.

He was expecting company at the hall. Thank goodness she had been able to move back to the dower house.

His mother was coming and perhaps other relatives too. His mother was determined to organize some sort of belated thirtieth birthday party for him, he had warned everyone at the Quentins' social evening, but everyone, of course, had been delighted. Imogen could not remember when there had last been company at Hardford Hall or any sort of party there. For Dicky's eighteenth birthday, perhaps?

She hoped she need not be involved in any way at all, with either the visit or the party. Perhaps it would all happen after she left for Penderris.

She *wished* he would just simply go away, though that seemed a remote hope now, at least for a while. Perhaps if he went away she would be able to recapture some of her serenity.

She made a cup of tea after washing the dishes she had used to make the cake, and took it into the sitting room, where Blossom kept guard over the fire. At least the cat was a live being, Imogen thought, setting down her cup and saucer and scratching her between her ears. She felt rather than heard a purr of contentment. She was so *glad* Blossom had come and stayed. She had never before thought of having a pet, some living creature to comfort her and keep her company.

There was a knock upon the door.

Imogen looked up, startled. It was not late, but it *was* February and already dark outside. It was also raining. She could hear it against the windows—the first they had had for some time.

Who . . . ?

There was another knock.

She hurried to open the door.

*   *   *

Until his hand released the knocker and it banged against the door, Percy convinced himself that he was merely out for an evening stroll but would check that the roof was still on the dower house while he was at it before circling back to the hall.

It was a dark evening but he had not brought a lantern with him. The twelve capes of his greatcoat did a decent job of keeping out the rain and the cold. The brim of his tall hat did a tolerable job of shielding his face, though only if he held his head at a certain angle, and even then there were little deluges every time enough water had collected at the edge of the brim to become a waterfall, one of which had found its way down the back of his neck. The path along which he had walked was becoming a bit slick underfoot and threatened to turn to mud if the rain continued. A wind was getting up. It was not exactly a gale, but it was neither a gentle breeze nor a warm one.

In other words, it was a miserable evening to be out, and only when his hand had released the knocker did he admit to himself that a stroll was not after all what he was out for. And here he was ending a sentence again, even if only in his own head, with a preposition.

She did not dash to open the door for him. Perhaps she had not heard the knocker. Perhaps he still had a chance to slink away, to retrace his steps and dry off before the library fire with a glass of port in one hand and the volume of Pope in the other.

He rapped the knocker against the door again, and within seconds the door opened.

She had come back here to escape from him. A fine time to remember that.

"Are you really all alone in the house?" he asked her. "It will not do, you know."

He had discovered only at breakfast this morning that her housekeeper did not live in. He had wondered if that had been the housekeeper's idea or hers. He would wager upon the latter.

"You had better step inside," she said none too graciously.

He did so and stood dripping all over the small hallway.

"No," he said firmly as she began to stretch out a hand. "You are not a butler, and there is no point in both of us being soggy." He removed his hat and coat as he spoke and set them down nearby while she folded her hands at her waist and looked inhospitable.

She watched as he ran a finger beneath the back of his cravat. There was nothing much he could do about its dampness except put up with it.

"The fact and propriety of my being alone in the house are absolutely none of your concern, Lord Hardford," she told him. "I will not have you play lord of the manor here in my own home."

He opened his mouth to dispute that last point, but closed it again without saying anything. It would be petty to argue. But he could not capitulate entirely. "Even opening the door after your servant has left could be dangerous," he said. "How did you know it was safe to do so now?"

"I did not," she said. "And clearly it *was* not. But I will not live in fear."

"The more fool you, then," he said. He had not missed the insult, but perhaps he had returned it. One did not normally call a lady a fool. "Are we to remain freezing out here in the hall?"

"I beg your pardon," she had the good grace to say as she turned to lead the way into the sitting room, which was invitingly cozy and warm. "I do hope, though, you have not come here to be disagreeable, Lord Hardford. Take the chair by the fire while I make some tea."

"Not on my account," he said, availing himself of the chair she indicated. "And I am not always or even often disagreeable."

"I know," she said. "You are charm right through to the heart."

Ah, a direct quotation from his own mouth. Well, and so he was with almost everyone he knew. Everyone, in fact, except Lady Barclay. He regarded her as she arranged her skirts about her on the love seat. It was unfair to think of her as being made of marble. On the other hand, she was not all feminine warmth either. He had no idea why he had come.

"I have no idea why I have come," he said.

Ah, the polished gentleman of consummate good manners with an endless supply of polite topics upon which to converse.

"You came to disapprove of me and find fault and scold," she said. "You came because I am an encumbrance upon your estate and you are too irritated simply to ignore me."

Well.

"Fustian!" he said. "You would not even be decently submissive enough to allow me to pay for your roof."

"Exactly," she agreed. "But you found a way of paying half anyway *and* of making me beholden to you for getting the job done without further delay."

"You are as irritated with me as I supposedly am with you," he told her.

"But I did not seek you out this evening," she pointed out with damnably faultless logic. "I did not go to *your* house, Lord Hardford. You came to *mine*. And if you dare to point out that my house is actually yours, I shall show you the door."

He sat back in his chair, not a particularly wise move, since it pressed his damp shirt against his back. He drummed his fingers on the chair arms. "I never quarrel with anyone," he said, "especially women. What *is* it about you?"

"I do not worship and adore you," she said.

He sighed. "I am lonely, Lady Barclay," he said.

Yes, what *was* it about her? What the devil *was* it?

"I think perhaps *bored* would be a more appropriate word," she said.

She was quite right.

"You presume to know me, then?" he asked.

She opened her mouth, drew breath, and—interestingly—flushed.

"I beg your pardon," she said. "Why are you lonely? Is it just that you are far from your family and friends? Are there many of them?"

"Family?" he said. "Hordes. All of whom love me, and all of whom I love in return. And friends? Another horde, most of them friendly acquaintances, a few closer than that. I am, as one of my cousins informed me on my birthday recently, the most fortunate of men. I have everything."

"Except?" she said.

He raised his eyebrows.

"What do you *not* have, Lord Hardford?" she asked. "For no one has everything, you know, or even nearly everything."

"Well, that is a relief to know." He grinned at her. "There is still something for which to live, then?"

"You do that very well," she said.

"What?"

"Giving the impression that there is nothing to you but . . . charm," she said.

"Ah, but you must not disappoint me, Lady Barclay, and become the typical female," he said. "You must not assume that somewhere inside me there is a heart."

His stomach turned a complete somersault then. She smiled back at him—lips, eyes, the whole face.

"Oh, I would never make that foolish assumption," she said. "Why are you lonely?"

She was not going to leave it alone, was she? Why had he used that stupid word when he had meant simply that he was bored?

She asked another question before he could answer. "What is one thing you have done in your lifetime that made you proud of yourself?" she asked. "There must be something."

"Must there?"

"Yes." She waited.

"I did rather well at Oxford," he said sheepishly.

She raised her eyebrows. "Did you?"

Well, that had surprised her and she looked skeptical. Suddenly he felt stung. "A double first," he said. "In the classics."

She stared at him. "I suppose," she said, "you really are reading that volume of Pope's poetry."

"You have been checking on me, have you?" he said. "Did you expect something from the Minerva press? Yes, I really have been forced to sink as low as to read poetry—in English—while I rusticate in Cornwall."

"Why are you lonely?" she asked yet again.

"Perhaps," he said, "or *probably* it is the need for sex,

Lady Barclay. I have not had any for a while. I have been lamentably celibate."

If he had expected any sign of shock, he was disappointed. She only nodded slowly. "I will not press the issue," she said. "You do not want to answer my question. Perhaps you cannot. Perhaps you do not *know* why you are lonely."

"Are you?" he asked her.

"Lonely?" she said. "Not often. Alone, yes. Solitary, yes. I choose those states as often as I can, though I will not allow myself to become a recluse. We all need other people. I am no exception to that rule."

"I suppose," he said, "you have been celibate for the past eight years. Do you miss sex? Do you long for it?"

Where the devil was all this coming from? If someone would just please be obliging enough to pinch him, he would gladly awake—but only after hearing her answer. She still did not appear shocked or offended or embarrassed. She was looking very directly back into his eyes. Good Lord, if she was thirty, she had not had sex since she was twenty-two. It was an awfully large chunk of her youthful years.

"Yes," she surprised him by saying. "Yes, I miss it. I choose not to long for it." She looked down at her hands, which were clasped loosely in her lap. "Chose," she said softly, changing the verb tense of what she had said and in the process changing the meaning too.

A piece of coal shifted in the hearth, sending sparks up the chimney and making Percy aware of a huge tension in the room. He still had no idea why he had come here, but he had certainly not expected any of this. This was not conversation. Nor was it flirtation. It was ... What the deuce *was* it?

"I think," he said, "I came to Cornwall in the hope of finding myself, though I did not realize that until this moment. I came because I needed to step away from my life and discover if from the age of thirty on I can find some new and worthwhile purpose to it. But my old life is about to catch up with me again in the form of unknown numbers of my family, led by my mother. I love them and I resent them, Lady Barclay. May I seek refuge here occasionally?"

What an asinine question to ask. She had moved here *to get away from him.* And he had been happy to see her go.

The cat awoke and stretched, its paws spread out before it, its back arched. It jumped to the floor, padded over to the love seat, and leaped onto Lady Barclay's lap, where it curled up and addressed itself to sleep again to recover from its exertions. Percy watched her hand smooth over the cat's back. She had slender fingers with well-manicured nails.

"You want me as a friend, Lord Hardford?" she said. "Someone not of your old world? Someone who does not adore you and fawn upon you?"

"I *want* you as a lover," he told her. "But failing that, friendship will do."

It was a good thing she was farther than arm's length away, he thought, and that her freedom of movement was hampered by the cat on her lap, or it was altogether possible he would be nursing a couple of stinging cheeks by now or a cracked jaw.

And was it true? *Did* he want her as a lover? *Lady Barclay?* The marble woman? She could not be less like his usual sort of amour if she tried.

But perhaps that was the point?

"Friendship seems unlikely but possible," she said. She was looking at the cat.

He did not say anything. He was even holding his breath, he realized before releasing it. She was going to allow him to come again, was she? And did he want to? Was it wise — in the evenings like this when there was not even a servant in the house, much less a chaperone? Did she care? Did he?

Her eyes were upon him.

"I am not sure about the other," she said.

Was he understanding her correctly? But she could not possibly mean anything else than what he *thought* she meant.

The air fairly sizzled — and it had nothing to do with the fire, which had burned rather low.

He got abruptly to his feet to put more coal on it.

"I must be on my way," he said when he had finished. "I have disturbed you enough for one evening. No, you need not move. I can see myself out. But remember to lock the door when you do get up."

He stood before her for a few moments, looking down at her. Then he bent over her, without disturbing the cat, and kissed her briefly. Her lips were soft and warm. Not responsive, but not *un*responsive either. He straightened up.

"Imogen," he said, purely for the sake of hearing her name on his tongue.

"Good night, Lord Hardford," she said softly.

The rain had eased a bit and the wind had dropped, he found as he stepped outside, although he was surrounded by almost pitch-blackness. He had started something tonight — perhaps. But what?

Friendship?

An affair?

Part of him was elated. Part was frankly terrified. But why? He had had friends before, though not many female friends, it was true. And he had certainly had plenty of affairs.

None of them, though, had been with Imogen Hayes, Lady Barclay.

12

"I must confess," Sir Matthew Quentin said, "that I have occasionally enjoyed a glass of good brandy with an acquaintance or neighbor without inquiring too closely into its place of origin."

"I suppose I have done the same," Percy admitted. "I have never been keen on the idea of smuggling, though. Not just because the government is thereby defrauded of revenue, but more because the people who really benefit are not the ordinary man who does the hardest work and takes the biggest risk, but those few who direct operations from afar and terrorize anyone who threatens their operation. They make a fortune out of terror and oppression and the sure knowledge that there will always be a market for luxury goods and that even people with no direct involvement will join a conspiracy of silence. No one wants to stick his neck out over something that cannot be stopped anyway."

"Oh, I agree," Sir Matthew said. "I suppose you have been discovering, have you, that the old earl encouraged the trade and allowed it safe haven on Hardford land in return for some creature comforts? More ale?"

They were sitting at their ease in Sir Matthew's library awaiting luncheon, to which Percy had been invited. Paul Knorr, his new steward, had arrived from Exeter the day before, three days after a letter from Higgins informed Percy of his appointment. The man was now conferring with Quentin's steward over luncheon and ale at the village inn. Percy was optimistic about Knorr. He was young and well educated, son of a gentleman of Higgins's acquaintance, and he was keen to get on with his new duties. He had managed his family's land for a number of years before his father's death, but now his elder brother had inherited and he had sought employment elsewhere.

"Thank you," Percy said, and waited for his glass to be refilled. "The beach and the cellar of the dower house, you mean? That was all stopped, though, was it not, when Lady Barclay took up residence there?"

"Was it?" Sir Matthew looked at him with raised eyebrows. "But even if not then, it probably did come to an end two years ago. One can hardly imagine Lady Lavinia being agreeable to the idea of having smugglers and their goods in her home."

In her home? Inside the house, did he mean?

"I suppose not," Percy said. "Now Mrs. Ferby . . ."

They both laughed.

They were interrupted by Lady Quentin, who came to inform them that luncheon was ready. She wanted to know more about Paul Knorr and whether Ratchett was likely to retire soon. Percy satisfied her curiosity as far as he was able. But mention of the elderly steward reminded him of something else.

"Ratchett has a nephew," he asked, "who went to the Peninsula with Viscount Barclay as his batman, I believe?"

"Instead of that poor boy who broke both his legs no more than a month or two later," Lady Quentin said. "He would have been safer in Portugal. What a dreadful accident that was, falling from the stable roof. We never did find out what he was doing up there."

"A great-nephew, I believe," Sir Matthew said. "He was appointed head gardener at Hardford after his return, though he was none too popular with some of us. He could give no account of what had happened to Barclay and his wife beyond the fact that they had been captured by a band of ferocious-looking French scouts while he was bringing them firewood and was without his musket. I suppose he could have done nothing to help them anyway. There were those, though, who felt that he ought at least to have waited until he *did* have word, one way or the other. If he *had* stayed, he might have helped escort Lady Barclay home. She was, I believe, in something of a state. Understandably so."

"Poor Imogen," Lady Quentin said. "She and her husband were quite devoted to each other. But that man, that so-called head gardener, does not know the difference between a geranium and a daisy, or between an oak tree and a gorse bush, I swear. His title is a sinecure. Oh, I do beg your pardon, Lord Hardford. I am being spiteful. You must be impatient for your mother's arrival. All your neighbors, ourselves included, are agog with eagerness to meet her."

The day was all but gone by the time Percy and Knorr returned to Hardford.

"I must remember to refer to you as the *under*steward," he said. "One would not wish to hurt the feelings of an octogenarian."

"Mr. Ratchett does have handwriting that I envy,"

Knorr said with a smile. "And the books are very clear and easy to understand."

He had missed a visit from Lady Barclay, Percy discovered. Lady Lavinia thought it a great pity. Percy did not. He went out of his way, in fact, to avoid her during the next couple of days, as he had done yesterday and today. He did not know what had possessed him that evening at the dower house. He still did not know why he had gone there. He also did not know why he had said some of the things he had.

I think I came to Cornwall in the hope of finding myself, though I did not realize that until this moment.

May I seek refuge here occasionally?

I want you as a lover. But failing that, friendship will do.

He squirmed at the memories, especially of that last exchange. Lord! He would swear that he had had no idea what was about to issue from his mouth when he had opened it.

Friendship seems unlikely but possible, she had replied. *I am not sure about the other.*

That was the point at which, far too late, he had leapt to his feet and fled. But *not,* he recalled, before kissing her.

No, he preferred to keep both his person and his thoughts well away from Lady Barclay until he had himself well in hand.

Whatever that meant.

Imogen did not set eyes upon the Earl of Hardford for four whole days after his evening visit to the dower house, even though she got up her courage on the second day to call upon Aunt Lavinia and Cousin Adelaide. He was out with the new understeward, acquainting him with Sir Matthew Quentin's well-run farms and experienced, efficient steward. Mr. Knorr was a young gentleman of keen intelligence and pleasing looks and manners, her aunt reported, though why Cousin Percy would go to the expense of hiring a second steward when there was already Mr. Ratchett, she did not know.

Imogen thought it was probably because an active steward was desperately needed for Hardford, but the earl was too kind to force Mr. Ratchett into retirement. She had conceded, albeit reluctantly, that he was indeed capable of kindness.

She had also conceded that she found him more attractive than she had found any other man—and that, disturbingly, included her late husband. She had never thought of being *attracted* to Dicky. He had been her best friend, and everything about him had pleased her— even *that*. Lord Hardford had dared give it a name, in her hearing. It had really been quite shocking of him. *Sex.* There. Yes, sex with Dicky had pleased her. It had pleased him too. But . . . *attraction*?

Was not attraction *just* sex? Divorced from liking or friendship or love? It seemed distasteful.

She wanted it.

She wanted to satisfy a craving she had suppressed for most of her adult life. More than eight years. And she wanted to do it with a man of obvious experience and expertise. She did not doubt Lord Hardford had both.

She had even expressed some willingness—*I am not sure about the other*.

He could not possibly have mistaken her meaning.

She was still not sure.

Perhaps it would not be so very wrong. It was not as

if she was planning to commit herself to any long-term relationship, after all, anything that would bring her real happiness. Only the satisfying of a natural craving. It *was* natural, was it not? For women as well as for men?

Perhaps she would be at peace again if she let it happen. He would go away after a while—she felt no doubt about that, especially now that he had hired another steward, who was young and intelligent and presumably competent. Lord Hardford would go away, probably never to return, and she would be at peace once more, or as much at peace as she ever could be.

In the meanwhile . . .

Would it be so wrong?

The thoughts and the mental debate teemed through Imogen's mind even while she listened to her aunt's animated chatter about the visitors that were expected, though she did not know how many were coming or even exactly when, and Cousin Percy did not know either. It was very unsettling. Aunt Lavinia went on to talk about the entertainments they must plan. It had been a veritable age, she said, since there was any evening entertainment at Hardford. Dear Brandon had not held with such things But now . . .

Imogen let her prattle happily on. And she was hugely relieved—and disappointed?—that the earl did not come home while she was there. He did not come back to the dower house either in four days, and Imogen paced, upstairs and down, unable to settle to any activity for longer than a few minutes at a time. She would have paced the cliff path and the beach too, but she was afraid of running into him. The farthest she went, except for that one visit to the hall, was the garden, where she found that the first snowdrop had bloomed.

He did not come, and she was safe from her own weakness and indecision. She did not have to decide if it would be wrong or not.

On the fifth day, Mrs. Primrose brought news with Imogen's luncheon. A pageboy, sent from the hall with fresh eggs, had brought word of the arrival of two grand traveling carriages full of passengers and a few riders in addition and a great deal of baggage and noise and bustle. And then later in the afternoon the same pageboy returned with a hastily scrawled note in Aunt Lavinia's hand inviting Imogen to dinner so that she might meet a number of long-lost cousins, though some of them were not strictly speaking relatives as they belonged to the maternal side of Cousin Percy's family.

His mother had indeed not come alone, then.

Even while Imogen was thinking up excuses for not going, her eyes focused upon the last two sentences— *Cousin Percy asked me particularly to write to you on his behalf, dearest Imogen, with apologies for not doing so himself. He is busy with his loved ones.*

The invitation came from him, then, even if the apology was probably Aunt Lavinia's invention. And it was only proper that he invite her, Imogen supposed reluctantly. She was, after all, the widow of his predecessor's only son. And by the same token, it would be unpardonably rude of her not to put in an appearance.

She sighed and went to the kitchen to inform Mrs. Primrose that she need not prepare an evening meal.

It could have been worse, Percy thought as he dressed for dinner. *All* his relatives, both paternal and maternal, might have descended upon him—as they still might, of course. There could be a dozen packed carriages bowling along the highway at this very moment in the general direction of Hardford. One could not know for sure.

Aunt Edna, his father's sister, had arrived late in the morning with Uncle Ted Eldridge. Their son, Cyril, had come with them, as had the three girls, Beth and the twins, Alma and Eva. They had been in London, kicking their heels according to Cyril, waiting for the Season to begin so that Beth could be fired off into society and onto the marriage mart. The prospect of passing some time by coming to see Percy in his proper milieu and to celebrate his thirtieth birthday, albeit belatedly, had appealed to them all, without exception.

Aunt Nora Herriott, his mother's sister, had been equally enthusiastic over the invitation and had come with Uncle Ernest and their sons, Leonard and Gregory. They also had come from London and had met the Eldridges by chance at a toll booth and traveled with them thereafter.

One big, happy family come to jollificate with him, Percy thought as he considered the fall of his neckcloth with a critical eye and gave Watkins a nod of approval. Was *jollificate* a verb? If it was not, then it ought to be, for it perfectly described what his family clearly had in mind for the next week or so. One shuddered at the very thought.

And it might not be just family. According to Cyril, Sidney Welby and Arnold Biggs, Viscount Marwood, were thinking of ambling down this way too and might already have begun ambling.

And then, in the middle of the afternoon, just when things had been calming down at the house, Percy's mother had arrived in company with Uncle Roderick Galliard, her brother, and his widowed daughter, Cousin Meredith, and her young son, Geoffrey.

The arrival of the infant had eclipsed all else and had brought everyone and his dog—or, rather, everyone and the Hardford strays, which had, as usual, escaped from the second housekeeper's room—converging upon the child to offer unsolicited hugs and kisses and squeals and exclamations and yips and barks and a growl from Prudence. He *was* admittedly a pretty child with his mop of fair curls and big blue eyes. Percy had done his bit too by snatching up the boy and tossing him toward the ceiling to shrieks of glee from said infant, cheers of encouragement from the male cousins, and assorted squeals of fright and cries of alarm from the female cousins and aunts—while Meredith looked placidly on.

His mother had been filled with ecstasy on her arrival. Even Mrs. Ferby, whom she insisted upon calling Cousin Adelaide, had been unable to escape her hugging arms and delighted exclamations of bonhomie. To find some shared blood between those two would probably take the dedicated researcher all the way back to Adam and Eve, but to his mother, Mrs. F was family. His mother and Lady Lavinia were, in fact, a matched pair and had taken to each other like bees to pollen.

He was already dreaming of availing himself of the peace and sanity of the dower house, Percy thought grimly as he raised his chin for Watkins to position his diamond pin just so in his neckcloth. Though *peace* was probably not quite the right word. Lady Barclay did not much like him, and he was not sure he greatly liked her. Except that he had told her he wanted to be her lover but would settle for friendship. And *she* had told *him* that friendship was possible though improbable and that she was not sure about the other.

So were they friends or were they not? *Could* they be?

Should they be?

He could not for the life of him make any sense of it.

She was coming for dinner. At least, she had been invited and would probably come out of a sense of duty if for no other reason. Anyway, she could not hope to hide out in the dower house for long before it was discovered and invaded by his family, and she must have the sense to realize that. His mother had already learned of her existence and simply could not *wait* to embrace her—not *meet*, but *embrace*.

It was enough to make a grown man wince.

"No, no," he said in response to the stricken look on his valet's face. "You did not stick the pin in me, Watkins. Carry on."

Lord, he hoped she would come. And he hoped she would not.

She came.

They were all gathered in the drawing room when Crutchley announced her—yes, he actually did, his chest puffed out, his voice projecting his words into the room, silencing the hubbub as everyone turned curious eyes his way. He was behaving like a majordomo at a grand *ton* ball. Having all these visitors under his charge had gone to his head.

It must have been a bit daunting to walk alone into the room in a sort of silence, with every eye turned her way, but she did it with calm grace. Her near blond hair was smooth and shining, but it was styled quite simply, especially when one compared it with all the curled and crimped and ringleted heads of his aunts and cousins. Her dress was of dark green velvet, long-sleeved, only very slightly scoop-necked and falling in loose folds from beneath her bosom to her ankles. It was quite unadorned, and she wore no jewelry except tiny pearls in her earlobes and her wedding ring. She was not sparkling with bright smiles, though she was not scowling either.

She set every other woman in the room in the shade, including Beth, who was wearing some of her new London finery and whom he was certain was destined to become one of the acclaimed beauties of the upcoming Season.

The devil! When had he started to think of her as stunning?

He stepped forward and bowed. "Lady Barclay, Cousin Imogen," he said, turning toward his avidly interested family members, "is the widow of Richard Hayes, Viscount Barclay, who would have been in my place here had he not died a hero's death in the Peninsula. She lives—by choice—in the dower house. May I present my mother, Cousin Imogen—Mrs. Hayes?"

His mother hurried forward and hugged her and exclaimed over her and called her Cousin Imogen.

Percy took her about the room, introducing everyone and explaining relationships. He was not sure she would remember afterward, but she paid close attention and murmured something to all of them. She was a true lady.

I want you as a lover, he had said to her less than a week ago. She seemed as remote as the moon tonight—and as desirable as ever. Any hope that he had been temporarily out of his mind that evening or that the intervening days would cool his ardor was squashed.

Crutchley, still in his majordomo persona, was soon back to announce that dinner was served. Percy took his mother on his arm, while Uncle Roderick offered his to Lady Barclay and Uncle Ted escorted Lady Lavinia.

It was rather dizzying to see such a crowd in the dining room, Percy thought a few times during dinner. Extra leaves had been added to the table, and Mrs. Evans in the kitchen had risen magnificently to the occasion, as she had said she would when he had suggested employing someone to assist her.

It ought not to be dizzying. He had spent much of his life in company with crowds of people. Even as a child, when he had remained at home with tutors rather than going away to school, there had always been cousins and other relatives and neighbors and friends of his parents in the house. He had not been here long, but already he had grown accustomed to the quiet of Hardford, give or take a few distant cousins and a menagerie. He rather liked it, he thought in some surprise, though he would not stay. He would leave when his family did. Now that Knorr had arrived, there was no real reason for him to remain. There would be crops this year, a thinning of the flock, a new barn, repairs to the sheep pens, and numerous other improvements. Ratchett would have more detail to add to his books—and that would keep him happy.

"You are unusually quiet, Percy," Aunt Edna remarked over the roast beef course.

"Am I?" He smiled. "It must be the sobering effect of being thirty years old."

"Or it could be," Uncle Roderick said, "that it is difficult to get a word in edgewise. Whatever must you think of us, Lady Lavinia?"

"I could positively weep with happiness," she replied. "All this time there has been an estrangement between the two branches of the family because of a foolish quarrel so long ago that no one even remembers its cause."

No one pointed out to her that about half their number were his mother's family and bore no relationship to her at all. She was clearly happy, and so was Percy's mother, who was beaming back at her and dabbing the corner of one eye with her handkerchief. No one could call his family unsentimental.

"And we have rediscovered one another, Cousin Lavinia, because Percy finally decided to come here where he belongs," his mother said. "And also because of the sad demise of Cousin Imogen's husband. How strange life is. Good things can arise from bad."

Everyone looked suitably solemn over this less-than-profound pronouncement. Percy's eyes locked upon Lady Barclay's. She was still looking a bit marble.

The female cousins appropriated her attention in the drawing room after dinner, and Percy, who sat with his uncles and found himself talking, of all things, about farming, realized from the snatches of conversation he overheard that they had discovered she had been in the Peninsula with her husband and were peppering her with questions about her experiences there. Alma wanted to know if she had been much in demand as a partner at regimental balls and thought it must be simply *divine* to be at a ball and no one but officers with whom to dance.

Fortunately, perhaps, Percy did not hear Lady Barclay's response, but she seemed to be humoring her listeners.

She rose to leave after the tea tray had been removed.

"You have your carriage, dear?" Aunt Nora asked.

"Oh, no," she replied. "The dower house is not far away."

"But the path is dark even on a bright night, Imogen," Lady Lavinia said. "Do take a footman to carry a lantern for you."

"I shall escort Cousin Imogen myself," Percy said.

"There is no need," she said.

"Ah, but there is," he told her. "I must impress my relatives with how well I play the part of responsible lord of the manor."

Most of the relatives laughed. She did not. She did not argue, though.

"I look forward to seeing your home, Cousin Imogen," his mother said. "May I call?"

"But of course, ma'am," Lady Barclay said. "I shall be delighted to see you and any other of Lord Hardford's guests who care to come visit me."

"We are a gregarious lot," Percy warned her after they had left the house together, without a lantern. "You cannot expect us to remain within the hall to mind our own business when there is another house close by and someone else's business to mind instead."

"You have an amiable family," she said.

"I do," he agreed. "Will you take my arm so that I may feel more protective and therefore more manly? I am fortunate to be a part of such a family—on both my father's and my mother's side. But sometimes they can be a little ... intrusive."

"Because they care," she said.

"Yes."

The night was reasonably bright. There seemed to be no clouds overhead. It was also crisply cold. She set her hand within his arm. Neither of them took up the conversational slack.

He could see the outline of the dower house ahead. It was, of course, in total darkness. He did not like the fact that there were no servants there waiting for her. But he could say nothing. She had made it clear that she would not tolerate his interference.

"Thank you," she said, sliding her hand free of his arm when they reached the gate. "I appreciate your accompanying me even though it was unnecessary. I have done the walk many times alone."

"I shall see you into the house," he said.

"I have set a lamp just inside the door, as I always do," she told him. "I shall light it as soon as I set foot inside to dispel the darkness and, with it, all the ghosts and monsters lurking there. You need come no farther."

"You do not *want* me to come farther?" he asked her.

Her face, turned up to his, was lit faintly by moonlight. It was impossible to see her expression, but her eyes were great pools of . . . something.

"No." She shook her head and spoke softly. "Not tonight."

Or any night? He did not ask the question out loud.

"Very well," he said. "You see how you have quelled the naturally domineering male in me? Not entirely, however. I shall stand here until you are inside and I see the light from your lamp."

He opened the gate as he spoke and closed it after she had stepped through.

"Very well," she said, turning to look at him. "You may come and break the door down if the light does not appear and you should hear a bloodcurdling scream."

And damn it, but she smiled again with what looked in the near darkness to be genuine amusement.

"Is it not customary," he asked her, "to offer a kiss to the man who has escorted you home?"

"Oh, goodness me," she said. "*Is* it? Times must have changed since I was a girl."

He grinned at her, and she reached up both gloved hands to cup his face before leaning across the gate and kissing him. It was not just a brief, amused token of a kiss either. Her lips lingered on his, soft and slightly parted and very warm in contrast to the chill of the night air.

He leaned into her, his arms going about her to draw her against him, and her arms slid about his neck. It was not a lascivious kiss. It was something far more delicious than that. It was very deliberate on both their parts. Their mouths opened and he explored the moist interior of hers with his tongue. This time when she sucked on it, he enjoyed the sensation. It was a kiss curiously devoid of full sexual intent, though. It was instead . . . sheer enjoyment.

It was a totally new experience for him. It was a bit alarming, actually.

She ended the embrace, though her arms stayed loosely about his neck.

"There, Lord Hardford," she said. "You have had your thank-you for tonight."

"May I escort you home *every* night?" he asked.

And she laughed.

He could have wept with happiness—to borrow a phrase from Lady Lavinia.

And then she was gone. He stood where he was, his hands on the gate, until she had opened the door with her key and stepped inside—without looking back—and closed it behind her. He waited until he saw faint light about the doorframe and then light moving into her sitting room. He turned then to leave.

And it was only as he did so that he realized Hector was at his heels. What was it about Hector and heels? Was *he* Achilles? And was Lady Hayes—Imogen—his Achilles' heel?

Or his salvation?

Curious thought.

"Damned foolish animal," he grumbled. "And how *do* you manage to get through closed doors? And *why*? It is cold out here and there was no need for you to come too."

The stunted tail waved as Hector fell into step slightly behind him.

13

Imogen's day started peacefully enough, though she did not expect that pleasant state to continue.

The morning post brought her two letters, both from wives of her fellow Survivors. She was always gratified to hear from them. She liked them all, though she had not yet met the Duchess of Worthingham, Ralph's wife, in person. She liked them not least because each had made one of her dearest friends happy. And she liked them because they were strong, interesting women in their own right. She was never sure, though, that they liked *her*. She was one of the Survivors, and during their annual reunions they spent time alone together, the seven of them, especially at night. The wives respected that need and never intruded, though at other times during those days they all mingled together and greatly enjoyed one another's company.

Imogen often wondered if the other women were wholly comfortable with her. She felt her difference from them and suspected that they must feel it too. She wondered if they sometimes found her aloof.

In any case, she always enjoyed having a letter from

one of them. And today there was the special gift of two. She settled down to a good read over breakfast. Ralph's wife, the Duchess of Worthingham—she had signed herself simply Chloe—had written to say she was very much looking forward to meeting her at Penderris Hall, as well as Sir Benedict and Lady Harper, whom she had also not yet met. And she was coming despite Ralph's concerns over her perfectly good health. Some people, of course, would insist upon calling it "delicate" health and frightening the poor man, but she had never felt better.

The duchess, Imogen inferred, was expecting a child. And so by the end of the year three of their number would be fathers.

Life had moved on for all of them except her—and George. But George, Duke of Stanbrook, was in his late forties and one assumed, perhaps wrongly, that he would never consider remarrying.

Imogen finished reading the duchess's delightfully long letter and then read Sophia, Viscountess Darleigh's. Their son, who had just had his first birthday, was *walking everywhere*—both words were underlined—and Vincent had developed an uncanny ability to follow him about to make sure he did not come to any greater harm than the occasional bump or scrape. Of course, Vincent's dog helped, having apparently decided that young Thomas was simply an extension of Vincent. Another one of their books for children had just been published— another nail-biting adventure of Bertha and Blind Dan. Sophia would bring a copy to Penderris.

Vincent was riding daily despite the cold weather. Indeed, he was *galloping* along the specially built race track about half the perimeter of their park. It was enough to make Sophia's hair stand on end—and her hair had grown *long* since last year—but since she was the one who had conceived the idea of the track for just such a purpose, she could hardly complain, could she?

Imogen was smiling by the time she rose from the breakfast table. Soon now she would be with them all. Looking out the window, she saw that the sun was shining from a clear blue sky. As far as she could tell from indoors, there was no significant wind either. She donned a warm pelisse and bonnet and went outside to make sure no new weeds had invaded her flower beds and to see if there were any more snowdrops in the grass. Blossom padded outside with her and curled up on the front step in the sunlight after prowling about the garden.

Imogen pulled out a few offending weeds and found five more snowdrops The air, though not exactly balmy, was at least not bitterly cold. One could believe in spring this morning.

She sat back on her heels and looked over to the garden gate.

She had stopped him from coming inside with her last night, but she had enjoyed some light banter with him just there. It seemed so long ago—a lifetime—since she had felt lighthearted, as she had for a few minutes last night. And she had kissed him quite voluntarily and quite ... eagerly, when it would have been the easiest thing in the world to avoid doing so.

Is it not customary to offer a kiss to the man who has escorted you home? he had asked her. And he had smiled. No, he had grinned. She had been able to see the difference even though they had not brought a lantern.

She smiled at the memory. She liked him *so much* in that mood—slightly flirtatious but in an amused, quite unthreatening way.

She had expected her peace to be shattered at some time in the course of today, and now was the time, it seemed. Through the gate she could see Mrs. Hayes coming along the path from the hall in company with her sister and sister-in-law. Imogen got to her feet, brushed the grass from her pelisse, and went to open the gate for them, since she guessed the dower house was their destination.

She had not looked forward to last evening, but she had surprised herself by almost enjoying the noise and the laughter and the sense of family she had got from Lord Hardford's relatives. It had been obvious that he was as fond of them as they were of him, but she understood why he felt somehow . . . invaded.

Perhaps he would come now that they were here—to take refuge at the dower house.

All three ladies hugged Imogen and kissed her on the cheek as though they were close relatives. All of them also exclaimed over the prettiness of the house and its position close to the cliffs but nestled cozily in its little hollow with its own well-tended garden.

"I could be perfectly happy living here myself," Mrs. Hayes declared. "It is an absolute delight, is it not, Edna and Nora?"

"We will come here to stay with you and Cousin Imogen, Julia," her sister replied, "and leave our husbands and offspring at home."

All three ladies laughed merrily, and Mrs. Hayes set an arm about Imogen's waist and hugged her to her side.

"You must not mind us, Cousin Imogen," she said. "We are a family that likes to joke and laugh. Laughter is always the best medicine for almost everything, would you not agree?"

They all proceeded inside for coffee and some of Mrs. Primrose's scones. The ladies talked with great enthusiasm about going visiting in the village during the afternoon with Cousin Lavinia—they all referred to her by that name. And Mrs. Hayes talked of her plan to *do* something about that dreadfully gloomy and neglected ballroom at Hardford Hall and make it suitable for a grand party, perhaps even a ball, to celebrate her son's thirtieth birthday—belatedly, unfortunately, because he had gone off to London for his actual birthday. And they would also celebrate his arrival at his new home, also belated.

"Oh, definitely a ball, Julia," Mrs. Herriott said. "Everyone loves to dance."

"You simply must come up to the hall and help with ideas and plans, Cousin Imogen," Mrs. Hayes said.

"I am going to steal your cook, Cousin Imogen," Mrs. Herriott told her. "These are surely the best scones I have ever tasted."

They left after a correct half hour or so, hugging Imogen again as they went and kissing her cheek and hoping they would see her at the hall again during the evening. She could only laugh softly to herself after they had gone. She felt rather as though she were emerging from a whirlwind.

She had scarcely finished her luncheon a couple of hours later when her home was invaded again, this time by the Eldridge twin sisters—was it possible to tell them apart?—and the two Herriott brothers and Mr. Cyril Eldridge. They were all first cousins of the earl, Imogen remembered from last evening. Today they were out for a walk and had called to beg Imogen to go with them.

"You simply *must* come, Cousin," one of the Eldridge sisters pleaded. "Our numbers are uneven."

"Percy says there is a way down onto the beach from close to here," Mr. Eldridge said, "and that you would be able to show it to us, Lady Barclay. Will you be so kind? Or are you busy with something else?"

"I would be delighted," she said, and was surprised to discover that she meant it. Four of the cousins were very young—all of them below the age of twenty, she guessed. The twins were probably fifteen or sixteen. The young men had a tendency to guffaw at the slightest provocation and the young ladies to giggle. But there was no guile in them, she had noticed last evening. They were merely acting their age. She was rather touched that they had thought of asking her to join them when she must appear quite elderly in their eyes. But of course, Mr. Eldridge was probably far closer to her in age than he was to them. Perhaps they had considered that.

"Beth went visiting with my mother and my aunts and Lady Lavinia," Mr. Eldridge explained as they set out along the cliff path. "They must have been horribly squashed in the carriage. Meredith stayed back to play with young Geoffrey when he wakes from his afternoon nap. My father and my uncles went off with Percy to look at sheep. He was actually soliciting their advice. It scarcely bears thinking of, Lady Barclay. Percy interested in farming? Next he will be talking about *settling* here. Oh, I beg your pardon."

"Because I might be offended that the very notion of someone's wanting to settle here appalls you, Mr. Eldridge?" she said. "I am not offended."

"It is only," he said, "that I cannot imagine Percy being contented here for long. He only came because he said he would when he was colossally bored and colossally drunk on his birthday, and Percy never likes to go back on his word. I'll wager he was already planning to leave here when Aunt Julia decided to come and bring us lot with her. I'll wager he just about had an apoplexy."

He was not far wrong, Imogen thought with an inward smile. But—*colossally bored*. And *colossally drunk*. And this was the man she had kissed voluntarily and with some pleasure last night? The man she had come to like? And the man with whom she was still half considering having an affair?

It was nothing she did not already know or guess about him, though. He was also a very intelligent, well-educated man, and a man who had somehow lost direction about ten years ago and not found it since. *Would* he find it? Ever? Here, perhaps? She hoped not here. Please not here. She might perhaps allow herself a little reprieve in company with him, but it could not be prolonged.

"Is this it?" one of the Herriott brothers—Leonard?—was calling from a little way ahead along the path.

"It is," Imogen called back. "The path looks a bit daunting, but you will see that it zigzags to minimize the steepness of the descent, and it is really quite wide and firm underfoot."

"I claim Gregory," one of the twins said. "He has a sturdier arm."

"Meaning I am fat, Alma?" Gregory Herriott said.

"Meaning that you have a sturdy arm," she said—and giggled. "And I am Eva."

"No, you are dashed well not," he said. "Not unless you changed frocks with your sister after luncheon."

There was a burst of laughter from the other three.

Imogen stepped forward to lead the way down.

If he had not been colossally drunk on his birthday,

perhaps it would not have occurred to him to come to Cornwall—ever. He had neglected it quite happily for two years. All this might not be happening if he had not got drunk. But if he had not, then she would still be at the hall herself now, waiting for the roof to be replaced on the dower house.

She would not go up to the hall this evening, she decided. She could not be expected to go there every night, after all.

May I escort you home every night? he had asked last evening after their kiss. He had asked it to make her laugh—and he had succeeded.

But she must not make a reality of that joke.

When had she last laughed before he came here, though? She had done it at least twice since that she could remember.

Oh, she did like him, she thought with a sigh as she allowed Mr. Eldridge, quite unnecessarily, to move ahead of her and help her down onto the beach.

She abandoned herself to an afternoon of frolicking by the sea.

Percy spent the morning with his family, though his mother and aunts went out for a walk, declaring their need for some air and exercise after several long days of travel. He suspected they would take the direction to the dower house and pay their respects to Cousin Imogen if she was at home.

Percy enjoyed the morning, taking everyone on a tour of the house and out to the stables—to see the kittens, of course—and playing billiards with some of the cousins, talking over coffee. He enjoyed a luncheon with brisk conversation, and he enjoyed an afternoon spent with his uncles, showing them about the farm, discussing with them some of his plans and some of Knorr's.

And it was a pleasure to return to the house to the discovery that there had been two more new arrivals. Sidney Welby and Arnold Biggs, Viscount Marwood, had indeed made the journey. There was much hand shaking and back slapping and noise and laughter—and that was when only Percy and they and Cyril were involved.

Once Welby's and Marwood's arrival was announced, the uncles and male cousins were pleased, and Percy's mother and aunts and Lady Lavinia delighted. The female cousins were dizzy with excitement that there were two young, personable gentlemen who were not their cousins staying at the house—one of them with a *title*. If they had twittered and giggled before, they soared to new heights now.

Dinner and the evening spent in the drawing room were occasions of such collective amity and glee that at one point Percy felt he could gladly step outside and bellow at the moon or some such thing. He might have done it too if there had not been the possibility that he would be overheard.

He did not know how it was possible to love one's family and friends and enjoy their company and feel grateful for them all—and yet to feel so constricted and constrained by them too. What was it about him? Whatever it was, it was a quite recent development. It had come with his thirtieth birthday, perhaps, this feeling that it was not enough to have everything, even family, even friends, even love.

It was the realization that there was a vast emptiness within that had gone unexplored his whole life because he had been too busy with what was going on outside himself. He felt like a hollow shell and remembered Lady Barclay's asking him if there was anything within the shield of charm he donned for public viewing.

He had joked about it, told her he was charm through to the very heart. He was not sure his heart did anything more than pump blood about his body. Except that he *did* love. He must not be too harsh with himself. He loved his family.

"You have gone very quiet again, Percy," Aunt Edna remarked.

"I am just enjoying the fact that you have all come such a distance for my sake," he told her. And the thing was that he was not lying—not entirely so, anyway.

He wanted his peace and quiet back.

What?

He had always avoided both as he would the plague.

The gathering began to break up after the tea tray had been removed. Some of the older generation as well as Meredith went off to bed. A few of the cousins were going to the billiard room and invited Sidney and Arnold to join them. A couple of the uncles were going to withdraw to the library for a drink and a look at the reading choices.

"Come with us, Percy?" Uncle Roderick suggested.

"I think I am going to get a breath of fresh air," he said. "Stretch my legs before I lie down."

"Do you want company, Perce?" Arnold asked.

"Not necessarily," he said.

His friend bent a look on him.

"Right," he said. "The outdoors by the sea on a February night does not really call to me, I must admit. Enjoy your ... solitude?" He raised his eyebrows.

"Billiards, Arnie?" Cyril asked, and the two of them

went off together in pursuit of most of the other young people.

Percy stepped outside after donning his greatcoat and gloves and hat and then deliberately going and fetching Hector from the second housekeeper's room, though why he bothered he did not know. The dog would surely have found a way of following him anyway. His name would more appropriately be Phantom rather than Hector.

It was a little before eleven o'clock. It was *not* too late for a stroll before retiring for the night. It *was* too late, far too late, to make a social call. But what about a call of necessity?

May I seek refuge here occasionally? he had asked her.

He could not possibly call on her at eleven o'clock at night. It would seem he had come for one thing only.

And would that be true?

His steps took him to the right outside the front doors and around the path that led past the dower house. Would he walk on past, though?

He would let her decide, he thought, or, rather, her lamp or candles or whatever she used to see in the dark when she was not sleeping. If her house was in darkness, he would walk on by. If there was light within, he would knock on her door—unless the light came from an upstairs room.

There was light in the sitting room.

Percy stood at the gate for what might have been five minutes until his feet inside his shoes—he had not changed into boots—turned numb with cold and his fingers inside his gloves tingled unpleasantly. Even his nose felt numb. He willed the light to move, to proceed upstairs, to give him the cue to move away and go home.

And he willed it to stay where it was.

Hector had given up sitting at his feet. He was lying there instead, his chin on his paws. He was beginning, Percy thought, looking down at him in the dim light of the moon, to look almost like a normal dog. Which was just as well, since he seemed to be stuck with the mutt. And, annoyingly, he felt love begin to creep up on him.

Damned dog.

The light stayed where it was.

Percy opened the gate and closed it quietly behind him after he and Hector had stepped through. He did not want to signal his arrival. There was still time to escape. He lifted the knocker away from the door, hesitated, and released it. It made a horrible din.

Lord, it was probably *after* eleven by this time.

The door opened almost immediately, long before he was ready.

And he said nothing. Not only could he not think of anything to say, but it did not even occur to him that perhaps he ought to say something.

She did not say anything either. They stared at each other, the lamp she held in one hand lighting their faces from below. It took Hector to break the spell. It must have occurred to the dog that the warmth inside the house was preferable to the cold outside. He trotted in and turned, as if by right of ownership, into the sitting room.

She stood to one side, mutely inviting Percy inside.

"It is not exactly what it seems," he said as she closed the door. "Late as it is, I have not come here expecting to sleep with you."

He never knew quite what happened to his tongue when he was in her presence. He had never spoken with any other lady as he very often seemed to speak to her.

"You have come to take refuge here." It was not a question. She turned to look at him with calm eyes and face. "Come, then."

And she led the way into the warmth of the sitting room.

14

Imogen had chosen not to go up to the hall for dinner even though Aunt Lavinia had sent a brief note again, assuring her that she would be welcome, that she was always welcome, as she knew, and did not need to wait for an invitation. And, she had added, there were two more guests—Cousin Percy's gentlemen friends from London.

Imogen liked all these people who had come to shatter her peace at Hardford, but she was finding the noise and bustle a little overwhelming. She was very thankful indeed for her own house, even if she must expect it to be invaded frequently during the daytime until everyone left.

She wondered if *he* was finding it overwhelming too. But they were of his world, and his world was a busy, noisy place, she guessed, with little room for quiet introspection. Perhaps he was enjoying their company and had forgotten all about that night when he had asked if he might retreat here occasionally.

But she remembered the book of Alexander Pope's poetry on a table beside his chair in the library—and his double first degree in the classics. And she remembered something he had said just before asking if he might come here — *I think I came to Cornwall in the hope of finding myself, though I did not realize that until this moment. I came because I needed to step away from my life and discover if from the age of thirty on I can find some new and worthwhile purpose to it.*

But he had not been allowed to step away from his life for long. It had caught up to him here.

She stayed up later than she ought, though the morning visit with the older ladies and the afternoon down on the beach with a group of exuberant youngsters had tired her. She could not settle to reading, which might have relaxed her. She thought of writing to her mother, but decided to wait until morning, when she would be wider awake. She crocheted but could not admire what she did. She went into the kitchen to make a cup of tea and ended up baking a batch of sweet biscuits and then washing up after herself. She crocheted again and petted Blossom, who was always fascinated by the fine silk thread and the flash of the crochet hook.

And finally she admitted that she was waiting for him to come and it simply would not do. She was allowing her peace and hard-won discipline to be shattered. She would go to bed, have a good night's sleep, and tomorrow take herself firmly in hand. This *would not do*.

She put her crochet away and got to her feet, remembering as she did so that she had not eaten any of the biscuits she had baked or made any tea after boiling the kettle and measuring the tea leaves into the teapot. It was too late now, though. And she was neither hungry nor thirsty. She reached for the lamp, glancing at the same time at the clock on the mantelpiece. It was ten minutes past eleven.

And that was when a knock sounded at the door, causing her to jump and Blossom to open her eyes.

Imogen picked up the lamp and went to open the door. It did not occur to her to be cautious about doing so.

For a dreadful moment they just stood looking at each other, one on each side of the door's threshold. A draft of cold air came in from outside. The lamp, lighting his face from below, made him look taller and a bit menacing, especially as he was neither smiling nor speaking. But she knew in that moment that she wanted him, that there was really no decision to make—or if there was, then she had already made it. And she knew too that it was not just *that*—oh, she might as well think of it as *sex*—that made her desire him. It was not just sex. It was ... more than that. That was what made it a truly dreadful moment.

And then he was inside and had said that about not having come expecting to sleep with her—had he *really* said it aloud and not shocked her beyond words? And she had acknowledged that he had come to seek refuge and led the way into the sitting room. Hector was already seated beside the chair on which she had been sitting all evening, the chair where *he* always sat when he was here.

Always?

How many times had he been here? It seemed as if he had always been here, as if that chair had always waited for him when he was not, as though when she sat on it she was drawing comfort from the fact that it was his.

This combination of tiredness and a late night was playing strange and dangerous tricks with her mind.

He waited for her to seat herself on the love seat and

then sat down himself. He had left his coat and hat out in the hall, she noticed. He was still unsmiling. He must have left his armor of easy charm out in the hall too.

"You must have been about to go to bed," he said. And then he did smile — a bit ruefully. "That was not the best conversational opener, was it?"

"I am still up," she said.

He looked about the room and at the fire, which had burned low. He got up, as she remembered his doing last time, picked up the poker to spread the coals, and then piled on more from the coal scuttle beside the hearth. He stayed on his feet, one forearm resting on the mantel. He watched the fire catch on the new coals.

"What if I had?" he asked her.

Strangely, she knew exactly what he was asking, but he elaborated anyway.

"What if I *had* come expecting to sleep with you?"

She considered her answer.

"Would you have tossed me out?" He turned his head to look at her over his shoulder.

She shook her head.

They gazed at each other for a few moments before he poked the fire again to give it more air and resumed his seat.

"Is it possible for people to change, Imogen?" he asked her.

She felt a little lurching of the stomach at the sound of her name on his lips — again.

"Yes," she said.

"How?"

"Sometimes it takes a great calamity," she said.

His eyes searched her face. "Like the loss of a spouse?"

She nodded slightly again.

"What were you like before?" he asked.

She spread her hands on her lap and pleated the fabric of her dress between her fingers—something she tended to do when her mind was agitated. She released the fabric and clasped her hands loosely in her lap.

"Full of life and energy and laughter," she said. "Sociable, gregarious. Tomboyish as a girl—I was the despair of my mother. Not really ladylike even after I grew up. Eager to live my life to the full."

His eyes roamed over her as if to see signs of that long-ago, long-gone girl she had been.

"Would you want to be that person again?" he asked.

She shook her head. "Have you read William Blake's *Songs of Innocence and Experience*?" she asked him.

"Yes."

"It is impossible to recapture innocence once it has been exposed for the illusion it is," she said.

"Illusion?" He frowned. "Why should innocence be more unreal, more *untrue,* than cynicism?"

"I am not cynical," she said. "But no, I could not go back."

"Can experience and suffering not be used to enrich one's life rather than deaden or impoverish it?" he asked.

"Yes." She thought of her fellow Survivors. They were in a vastly different place in their lives than could have been predicted eight or nine years ago, but five of them at least had risen above the suffering and forged lives that were rich and apparently happy. Perhaps they would not be so happy now if they had not had to go through that long, dark night of pain and brokenness. Disturbing thought.

"You are in some ways fortunate, Imogen," he said

softly, and her eyes snapped to his. "How can one, at the age of thirty, learn from the experience of nothing but empty pleasure and frivolity?"

"And *love*," she said fiercely. "Your life has been so full of love, Lord Hardford, that it is fairly bursting at the seams with it. Even that *dog* loves you, and you love it. It is *not* unmanly to admit it. And your life has included a period of intense learning about two of the greatest civilizations our world has known. You may have largely wasted the years since you left Oxford, but even *that* experience does not have to be for nothing. No time is *really* wasted unless one never learns the lessons that it offers."

He had sat back in his chair and was regarding her with a half smile on his lips. "You are expending passion over a wastrel, Lady Barclay?" he said. "*What* lessons?"

She sighed. She *had* allowed herself to become rather wrought up. But he was not a wastrel. A week or so ago she might have believed it, but no longer. He might have lived the life of a wastrel, but that did not make him one. He was not defined by what he had done or not done in the past ten years.

"Perhaps in recognizing how one ought *not* to live, one can learn how *to* live," she said.

"It is that easy?" he asked her. "I should turn overnight, you think, into a worthy country gentleman, a Cornish country gentleman, and bury myself for the rest of my life in the back of beyond with my crops and my sheep and the ugly dog I have supposedly come to love? Breeding heirs and spares and hopeful daughters? Loving my wife and helpmeet and cleaving only unto her for as long as we both shall live?"

And she laughed. Despite the almost unbearable tension that his words had begun to build, he had also created an image that was just too absurd.

His eyes smiled—oh, goodness!—and then his lips.

"You are really quite stunning when you laugh like that," he said.

That sobered her. But she had been having exactly the same thought about him and his smile.

"It gives a glimpse into the person you say you were and the person you were meant always to be," he said. "Can you not be happy again, Imogen? *Will* you not be?"

She smiled, found that she could not see him clearly, and realized that her eyes had filled with tears.

"No, don't cry," he said softly. "I did not mean to make you unhappy. Will you come to bed with me?"

She blinked away her tears. And her self-imposed exile from her own life seemed suddenly pointless. Wasted time—between eight and nine years to match his ten.

He had asked a question.

"Yes," she said.

And he got to his feet and came toward her. He reached out a hand. She looked at it for several moments, a man's hand, a hand that would touch her . . . She placed her own in it and stood. He had not left much room between himself and the love seat. She put her arms up about his neck and leaned into him as his own arms came about her, and their mouths met.

It was a very deliberate thing, she decided. It was not seduction, and it was not unbridled temptation. It was not something for which she would feel guilt, something she would regret. It was something she wanted and would allow. No, nothing as passive as that. It was something for which she would step back into life, something to which she would give herself unreservedly, something she would allow herself to enjoy. But not alone. Together. It was something they would enjoy together.

Just for a brief while. A short vacation from the life she had imposed upon herself and must live until the end.

She drew back her head and looked into his eyes, which were very blue even in the dimness of the lamplight.

"I do not expect forever," she told him, "or want it. I do not expect you to come back here in the morning out of any sense of guilt to offer me marriage. I would say no if you did. This is just for now. For a little while."

His eyes smiled again before his mouth followed suit. It was a devastating expression and quite unconscious and therefore unpracticed, she guessed. She was seeing him, or at least a part of him, as he really was.

"If I were to offer forever, I would be a fool," he said. "No one has forever in his possession. Take the lamp, and I will set the guard about the fire."

She turned to lead the way upstairs. Blossom was padding off to her bed in the kitchen.

"Stay," she heard him say to Hector.

A fire had been lit in the bedchamber. A few of the coals, now turned almost to ash, still glowed faintly red. The room was not exactly warm, but it was not frigid either.

She set down the lamp on the dressing table, lit a candle, and extinguished the lamp. Immediately the light was dimmer, more intimate. It was a pretty room, not small, but given a cozy effect by a ceiling that followed the slope of the roof on one side and a square window that reached almost to the floor. She drew the curtains across it—pretty white curtains with a bold flower pattern in pastel shades to match the bedcover. He did not usually notice such things, but he suspected they had been chosen, even if unconsciously, to suit Imogen Hayes as she had been before the death of her husband.

Percy stood inside the door, his hands clasped behind him, savoring the strangeness of the moment. This was not seduction on his part or even skilled persuasion. She was fully acquiescent. There had not even been any flirtation. This was a new experience for him and he was not sure what to expect. *That* was a new experience too.

She lifted her arms, facing away from him, and began to remove the pins from her hair. He moved then to stride toward her.

"Allow me," he said.

She lowered her arms without turning.

Her hair was warm and thick and shining in the candlelight. It was also absolutely straight and reached almost to her waist. It would be a maid's nightmare, he guessed, when the fashion was for curls and ringlets and waving tendrils. It was glorious and several shades of blond. He combed his fingers through it. There were no tangles that would need a brush.

Her crowning glory, he thought on a foolish flight of clichéd fancy and was glad he had not spoken aloud.

He turned her by the shoulders. She looked years younger with her hair down, and she looked twice as . . . No, she could not possibly look more desirable to him than she had downstairs, telling him earnestly that his time during the past ten years had not been wasted, eyes filling with tears when he had asked if she would allow herself to be happy again.

He would make her happy. No, perhaps not that. Good

sex was not synonymous with happiness. He would give her good sex. It was the only thing of value that he *could* give. No experience was ever wasted, she had said. Well, he had plenty of that.

He smiled at her. She did not smile back, but there was a softness and an openness to her that he knew was deliberate. She was allowing this, both for him and for herself. She had chosen *him,* he thought in some wonder. There must have been other men in more than eight years, other candidates more worthy than he. He knew of a couple right here in this neighborhood. But she had chosen him—just for now. *For a little while.*

Perhaps because she knew he would go away as soon as his family left? Perhaps because she knew there was no chance of permanence? He was not a permanent sort of man. Or perhaps because she really did not want permanence but merely a brief affair with good sex.

Did it matter why she had chosen him? Or why he had chosen her?

He reached behind her and undid the fastenings of her dress. He drew it off her shoulders and down her arms. It slid to the floor to pool about her feet. She was not wearing stays. He had realized that downstairs earlier. She did not need them. He kneeled down, removed first one slipper and then the other, rolled her silk stockings down over her calves and off her feet. Her legs were long and well shaped. He stood. She was wearing only her shift, which barely covered her bosom and reached not quite to her knees.

He drew a slow breath and reached for the hem, but her fingertips came lightly to his wrists.

"I would be uncomfortable," she said.

With her own nakedness? He nodded. He would

make her comfortable when they were on the bed. There was no hurry. Experience had taught him that, and he was glad tonight to be experienced, though his mind did not even touch upon all the women with whom he had acquired it.

For tonight there was only her. Imogen. A bit of a clumsy name, he had thought at first. Now he thought it perfect for her. Individual. Strong. Beautiful. Imogen.

He did not have any inhibitions about his own nakedness. He undressed while she watched, setting his clothes on a chair beside the window. And he did not stop when he came to his drawers, his last remaining garment. He removed them, then came back to her and cupped her face with his hands, and brushed his lips across hers. He was almost fully aroused, but she was no virgin to become vaporish at the sight. She had seen a man in his desire before.

"I knew you would be as beautiful without your clothes as you are with," she said, sounding almost resentful.

"I am sorry if I offend you." He smiled. "And I will wager you are as beautiful without yours as you are with too. A man does not necessarily like to be described as *beautiful,* you know."

"Not even when he *is*?"

Her shoulders and her arms, he noticed, were pebbled with goose bumps.

"But I leave you cold, do I?" He moved his hands down to her shoulders and drew her against him. "I must be losing my touch."

"I very much doubt it," she said, her hands—her *cold* hands—spreading over his chest.

"Come," he said, leading her to the bed and throwing back the covers. "Let me warm you up."

It did not take long. Not that he did all the warming. She had decided that she would let this happen, he had already realized, but there was nothing passive about the letting. She was going to *make* it happen, and abandoned herself to passion as soon as her back encountered the mattress. He doubted she even realized when her shift was peeled off over her head or that they had left the candle burning. She kissed him as though she would never have enough of him—just as he kissed her, in fact. And when his hands and his mouth explored every inch of her, teasing and arousing as they went, *her* hands and mouth were busy on him. They did not need either a fire in the hearth or blankets on the bed. They created their own roaring furnace of heat and desire and passion.

When his hand went between her legs, she opened and lifted to him. She was hot and wet to his fingers, and his thumb caressed her to an almost instant cresting and release. She sighed out loud and rolled into him, relaxed for the moment but unsated. Her mouth found his.

"Percy," she whispered against his lips.

It tipped him over the edge—just that, the sound of his name on her lips.

He drew her beneath him, slid his hands under her as she lifted her long legs and twined them about his, and went hard into her. Experience almost let him down then. He almost went off in her like a randy schoolboy. She was hot and moist and welcomed him with a slow, firm clenching of inner muscles.

It took him a few moments to control himself while he held deep in her, in a near ecstasy of pain.

And then they made slow, deliberate, exquisitely satisfying love. He had never before thought of sex with that particular euphemism. There was no love involved with having sex. It was purely, earthily, wondrously physical. But with her—with Imogen—sex was more than just that. Not love, but . . . But there was a deficiency of language.

It was strange how the thoughts were present in his mind even while his body was fully concentrated upon the sex act. Or upon making love. Or whatever the devil . . .

Then her inner muscles clenched as he thrust but did not unclench as they had done for the past several minutes in perfect rhythm with his withdrawals. And it was not just the inner muscles. Her whole body was taut and straining and lifting harder against his. He pressed deep again and held still. And . . .

Good Lord. Heaven help him . . . *Good Lord*.

He had been going to wait for her to climax and then continue toward his own release. But there was some sort of explosion that happened simultaneously inside his head and in his loins—and in her too.

And sometimes there was no experience to draw upon.

And absolutely no vocabulary.

He lay spent and heavy and panting on her, and she panted beneath him, all relaxed and hot and sweaty, and what had happened to all her goose bumps?

"Sorry," he murmured, disengaging from her and rolling off her and reaching down to pull the bedcovers over them. "I was squashing you."

"Mmm." She rolled into his side, all soft woman and warm, silky hair.

Maybe she had the same problems with vocabulary.

"Thank you," he murmured. He was sinking fast into warm, comfortable oblivion.

"Mmm," she said again. Very eloquent.

He shifted position, slid an arm beneath her neck to cup her shoulder with his hand.

"Do you mind if I sleep here for a little while?" he asked her.

"No."

He was sliding deeper, as he guessed she was, when a trot-trot-trotting sound was followed by a great warm lump of something landing heavily on the bed and worming its way between their legs.

"Damned dog," he muttered, but he was too sleepy to apologize for his language or to order the damned dog to get down and leave a man alone with his lover.

Imogen awoke when warm lips closed briefly over her own. She kept her eyes shut for a few moments. She did not want to disturb the dream. She knew it was not a dream, that it was real, but she half wished it were just a dream, something for which she need not bear responsibility.

But she only *half* wished it.

His face was above her own. She could see him quite clearly. The candle was still burning. She had no idea what time it was, how long they had slept. The dog, she realized, had gone from between them.

"I should take myself off back home," he said, "before any of the servants are about."

He looked predictably gorgeous, his dark hair disheveled, his eyelids sleepy, his shoulders bare. He was in her own bed with her, she thought foolishly. They had done *that* together, and it had been wonderful. If there was to be guilt, she was not going to feel it yet. Or at all. She had quite consciously decided to do this, to enjoy it and him. She slid her hands over his shoulders, cupped the sides of his neck, rubbed her thumbs over the underside of his jaw.

"You need a shave," she said.

He smiled slowly, that genuine, devastatingly attractive smile that began with his eyes.

"Are you afraid of whisker burn, Lady Barclay?" he asked.

"No." She found herself smiling back at him. "You are leaving, are you not, Lord Hardford?"

"Yes," he said. "After."

"After?"

"After I have said a thorough good-bye," he said. "No, that sounds too final. After I have said a thorough farewell. May I?"

She drew his face down to hers in reply.

"Let me do it," he murmured against her lips as he moved over and onto her between her thighs and came into her, hard and ready and deep. "Relax."

It was not what she had intended but . . . well, he was the expert.

It was delicious beyond words—to lie open on her back, all her muscles relaxed, even the inner ones that ached to close about him. To feel the hard, steady rhythm of his lovemaking into the soft heat of her body. To surrender. To receive and give nothing in return *except* her surrender. It was against her very nature to be submissive. It was something entirely new to her.

It was . . . well, it was delicious beyond words.

And, totally surprisingly, she shivered into release— but release from *what*?—after a few minutes. He felt it and held still and firm in her until she was finished, and then he continued until he was done and she felt the hot gush of his release deep inside.

For a moment—ah, foolishness indeed!—she wished she was not barren. But she let the thought go and enjoyed the full weight of his body relaxing onto her.

She could hear the dog snuffling in his sleep from somewhere in the room.

What was it going to be like, she found herself wondering as she stared up at the slope of the ceiling, after he had gone? Not just from her house tonight, but ... after he had gone from Hardford and Cornwall, perhaps never to return.

He inhaled deeply and audibly and lifted himself away from her and off the bed. She watched him get dressed. He turned to watch *her* as he did so. He was totally unself-conscious about his body, she realized. She desperately wanted to pull the blankets up from her waist but did not do so. It would be absurd to cover herself out of embarrassment in light of what they had done twice in the past few hours.

"When I seek refuge here again," he said as he pulled on his coat, "I will be quite happy with conversation and perhaps some tea. And I will not have a temper tantrum even if you turn me away altogether. I do not want you to think that I will come here in the future only to bed you. I do not want to think of you as my mistress. You are not that."

"But how disappointing," she said. "I was looking forward to negotiating with you on the size of my salary."

"What?" he said. "Half a roof is not enough?"

"Ah, but both halves actually belong to you," she reminded him, "as does the house beneath them. You have said so yourself. You became very lord-of-the-manorish and quite obnoxious, in fact, when you said it."

"Did I?" He tipped his head to one side and looked at her with a lazy smile—another new expression. "But I do not own the woman inside the house, do I? Nor do I wish to. You may turn me away whenever you choose, Imogen, or ply me with tea, or bring me to bed."

And there it was. The real man. The real Percy Hayes, Earl of Hardford, all artifice stripped away. A decent, principled man, whom she liked. Oh, too tame a word. She liked him enormously.

"You can bring my dog to bed too if you wish," he said, "to cuddle between us *after*."

She laughed.

His head tipped a little farther to the side.

"Imogen," he said, "let yourself do that more often. Please?"

But he did not wait for an answer. He strode toward the bed, kissed her firmly on the lips, and pulled the blankets up to her chin.

"I know you have been longing to do that for the last ten minutes," he said. "Stay there. I will see myself out. That key I saw hanging beside the door in the hall is not the only one you possess, is it?"

She shook her head.

"I will take it, then," he said, "and lock the door behind me. I will not also *un*lock it at any time to let myself in, though. That will be by invitation only after I have knocked. Good night."

"Good night, Percy," she said, and saw a flicker of something—desire?—in his eyes before he turned away.

"Come along, Hector," he said. "This is a time when you definitely *must* follow along at your master's heels."

Imogen listened to their footsteps descending the

stairs—he had not taken the candle with him—and the front door opening and then closing. She heard the scrape of the key turning in the lock. And she set the heels of both hands over her eyes and wept.

She did not know why. They were not tears of sadness—or joy.

15

*P*ercy had no idea what time it was when he arrived home, but at least he could see no light in any windows as he approached. He hoped that meant everyone, including his newly arrived friends, was in bed. No one was going to believe he had been out stretching his legs for several hours. And he was not in the mood for any male bragging on his own part or ribbing on theirs.

She lived in a house that *he* owned in a corner of *his* park surrounding *his* principal seat. She shared his name and still bore the female half of one of the titles that was his. He was Viscount Barclay; she was the viscountess. It was all rather bothersome. And he had no idea if she knew how to prevent conception. He had not thought to ask. He never did, but all the women who had been his mistresses or his casual amours from among the *ton* had known how to look after themselves and had not needed to be asked. He suspected that Imogen Hayes, Lady Barclay, was not that kind of woman.

She would *not* be pleased if she was forced to marry him.

Neither would he.

He lit a candle and looked down at Hector, who was looking back with his bulging eyes and ever-hopeful expression.

"The trouble is, Hector," he said, though he kept his voice down out of deference to the sleeping house, "that I am not accustomed to thinking and behaving responsibly. Is it time I learned, do you think?"

Hector gazed earnestly back and waved his apology for a tail.

"Yes?" Percy said. "I was afraid you would say that. I do not want to give her up, though. Not yet. And she needs me. What the devil am I saying? How could anyone possibly need *me*? She needs . . . something, though. Laughter. She needs laughter. Heck, I can make her laugh."

Lord, here he was talking to a dog and he was not even drunk.

If he took Hector back to the second housekeeper's room—why *was* it called that?—he would probably end up letting the whole menagerie out.

"Oh, come on, then," he said ungraciously, and made his way upstairs. Hector trotted after him, looking almost cocky.

Man and faithful hound.

He was not ready to give her up. He had only just had her. She had been a one-man woman until now. He had no doubt whatsoever of that. And that one man had been gone longer than eight years—after a four-year marriage. She had been a powder keg of passion tonight. It had not been just the outpouring of eight years of suppressed sexuality, though. At least, he did not think so. It had been very deliberate. She had been right there with him. She had called him by name.

Damn it—could he not just enjoy the feeling of relaxation left over from some vigorous and thoroughly pleasurable sex? It was unlike him to *think* about the experience. To worry about it, even.

He was worried.

Was she going to regret what she had done? *Had* he seduced her or at least led her into temptation? *Was she with child?* Or in danger of being if they continued their liaison? He was *not* ready for fatherhood. Or husbandhood either. Was that a word? *Husbandhood?* Probably not. He ought to write his own dictionary. It would give him something marginally useful to do.

Watkins, the idiot, was sitting quietly in his dressing room, waiting up for him.

"What the devil time is it?" Percy asked, frowning.

Watkins looked at the clock, visible now that Percy had brought a candle into the room. "Twelve minutes after three, my lord."

There was no point in scolding or what-the-deviling. Percy allowed his valet to undress him and produce a nightshirt warmed by the fire in the bedchamber. And then he climbed into bed and promptly fell asleep with Hector curled and huffing contentedly beside him.

Mrs. Wilkes, who asked to be called Meredith, called at the dower house the following morning with Mr. Galliard, her father, and her young son. Mr. Galliard, Imogen remembered, was Mrs. Hayes's brother. She was gradually sorting out who was who among the relatives.

They had not come to visit, however, and declined her offer of coffee with thanks. They were taking Geoffrey down onto the sands so that he could run free and work off some energy. The child was currently sitting on the doorstep, his arms around a happily purring Blossom. They had called in with a message. The older ladies were going into the ballroom after morning coffee and intended to make plans for the upcoming birthday party.

"And of course," Meredith said with a smile, "it is to be the grandest entertainment this part of the country has ever seen. Poor Percy—he will hate it. Though I daresay he will survive the ordeal. And he deserves it anyway after running off to London in order to escape just such a party in Derbyshire right _on_ his birthday. Aunt Julia was crushed with disappointment."

"That young man has been spoiled all his life," Mr. Galliard added fondly. "Though he has come out of it relatively unscathed. What Meredith has forgotten to add, Lady Barclay, is that you are to take yourself off to the hall as fast as your feet will convey you—_if you will be so good_. Your opinion is being solicited, young lady. And my sisters are not to be trifled with when they are making plans. Neither is Edna Eldridge. I have not yet sized up Lady Lavinia, though she appears to be happy enough to be drawn into action. The dragon, however, will have nothing to do with any plans to celebrate anything that concerns a _man_."

"_Papa!_" Meredith exclaimed, laughing. "Was Mrs. Ferby _really_ married for just a few months when she was seventeen, Cousin Imogen? And did she _really_ worry her husband to death?"

Less than half an hour later Imogen walked up to the hall on another brilliantly sunny morning. She hoped, hoped, _hoped_ she could reach the ballroom without running into the Earl of Hardford. The events of last night seemed unreal today despite the physical evidence of a slight and pleasurable soreness. It was going to seem strange and a little embarrassing to see him again. Today she could not even think of him as *Percy*.

As luck would have it, she spotted him in the distance over by the stables with Mr. Cyril Eldridge and two strange gentlemen who she assumed were his newly arrived friends from London. They were talking with James Mawgan, Dicky's former batman, now the head gardener.

Lord Hardford saw her, raised a staying hand, and came striding across the lawn, the other gentlemen with him. She clasped her own gloved hands at her waist and waited. Oh, dear, he looked very handsome and virile in his riding clothes. And they must have *been* riding. He was carrying a crop. Imogen felt a dull throbbing memory of where he had been last night.

"Lady Barclay." He touched the brim of his tall hat with the crop. "May I have the pleasure of presenting Viscount Marwood and Sidney Welby? Lady Barclay is the widow of my predecessor's son, who died in the Peninsula. She lives at the dower house over there." He nodded in the direction from which she had come.

The gentlemen bowed and Imogen curtsied.

"You will stay out of the way of my mother and my aunts if you know what is good for you, Lady Barclay," Mr. Eldridge said, and grinned. "They are about to force the entire neighborhood to celebrate in grand fashion Percy's long-gone birthday."

"A grand ball, I understand," she said. "I have been summoned to discuss what might be done with the ballroom."

"Well, we all know what ballrooms are for," Mr. Welby said. "You are doomed to be doing the dainty with all the village maidens, Perce."

"You too, Sid," he said. "Why else did you come all the way from London? For a private and decorous birthday tea? You *have* met my mother before, have you not? Allow me to escort you to the ballroom, Lady Barclay." He offered her his arm.

Imogen hesitated. She would have said no, but his friends might consider it ill-mannered and she might leave him feeling foolish.

"Thank you," she said, slipping her hand through his arm.

"I'll show you the way down to the beach," she heard Mr. Eldridge say to the other two gentlemen. "I was down there yesterday."

"Imogen," the earl said softly as they approached the house. He was looking directly down at her.

"Lord Hardford."

"I am *Lord Hardford* this morning, am I?" he asked her.

She turned her face unwillingly to his. She wished his eyes were not quite so blue.

"Are you sorry?" he asked her.

"No."

She would never be sorry. She was determined not to be.

"*May* I come again?" he asked. "If you have not changed your mind in the cold light of day. Though not necessarily to go to bed."

She drew a slow breath. "You may come," she said, "for tea and conversation. And to go to bed too. I hope."

Having decided to take a sort of vacation from her life, to have an affair with a man who would be here just a short while, she wanted the whole of it. He would be gone soon. And *she* would be gone soon—to Penderris

Hall. She wanted to sleep with him again and again and again in the meanwhile—even if the price was to be tears, as it had been last night after he left.

"I will come, then," he said. "For all three. Imogen."

With those words, they were inside the house, and the young twins were chasing Prudence through the hall, trying to catch her in what was clearly a lost cause. They were flushed and giggling and announced their intention of going out to see the kittens if someone would care to accompany them. One of them—it was impossible to tell them apart—batted her eyelids at Lord Hardford, and they both giggled again. The other asked where Mr. Welby and Lord Marwood had gone—and they both giggled. There was no further chance for private talk. The earl abandoned Imogen at the open doors of the ballroom after grimacing at the sight of his mother and aunts and Aunt Lavinia in a huddle inside.

"Enjoy yourself," he said.

"Oh," she assured him, "I shall. I want to see you dancing in surroundings as splendid as they can be made."

"You had better save all the waltzes for me," he said.

"If you ask nicely," she told him, "perhaps I will save one."

He laughed and strode away, and she realized she was smiling after him.

Percy's shoulder was propped against the wooden partition that had been built around Fluff's nest in the stables, his arms crossed over his chest, faithful hound seated alertly at his booted feet. He had always been fond of the youngsters in the family, especially those in the obnoxious age range between five and eighteen, when they giggled or guffawed or climbed trees they were not supposed to climb or swam in lakes in which they were not supposed to swim or put toads in their tutors' beds or spiders down their governesses' necks. The age, in fact, when most adults found them trying and tiresome and occasionally loathsome and best appreciated in their absence.

He liked them.

His family abounded with such youngsters as well as with the under-fives, whom everyone adored for their fat cheeks and plump legs and lisping voices. But today only Alma and Eva were available, so here he was because they had wanted him to come. They were squealing over the kittens and picking them up one by one while Fluff looked uneasily on. They were trying to decide which one they would like to take home with them—they seemed to be agreed upon the communal possession of just one. The kittens would not be ready to leave their mother until sometime after they left, of course, but he let them dream.

As a result of his mother's and aunts' visit to the village yesterday afternoon with Lady Lavinia, it seemed that four of the six kittens were already spoken for. And the Misses Kramer and their mother had apparently met Biddy, the sausage dog, at some time and had declared her to be the sweetest little thing they had ever seen. Perhaps, Lady Lavinia had said at dinner last night, they could be persuaded to take her, though she would be missed.

He had heard himself agreeing but insisting that it would happen *only* if they would take Benny too, Biddy's tall friend, since the two were inseparable. And he had said it, he had realized, not so much in the hope of getting rid of two of the strays instead of just one as out of concern for the well-being of both dogs. Though it *would* be good to deplete the menagerie. Blossom was firmly established at the dower house. Fluff had learned mousing skills somewhere during her pre-Hardford days, it seemed, and had been demonstrating them with remarkable success since her move to the stables. She would remain here.

However ... If Percy's eyesight had not deceived him, a hideously large and ugly feline of hopelessly mixed breed and unknown sex, with matted coat and fierce face and long whiskers, had darted across his path when he was coming downstairs for breakfast this morning. A stranger, no less. But soon to become a resident? Was Lady Lavinia hoping he would not notice? Or had she sized him up and drawn her own conclusions. A disturbing possibility, that.

There was a disagreement. The girls were squabbling with raised, indignant voices—until they dissolved into giggles again.

Percy's eyes rested thoughtfully upon Bains, the bandy-legged stable hand, who was spreading fresh straw in the stall being used for Sidney's horse. And he thought about Mawgan, the head gardener, with whom he had been having a few words earlier before he spotted Lady Barclay. Bains had had a raw deal. He had been left behind when he had volunteered to go to the Peninsula and had had his legs and his spirit broken. He was still a mere hand in the stables. Mawgan, by contrast, had gone off to war as Barclay's batman, had returned with the slight, though perhaps unjustified, taint of coward about him, and had been rewarded with what appeared to be a sinecure. He was head gardener, but, according to Knorr, it was another man who actually performed that function, since the other gardeners turned to him for instructions. Knorr had so far been unable to ascertain what exactly Mawgan did to earn his salary, though it was still only February and not high gardening season.

Perhaps he should just leave well enough alone, Percy thought. Perhaps the man had earned some recognition for his service to Barclay but was not suited to any particular task on the estate. He had grown up in the lower village, the son of a fisherman, now deceased. He had apparently had no aptitude for fishing either.

The girls had had enough of the kittens for now and were cooing over Hector, whom they were declaring to be *so* ugly, poor thing, but *so-o-o* sweet. He should take them down onto the beach, Percy thought. But there was something that had been nagging at him.

It was something to do with leaving well enough alone, letting sleeping dogs lie. He seemed to be thinking those phrases rather often, perhaps for a good reason. Why stick one's neck out and perhaps stir up a hornet's nest. And what a ghastly mix-up of images.

"You ought to go down onto the beach," he suggested. "It is a beautiful day for the time of year. Cyril is down there with Welby and Marwood. Take Beth with you."

"No, indeed," they cried in unison.

"If Beth comes," Eva explained—he had always been able to tell the twins apart, sometimes to their chagrin—"then she will surely *wilt* from climbing down that steep path and simply *have* to lean upon Viscount Marwood's arm or Mr. Welby's, and either Alma or I will be stuck walking with *Cyril*."

"To be fair," he said, grinning, "that would probably be as much of a trial for your brother as it would for you."

They both pulled identical faces at him and hurried off in the direction of the cliff path before he could try insisting that they include their sister in the party.

Percy made his way back to the house. He found Crutchley appropriately enough in the butler's pantry, wearing a large apron and cleaning an ornate pair of silver candlesticks that usually lived on the mantelpiece in the dining room.

"I am going to take a look around the cellar," Percy told him, and received rather a sharp look in return. "It is the only part of the house I have not seen."

"There is nothing much down there, my lord," the butler said, "apart from cobwebs and wine."

"Perhaps," Percy said, "either you or Mrs. Attlee could give the order to remove the webs sometime, Crutchley, and the spiders that go with them. In the meanwhile, I shall descend to the bowels of the earth anyway, since I am not afraid of spiders—or wine. You may accompany me if you wish, though it is not necessary to abandon your important task here. I shall take a candle with me and hope it does not shiver out and leave me stranded in the sort of darkness I experienced in my room the night after you had those heavy curtains erected across my window."

Crutchley came with him.

There was actually considerably more down there than just wine—all the usual paraphernalia one expects to discover either in the cellar or in the attic of any house, in fact. And, interestingly enough, not a single cobweb as far as Percy could see. A door at one side, shut and locked, opened into the wine cellar, which was adequately though not overabundantly stocked. A door on the other side, also shut and locked, opened into ...

Well, actually it did not open at all. Crutchley searched his ring of keys, grunted, and remembered that that particular key had been missing for a while and he did not know what had happened to it. It did not really matter, though. Nothing was ever kept in there.

"Ah," Percy said. "I daresay that is why there is a door, then, with a lock. One can never be too careful about empty spaces. The emptiness might escape and do untold damage."

The butler squinted at him and looked uncomprehending.

"If the door—and the lock—serve no purpose," Percy continued, "then we will just have the door chopped down and open up more space for storage. There is some considerable space in there, I would guess. The cellar extends beneath the whole house?"

"I believe so, my lord," the butler said. "I have never thought about it. I do not remember that room as being very large, though. And it is damp. That was why the old earl had it walled up and the door added—to keep the damp out."

Percy looked back at the door into the wine cellar. It was out of the range of the light from his candle, however, and he was forced to walk back. And yes, he could see now that this door and the wall in which it was set were considerably more ancient than those that led into the empty, damp room.

"I daresay, then," he said, "it would be as well to leave the door in place and forget about the lost key."

"Yes, my lord," the butler agreed.

Percy left the house by the front door and turned to walk about to the back. There were back doors, he knew, leading out to the kitchen gardens and other areas most frequented by the servants. There was also a servants' entrance at the side of the house closest to the stables—the same side of the house as the wine cellar. Percy had seen that before. Now he went to look at the other side. And sure enough, there was a door there too, one that was closed and securely locked—no surprise there. It also looked neglected, as though it had not been used in years. There was no path leading to it and no evidence of its having been approached by any large number of feet recently. On closer inspection, though, there was perhaps some sign of new sod having been set down for several feet stretching from the door. He could see the faint mark of straight lines in the grass dividing the pieces.

Damn it all, he thought, the old earl, his predecessor, had shut up the cellar at the dower house so smugglers couldn't use it. But had they replaced it with a good chunk of the cellar at the hall? If Percy was not mistaken, those pieces of sod were of a more recent date than two years ago, when the old earl had died.

There must have been general dismay when he turned up here a couple of weeks ago. A valiant effort had been made to move him at least to the back of the hall, where he was less likely to see a band of smugglers hauling their goods up to the house one dark and stormy night. And, that plan having met with defeat, a desperate attempt had been made to see to it that no light of outside activity could possibly penetrate the darkness of his bedchamber.

Did this mean that Crutchley was involved? And who else among the servants? *All* of them?

Damn it all to hell. He was going to have to either turn a blind eye—that phrase again—or *do* something about the situation.

The habit of a lifetime was to turn a blind eye, preferably two. It seemed to be a habit with his neighbors too, whether they benefited from the trade or not.

What did it matter to him if people in these parts liked their brandy and other luxury goods, and if someone—probably literally some *one*—was exploiting and terrorizing the locals, *including, perhaps, his own servants*, and getting very rich from the trade? And breaking the legs of a mere lad who had probably found the mad courage to voice an objection because his hero, Lord Barclay, had spoken out before going off to war.

Who was that someone? Anyone he knew?

He hoped not.

And of course it mattered. Dash it all, it mattered. And here he was. Decision time. Was he going to continue floating along in life, seeking out pleasure and avoiding pain, as he had done for at least the last ten years? Or was he going to wade in like a damned crusader and martyr, stirring hornets' nests and upsetting apple carts, disturbing the peace of the neighborhood and everyone in it, and all for what? So that everyone could drink inferior brandy? Or so that *he* could get *his* legs broken?

He considered his options rather grimly.

Forever after on his birthdays, he was not only going to sit alone before his own fire, wrapped in a shawl, a nightcap on his head, slippers on his feet, drinking tea laced with milk. He was also going to take up knitting. Why *the devil* had he decided to come here?

He had *everything*. No. He had *had* everything. He no longer did. Something was lacking. Self-respect, perhaps.

And he would not have met *her* if he had not come, he thought as he made his way back to the front of the house. And he would not have debauched her on his own land. No, nonsense, there had been no debauchery involved. What had happened last night had been absolutely mutual and dashed good too. In fact, he was going to have to devise a way of going back tonight. She had issued the invitation, had she not? To conversation and tea and sex?

There was something bothersome about it all, though, and he was not sure what it was.

He was not sure about *anything*. That was the whole trouble.

16

*T*he ball was to be held in ten days' time, two days before Imogen was expected at Penderris Hall. She had half hoped the ball would be later. She did not want to get too deeply drawn into . . . what? The lure of family and laughter? Living again?

Her thoughts troubled her as she participated in the plans and helped Aunt Lavinia remember every person for miles around who must be invited.

Cleaners were to be sent into the ballroom. Every inch of it from top to bottom was to be washed and scoured and dusted and polished to within an inch of its life. There were to be banks of flowers everywhere—a challenge for the first week of March, but not an insurmountable one—and there was to be a lavish banquet for supper and a full orchestra. There were to be card rooms— and card games, of course, for those so inclined—and a quiet lounge or two where guests might relax away from the bustle of the ballroom.

Despite her thoughts, Imogen was surprised at how much she enjoyed the morning and the interaction with the other ladies, who all bubbled with energy and enthusiasm. She was glad she was not living at the hall, though. It was a relief to know that she had her own house for retreat. She must never lose sight of who she was or of the life she had chosen to live.

And, oh, it would be very easy to be drawn off course. Every nerve ending in her body quivered when the earl stepped into the library—or so it seemed. She could tell by the amiable look on his face that he had been taken by surprise and was not too happy about it.

How did she *know* that?

She refused an invitation to stay for luncheon but promised to avail herself of a seat in one of the carriages after dinner. They had been invited, all of them, to an informal evening with Admiral and Mrs. Payne. It was rather brave of them, Imogen thought, to open their home to such a large crowd of people, most of them strangers.

"You must escort our cousin home, Percival," his mother said.

Imogen opened her mouth to protest but was forestalled.

"But of course, Mama," he said, and smiled politely at Imogen.

"This is quite unnecessary," she said when they were outside. "It is broad daylight." And yet, alarmingly, her heart sang.

"On the contrary." He offered his arm and she took it. "It is the most necessary thing in the world. I always do what my mother tells me, except when I do not. Besides, there may be wolves."

She laughed. Even to her own ears the sound was strange. But the world seemed a bright place today. The sun was shining and there was a suggestion of warmth in its rays. He had asked her just a couple of hours ago if he might come to the dower house again. He *wanted* to come, then. And life seemed perfect—for the next week. *Only* for the next week. And then there would be Penderris, and after that a resumption of her normal life. In the meanwhile his arm was solid, his shoulder was broad even without the help of all the capes on his greatcoat, and his usual aura of masculinity reached out and enveloped her.

"Imogen," he asked, "do you know how to prevent conception?"

And the spell was broken. Her stomach muscles clenched with shock and embarrassment.

"It is unnecessary," she assured him. "I am barren."

"In four years of marriage," he said, "there were no miscarriages? No stillbirths?"

"No," she said, "nothing." They were taking the short-cut across the lawn, she realized.

"And how do you know," he asked her, "that the ... fault, if that is the correct word, was not in your husband? Did he have other children?"

"No!" She glared indignantly at him. "He did not. He was not *like* that. I saw a physician." Her cheeks grew hot at the memory.

"Who?" he asked her. "Soames?"

"Yes." It had been a long time ago—more than ten years. It was long enough ago that she could be in company with the doctor without thinking about it, without that remembered embarrassment. And even at the time she had kept reminding herself that he delivered babies and was accustomed to all sorts of sights.

"And he told you that you were barren?" he said. "Did your husband also *see* him?"

"No," she said. "There was no need. The fault was in me. You need not fear being trapped into marriage, Lord Hardford."

"Percy is not the best name in the world to be saddled with," he said, "and Percival is worse. But I prefer either one to *Lord Hardford.* On your lips, anyway."

"I will not trap you into marriage, Percy," she said.

"Nor I you," he assured her, "though I did recklessly endanger you last night before I knew there *was* no danger."

A stream of people was pushing its way through a gap in the gorse bushes at the bottom of the lawn, accompanied by noise and laughter and general exuberance—Mr. Eldridge; his twin sisters; Mr. Galliard with young Geoffrey held firmly by the hand; Meredith; and the two gentlemen who had been riding earlier with the earl. The little boy slipped his hand free of his grandfather's at sight of the earl and came hurtling across the lawn, arms spread wide, mouth piping high-pitched news about building a sand castle and getting his shoes and stockings wet in the sea and going inside a big, dark cave and not being one little bit frightened.

The earl opened his own arms, caught the hurtling figure, and swung him about in a high circle before setting him down again.

Imogen's heart constricted a little. She had disciplined herself into thinking of her barrenness as a blessing in disguise. If there had been children, she would not have been able to accompany Dicky to the Peninsula. She would have been without the memory of that last year and a bit with him—the *good* memories. But perhaps, she thought now, if there had been children he would not have gone himself. Perhaps he would have stayed and somehow reconciled himself to the difficult situation with his father. Perhaps he would still be alive and here now.

Pointless thoughts!

It was disconcerting, though, to see that the Earl of Hardford was fond of children, or of this child, anyway. Would he make a good father? Or would he be neglectful of his own, leaving them to the care of his wife and nurses and tutors and governesses? He had the example of loving parents, though, and of a close-knit larger family.

For a moment she allowed herself the indulgence of longing for life the way it might have been, but she soon stifled the feeling. That was the trouble with letting down some of her guard. She had allowed herself a short vacation in which to take a lover, and now other thoughts and feelings were trying to creep—or gallop in.

"And are we to look forward to a grand ball in celebration of Percy's birthday, Lady Barclay?" Viscount Marwood asked her with a grin as the rest of the group came up with them. He had a smugly happy-looking twin on each arm. Meredith was on Mr. Welby's arm.

"Oh, grander even than that," Imogen assured him, and there was general whooping and laughter as though she had made the joke of the decade.

"And you thought you could turn thirty only once, Perce," Mr. Welby said. "Hard luck, old chap."

She and Percy continued on to the dower house as the group continued on its way back to the hall, but Imogen did not miss the wink Mr. Welby directed at the earl.

They walked in silence the rest of the way to the dower house.

"Entertainments in the country usually end at a decent hour of late evening rather than at an indecent hour of the early morning as they do in town," he said when they were standing at the gate, one on each side of it. "Will we be back before midnight tonight, do you suppose?"

"Normally I would say a definite yes," she said. "However, the neighborhood will be buzzing with excitement at the presence of so many visitors at the hall, and Mrs. Payne likes to demonstrate that she is no rustic. It may be later."

He set his hands on either side of her own on the gate without actually touching them.

"And how late would be *too* late, Lady Barclay?" he asked her.

"Dawn," she said. "Dawn would be too late."

"We must hope, then," he said, "that Mrs. Payne will let us go significantly before dawn. I do not like to be rushed in the pursuit of my pleasure."

"We will hope," she agreed. Beneath the brim of his tall hat, his eyes looked one shade darker than the sky.

He nodded, patted the back of her right hand, and turned to stride away back across the lawn, the heavy folds of his greatcoat swinging enticingly against the outsides of his boots.

Imogen went to look for snowdrops. There were five new blooms.

Spring had been defined for the past five years by the reunion with her fellow members of the Survivors' Club in March. And now? Oh, and now there was an awakening of gladness in her that the earth was coming alive again, as it always did without fail, to overcome winter. Light to dispel darkness, color to replace drabness, hope to . . .

But no. She would keep it as an external rejoicing. The world was out there, beyond the bounds of her own being. And it was sprouting to new and exuberant life again, as it always would. Her heart lifted a little with it.

She blinked away tears—again?—before going indoors.

Mrs. Payne would be well able to hold her own as the hostess of a London drawing room, Percy decided during the evening. She was a bit brittle and hard-edged when not laying on the charm for him and his guests, but she knew how to control a largish party of diverse individuals.

The Kramer sisters, who seemed to like to *take charge*—he would wager they were on every committee ever devised by the local church—suggested music soon after everyone had arrived and even pulled their chairs and their mother's into the small makings of a circle about the pianoforte that sat at one side of the drawing room. They would indeed have music, Mrs. Payne said with a graciousness that cut like a knife, *after* supper when it could make them mellow before they went home.

She directed the admiral to see that everyone had a drink—there was an impressive array of bottles and decanters on a long sideboard as well as a jug of lemonade and a large silver coffeepot and matching teapot covered with a plump cozy. She ushered some of the older guests into a smaller room that adjoined the drawing room and settled them about a few tables that had been set up for cards. She selected Sidney and Arnold as team leaders to pick teams for charades—a perfect choice of activity when a largish number of her guests were young people. And even some older folk enjoyed being silly once in a while. Miss Wenzel, almost bouncing with excitement on her chair, was particularly good at guessing even the most obtusely acted-out words, and Alton was an excellent actor and did not appear to mind making an ass of himself.

Before the excitement of the game could pall, Mrs. Payne summoned a group of servants to roll back the carpet and then took to the pianoforte herself to play a few vigorous country dances for the young people. Four couples might have stood up with ease, six at a bit of a squash. There were eight couples for every dance and a few bumped elbows and trodden toes and one slightly torn hem and a good deal of laughter. A ninth couple was a physical impossibility, however, Percy discovered during the third such dance when he tried to edge onto the end of the line with Lady Quentin. Mrs. Payne actually stopped playing in order to tell them so.

An excellent supper was served in a spacious dining room to the accompaniment of lively conversation. Afterward, as promised, a select few of the guests provided music until Mrs. Payne directed her butler to have the carriages brought up to the door. It was a little before half past eleven. They were home before midnight.

The female cousins and aunts and Percy's mother all retired to bed after a lengthy bit of animated chatter in the hall. Most of the men did not go up with them but assembled instead in the library, where they laid siege to Percy's liquor and ensconced themselves in all the most comfortable chairs. The menagerie was there too in force, someone having grown lax about seeing to it that they remained inside the second housekeeper's room when they were not being exercised under supervision. Or perhaps it would be more accurate to say that someone had continued to be lax, since that particular rule had never been enforced with any strict regularity as far as Percy could see.

The strays included the new cat, which had been assigned the unlikely name of Pansy, though Percy suspected it was a male. It was curled up at the edge of the hearth next to the coal scuttle and glared ferociously at the newcomers as though expecting to find itself flying off the toe of someone's boot at any moment. It was indescribably thin and scruffy.

The uncles and male cousins and friends settled into the sort of late-night conversation that would drone on for hours. After half an hour Percy looked hard at Hector, who was hiding beneath the desk, and the dog, bless its heart, came trotting out to stand before him and regard him fixedly with bulging eyes and lolling tongue and one and a half ears and three quarters of a tail all erect.

"You need to be taken outside, do you, Heck?" Percy asked with a sigh. "And you expect me to do the taking? Oh, very well. I need to stretch my legs anyway."

Sidney Welby was not deceived for a moment. He favored Percy with a slow wink as the latter got to his feet, and said not a word.

"Good Lord, Percival," Uncle Roderick said, sounding outraged, "there are servants to take dogs out to relieve themselves, if they need to be accompanied at all. I would count myself fortunate if I were to let that dog out and it never returned. It is the epitome of pathetic ugliness, if you will excuse my saying so. It is an affront to any lover of beauty."

"But he has a grand name," Percy said, "and is doing his mortal best to live up to it. Anyone with the name of Achilles had better watch his heels."

And he sauntered out to get his coat and hat while Hector came trotting after him.

Sidney had voiced his thoughts earlier in the afternoon. "You and the merry widow, is it, then, Perce?" he had said. "She is handsome enough, by Jove. But a little more formidable than your usual sort, perhaps?"

"And to which merry widow do you refer?" Percy had asked. But it had been a weak retort, he had had to admit even to himself, though he had accompanied it by raising his quizzing glass.

"She missed acquiring the other half of the title when her husband was killed, did she?" Arnold had added. "Beware, Perce. She may have designs on the other half by marrying the new Earl of Hardford."

"You may both," Percy had said pleasantly, his quizzing glass almost all the way to his eye, "take yourselves off to hell with my blessing. And you will both desist from bandying the lady's name about when she lives on my land in a home I own and is therefore deserving of respect from any visitors of mine."

"He is on his high horse, Sid," Arnold had said. "One does not use the phrase *desist from* in ordinary discourse. And did we mention any particular lady's name, Perce?"

"Something has fuddled his brain, Arnie," Sidney had added. "One consigns someone to hell with one's *curses,* not one's *blessing,* does one not? A contradiction in terms, Perce, old boy. I believe it *is* Percy and the merry widow, Arnie."

"I believe you are right, Sid," Arnold had said. "A definite item."

Percy had consigned them both to the devil again— *with his blessing*—and changed the subject.

It was too much to hope, Percy thought as he strode

along the path to the dower house—it was a devilish dark night, but he would not go back for a lantern—that there would be no talk among his relatives as there already was with his two friends. They were not an unintelligent lot, and the females among them could smell out a potential romance from five hundred miles away. However, the men would keep quiet, give or take a bit of good-natured ribbing when there was no lady within hearing distance. And the ladies would think only in terms of courtship and marriage. If he was not careful, they would be planning his wedding even before they had finished with his birthday ball.

He just hoped there would be no gossip among the neighbors. It would not matter for him—he would be leaving soon. But she would go on living here. He did not believe there would be any gossip, though. He had been careful tonight not to ignore her—that in itself might have looked suspicious—but not to single her out for any particular attention either. He had waltzed with her at the assembly, but that had been almost two weeks ago.

He had spent half the evening trying to ignore the fact that Wenzel had rarely left her side all evening, even though they were on opposite teams for charades, and the other half noticing that Alton had an eye for her too. It—the fact that he *noticed*, that was—was enough to make a man take up grinding his teeth.

There was still a light in the sitting room window.

Tonight he did not try to close the gate quietly. Nor did he hold the knocker suspended above the door for several seconds before letting it fall. And tonight he was prepared for the door opening quickly. She was still dressed as she had been for the evening's entertainment. Her cheeks were flushed, her eyes bright. He stepped over the threshold while Hector trotted past and into the sitting room, took the lamp from her hand and set it down on the chair where he had left his outdoor clothes last night, took her in his arms without first shutting the door, and kissed her.

He felt like a man coming home to his woman after a day of hard labor—a mildly alarming thought.

"Just don't ever marry either Wenzel or Alton," he heard himself say when he came up for air. "Promise me."

It would be a good thing if just sometimes his head would warn his mouth in advance of what it was about to say.

She raised her eyebrows and edged past him to shut the door. "You have come for a cup of tea, have you, Lord Hardford?" she asked him.

17

Imogen was feeling shaken. He had swept her up in his arms again after she had closed the door. He had been laughing.

"I intend to be a jealous, possessive, dictatorial, thoroughly obnoxious lover whom no woman could resist," he had said before kissing her hard again.

And instead of being indignant or outraged or any of a number of other things that she ought to have been—for he had been at least half serious when he had told her never to marry Mr. Wenzel or Mr. Alton—she had laughed too.

"Ah," she had said with an exaggerated sigh, batting eyelashes, "*just* my kind of man. Masterful."

And they had come straight up to bed—after he had gone into the sitting room to set the guard about the fire, to the probable disappointment of Blossom and Hector, and then taken the lamp from the chair beside the door, handed it to her, and put his greatcoat and hat there instead.

Not long after, she realized she did not even know where all their clothes were. They were inside her bedchamber somewhere, but not a single garment had found its way onto the chair by the window or onto the bench before the dressing table. She suspected they were strewn all over the floor getting horribly creased.

They were lying in her bed now, having made love twice in quick succession, with great vigor both times. The lamp was on the dressing table, its glow doubled by its reflection in the mirror. The bedcovers were up about them to keep them warm against the chill of the night, though she had lit a fire up here after arriving home earlier. She could not remember how the covers had got here from the foot of the bed, where they had been kicked while they were too busy to think about being cold, but she was thankful they were. He was sprawled half across her, his face against her bosom, one arm flung about her waist, his hand on her arm, one leg nestled between hers. His hair tickled her chin. She smoothed her fingers through it. It was warm and thick and soft to the touch.

He was sleeping, exhaling warm breath between her breasts, and she thought there was nothing more endearing than a man in all the helpless vulnerability of sleep.

She was not anywhere close to sleeping, even though her body was sated and languorous. She was also feeling shaken—by her own terrible ignorance. For having an affair with an attractive man was not just a physical thing. It was not even just a mental thing—it was with her mind that she had made the decision to allow herself this short break from her life.

She was finding it was also a thing of the emotions. Indeed, it seemed to her now that it must be *primarily* of the emotions. Her body would recover from the deprivation that would follow the end of the affair. So would her mind, with a bit of discipline—she was good at mental discipline. She had spent three years honing the necessary skills and the five years since constantly practicing them.

But her emotions? How would *they* fare in the months and perhaps years ahead? How long would it take her to regain her equilibrium and tranquillity? Would she ever do it? For body, mind, and emotions were not separate things. They were somehow all bundled up in one, and if one of the three dominated, it was probably emotion. She had not taken that into account when she made him her lover.

Lover. But she was not in love with him. She liked him. She enjoyed being in bed with him, and that was an understatement. Neither of those things was being in love. But then she did not know what being in love felt like. She had never felt the kind of romantic euphoria with Dicky that is described in all the great love poetry. She had not needed to. She had *loved* him.

What *did* it feel like, being in love? But she would never know. For even if it was possible for her, she would never allow herself to know. She had no right.

She was going to suffer, she knew. She deserved to.

He inhaled deeply and exhaled on a long sigh of contentment.

"This is the best pillow ever," he said.

She lowered her face into his hair and kissed the top of his head. "I am feeling deprived," she said, "of tea and conversation."

When he lifted his face, it was full of laughter and sexual contentment. He raised himself on one elbow and propped his head on his hand. He trailed the backs of the fingers of the other hand down one side of her jaw and up the other.

"When you were a child," he said, "did you often wish you could start a meal with dessert and leave the more solid, stalwart fare for later? I am still a child at heart, Imogen."

She turned her head to kiss his palm where it joined his wrist. "But *two* helpings of dessert?" she said.

"When it is especially delicious, yes, indeed, and with great, hearty, unapologetic appetite," he told her. "Do you have a warm dressing gown?"

"Yes."

"Put it on," he said, "and go down and set the kettle on to boil. This is me being the dictatorial lover. I shall get dressed and follow you, at which point I will turn into the meek lover and build up the fire in the sitting room and come to carry in the tea tray. Then we will proceed to drink and converse. It cannot be much later than two in the morning."

It was with a curious mixture of elation and uneasiness that Imogen went downstairs a few minutes later, wrapped warmly in her nightgown and old dressing gown, lamp in hand—he had lit a candle for his own use. There was something wonderfully, and disturbingly, domestic about all this. He was going to build up the fire for her? And carry in the tray? And stay to talk—at two in the morning?

He was mad.

They were mad.

Ah, but sometimes insanity felt so . . . freeing.

It was twelve minutes past two, Percy could see from the clock on the mantel, maybe thirteen. The fire was roaring up the chimney. He had a cup of tea at his elbow with two sugar-sprinkled biscuits in the saucer. And he was seated a short distance from the fire on one half of the love seat, as close to the center as possible, just as she was on her side. This sofa would accommodate four people in a row if necessary, especially if the middle two were pressed together, his arm about her shoulders, her head on one of his.

When he had mentioned a dressing gown, he had expected . . . well, a froth of lace and ribbons. Hers was of heavy velvet and at least a million years old. Its nap was worn almost threadbare in places, notably—and interestingly—in the region of her derriere. It was at least one size too large and had grown a bit shapeless. It covered every inch of her from neck to wrists to ankles. It ought to make her look like the veriest dowd, especially when combined with a pair of slippers that were surely *half* a million years old. She had not put her hair up or left it down. She had hauled it back to her neck and secured it there with a thin strip of ribbon.

She looked deliciously gorgeous—too good for dessert. She was the whole feast.

He was a trifle alarmed by the thought. She ought *not* to look appetizing at all, especially when compared with . . . well, with all his other women. And what the devil sort of performance had he put on upstairs in her bed? He had had her twice, and all within fifteen minutes at the longest. No, correction—they had had each other. But he had no complaint at all about *her* performance, though she had used no feminine wiles to prolong or intensify his pleasure. She had just . . . gone at it.

He took a biscuit from his saucer and bit into it.

"If you merely go to sleep on my shoulder," he said, "I shall be peeved. It is conversation time, Lady Barclay. On what topic do you wish to converse? The weather? Our own health and that of everyone else we know, the more gruesome the detail the better? Bonnets or parasols? Snuffboxes?"

Hector had come closer while he spoke and plumped down across one of his feet. The cat, which had been comfortably disposed upon its own bed when he went into the kitchen, had jumped onto the empty space at the other side of the love seat and curled up there to recover from the exertions of walking all the way to the sitting room.

"Oh, I would love to know about the latest fashions in bonnets," she said. "Large brimmed or small? Ostentatiously trimmed or elegantly unadorned? Straw or felt? Tied beneath the chin or perched on the head to tempt the wind? But I suppose that being a man, you cannot give me the answers I crave."

"Hmm," he said. "How about snuffboxes, then? I can perhaps acquit myself more knowledgeably upon them."

"But, alas," she said, "I have not the smallest modicum of interest in snuffboxes."

"Hmm." He chewed the rest of the biscuit and frowned in thought. "Quizzing glasses?"

"I am about to break into a snore," she said.

"Hmm." He picked up the other biscuit. "Must we come, then, Lady Barclay, to the regrettable conclusion that we are quite incompatible in everything except sex?"

"Alas," she said with a huge sigh—and then burst into laughter.

It was a sound of sheer silliness, and the thought occurred to him with a jolt of alarm that he might just possibly be falling in love with this woman—whatever the devil falling in love *was*.

He silenced her with his mouth.

"Alas that we are sexually compatible, did you mean?" he asked.

"You taste sweet." She raised a finger, brushed what he supposed was a crystal of sugar from the corner of his mouth, and put the top joint of the finger in her mouth.

The minx. She was sheer blatant courtesan at that moment, and he was not at all sure she did not know it. Her eyes were steady on his.

"Sweet?" he said.

"It was not you after all." She smiled at him. "It was the sugar on the biscuit."

"Hmm," he said.

"Tell me more about your childhood," she said.

"It was really quite dull and uneventful," he assured her, stretching his legs out before him and crossing them at the ankles—Hector made the necessary adjustments. "The greatest adventure by far was that episode on the cliff face I told you about. Apart from that, I was a docile, obedient lad. How could I not be? I was constrained by love. My parents adored me, as did my nurse, who, to my chagrin, stayed with me until I went away to Oxford at the age of seventeen. My tutors too, even the one who liked to swish his cane to punctuate his instruction and did not hesitate to use it on my backside when I was particularly thick about providing the right answers to his questions or when in a piece of writing I attached a plural verb to a singular subject or some such outrage. He loved me. He told me I had been blessed with a fine mind and that he was being paid to see to it that I learned how to use it properly, but I do believe he was motivated by more than just money."

"Did you hate your lessons?" she asked.

"Not at all," he told her. "I was that rarest of all breeds of boy—I enjoyed learning, and I enjoyed pleasing the adults who had the care of me. You would not have recognized me in those days, Imogen."

"Were you lonely?" she asked.

"Oh, Lord, no," he said. "There were regiments of relatives and others. Aunts and uncles galore and cousins abounding. I did not see the relatives with any great regularity, but when I did I had a grand old time. I was among the oldest of the cousins and I was always big for my age—*and* I was a boy. I quite undeservedly found myself the leader of the pack, and I was expected to lead my youngers into mischief. Even the adults expected it. I almost always did what was expected of me. But it was innocent mischief—climbing forbidden trees, swimming in forbidden lakes, stamping through forbidden muddy puddles for the sheer joy of getting ourselves thoroughly dirty, hiding in hedgerows and jumping out at unwary travelers, shrieking like demented things."

Her head was turned on his shoulder and the side of her forefinger stroked lightly along his jaw.

"I ought to have been sent away to school," he said.

"You *were* lonely."

"If I was," he said, "I am not sure I particularly noticed. I was so terribly innocent, though. I was shocked down to my toenails when I discovered that studying was the very *last* thing a fellow was supposed to do at university. The height of accomplishment there was to drink one's fellow imbibers under the table and to sleep with every barmaid in Oxford and its environs. Well, you know, Imogen, you *did* ask."

"About your *childhood*," she reminded him. "And you acquired these accomplishments, did you?"

"Not at all," he said. "I thought I was there to learn, and that is what I did. It was not until the end that it suddenly dawned upon me that I was a thoroughly odd fellow and quite out of step with what being a gentleman was all about. I was a virgin when I came down from Oxford. And *that,* my lady, is something I have not told any other living soul. I am discovering that it is fatal to engage in conversation with a woman after two o' clock in the morning."

Deuced embarrassing, actually. What the devil had possessed him to divulge that particular detail from his inglorious past? A twenty-year-old male virgin, no less.

"I wish you had not told me," she said. "I would have preferred to cling, at least in part, to my original impression of you."

"Oh, cling away," he said. He removed his arm from about her and sat forward in order to drink his tea before it turned quite cold. "I very soon became the man you think me, Imogen—and you do not know the half of it. That old innocent who was once me has long faded into ancient history."

"Of course he has not," she said. "We are made up of everything we have ever been, Percy. It is the joy and the pain of our individuality. There are no two of us the same."

He set his cup down and looked at her over his shoulder.

"The world will be very glad there is only one of me," he said.

"But you have told me far more than the fact that you were still a virgin at the age of twenty or so," she said. "And it is something else that probably no one else knows. Your image of yourself has taken a severe battering during the past ten years. Your life has become unbalanced, perhaps because the first twenty years were almost unalloyed happiness and diligence and security. You were both fortunate and unfortunate in that, Percy. And now you feel *in*secure and a bit worthless and not even sure that you like yourself. You need to find balance, but do not know quite how."

He stared at her for several moments before getting abruptly to his feet, dislodging poor Hector again as he did so. He busied himself with poking the fire and putting on a few more coals.

"But not many of us ever do know quite how," she continued quietly into the silence, and he had the feeling she was talking more to herself than to him. "Life is made up of opposing pairs—life and death, love and hatred, happiness and misery, light and darkness, and on and on to infinity. Finding balance and contentment is like trying to walk a tightrope between all those opposites without falling off on one side or the other and believing that life must be all light or all darkness, when neither one is the truth in itself."

Good Lord! What *was* it about late, late-night conversations?

"You and me," he said, turning fully to face her. "Another pair of opposites."

The cat was on her lap. She was stroking its back and ears, and it was purring, its eyes closed in ecstasy. He was envious.

"I do beg your pardon," she said. "How presumptuous of me to try analyzing your life and preaching at you."

He set one foot on the hearth and rested one arm along the mantel. What *was* it about her? Her hair was scraped back so severely from her face that it almost made her eyes slant. Her shapeless dressing gown was belted about her waist like a sack. She had just been haranguing him like a prissy governess.

And he wanted her more than he had ever wanted any other woman.

She was not even particularly feminine—not in a frills and lace and powdered, fragrant, swelling bosom sort of way, anyway. She was not lisping and big-eyed and worshipful with a head stuffed full of fluff.

Devil take it, was he describing the sort of woman whose bed he usually sought?

She was . . . What was the word Sidney had used earlier—or yesterday, to be precise? *Formidable.* That was it. She *was* formidable. That fact ought to repel him. Instead it attracted. Ah, another pair of opposites—attraction and repulsion.

"You and me," he said again. "But there has been no balance tonight, Imogen. It has been all me, as is only right for a domineering male lover."

She smiled at him—and the uncomfortable suspicion grew again that he was falling in love with her. *Something* unfamiliar was happening to him, anyway, something that was attacking his gut. And it was not just the desire to take her to bed and have his way with her until they were both panting with exhaustion. It was what was left beyond the sexual desire that was unfamiliar and unidentified—unless that *was* being in love. He hoped not.

She should never smile.

She should *always* smile.

He felt as if he were on her balancing scale of opposites.

"Yes, lord and master," she said.

He pointed a finger directly at her.

"It will be your turn next time," he said. "You have stripped me naked, Imogen, and I do not mean just abovestairs in your bedchamber. I will strip you next time—and I do not mean *just* abovestairs in your bedchamber."

He smiled at her even as her own smile faded.

"Not tonight, though," he said. "I have a valet to consider. No matter what I say to him, he will insist upon waiting up for me. He will be sitting in my dressing room at this very moment, without a fire, without a light, like patience on a monument. It is time I went home."

She lifted the cat gently off her lap and set it down beside her—the animal thanked her with an indignant meow. And she stood and brushed cat hairs from the ancient velvet of her dressing gown and looked up at him.

He closed the distance between them and kissed her, his arms about her. There was no desire, though, to take her back up to bed, and that in itself was a bit unnerving. There was only the warmth of embracing a woman with whom he was becoming increasingly comfortable, even if she *did* harangue him when she could get him alone at two in the morning.

She saw him on his way, holding the lamp aloft with one hand to light the path to the gate and clutching her dressing gown to her throat with the other. He looked back after closing the gate behind him and tried to convince himself that she did not present the most appealing sight he had ever seen in his life.

The sooner he left here after this infernal ball, he thought, the better it would be for his peace of mind. He touched the brim of his hat with one gloved hand and turned away.

18

The ladies had taken possession of the library and the ballroom again. Imogen, Beth, and Meredith, at last sighting, were writing invitations. A couple of the uncles had gone off with Knorr to watch as part of the park wall was rebuilt without mortar. Leonard and Gregory had walked to Porthmare with Alma and Eva to deliver some invitations and visit some new acquaintances. Uncle Roderick and Cyril had taken Geoffrey down onto the beach again.

Percy was riding along the top of the valley with Sidney and Arnold.

"If I were you, Perce," Arnold was saying, "I would turn a blind eye. You say nothing specific has happened since you came here to compel you to act."

"Apart from one soggy bed, one sooty floor complete with dead, sooty bird, and one window curtain designed to keep out the light even of the sun on midsummer day, no," Percy admitted. "Nothing of which I am aware."

"You will be gone from here soon, Perce," Sidney said. "And I doubt you will be back soon. There is not much here for you, is there? Apart from the widow, that is."

That drew Percy up short—and his horse too. "The *widow*?" he asked, frost in his voice.

Arnold's mount pranced about as he reined it in. He was grinning. "The last of us staggered off to bed just before three last night," he said. "One of your uncles remarked that you were wiser than the rest of us and must have taken yourself off to bed after walking with the dog. Sid and I took a brief peek into your room. Fire crackling, nightshirt spread over a chair before the blaze, bedcovers turned neatly down, no Percy."

And the thing was, Percy thought as he contemplated dragging both men from their horses and banging their heads together, that they fully expected him to grin back, confess to his whereabouts at that ungodly hour, and make some bawdy boast about his newest conquest. They had every reason to expect it. It was what he would normally do. What was so different this time?

Could it be that *he* was different? That he had changed, or, since a change of character did not happen overnight or even over a hundred nights, that he was *changing*? Devil take it, he needed to leave this place.

He looked down to the valley, peacefully green, the river flowing through it, the village farther back toward the sea.

"I will be leaving soon," he said. "And I doubt I will ever come back. It is the damnedest backwater."

And yet he felt disloyal saying so—disloyal to Lady Lavinia, to the Quentins and Alton and even Wenzel, to the vicar and the physician and the Kramer ladies and the sturdy fisherfolk. And there was Bains with his bandy legs and broken spirit, and Crutchley, who might have some voluntary involvement with smuggling or who just might be the victim of intimidation. There was that half cellar below his house that might be stuffed with contraband or awaiting a new shipment. There was . . . Imogen.

How long had he been here? Two weeks? Three? It was no time at all. A mere blink of the eye. He would forget it all in another blink once he was away from here.

He would forget *her*.

They continued their ride.

He could not recall regretting any of the liaisons he had had with women. He had ended most of them himself, but never because he had regretted starting them. He *liked* having affairs. They were mindless mutual enjoyment with no commitment or responsibilities attached.

He already regretted what he had started with Imogen.

He would forget her, though. She was leaving here herself a few days after this infernal ball. He would be gone before she returned.

It was just dashed stupid of him to have fallen in love. He presumed that was what had happened to him. Certainly he could not explain his feelings any other way. He did not like being in love one little bit.

"He does not want to talk about the widow, Arnie," Sidney said.

"I have come to the same conclusion, Sid," Arnold agreed. "But I would ignore the smuggling if I were you, Perce. Everyone else does. You are not going to stop it anyway. Those revenue men never can. And you must admit, they are a humorless lot. It is a pleasure to see them hoodwinked."

"And you must admit, Perce," Sidney added, "that brandy that comes into the country by the back door, so to speak, always seems to taste better than the legal stuff. It costs a lot less too."

The whole world was in agreement, it seemed, that it was best to ignore what was going on under everyone's nose. Who was he to become a crusader? It had never occurred to him to be one until he came here. Having a conscience and acting upon it made him seem suspiciously like his old studious self—out of tune and out of step with all the rest of the world. A killjoy. A poor sport. An idiot.

"Quite so," he said. "There are supposed to be some old tin mines over there on the other side of the valley. I'll find out exactly where and get up a party to go exploring one day."

And the conversation moved away from both smuggling and his affair.

By the end of the morning the invitations had all been written. Imogen allowed her spirits to be seduced by a sense of family as the older ladies flitted in and out of the library and the younger two chattered between invitations.

Mrs. Hayes and her sister and sister-in-law often had disagreements, a few of them quite heated. But they never seemed to bear a grudge, and somehow they always found a compromise over a disputed plan for the grand party. The young cousins too, she had noticed on previous occasions, frequently squabbled among themselves, but always ended up giggling or guffawing. The twins sometimes avoided their older sister quite deliberately, but once she had seen them sitting on either side of her on the pianoforte bench while she picked out a melody, each with an arm about her shoulders. Mrs.

Hayes's brother seemed to prefer the company of his daughter and grandson to that of anyone else, but he was perfectly amiable when he *was* in company, and had even invited Mr. Cyril Eldridge, who was no blood relation, to walk on the beach with him and the little boy this morning. The other two older gentlemen were often discussing current affairs with each other and growing quite heated in their disagreements, but they also seemed ultimately content to agree to disagree.

Imogen suddenly missed her brother—and her mother in far-off Cumberland. Family—that deep sense of connection as opposed to a mere dutiful visiting and letter writing—was something she had given up with everything else five years ago. She was not entitled to the warmth and comfort it provided—or to the bickering and the laughter.

She felt a bit as though her heart had been in cold storage for a long time and was gradually thawing. She could not allow it to happen completely, of course, but for the next week and a half she would perhaps allow herself to relax a little. She would put herself back together when she was at Penderris, surrounded by her friends. She would ask for their help if she needed it, though just an awareness of their love and support would probably be sufficient. She *would* do it, though. She had never been much lacking in willpower.

In the meantime, she would now permit herself some enjoyment. It seemed a long age—another lifetime— since she had last enjoyed herself.

If only she had been able to have a child or two with Dicky, she thought as she left the hall to return home and drew her cloak more closely about her against the chill of a colder day. Geoffrey was coming across the lawn, one hand in his grandfather's, the other in Mr. Eldridge's, and she could hear the chant of their three voices, "One, two, three, *j-u-u-m-p*." The two men lifted the shrieking child high between them on the last word.

Imogen did not often regret her barrenness. What was the point? And it would have changed everything if she had been fertile. She would not be standing here now, smiling wistfully at a child who had not even been born when Dicky died. Who knew what she would have been doing? It was foolish even to think of it.

Percy was approaching from the stables with his two friends and Hector frolicking along beside them—yes, actually frolicking. The child, seeing them, abandoned the other two gentlemen and went racing off to be lifted high and spun around and deposited astride Percy's shoulders. A burst of laughter and a high-pitched shriek and giggle ensued when Percy's tall hat was knocked off and he insisted upon bending to retrieve it himself, deliberately almost spilling the little boy over his head as he did so.

There was a general exchange of pleasantries as everyone approached the house.

"The invitations are all written, are they, Lady Barclay?" Mr. Galliard asked.

"They are," she told him. "We are all agreed that we cannot expect quite the sort of sad squeeze we might have hoped for if this were a London ball during the Season that we were planning, but the ballroom should be quite creditably filled."

"Hard luck, old chap," Mr. Welby said, clapping Percy on the shoulder and lifting Geoffrey down to play with Hector.

"One must always look on the bright side," Percy said.

"How lowering it would be if I could expect no more than my own family members and two friends already assembled here, huddled in one corner of the ballroom pretending to enjoy my belated birthday ball. I am not at all sure it is a good idea to let Heck *kiss* you, Geoff, my lad."

"Are you on the way home, Lady Barclay?" Viscount Marwood asked her. "Do allow me to escort you, ma'am." And he offered his arm together with what seemed like a mischievous grin.

"And since you are in possession of *two* arms, ma'am," Mr. Welby said, bowing to her with a courtly flourish, "do allow me to escort you too."

Imogen laughed and dipped into a deep curtsy. "Why, thank you, gentlemen," she said, taking an arm of each. "I was warned just yesterday that there might be wolves."

"Plural," Percy said. "At least three of the beasts, or so I have been told. I had better come too."

And they set off, the four of them, across the lawn in the direction of the dower house with a continuation of the silly, mindless banter—in which Imogen joined. She found herself almost wishing someone would suggest the one-two-three-jump game. And then, when they came to her house, Percy opened the gate with a flourish, she stepped inside, he closed it, and the men took turns, the foolish idiots, raising the back of her hand to their lips and assuring her that she had brightened their day and made the fact of the hidden sun quite irrelevant.

She stood at the gate, watching them walk away, Hector trotting along behind. They were still talking, still laughing, and she realized she was smiling—and realized too that it was an unfamiliar feeling. And then she was blinking back tears—yet again. Another unfamiliar feeling.

Percy turned his head briefly before they disappeared from sight behind a tree and smiled at her. And she was still smiling herself, tears notwithstanding.

Oh, goodness, oh, goodness—she was so very deeply in love with him.

And it was all her own fault. She had no one to blame but herself.

"You have my permission," she said, "to use my key at night—to let yourself in as well as out. Then I will not have to wait up, wondering if you are coming or not, for you will not always be able to come, will you?"

He backed her against the wall of the hallway and kissed her openmouthed. It was closer to half past twelve than to midnight. He had half expected to find the dower house in darkness and had not known if he would knock on her door anyway. Her key had been burning a hole in his pocket.

"I am sorry," he told her. "I could not get away any sooner. We had a visitor."

"I know," she said. "Mr. Wenzel, was it not? He brought Tilly and Elizabeth Quentin here and went to the hall rather than return home and come back for them later. But I am glad you came."

"So am I." He rubbed his nose across hers.

She was wearing her ancient fossil of a dressing gown again, and he marveled at the fact that she had not titivated herself for her lover, as every other woman with whom he had been intimate had always done. Her hair was tied at the neck again, though it was draped loosely over her ears and back tonight. Her lips were slightly parted, the upper one with its engaging lift. Her eyes were . . . open. He still had not thought of a better word than that. Her hands were resting on his shoulders, pushed beneath the capes of his greatcoat.

Deuce take it, but I love you.

He gazed into her eyes, frozen for a moment. He had not spoken aloud, had he? But he heard no echo of the words and saw no shock in her face.

"Are you inviting me in?" he asked.

"Are you not already in?" she said. "But where do you wish to go? Upstairs? The sitting room?"

It ought to have been obvious. It was almost half past midnight and they were new lovers.

"The sitting room," he said. "But no tea, thank you. I have drunk enough of the stuff since the arrival of my family to sail away on. Even poor Wenzel was plied with it twice this evening."

She picked up the lamp so that he could set his outdoor things on the chair and led the way into the sitting room. Was he *mad*? Or going senile? It was the middle of the night, there was a wide, comfortable bed upstairs, she was willing to welcome him into it and into *her*, she looked as delicious as the cake and the icing and the cream filling all in one despite the fact that she had not titivated herself or perhaps because of it—and he had chosen the *sitting room* instead?

"I am surprised he did not stay *here* instead of calling on us," he said.

"Mr. Wenzel? With Tilly and Elizabeth, you mean?" she asked. "He never does. Nor does Sir Matthew when it is his turn to bring them. We like to discuss our books just among ourselves."

"A *reading* club?" he said.

"We have been meeting monthly for the past three years," she explained as she set down the lamp on the mantel and reached for the poker. But it was already in his hand, and she sat down on the love seat while he stirred the coals and put on a few more. The animals had settled comfortably close to the heat. "We all read the same book or set of poems or essays and then discuss them over tea and biscuits or cake. We enjoy that one evening of the month immensely."

"And what was it tonight?" he asked as he straightened up.

"Just one poem, though a longish one," she said. "William Wordsworth's 'Lines Written a Few Miles Above Tintern Abbey.' Have you read it? One of my friends, one of my fellow Survivors, lives in Wales, though his home is on the western side of it rather than in the Wye valley in the east. I went there with George last year for his wedding."

"George?" That was not *jealousy* flaring in him, was it?

"Duke of Stanbrook, owner of Penderris Hall," she explained. "A sort of cousin though a closer relationship than yours and mine. He is another of the Survivors."

"The one whose wife jumped off a cliff?"

"Yes," she said.

He wished he had not remembered that particular detail. The man had also lost a son to the wars and must be as old as the hills. Percy tried to remember him from the House of Lords but without any success. Perhaps he would recognize him if he saw him.

He eyed the empty chair beside the fire and went to sit on the love seat. He turned and scooped her up and set her on his lap with her feet on the seat beside them. She was on the tall side, but she wriggled downward—heaven help him—until she was snuggled against him, the side of her head on his shoulder. She inhaled audibly.

"I love the way you smell," she said. "It is always the same."

"Mingled liberally with sweat on two recent occasions," he said.

"Yes." She laughed softly.

"And I love the sound of your laughter," he said. And if he had met her for the first time today, he realized, or even yesterday, it would not even have occurred to him to think of her as the marble lady. He wondered if she was falling in love with him, or if it was just the sex.

It was *not* just the sex, though, was it? If it were, then they would be upstairs now, naked on her bed, going at it.

For a moment he felt almost dizzy with alarm. That was what they really ought to be doing.

"I am not much given to laughing," she said.

"And that," he said, "is why your laughter is so precious. No, correct that. It would be just as precious if you laughed frequently. You used to?"

She inhaled and exhaled, but she had not tensed up, he noticed.

"In another lifetime," she said. "I like your friends."

"They do not have two brain cells between them to rub together," he said fondly.

"Oh, but of course they do," she said. "I might have said that of you if I had seen you only with them. Sometimes we need friends with whom we can simply be silly. Silliness can be . . . healing."

"Are you ever silly with your friends?" he asked her.

"Yes, sometimes." He could feel her smiling against the side of his neck. "Friendship is a very, very precious thing, Percy."

"Are we friends?" Now where the devil had that infantile question come from? He felt foolish.

She raised her head and looked into his face. She was not smiling.

"Oh, I believe we could be." She sounded almost surprised. "We will not be, though. We will not know each other long enough. It will be enough that we are lovers, will it not? Just for a brief spell. That is all either of us wants. I shall not try to cling to you when it is over, and that is a very firm promise."

He felt as though someone had dropped a very large iceberg down the chimney and doused the fire and all memory of it.

Yes, that was all either of them wanted. That was all *he* wanted—a vigorous and pleasurable sexual liaison while he was living out here in a social desert.

Why, then, were they sitting in her sitting room?

He drew her head back to his shoulder. "Would you be surprised to know," he said, "that smuggling is still active in this area? Even on this land?"

There was a lengthy silence. "I would not be terribly *shocked*," she said eventually, "though I know nothing of it."

"Nothing of the involvement of any of the servants here?" he asked her. "Or whether their involvement is voluntary or forced? Nothing of the use of the cellar at the hall for the stowing of contraband?"

"Oh." She paused. "*Definitely* not that. With Aunt Lavinia and Cousin Adelaide in the house? Is it *true*?"

"Both the inside and the outside doors leading into one half of the cellar are locked, and both keys are missing," he told her. "No one is trying hard to find them, for apparently that area was shut off to keep the damp from the rest of the cellar."

"Oh," she said again. "I thought—I hoped—it had all ended with my father-in-law's passing and even before that when I moved here."

"I have been advised," he said, "by everyone to whom I have spoken, to leave well enough alone, to turn a blind eye, to let sleeping dogs lie and so on. The trade will go on, I am told, and no one is really hurt by it."

She was silent. What the devil had induced him to raise this topic of conversation to a lady, and at something close to one in the morning? He glanced at the clock. It was five to.

"Who *is* harmed by it, Imogen?"

"Colin Bains was," she said.

"Yes."

"He was *such* a bright, eager boy," she told him. "He worshiped Dicky. He *so* much wanted to come to the Peninsula with us."

"Your husband was quite vocally opposed to the smuggling?" he asked.

"He was," she said. "But he could not persuade his father that there was anything so very wrong with it. On the surface there was not and *is* not. There is a little loss of revenue to the government and a lot of enjoyment of superior luxury goods—particularly brandy by the gentlemen, of course. But I think what we see and know is the veriest tip of the iceberg, and what we do *not* see is ugly and vicious. Even the visible tip can be nasty. He received threats before we went away."

"Bains?"

"No, Dicky," she said. "There were two letters, one threatening his life, one mine. They were written in a childish, nearly illiterate hand, and his father laughed at them. But Dicky was already in the process of purchasing his commission. We never knew if the threats were serious or not."

Good God. What if they had been? What if they had been very serious indeed?

Good God.

"Oh," she said, "I have been *such* a coward. I have known nothing lately because I have chosen to ask no questions and not to look out my windows late on dark nights."

He lifted her chin with the hand that was about her shoulders. "I beg your pardon, Imogen," he said. "I *do* beg your pardon for raising this topic with you. Forget I did. Keep on knowing nothing. Promise me? *Promise.*"

She nodded after a moment. "I promise," she said, and he kissed her.

"I am feeling too lazy even to come upstairs with you tonight," he said, laying his head back against a cushion. "Have you ever made love on a love seat? It sounds like a logical place to do it, does it not?"

"It would not be long enough," she said, "unless we were uncommonly short."

"Shall I show you?"

"It sounds . . . uncomfortable," she said, but she was half smiling back at him.

"Not at all," he said. "What are you wearing beneath your dressing gown and nightgown?"

"Nothing." Her cheeks turned a little pink.

"Perfect," he said. "I, on the other hand, need to make a few adjustments. I could hardly leave the main hall clad only in my nightshirt."

He lifted her off his lap and set her down beside him

while he undid the buttons at his waist and lowered the flap of his breeches and parted the folds of his drawers. And he reached for her again, his hands going beneath her garments to lift them out of the way. She came astride him, braced herself on her knees, and set her hands on his shoulders while she leaned slightly back and looked down. She watched—they both did—while he put himself inside her and drew her downward with his hands on her hips until he was fully embedded. Her muscles slowly clenched about him.

"Oh," she said.

Oh, indeed. He was enveloped in wet heat and the agony of full desire.

He kept a firm grasp on her hips and lifted her partly away from him so that he could work her with firm upward strokes. And she rode him with a bold rhythm that matched his own, and he wanted it never to end, and he needed to end it *now,* and he would continue with it forever because it was the most exquisite feeling in the world and she felt it too and they must end *now* but they must prolong the pleasure just a little longer.

He did not know for how many minutes they made love. He did not know which of them broke rhythm first. It did not matter. They finished together, and it was like—ah, that old cliché, though it had never had any meaning for him before now—it was like a little death.

It was ... exquisite. He was going to have to invent a vocabulary all his own, since the English language was often totally inadequate to his needs.

When he came more or less to himself, she was relaxed on him, her knees hugging his sides, her head on his shoulder, her face turned away from his, and she was sleeping. He was still buried in her, still slightly throbbing. The cat was on the love seat beside them. Hector was draped across one of his shoes.

He had never felt more relaxed in his life, Percy thought.

And never so happy.

He was too relaxed even to be alarmed at the thought.

19

"*All* the servants?" Paul Knorr said. "Inside and out?"

"The butler, the head steward, the cook, the bootboy, the head groom, and lowliest gardener and stable hand, Lady Lavinia's maid, the scullery maids," Percy said. "All except those brought by my visitors."

"The cook is sure to have something in the oven at ten o'clock in the morning," Knorr said with a cheerful grin. "And she is a tyrant. I quake and tremble."

"If she comes at you with a rolling pin," Percy said, "run fast."

"Has Mr. Ratchett ever ventured beyond the steward's room?" Knorr asked.

"He will today," Percy told him. "You will see to it, Knorr, by being your usual deeply deferential self. You do it very well. Go."

Knorr departed to fulfill his task of rounding up everyone who worked within the boundaries of the park, even Imogen's housekeeper, even Watkins and Mimms and Percy's coachman.

Everyone had dispersed after breakfast, except Mrs.

Ferby, who kept guard over the fire in the drawing room. Percy's mother had gone with Aunt Nora, Lady Lavinia, and Imogen the Lord knew where to make arrangements about flowers and music for the ball. Aunt Edna and Beth and the twins were out in the stables with Geoffrey, kitten gazing. Meredith had gone off in Percy's own curricle, driven by Sidney, to call upon Miss Wenzel and her brother—Percy thought there had been a bit of mutual attraction between his widowed cousin and Imogen's would-be suitor last evening. Arnold was exploring the cliff walk with Uncle Ernest and his two boys—they intended to take a look at the fishing village too. Uncles Roderick and Ted had gone riding up the valley in the opposite direction. Everyone was accounted for.

"You are staying home on *estate business,* Perce?" Arnie had asked with a look of incredulity when Percy had explained why he would not join in the cliff walk. "That is more than a bit alarming, I must say."

"You are staying in order to confer with *your steward,* Percy?" Uncle Ted had said when his nephew declined the request to go riding. "I am impressed, my boy. Turning thirty has done wonders for you. Your father would be proud."

"I hope so," Percy had said meekly.

He had steeled every nerve. He was probably about to do *entirely* the wrong thing. But for once he was determined to *do* something that needed doing, even if like an idiot he must stand alone against the whole world and even if nothing of any significance could possibly be accomplished. Even if he was going to be merely tilting at windmills.

He had been raised, after all, to stand alone and always to do what he believed to be right. He had not fully realized that before now. He had not gone away to school, where, at an impressionable age, he would have learned to become just like every other boy of his social class. He had remained at home to be educated and trained—and loved—by a number of straight-thinking adults. He had remained under the influence of that upbringing through his university years and had stuck out from his fellows like a sore thumb while acquiring an excellent education in his chosen field. He had spent the past ten years more or less repudiating his past and making up for lost time—with interest. He was now like every other idle gentleman of his generation, but even more so.

But one's upbringing could never be quite erased. If his could be, he would cheerfully do it, for then perhaps he would not be feeling this sudden dissatisfaction with his life, this onslaught of conscience, this urge to go crusading.

It *was* idiotic. It *was* nonsensical. He might—and probably would—regret it. But it was perhaps better to act from conscience and be sorry than to bury his head in the sand and sidle by his own life because he could not be bothered to live it.

Someone had *organized* the staff, Percy saw as soon as he entered the seldom-used visitors' salon on the ground floor. They were standing to rigid attention in such straight lines that someone had surely used a long ruler. And they were arranged strictly according to rank. All eyes faced forward. Percy felt a bit like a general about to inspect his troops—the Duke of Wellington, perhaps.

"At ease," he said, standing just inside the door with his hands clasped behind him.

There was an infinitesimal relaxing of posture. *Very* infinitesimal.

"I am declaring war," he said, and at least twenty pairs of eyes swiveled his way though the heads belonging to the eyes did not follow suit, "against smuggling."

The eyes went forward again. Every face remained blank. Ratchett, Percy saw, was having a hard time keeping his spine straight. In fact, he looked like a bow just waiting to be strung.

"Mr. Knorr," Percy said, "will you set a chair for your superior, if you please. You may sit, Mr. Ratchett."

The head steward's head turned and he squinted at Percy's left ear, but he made no protest when Paul Knorr set a chair behind him. He sat.

"I am *not* intending to gather together an army to sally forth for a fight against the forces of evil, you will no doubt be relieved to know," Percy continued. "What goes on beyond the borders of my own land is, at least for the present, not my concern. And I am aware that it would take a very large army indeed to rid the land entirely of smuggling. But it *will* end within the borders of what is mine. That includes the house, the park, and the farm, and even the beach below my land, since the only landward route away from the beach is the path up the cliff face and across the park. Anyone who takes exception to my decision is welcome to collect what wages he is owed from Mr. Ratchett or Mr. Knorr, without any penalty, and leave here with his belongings. Everyone who stays is my employee and will live and work here according to my rules, whether he or she is on duty or off. Are there any questions?"

The pause that followed reminded Percy of the one in the nuptial service when the members of the congregation were invited to report any impediment to the marriage of which they were aware. He did not expect the silence to be broken, and it was not.

"If," he said, "there are any smuggled goods anywhere on my land at present—in the cellar of this house, for example—I will allow two days, today and tomorrow, for them to be removed. After that, there will be no more, and I will expect Mr. Ratchett or Mr. Crutchley or Mrs. Attlee to be in possession of both keys to the locked room in the cellar—the inside and the outside keys. If they remain lost after the two days, then the locks will be forced and new locks installed—and I will myself retain one set of the new keys."

One maid—the deaf-mute—had her head slightly turned and her eyes fixed to his lips, Percy noticed for the first time. He strolled down the center of the lines, looking first one way and then the other. He felt more martial than ever.

"Anyone who fears reprisal," he said, stopping and looking steadily into the face of the stable hand beside Colin Bains, a ginger-haired lad with freckles half the size of farthings, "will speak either to Mr. Knorr or to me."

That was a tricky point, actually. Anyone who feared how the gang would react to his—or her—withdrawal from the trade would hardly make a public complaint and draw even more attention to him- or herself. Would they *all* be in danger of reprisal? It was a risk he had chosen to take.

"I will speak openly of this wherever I go over the next few days," Percy said, returning to his place by the door and letting his eyes move from face to face along the rows. There was absolutely nothing to be read in any of them. "I will make sure it is clearly understood that this is *my* rule and that everyone in my employ is required to live by it or lose his or her position. Are there any questions?"

"Mr. Crutchley," he said when no one spoke up, "you will send the servants about their business, if you please. James Mawgan, I will see you in the library as soon as you have been dismissed."

The head gardener's face turned in sharp surprise and became almost instantly blank again.

The morning room that seemed more like a library to him was unoccupied by any human, Percy was happy to discover. It was, however, occupied by the remnants of the menagerie. The bulldog—Bruce?—had claimed the hearth, and was flanked by his usual cohorts, two of the cats. The new one was beside the coal scuttle, cleaning his paws with his tongue. Hector sat erect and alert beside the chair Percy usually occupied. He was neither cowering nor hiding, an interesting development. The other two dogs—the long and the short—had been taken yesterday to the Kramer house, where apparently they had been given an effusive welcome and a large bowl of tasty tidbits apiece. All of Fluff's kittens had now been spoken for, though they were not to leave their mother for a while yet.

Percy wondered if he had just set the cat among the pigeons, or stepped on a hornet's nest, or awakened a sleeping dog, or otherwise done what it would have been altogether better for him *not* to do. Time would tell.

"Come," he called when someone tapped on the door.

Mawgan stepped inside, closed the door behind him, and stood with his arms hanging at his sides and his gaze fixed on the carpet two feet in front of him.

"You were the late Viscount Barclay's batman for almost two years, Mawgan?" Percy said.

"Yes, my lord."

"You did not like the life of a fisherman?" Percy asked.

"I did not mind it," Mawgan said.

"How did it come about, then? Did Barclay not have a valet?" He surely would have been the obvious choice for the position of batman. He might have been elderly, of course, but it was unlikely when Barclay himself had been a very young man.

"He died, my lord."

"The valet?"

"He drowned," Mawgan explained. "He was on a day off and wanted to go out fishing in my father's boat. He fell in. He couldn't swim. I jumped in and tried to save him, but he fought me in his panic and we went under the boat and I got knocked on the head. Someone pulled me out, but I didn't come round for two whole days after. He didn't make it, poor bugger—begging your pardon, my lord."

Percy stared at him. Mawgan had not changed posture at all. He was still staring at the carpet.

"Your appointment was in the nature of being a reward, then, for trying to save the valet's life?" he asked. "You are the great-nephew of Mr. Ratchett, I believe?"

"I think he put in a word for me, my lord," Mawgan said, "after Bains would not let his boy go. But his lordship called at our house to see me after I came around, and I asked myself."

"You saw him and the viscountess being captured by a French scouting party?" Percy asked.

"I did, my lord," Mawgan said. "There were nothing I could do to stop it. There were six of them, and I did not

even have my musket with me. It would have been suicide if I had tried. I thought the best thing to do was get
back to the regiment as fast as I could and fetch help.
But it was a long way and I got lost in the hills in the
night. It took me more than a day."

"You assumed, did you," Percy asked, "that they had
both been killed?"

"They was obviously not French," Mawgan said, "and
his lordship was not in uniform and had nothing on him
to prove he was an officer. I thought they were for sure
both dead. I would have stayed on in the Peninsula if I
had believed there was any hope. But I was not even
allowed to go with the party that went looking for them.
Like looking for a needle in a haystack, that was, but I
wanted to go all the same. It would have been something
to do. It is worst of all to have nothing to do."

And yet, Percy thought, his head gardener seemed to
be making a career of doing just that. "And so you came
home," he said.

"I wish I had stayed, my lord," Mawgan assured him.
"I felt that bad when I knew her ladyship was still alive
and had been released and brought home all out of her
mind like. I might have been some comfort to her, a familiar face."

. . . *all out of her mind like.*

Imogen!

"Thank you," Percy said briskly. "I wish I had known
Viscount Barclay. He was a distant cousin of mine and a
brave man. A hero. You were privileged to know and
serve him."

"I was, my lord," the man agreed.

"What do you know about this smuggling business?"
Percy asked.

"Oh, I don't know nothing," Mawgan assured him. "And it would not surprise me, my lord, if there isn't nothing to know. I think someone must of been spinning yarns at you to make you think there is smuggling going on here. Once upon a time maybe, but not now. I know most of the servants don't tell me nothing because I am head gardener, but I would have caught some whisperings. I haven't heard nothing."

Percy knew a great deal about double negatives. Some of his knowledge had entered his person via the cane of one of his tutors across his backside, though most of it had entered through the front door of his brain. *I don't know nothing* was probably the exact truth. But short of applying hot needles to Mawgan's fingernails, there was no more information to be gathered, he understood. He had just wanted to be quite clear on the matter. He sighed aloud.

"Perhaps you are right," he said. "However, it is as well that everyone here understand just where I stand. You will keep your ear to the ground, Mawgan? And let me know if you hear anything? You have been a loyal servant, I can see."

"I certainly will, my lord," Mawgan said, "though I don't expect there will be nothing to tell. These are good people here. My great-uncle has always said so and I have seen so for myself."

"Thank you," Percy said. "I will not keep you from your busy duties any longer."

Mawgan backed out without once looking up.

Percy was feeling cold even though he stood with his back to the fire. Barclay had received two threatening letters before he went to the Peninsula. His valet, who would surely have accompanied him as his batman, had died accidentally in a boating accident. Bains, who had pleaded to go in his place, had been deemed by his father to be too young, though fourteen was really not *very* young for a boy. Mawgan had been appointed through a combination of heroism in a losing cause and the influence of Ratchett, who was his mother's uncle. Mawgan had been conveniently out of the way—without his musket—when the French scouting party took Barclay and Imogen. Then he got lost on the way back for help. When he came home here, he was given the post of head gardener.

There was nothing sinister in any of those details, except the threatening letters. Even when one put them all together, there was nothing convincing, nothing that would not be laughed out of any court in the land.

. . . when I knew her ladyship was still alive and had been released and brought home all out of her mind like.

The bottom felt as if it had fallen out of Percy's stomach at the remembered words.

Imogen *all out of her mind.* Living for a while at her brother's house unable to sleep, eat, or leave her room. Living for three years at Penderris Hall until she had transformed herself into a marble lady and could cope once again with the outside world from within her rigid shield.

And then, Imogen laughing and curled up in his arms. Sleeping with her head on his shoulder and grumbling incoherently when he awoke her.

. . . all out of her mind like.

Love, he thought almost viciously, was the damnedest thing, and he had been wise to avoid it all these years. *Not* the sort of love he felt for his family, but the sort of which the great poets wrote. Euphoria for one minute, if that, and blackest despair for an eternity after.

But how did one *un*love?

He loved Imogen Hayes, Viscountess Barclay, so deeply that he almost hated her.

And let his mind work *that* one out if it dared.

He had to see her.

But first . . .

Imogen ought to have been reading or crocheting or writing a letter. She ought at the very least to have been sitting upright in her chair like a lady, her back straight as she had been taught to sit when she was a girl. Instead she was slouched down in one of the chairs by the fire, her back in an inelegant arch, her legs stretched out in front of her and crossed at the ankles. Her head was nestled in a cushion. Blossom was curled up on her lap and Imogen had one hand buried in the cat's fur. She was drifting pleasantly in and out of consciousness. She had not had much sleep last night or the two nights before—her lips curved into a smile at the remembered reason for that— and it had been a long and busy morning. Now it was late afternoon and she intended to relax. She expected, and hoped for, another night of little sleep tonight.

She was just drifting off to sleep when something solid came between her and the heat of the fire and a shadow obstructed its light. At the same time her incoherent dream became fragrant with a familiar smell and she smiled one of her smug smiles. Blossom purred. Imogen made a sound that was very similar.

"Sleeping Beauty," the fragrant shadow murmured, and then his lips were light and warm and parted on hers and she moved deeper into her dream.

"Mmm." She smiled at him and lifted her hands to his shoulders.

His legs were on either side of hers, his hands braced on the arms of the chair, his face a few inches from her own. He looked large and looming and gorgeous. He smelled delicious.

"I did *not* use the key," he assured her. "I was let in quite respectably by your housekeeper, though she was looking rather like a prune. I had better not be alone in here with you for long. She will be getting ideas."

Blossom jumped down off her lap, contemptuously close to Hector, and Hector barked once sharply, bared his teeth, growled, and then barked once again. The cat crossed to the other chair in rather ungainly haste.

"Goodness," Imogen said. "That is the first time I have heard Hector's voice."

"I am training him to be fierce," Percy said, straightening up.

"What you *are* training him to do," she said, "is to have some confidence in himself."

"Come down onto the beach with me," he said.

Imogen raised her eyebrows as she sat up. "Is that a request, Lord Hardford, or a command?"

"A command," he said. "Please? I need you."

She looked closely at him. He was looking grim about the mouth. She got to her feet and went to fetch her cloak and bonnet and put on shoes suitable for walking on the sand.

There were several snowdrops blooming in her garden, and a clump of primroses was beginning to stir into life in one corner. She did not stop either to look at them or to draw attention to them. She led the way out through the gate.

"You are not with any of your guests this afternoon?" she asked, though the answer was perfectly obvious.

"All the over-forties tired themselves out this morning," he said, "and are variously disposed about the house with sedentary activities. The younger lot have gone off in a body with young Soames and his sisters to have a look at some ruined castle on the other side of the valley. It is said to be picturesque, and I daresay it is."

"And you chose to drag me down onto the beach rather than go with them?" she said.

He did not answer. And she was interested to note that when they came to the path down to the beach, he turned onto it without hesitation and led the way with bold, almost reckless strides. There was a great deal of unleashed energy inside him, she sensed. Perhaps an *angry* energy.

She would not pry, she decided. It might explode out of him before he was ready to do something more constructive with it. Perhaps, despite his words and his kiss when he came upon her asleep a short while ago, he was regretting their affair. Perhaps he did not know how to break the news to her that it was over.

Oh, please, please let it not be that. Not yet. Not just yet.

He turned and lifted her down from the rock above the beach without waiting for her to move onto the last short section of the path and descend on her own. He set her down and gazed grimly at her, his hands hard on her waist.

"You did not mention the valet," he said.

She waited for some explanation. None came, only an accusing glare. "The valet?" She raised her eyebrows.

"Your husband's," he said.

Comprehension dawned. "Mr. Cooper? Oh, it was a terrible tragedy. He drowned."

"He would have been your husband's batman," he said.

"He was looking forward to it," she told him, "though Dicky offered to release him and give him a good character if he preferred to stay and look for a new position. It was terribly sad. He was only twenty-five."

"And then Bains volunteered to go in his stead," he said.

"Yes," she said. "Dicky was fond of him, and he was very eager to go. We were surprised that his father would not agree. We expected that he would see it as a great opportunity for his son. But I suppose he wanted to keep him home, where he would be safe."

"And so Mawgan went," he said. "He had risked his own life trying to save the valet's."

"Yes, I believe he did try," she said. "But it was not just that. Mr. Ratchett had a word with my father-in-law and he had a word with my husband, and Dicky needed a batman in a hurry."

"Was it a reluctant choice?" he asked.

"Not particularly." She frowned. "We did not know him at all well and there was no time to get to know him before we all sailed. But Dicky never complained about him. He was just a bit . . . sullen. Or perhaps that is too harsh a word. He was reticent."

What was this all about?

"I went to pay a call upon Bains's father this morning," he said. He was still holding her by the waist, and he was still frowning at her.

"Oh, but he died," she said, "not long before Christmas. I baked a cake and took it to Mrs. Bains because Dicky—and I—had always been fond of Colin. I was still at the dower house, so it must have been before the roof blew off."

"Bains Senior was over the moon with pride and joy,

or words to that effect, when he first knew that Viscount Barclay had chosen to take his boy to the Peninsula with him as his batman," he said.

Imogen frowned back at him and shook her head slowly. "That is what Mrs. Bains told you?"

"And then suddenly, for no discernible reason, he changed his mind," Percy said. "And he was quite adamant. Mountains would not have moved him. Neither would the pleadings and even the tears of his son. He would give no reason—not then or ever."

"What?" Her frown had deepened.

He released her suddenly and turned to look at the cliff face on the west side of the path. He looked more than grim now. He looked like granite.

"I am going up," he said.

They had not taken even one step along the beach after coming all the way down here. Neither had Hector. He was seated at their feet.

"Very well," she said. Her mind was feeling a bit addled. There had been a number of threads to their conversation for the past few minutes, seemingly random threads that nevertheless should somehow connect themselves into a weave and a pattern, she felt. But she had not made the connections yet. Or perhaps she was afraid to try too hard.

"I mean up there," he said, pointing off to the left of the path down to the beach.

"Up the cliff face?" she asked him. "You are going to *climb*?"

"I am," he said, and he took off his hat and dropped it to the sand. His gloves and his greatcoat followed and then his neckcloth and cravat—and his coat. It was not a particularly cold day, but neither was it by any means a warm one in which to be standing on the beach in shirt-sleeves and waistcoat.

"But why?" she asked. "You are afraid of the cliffs."

"For precisely that reason."

And he strode away from her.

20

It was what he had intended from the moment he had seen his cousins and friends off on their afternoon excursion. They had been disappointed that he was not going with them, and his friends had looked downright puzzled.

Percy had known he was going to climb the cliffs. Why he had not stridden off to perform the foolish feat alone, he did not know. Why drag Imogen along with him? To rescue him if he got stuck or to go tearing off to fetch help? To watch and admire while he defied death in such a daring escapade? To pick up the pieces if he fell? He had dashed well better *not* fall. She did not need that memory to add to all her others.

He had chosen what looked like a climbable route to the top while he was standing beside her, and strode toward the base of it. He noticed that he had picked a climb that was not too far left of the path, the unconscious idea being perhaps that if he got to a point at which there was no feasible way up, he would not have to find his way back down—perish the thought—but could edge sideways and walk the rest of the way to the top.

He looked down when he was probably not much more than his own height above the beach and decided on the instant that he would not do *that* again. Neither did he look up except to his next hand- and foothold. Climbing, he discovered, was like a number of other concentrated activities. It was a moment-by-moment-by-moment thing—don't look ahead, don't look back, focus upon what must be done now.

Terror started in his mind, then engulfed his heart and set it to pumping and thumping through his chest and up into his ears and his head, and then took up residence in every bone and muscle and nerve-ending in his body. At one point he was all pins and needles. At another he was so weak that he felt like a newborn babe. Everything in him screamed to stop while he was still safe. Except that he had never been farther from being safe in his life and stopping was out of the question. If he stopped, he would never move again—not until his tutor and a boatman arrived to pry him off the face of the cliff and carry him down to the boat.

There was a wind, which he had not noticed when he left the house or when he descended the path to the beach. It roared about his head and his feet at what must surely be hurricane force. The rocks to which he clung were slick with ice, and the sun baked his back and the top of his head. And such imaginings meant that he was going out of his mind—which might be the best place to be at the moment. All the better if he could go out of his body too.

Climb. Don't think. Climb. Don't stop. Don't wonder how far you have come. Climb. Don't wonder how far there is to go. Don't wonder where Imogen is. Don't wonder if that valet was murdered. Stop thinking and climb. Don't wonder if Bains's father was threatened and intimidated. Don't think. Don't stop. Don't wonder if Barclay was lured to his death and if Imogen had escaped by the skin of her teeth. Climb. Don't stop.

At one point he looked down inadvertently. He knew the sea was not directly below him—the tide did not come in that far. Nevertheless, the sea was all he saw, gray and choppy and far, far below the hurricane that was roaring about his feet. He wished he had taken off his waistcoat. He wished all the bones from his knees had not migrated elsewhere. He hoped like the devil that he was not going to arrive at the top with wet breeches. He hoped like a thousand devils that he was going to arrive at the top.

Climb. Don't stop. Climb.

He should have worn his other boots.

A couple of times he was stuck with seemingly nowhere else to go. Each time he found a way. The third time it happened he was scared out of his wits—what was left of them. There was nothing there above him. There was nowhere else to go even though he pawed about with one hand to find solid rock. He crawled along a horizontal surface, still looking, and something came down flat on his back—a hand?

"Don't ever, *ever* do that again," a shaking voice said, and for a moment he mistook it for an angel's voice and thought perhaps he was crawling on his belly toward the pearly gates. "Not *ever*, do you hear me? I could *kill* you."

"That would be a bit of a shame," he said to the grass on the cliff top—he was grasping two fistfuls of it, "when I seem to have survived the cliff face."

He rolled over onto his back, and she came to her

knees beside him, and somehow—for some idiotic reason—they were both laughing. He wrapped his arms about her—they felt a bit like jelly—and drew her down on top of him while they snorted and shook with mirth.

By Jove, he had done it.

"By Jove, I've done it!"

"Why?" she asked, rising to her knees again.

Two bulging eyes, gazing steadily at him from his other side, asked the same question.

"I have some dragons to slay," he explained. "But first I had to slay the one at my back."

She shook her head and tutted but did not say what she obviously *wanted* to say. Hector merely looked.

"Percy," she said then, "you must be frozen."

"Frozen?" he said. "Are you sure someone has not shoveled more coals onto the sun?"

She looked upward and smiled. "What sun?"

Lord, but he loved to see her smile. He was glad he had survived just to see that.

Clouds stretched unbroken from horizon to horizon. No sun. And what had happened to the hurricane?

"What dragons?" she asked him. Her hands were clasped tightly in her lap.

"I called a staff meeting this morning," he told her.

"Yes. Mrs. Primrose told me," she said, "though she would not tell me what it was about. She would only say it was business. *You* called it?"

"I made it clear," he said, "that my land and the beach below here are now and forever out of bounds to smuggling, and that no employee of mine will be involved in any way in the trade. I have allowed a couple of days for any voluntary resignations and for the removal of any illegal goods from the house and grounds while I look studiously the other way. Everyone has advised me to turn a blind eye, but I have not turned it."

She gazed steadily at him for several silent moments before leaning over him and kissing him on the lips. "When I first knew you," she told him, "I would have said that you were as different from Dicky in every imaginable way as it is humanly possible to be. I would have been wrong."

It was not the best feeling in the world for a man to be compared to his lover's dead husband, even if it was a favorable comparison—especially then, in fact.

But her eyes were bright with unshed tears.

"That is *exactly* what he would have done," she said. "You fool, Percy."

It was not great to have your lover call you a fool either.

"I l—" She clamped her lips together and returned to the upright. "I *honor* you."

I love you? Was that what she had stopped herself from saying just in time?

He covered the hands in her lap with one of his own.

"I am a bit of a fool actually," he said. "Having conquered the impossible heights, I now have to trot back down the path to haul up my belongings."

"There." She pointed behind herself, and he saw both of his coats and his hat and cravat and neckcloth. They were even neatly folded and stacked. "How can you possibly walk around wearing all that, Percy? They weigh a *ton*."

"Because I am tough. A real *man,* in fact." He grinned at her. "I knew the little woman would carry them up for me."

He caught her fist before it thumped against his shoulder and brought it to his lips. "I am sorry, Imogen," he said. "I am sorry for all of this. You probably had other, more congenial plans for the afternoon."

"No," she said. "I have given myself time off for this, and I intend to enjoy every moment that offers itself."

She bit her lower lip then, reclaimed her hand, and got to her feet

Time off? From what? Her marble existence?

I intend to enjoy every moment that offers itself. As though there were a time limit.

As there was. That had been clearly agreed between them. He had set one for himself. He intended to leave here soon after the ball, probably never to return. She was going off to her reunion with that Survivors' Club group.

Was he too merely taking time off, then? From what, though? His meaningless existence? Was he going to go back to pranks and dares and mistresses and the occasional appearance in the House as a sop to his conscience?

"Tonight," he said, "I will make sure I come with enough energy to climb the stairs to your bed. And we will make full use of it, Imogen, for hours and hours. Be prepared."

"Oh, I will be," she said, but she did not look at him. She was busy pulling on her gloves as he stood up.

And standing up, of course, put him in sight of the house over the gorse bushes and up the lawn. It would not do to pull her into his arms and kiss her. All the elder relatives as well as assorted servants might well be lined up in the windows gazing seaward.

His legs were still feeling decidedly unsteady, and one glance at the long drop not far from his feet assured him that he still had a very healthy fear of getting too close to the edge. But by Jove, he had climbed up.

They walked back to the dower house without talking, and he took her hand when they were on either side of the gate and squeezed it without raising it to his lips. He had not forgotten the look on her housekeeper's face when she opened the door to him earlier.

He feared that he really had stepped into some hornet's nest this morning.

"Until later," he said.

"Yes."

He strode away across the lawn without looking back.

To her shame, Imogen was almost an hour later than usual rising the following morning. She intended walking into the village and calling upon a few people, including Tilly and Elizabeth. She was marvelously well blessed, she realized, to have two such close women friends—close in mind and temperament as well as in age.

She was going to need them in the foreseeable future.

But she would not think of that yet. She stretched luxuriously and turned her head toward the pillow beside her own. No, she had not mistaken. He *had* left something of the smell of his cologne behind.

He had come just before midnight and not left until well after half past four. And, as he had promised, he had kept her very busy indeed during the intervening hours, with only brief respites for relaxation and snatches of sleep. They had made love four separate times. But making love with Percy, she was discovering, consisted not just in the joining of their bodies and the brisk activity that followed. It was also about talking—often utter nonsense—and laughing and touching and kissing and rolling about and—yes!—hurling pillows at each other and forgetting all about reserve and decorum and adult dignity. It was about sexual play that preceded penetration. But she had learned to give as good as she got in *that* aspect of lovemaking. If he could make her beg—and he could—then she could make him beg too. Oh, yes, she could.

And the joining of their bodies! Ah, there was nothing more wonderful in this life after lengthy romping and even more lengthy sex play. And the hard rhythms of lovemaking, and the rhythmic sounds of wetness and labored breathing, and the gradual building of tension and excitement. And the release at the end of it all—the most wonderful moment of all, and the saddest, for following that moment, there came the gradual awareness of separation even while they were still joined, the knowledge that they were two.

But there was the knowledge too that they still had some time left—more than a week.

He had left after sitting, fully clothed, on the side of the bed and kissing her slowly and thoroughly as though the previous hours had not been enough, would never be enough.

"Tonight," he had murmured against her lips, "and tomorrow night and . . ."

She had laughed then, for Hector had been peering over the side of the bed, his chin on the bedcovers, his eyes bulging. He was such an ugly, adorable dog.

She had listened to them leave, to the sound of the key turning in the lock, and she had indulged in her usual little weep before falling so deeply asleep that she could not even remember if she had dreamed.

And now she was late waking, though it really did not matter.

Mrs. Primrose brought her breakfast to the dining room as soon as she came downstairs.

"You was wise to sleep late, my lady," she said as she poured Imogen's coffee. "A nasty, dismal day it is out there."

It was too. Imogen had not noticed. There was rain on the windows, and they were even rattling in the wind. The sky beyond was leaden.

"At least," she said, "we do not have to run upstairs with all the pails to catch the drips."

She stirred her coffee and turned her attention to the letters beside her plate. One was from George, Duke of Stanbrook—she recognized his writing. Another was from Elizabeth—an invitation, probably, to some entertainment that included all the guests at the hall. Elizabeth had talked about it at their reading club meeting. The other letter was addressed in a round, childish hand. One of her nieces or nephews, perhaps? It had not happened before. She broke the seal of that one first out of curiosity.

It was a totally untutored hand, a jumbled mixture of capital and lowercase letters, some large, some small, some cramped, most looping. Who on earth . . . ?

You will perswaid that luver of your's to leve here and stay away, it read, *or you may cum to harm, yore laidyship. This is a frendly warning. Heed it.*

There was no signature.

Imogen held the paper with both hands, both of them pulsing with pins and needles. She ought to have understood as soon as she saw the outside of it. More than ten years had passed, but she should have realized anyway. If she was not mistaken, the same person who had written the threatening letters to Dicky and herself before they left for the Peninsula had written this.

Oh, Percy, she thought, *what have you started?*

Imogen had learned a great deal about self-control and self-containment during the past eight years. She did not open her other letters, but she did eat her way through a whole round of toast and drink her coffee before folding her napkin and leaving it neatly beside her plate and getting to her feet.

"I will be going up to the hall this morning," she told her housekeeper. "You may let the fire die down in the sitting room."

"Take your umbrella, my lady," Mrs. Primrose advised, "if you can keep it from blowing inside out, that is."

Percy was in the drawing room, as was almost everyone else except the older ladies, who were at their meeting in the morning room. Percy was devising a tournament that included, among other things, card games, billiards, dart throwing, and a treasure hunt. Everyone was in high spirits despite the rain that was lashing against the windows. Everyone, it seemed, turned a laughing face toward Imogen.

"You are just in time to join us, Lady Barclay," Viscount Marwood told her. "You can be on my team. That will give us one more player than the other team, but the others have Percy, who really counts for two when it comes to games. Are you good at darts? You may pick off one or two of our foes, if you wish—as long as you do not do any permanent harm, I suppose. That might upset the other ladies."

And the bizarre thing was that she *did* join in, though the contest lasted a great deal longer than she expected. Indeed, there was even a break halfway through for luncheon, which was supposed to last an hour and actually lasted an hour and a half.

Everyone was having a merry old time, including the older gentlemen. And even Cousin Adelaide, who did not participate, was looking less crusty than usual, though she did complain that too many of the activities were taking place beyond the drawing room doors.

Cats darted everywhere. Bruce did not move from the hearthrug. Hector sat beside Percy's empty chair, thumping his tail at any sign of action.

It was all that a family house party *ought* to be, Imogen thought. The twins squabbled with each other at least half a dozen times, though they were on the same team. Leonard Herriott accused his brother of cheating during the treasure hunt and found himself at the wrong end of a blistering retort before their father stepped in to restore order and remind them that there were ladies present. But good nature and laughter prevailed every time, as well as a hotly competitive spirit, until finally everyone had completed every activity and the scores were added up by a committee of two—one person from each team—and it was discovered that Percy's team had won by the slimmest of margins.

Boos from the losers mingled with unruly cheers from the winners, and Aunt Lavinia rang for the tea tray, the ladies' meeting having long ago come to an end.

"Lord Hardford," Imogen said, "may I have a private word with you?"

It was perhaps not the best way of going about it, she realized too late. He looked surprised—and perhaps a little annoyed?—and everyone else looked a bit surprised too. Imogen flinched slightly as she noticed Mr. Welby winking at Viscount Marwood.

"It is a matter of business," she added.

"But of course, Cousin." He led the way to the door and opened it for her to pass through. He preceded her to the morning room and followed her inside before closing the door behind them.

He looked a bit grim, she thought as she turned to face him.

"What is it?" he asked.

She took the letter from a pocket of her dress and handed it to him.

He opened it and stared at it, then spoke a word she had only ever heard before in Portugal, on the lips of soldiers who had not realized they were being overheard by a woman. He did not apologize.

He raised his head and looked at her for a long while in silence. "He could do with a few spelling lessons, could he not?" he remarked. "Not to mention penmanship."

"It is no joke, Percy," she said.

"No, indeed it is not," he agreed. "Instead of threatening me, which I might have taken as a joke, he has threatened my lady and very seriously annoyed me."

She might have taken exception to that description of herself as *my lady* at any other time, but this was not any other time.

He continued to look at her without moving for a few moments longer. "With your permission," he said then, "I will summon a few more people here. Men. Shall I summon my mother too? Or Lady Lavinia, perhaps?"

"No," she said, remembering one phrase of the letter—*that luver of your's.* "Which men?"

"My steward," he said. "Mr. Knorr, that is. My two friends. Cyril Eldridge. My uncles."

It suddenly occurred to Imogen that it really was possible that Dicky's valet had been murdered; that Mr. Bains had been coerced into withdrawing his permission for Colin to accompany them to Portugal as Dicky's batman; that James Mawgan had been planted quite deliberately in that position. Yesterday it had all seemed too preposterous to be taken seriously. It still did today. But someone had just threatened her life—again. That seemed too ridiculously melodramatic as well, but it had happened.

"Very well," she said.

He strode to the door, gave some instructions to Mr. Crutchley, and came toward her after closing the door again. He took both her hands in a bruising grip.

"Perhaps I should be horsewhipped," he said, "except that this is *precisely* the reason they need to be confronted. I am sorry, my l—. Ah, dash it all, I am sorry, *my love*. I will *not* allow anything to happen to you. I *will* not. Of that you may rest assured. And when this is over, you may consign me to hell and I will go there without a murmur."

He raised her hands one at a time to his lips and kissed them fiercely before releasing them and striding over to the window to stand with his back to the room. The letter was sticking out of one of the pockets of his coat.

The uncles and cousin and friends were the first to arrive, all in a body, all clearly bursting with curiosity.

"We will wait for Knorr," Percy said after one glance over his shoulder.

They waited in silence until there was a firm tap on the door and Mr. Knorr stepped inside.

A mere moment later it opened again, and Mr. Crutchley admitted—of all people—Cousin Adelaide.

She looked about her disagreeably and made for the chair closest to the fire.

"The others may say until they are blue in the face," she said, "that the ladies have not been invited, but there is a lady down here already, a young one, and she will not be left alone at the mercy of a roomful of *men* while I have anything to say in the matter."

She seated herself and continued to look disagreeable.

21

*P*ercy had realized from the start that he was playing a dangerous sort of game of dare, something
with which he was long familiar. The difference this time
was that he was not doing it merely for his own amusement. He had not expected it to be easy. Hardford was a
convenient base for smuggling—right on the coast but
up away from the valley, with a secluded, relatively safe
landing place and a way up to the top, which was private
ground—an earl's property, in fact—and hence less
likely to be the target of patrols by customs officers.
There were roomy cellars in both the dower house and
the hall itself, and until recently the owner of both was
willing to aid and abet the trade even if he was not ac-
tively involved in it. And even after the death of that
earl, the new one had been obliging enough to stay away
for two full years.

Oh, he had not expected that rousting them permanently off Hardford property would be easy. He had
even realized that he was putting himself in possible
danger by being so open and determined in his opposi-
tion. He could not forget Colin Bains with his broken

legs. He had never suffered from a wild imagination, but he did not believe he was weaving too fantastical a tale about the series of events that had preceded—and followed—the departure of the late Richard, Viscount Barclay, for the Peninsula. Nevertheless, the possibility of danger had not particularly bothered him. He had thrived upon it, after all, for ten years.

Never in his wildest fancy had he imagined that the threat of danger would come, not to him, but to Imogen.

How fiendishly clever, had been his first thought upon reading the letter. *How did he know?* had been his second thought. But it was not altogether surprising. Percy had really quite recklessly endangered her reputation by trotting off to the dower house for each of the last several nights and not leaving it until early morning. It would be more surprising if no one knew. The whole *world* probably knew.

He was more angry than he had ever been in his life. But it was a quiet, leashed anger. There was no point whatsoever in blustering and lashing out with either words or fists—not unless or until he had a target for those fists, anyway. And at least half of his anger was directed against himself.

He drew the letter from his pocket and turned from the window.

"Smuggling is rife along this stretch of the coastline," he said. "I called a meeting of the whole of my staff yesterday morning and made it clear that I would no longer harbor either smugglers or their contraband on my land."

"Smuggling is rife along *every* stretch of coastline, Percy," Uncle Roderick said. "There is no way of stopping it, I am afraid. And I must admit that I enjoy a drop of good French brandy now and then, though I am careful never to ask my host where it came from." He chuckled.

"That was probably not wise of you, Percy," Uncle Ernest said. "And it will do no good, you know. Your servants may pay you lip service for a while, but they will surely slip back to their old ways soon enough. If I were you, I would let the matter drop now that you have made your point."

"You had better sharpen your cutlass even so, Perce," Sidney said with a grin.

"And load your pistol," Cyril added.

"The sooner we get you back to London, Perce," Arnold said, "the better for everyone, I think." But he did turn and look at Imogen, Percy noticed. She had gone to sit on a chair beside Mrs. Ferby, who was patting her arm.

"But there is viciousness underlying it all," Percy said. "A bit of brandy, a bit of lace I might be tempted to ignore. Broken legs and murder I cannot."

"Murder?" Uncle Ted said sharply.

"I have no proof," Percy said, "but yes, murder. Ten years ago there were threatening letters when the late Viscount Barclay voiced his concerns about the trade encroaching upon his father's land. Today Lady Barclay received another such letter. I did not ask, but I believe I can guess the answer. As far as you can recall, Lady Barclay, does this one appear to be written in the same hand?"

Mrs. Ferby had Imogen's hand clasped in her own, their fingers laced.

"Yes," Imogen said.

"I would like you all to read it," Percy said, "with Lady Barclay's permission."

"Yes," she said again.

Percy handed the letter to Cyril, who was closest to him, and it was passed from hand to hand until all the men had read it. Mrs. Ferby stretched out her free hand, and Knorr handed it to her.

"Somewhat illiterate, is it not?" Uncle Ted remarked. "The man can scarcely write."

"It is upsetting for any lady to receive something like this," Uncle Roderick said. "But it is a little difficult to take it seriously. It is all nonsense, in my opinion. Slanderous, though."

"I tend to agree," Uncle Ernest said. "But if this comes from one of the servants here, Percy, the man must be rousted out and dismissed immediately. He has not signed it, of course, even with an X."

"Lady Barclay must be offered protection, Perce," Arnold said. "You live alone, ma'am, at the dower house with only a servant, do you not? And I understand even she leaves at night?"

"You must move to the hall immediately, Cousin Imogen," Uncle Roderick said, "until this matter has been investigated, as I suppose it must be. You must never be alone. Your maid must sleep in your room with you at night."

"But I have no wish to leave my own home," Imogen protested, speaking for the first time.

"It would be better if you did, ma'am," Sidney said, "temporarily at least. There are enough of us here to offer you proper protection on the unlikely assumption that there is a madman on the loose."

"Hardly a *madman*," Mrs. Ferby said, and all eyes turned her way. "This," she said, waving the letter in her hand, "was written by a very clever man. I would not underestimate him if I were you, Lord Hardford."

"I do not believe I am underestimating him, ma'am," Percy said.

"Clever?" Sidney asked.

"The multiplicity of errors in the letter suggests someone who is making them quite deliberately," Knorr said. "And the vast changes in style of handwriting in the course of such a short note suggest a deliberate attempt to deceive. But there is a certain menace about the tone, which goes beyond the words themselves. Perhaps it is the contrast between the childish appearance of the note and the message it conveys."

Percy looked at his new steward with approval.

"Where did it come from?" Cyril asked. "From here or from somewhere outside?"

"That meeting was yesterday morning, you said, Percy?" Uncle Ted asked. "Who left the house or estate during the rest of the day?"

"Apart from us, do you mean?" Percy asked. "Knorr, do you know?"

"No one as far as I know, my lord," Knorr said after giving the matter some thought. "But it is hard to say for certain. We all know how news and gossip seems to travel on the wind."

"Whoever it is," Mrs. Ferby said, "it is someone whose handwriting is well known."

"Yes, ma'am," Arnold agreed. "He has certainly gone out of his way to disguise it."

"We are assuming it *is* a man, are we?" Sidney asked.

"Oh, it is a man," Mrs. Ferby assured him with some spirit. "A woman would make her threat directly to the man. A woman would stab straight to the heart or shoot right between the eyes. Only a man would threaten the woman for whom his enemy cares."

Imogen, Percy noticed, had turned as white as chalk. Her lips looked blue in contrast. He almost strode toward her to catch her lest she faint, but the letter had done enough damage to her reputation as it was. And she was holding herself very upright. Mrs. Ferby still had a tight hold of her hand.

"Are we making a mountain out of a molehill?" Uncle Roderick asked. "Are we in reality dealing merely with a mischief maker?"

"No." Several voices spoke together.

"I suppose," Percy said, "it was rash of me to stir up all this trouble at a time when I have a houseful of guests and a ball is being planned."

"You would not perhaps consider letting it be known that you will be leaving here after the ball, Percy?" Uncle Ernest asked. "I suppose you *will* be going up to town for the Session? And that no more will be said on the subject of smuggling?"

Percy drew breath to answer.

"No," Imogen said.

Everyone turned toward her.

"No," she said again. "Lord Hardford has done the right thing. It is what my husband would have done on his return from the wars if he had survived. What Lord Hardford can accomplish is a mere drop in the ocean, of course. It will be a long time, if ever, before smuggling loses its lure for the criminally minded or before it ceases to be hugely profitable. But even one drop of the ocean is an essential part of the whole. Violence and intimidation and even murder have been allowed to flourish uncontested for long enough. Too many blind eyes have been turned."

There was a short silence.

"Bravo, Imogen," Mrs. Ferby said in her baritone voice. "You will restore my faith in your whole sex, Lord Hardford, if you continue what you began yesterday— even if *I* should be the next one to be threatened."

How Percy could grin and feel genuinely amused, he did not know. But there was ever a fine line between comedy and tragedy. "I shall keep that in mind, ma'am," he said.

"It would be foolhardy of me," Imogen said with a sigh, "to remain at the dower house, and it would cause unnecessary trouble while everyone tried to see to it that I was properly protected there. I will move here until it is safe to go home."

"Thank you," Percy said, and for a few moments their eyes met and held and he could hear in memory the words he had spoken very early this morning—*tonight and tomorrow night and . . .* "Remain here at the house, and I will have your belongings brought over."

Mrs. Ferby pushed herself to her feet, drawing Imogen up with her.

"Come, Imogen," she said. "We have missed our tea. We will have Lavinia ring for a fresh pot."

Paul Knorr held the door open for them.

The letter was left lying on Mrs. Ferby's abandoned chair.

After several minutes of mulling over the situation to no practical purpose, Percy suggested that everyone return to the drawing room to resume their interrupted tea. He and Knorr stayed, however.

"What is your considered opinion, Paul?" he asked when they were alone.

"If there is a highly organized gang of long standing," Knorr said, "and everything points to that being the case, then it almost certainly encompasses a large area—the whole of the estuary and river valley and more. Such an organization would not tolerate competition. It will be extremely difficult to dislodge."

"That is not my intent," Percy said. "I will leave that to the customs officers. But I own this land, Paul. I am responsible for the safety and well-being of all who live and work on it. That may sound somewhat pretentious, but there is a general atmosphere of secrecy and fear here. Is *fear* too strong a word? No, I do not think it is. And there is that stable hand with his broken legs and that probably murdered valet of the late Barclay's. Perhaps even Barclay himself, though indirectly rather than directly, since he was certainly captured and tortured and executed by the French."

He had already told his new steward all those details. Knorr at least was someone he knew he could trust. He drew breath to say more.

"But you are thinking, are you not," Knorr said before Percy could speak, "that the core of the gang is right here? The leader, at least? And I think you are right."

Percy stared at him and nodded slowly. Something inside him turned cold. He must be thankful at least that Imogen had been sensible enough to agree to stay at the hall, where she must never be allowed to be alone. But . . . right in the lion's den?

But devil take it, it was *his* den. And she was *his* woman, though he did not doubt she would not like that description of herself. It would probably make him uneasy too if he stopped to consider it, but he did not have the leisure to think about the state of his heart.

"Call Crutchley in, if you will," he said. "Tell him to bring more port."

The butler came creaking in a couple of minutes later, bearing a tray.

"Set it down," Percy instructed him. "I will not keep you long enough for anyone to become suspicious. I have a very few questions for you. I do not expect you to give me the name of the person who ordered you to persuade me to move from my bedchamber overlooking the bay to one at the back of the house. But I do ask this. Was it a willing loyalty that caused you to obey, or fear of reprisal if you did not?"

The butler stared at him with apparent incomprehension.

"I have no intention," Percy added, "of disciplining you in any way at all for damp sheets and a dead bird and soot."

"Who is there of importance in your life, Mr. Crutchley, apart from yourself?" Paul Knorr asked.

Crutchley's head turned toward him. His expression did not change, but he spoke. "I have a daughter down in the village," he said, "and two grandsons, and one of them has a wife and two little ones."

"Thank you," Percy said. "Again I do not ask for a name, unless you choose to volunteer it, but do you know who the leader of this particular gang is?"

Crutchley nodded once after a longish while.

"Is his identity generally known?" Percy asked.

A quick shake of the head.

"And does he live and work within this estate?" Percy asked.

But there was no response this time—only a slight tightening of the butler's lips and a blanking of his expression.

"Thank you," Percy said. "You may leave."

He stared at the closed door for some time before looking at Knorr.

"Where is Mawgan to be found when he is not busy head gardening?" he asked.

They left the house together a few minutes later rather than summon the man to the house.

"Whatever must you think of me?" Imogen said as they climbed the stairs together. Cousin Adelaide had drawn her arm through her own.

"I never did find a man I could both love and admire, Imogen," she said. "I have always been convinced that such a man did not exist, though I never knew your Richard except once or twice perhaps when he was just a lad. Until very recently I would have said Lord Hardford was among the most worthless of them all. I am changing my mind about him even if he *does* have an air of carelessness about him and is too handsome for his own good. I think if I were your age, I might fall in love with him too." She laughed, a deep bass rumble that Imogen could not remember hearing ever before.

"Oh, but I am not in love with him," she protested.

They were approaching the head of the stairs and the drawing room.

"Then you have no excuse for dallying with him," Cousin Adelaide said firmly. "Or would have no excuse if you were telling the truth. I never thought I would tell any girl to go with her heart, but that is what I am telling you."

Cousin Adelaide had been living here for some time. Imogen had never disliked her, but it had never occurred to her to *love* Cousin Adelaide. Not until now.

"Thank you," she said, "for coming down and offering your chaperonage."

"Chaperonage?" Cousin Adelaide laughed again. "I came because I was burning with curiosity."

And it was Imogen's turn not to believe.

One of the twins was sitting in the old lady's chair when they went into the drawing room, and the girl immediately jumped to her feet and moved away. Cousin Adelaide looked her old self by the time she was seated and supposed out loud and with obvious displeasure that the tea was probably stone cold in the pot.

Everyone looked expectantly at Imogen, and she made a hasty decision. She told them everything—omitting the one detail in the letter that had referred to Percy as her lover.

Almost before the ladies had stopped exclaiming and Mrs. Hayes had hurried over to sit beside Imogen and take both her hands in her own, the men returned to the room—all except Percy, that was. Everyone buzzed with the shock and outrage while fresh tea was brought in and another plate of cake.

Then, amazingly, the rest of the day proceeded with near normality except for the fact that Imogen was back in her room upstairs, almost as if the dower house was still without its roof. A truckle bed was set up in her small dressing room for Mrs. Hayes's own maid. Imogen did not question the choice of that particular maid, but she guessed that whoever had made the decision was afraid to trust any of the servants from the hall, including her own Mrs. Primrose.

Privacy, of course, was out of the question. Everywhere she went, someone went with her, usually more than one person, including at least one gentleman except within the confines of her own rooms. It was all very well done, of course. There was never a sense of being hedged about by guards.

The evening was spent around the pianoforte in the drawing room or seated about two card tables. The following morning, Sunday, they all went off to church, Imogen squeezed inside a closed carriage with two of Percy's uncles and two aunts. She was seated between the same couples on a church pew with family both in front of them and behind. She was flanked by Mr. Welby and Mr. Cyril Eldridge when they all stepped outside the church and stood for a while in the churchyard exchanging news and pleasantries with neighbors. Mr. Eldridge handed her back into the carriage for the return journey, and she squeezed her way between the aunts.

It was all quite ghastly, perhaps the more so because the whole family remained as cheerful as ever, as though nothing had happened, as though they had not all just made the discovery that they were living among a gang of ruthless smugglers and that her life was in danger if she could not persuade Percy, *her lover,* to go away and forget about his campaign to rid his land of the scourge. She had no doubt that everyone knew she had been accused of being his lover, even though she had not told the ladies and was quite sure Cousin Adelaide would not have done so. Perhaps none of the gentlemen had said anything to the ladies either, but they were not stupid. The letter had threatened her harm if she did not get him to leave. Why her? The answer must surely be obvious.

And through it all Imogen missed him dreadfully. There was no way, of course, that their affair could continue while she remained at the hall. But even if she was able to return home within the next few days, some of the new situation would not change. Everyone now *knew* or suspected. It would be sordid to continue. It had not seemed sordid before, even though perhaps it had been.

Their affair, her little vacation from her life, was over. It had ended quite abruptly and long before she was ready. But perhaps it was as well. She had been enjoying it far too much. And her feelings had become far too deeply involved. It was as well that it end now before she became even more deeply entangled.

But oh, the pain of it.

The end of her affair felt in some ways more dreadful than the terrible threat of that letter, even though it had revealed that someone *knew* and was prepared to use that knowledge quite ruthlessly. It was even worse to know that there was some connection between now and *then*. Those events of ten years ago had seemed only very sad at the time, but they might well have been horribly sinister. Ten years was a long time. But she was as sure as she could be that the person who had written *this* letter had also written *those* earlier ones.

She was badly frightened. Not just for herself—she was being very closely protected—but for Percy, who was pursuing the matter quite aggressively. She was terrified for him. They had killed Dicky's valet. She was convinced of that now, though it had never occurred to her at the time. *But why?* And they had broken Colin Bains's legs.

And yet, all mingled in with the terror, perhaps even surpassing it, was the pain of the abrupt ending of a love affair.

22

*A*nger became a permanent state for Percy, though he kept it under control as he continued to mingle with his family and friends. He avoided being alone with Imogen. He had asked his uncles and his friends to keep an eye on her, and they did. Not that they had needed telling. Neither had the aunts and female cousins and younger male cousins, who had been informed about the situation, though they had not been shown the letter. They closed about her, the lot of them, like the petals about the core of a rosebud.

The bulk of Percy's anger was directed against himself. He had put Imogen at risk in more ways than one when he had been self-indulgent enough to begin an affair with her. And making an open declaration of war against smuggling on his property had no doubt been rash and ill considered.

He deserved to be horsewhipped.

Unfortunately, he could not go back. One never could. He could not relive the past three weeks and make different decisions. Neither could he relive the past ten years. He could only move forward.

He missed Imogen with an ache of longing that was almost welcome. He deserved every pang and worse.

His determination to get to the bottom of things in response to that letter had met with some frustration. James Mawgan had a cottage up behind the stables, in a little cluster of such houses. He had not been home when Percy called there with Knorr on the Saturday afternoon. It was Mr. Mawgan's half day, a neighbor had explained after curtsying to Percy, and he sometimes went to see his mam.

He was not there on Sunday either, a full day off for most of the outdoor workers. And on Monday he rode off early with another of the gardeners to see about getting some new bulbs and seedlings for the flower beds and kitchen gardens.

"Finally," Knorr commented dryly, "the man is doing something to earn his salary. I'll collar him when he gets back, my lord."

After luncheon, Percy and a group of the younger cousins, including Meredith and Geoffrey, climbed to the top of the rocks behind the house, where they were rewarded with a brisk wind and scudding clouds across a blue expanse of sky and a magnificent view in all four directions. It would not have surprised Percy if someone had told him that on a really clear day one could see Wales to the north and Ireland to the west and France to the south.

And it had grabbed at something in him. *His heart?* Should it not be turning his knees to jelly?

Geoffrey was running along the top, his arms stretched to the sides, a racing yacht screeching into the wind. Gregory was in hot pursuit.

Evil could not be allowed to continue thriving here,

Percy thought, like a cancerous growth upon the body of his own people. It *would* not be allowed.

Mr. Knorr was awaiting him in the visitors' salon, Crutchley informed him when they returned to the house.

Mawgan was in there too.

"Ah," Percy said as the butler closed the door behind him, "I trust you will soon have the flower beds blazing with splendor, Mawgan?"

"It is my plan, my lord," Mawgan said.

"Good," Percy said. "I shall look forward to seeing it through spring and summer and autumn."

There! That was a gauntlet flung down between them. Whether he really would stay was uncertain. But it was as well that those who wanted him gone believe that he was planning to stay, that his resolve had not been shaken by any threat.

"Tell me, Mawgan," Percy said, "Are you a strong swimmer?"

The man looked a bit mystified. "You have to be if you are a fisherman," he said.

"But you could not save one man who fell overboard?" Percy asked. "I do not imagine the sea was particularly rough. As an experienced fisherman you would not have been out if it had been, would you? Certainly not with an inexperienced guest."

"He fought me," Mawgan said. "The silly bugger. He panicked."

Knorr cleared his throat.

"And then he went under the boat, and hit his head," Mawgan added.

"I thought that was you." Percy looked closely at him.

"We both did," Mawgan said. "I was trying to get him."

"Who else was in the boat?" Percy asked him.

"My father, a few others," Mawgan said vaguely. "I can't remember."

"I would have thought," Percy said, "that every detail concerning that tragic incident would be seared upon your memory."

"I hit my head," Mawgan said.

"And while you were recovering," Percy said, "Colin Bains volunteered to take the valet's place and his father was first puffed up with pride at the prospect of having a son as batman to a viscount, heir to an earldom, and then suddenly, in a peculiar reversal of attitude, flatly refused to allow his son to go."

"I don't know nothing about that," Mawgan said.

"Then Mr. Ratchett got you the job," Percy said.

"He spoke for me," Mawgan replied. "And Lord Barclay come to see me."

"And when you returned from the Peninsula," Percy said, "you were rewarded for your service with your present senior position on my outdoor staff."

"It weren't my fault, what happened to his lordship," Mawgan said.

"Was it not?" Percy asked softly, and the man's eyes met his for the first time. "Or were you sent to make sure that somehow, by fair means or foul, Viscount Barclay did not come home?"

And there went another gauntlet. There was really no going back now, was there?

They stared at each other. Percy expected incredulity, shock, outrage, *some* look of strong denial. Instead he got only the squinted stare, which finally slid away from him, and then the oldest answer known to man.

"I don't know what you are talking about," he said. "My lord."

"I am not at all sure *how* it was done," Percy told him, "but I *am* sure that it *was* done. You were given your orders and you followed them. Someone must have had a great deal of trust in you. It was an important mission, was it not, but not an impossibly difficult one—far away from home, a war that was killing thousands of both high and low degree, no wind of blame to blow upon this particular part of Cornwall. The odds were high that it would happen anyway without any intervention on your part. But you *had* been there longer than a year, I understand. You must have been growing impatient and a bit anxious."

"I don't know what you are talking about," Mawgan said again. "If you think I killed him, then you had better ask your— You had better ask Lady Barclay. The French took him and killed him. She was there. She will tell you."

Your—? Lover, perhaps? It was the closest he had come to a slip of the tongue.

"Your orders came, I suppose," Percy said, "from your uncle. But tell me, Mawgan, was he acting merely as an agent for someone above him? The head man, maybe, the leader of the gang, the kingpin? Or was he acting for *himself*?"

It seemed impossible, incredible, laughable—that dusty, shambling old man, surrounded by the estate books, forever writing in them in his meticulous, perfect handwriting, almost never leaving his study. But what other books and accounts did he work on in there? And he had not always been old, had he?

Paul Knorr had not moved since Percy came into the room. The clock on the mantelpiece, which Percy had not noticed until now, ticked loudly.

Was one allowed a third gauntlet? If so, he had flung that too.

"I don't know what you are talking about," Mawgan said. "My lord."

"In that case," Percy said, "you had better return to your house. Mr. Knorr, will you ask Mimms, my personal groom, to accompany Mr. Mawgan, if you please, and remain with him? I have spoken to him—he will know what you are asking."

When they were gone, Percy stared glumly into the unlit fire for a minute or so and then took himself off with firm step to the steward's office. He probably should have summoned revenue officers, he thought. But how could one summon them for the mere whiff of an idea without even a shred of real evidence? He would be the laughingstock.

He supposed everyone concerned realized—or had been told—that if no one said any more than *I don't know what you are talking about* in answer to any question on the topic, they were all perfectly safe. There was no evidence against anyone.

The only real error made so far was that letter to Imogen. For someone who was obviously very intelligent, it had been a stupid mistake. But it was not evidence.

He opened the office door without first tapping upon it.

The estate books were piled neatly on shelves and tabletops and upon one side of the desk. But surely half their usual number was missing.

So was the steward.

He had better not ever think of applying for a position as an investigator with the Bow Street Runners, Percy thought. He had been signaling his suspicions ever since Saturday afternoon, when he had gone knocking upon Mawgan's door.

Ratchett was gone, and so were all the books and ledgers that were, presumably, *not* estate records.

They were down on the beach again, a large party of them, on a gloriously sunny afternoon that felt more like full spring than very early March. And everyone was merry after all the tensions of the day before.

Imogen still felt a bit numb with shock. Mr. Ratchett! Not only was he involved in the smuggling ring that had plagued their part of the coast for years, but it also seemed very possible that he was the leader, the ruthless organizer and beneficiary of the trade, the man who ruled his subordinates with a fist of iron but whose identity very few even of his own men knew or suspected. There was no proof that would stand up in a court of law, but the fact that he had disappeared and that he had apparently taken with him half the contents of the steward's office was strong corroborative evidence.

He had been living among them for years and years, a seemingly harmless eccentric.

Imogen wondered if her father-in-law had had any inkling.

It was no wonder they had tried to get Percy to leave almost as soon as he had arrived. It was no wonder they had resorted to threats when he had not only refused to budge but had also declared war on the trade on his land.

Oh, how they had had everything their own way for

the past two years, with only two unsuspecting women living in the main house and one at the dower house!

And it seemed more than probable that Mr. Mawgan had drowned Dicky's valet. But what had upset Imogen more than anything else and kept her awake through much of last night, listening to the light snoring of Mrs. Hayes's maid, was the equally unproven theory that James Mawgan was a trusted lieutenant of Mr. Ratchett's army, perhaps even his heir apparent, and that it had been carefully arranged that he accompany Dicky to the Peninsula to ensure that he did not return.

But ... it was a French scouting party that had come upon them in the Portuguese hills and captured them. James Mawgan could not have had anything to do with that. Could he?

He had been put briefly under house arrest yesterday. But with the disappearance of Mr. Ratchett there had been no grounds upon which to hold him, and Percy's groom, who had been guarding his cottage, had been called off.

James Mawgan had also disappeared by the time Sir Matthew Quentin had sent for him later in the evening to question him further in his capacity as the local magistrate.

Percy had sent for him, and Sir Matthew in his turn had summoned a customs officer, who had arrived late in the evening. The three of them, as well as Mr. Knorr, had conferred well into the night. Meanwhile Elizabeth, who had come with her husband, had sat in the drawing room holding one of Imogen's hands and listening to the story being told and retold and told again by everyone else who was gathered there.

The four men had spent the morning together again,

conducting interviews both at the house and in Porthmare. The ladies, with a male escort, had buzzed about in
what Imogen deemed pointless preparations for the ball
in four days' time. The servants had the mammoth cleaning chores well under way, and the cook had the menu
fully organized.

Now this afternoon, at last, they were relaxing. Mr.
Wenzel and Tilly had arrived at the house soon after luncheon, full of concern over the news. The three Soames
sisters arrived soon after with their brother to see if the
young people cared to walk with them. Mr. Alden Alton
came on their heels, escorting Elizabeth, who had come
to be with Imogen since Sir Matthew had not been able
to deliver any very comforting news at luncheon. And
everyone in the house was bursting for air and exercise.
At least, the younger element was. The older people
seemed quite thankful to watch Imogen being borne
away, safely surrounded by a large body of exuberant
youngsters as well as Mr. Welby, Viscount Marwood, Mr.
Cyril Eldridge, and Percy.

A number of possible destinations had been suggested, but almost inevitably they had ended up descending the path to the beach like a long, slow-moving
snake and then frolicking on the sand. Parasols were
raised above bonnets while their owners chatted and giggled and flirted. Tall hats were pressed more firmly upon
heads though there was not much of a wind, and their
owners looked ruefully down upon boots quickly losing
their shine beneath a thin coating of sand. Hector, with
so many people wanting to throw items for him to chase,
ended up chasing his stunted tail.

And yet, Imogen noticed, the scene was not quite as
carefree as it might have appeared to a stranger. She

walked for a while with her two friends, one on either side of her, each with an arm linked through her own. But a number of the gentlemen, without making it at all obvious, formed a loose ring about her and directed frequent glances to the top of the cliffs.

Mr. Wenzel, Imogen was interested to note, after showing her all due concern up at the house, was walking arm in arm with Meredith, a little apart from everyone else.

And then, almost as though the move had been orchestrated, both Elizabeth and Tilly moved away to talk with other members of the group, everyone else moved back a little so that the circle about Imogen became larger, and she found herself walking beside Percy. He did not offer his arm, and she clasped her hands firmly behind her back. They seemed suddenly isolated in a little cocoon of near privacy.

"I miss you," he said softly.

She ached for him as she lifted her face to the blue sky and watched a couple of seagulls chase each other overhead.

"Dicky was not ever going to come home, was he?" she said. "It must be a hugely lucrative business. Mr. Ratchett, if it is indeed he, must be enormously wealthy as well as powerful. Please find him, Percy, and destroy his power and release all the people who do his bidding out of fear."

"I will," he promised, though they both knew his chances of fulfilling that promise were slim at best.

"Imogen," he said, "save every waltz at the ball for me. Please?"

She turned her head and looked at him briefly. It was almost her undoing.

"I cannot do that," she said. "Perhaps not even one. All these people — *all* of them — believe us to be lovers, and the dreadful thing is that they are right. Or *were* right. I have been justly punished. You will be leaving here after the ball, when all your guests leave?"

"Probably," he said, "even if only temporarily. I want to take you to safety. I want to take you to London."

"I will be going to Penderris next week," she reminded him. "I will be there for three weeks. I would guess that George will try to persuade me to stay longer and that each of the others will try to persuade me to go with him. They are good friends."

"And I am your *lover*," he said. "Go there first, if you will, but then come to London with me and marry me. I rather fancy a grand *ton* wedding at St. George's on Hanover Square. Don't you? And I never thought I would hear myself say that. Come with me and marry me, Imogen, and let me keep you safe for the rest of your life."

Unhappiness assailed her like a great ball of lead in her stomach, weighing her down, freezing her so that she no longer saw the blue sky and the sun. The two gulls, playing a moment ago, were now crying mournfully.

"I cannot marry you, Percy," she said.

"You do not love me?" he asked.

She closed her eyes briefly as he stopped to pat Hector on the head and then squinted up at the cliff top.

"I am very fond of you," she said.

He spoke the same shocking word he had uttered when he saw her letter. This time he apologized.

"But I would rather you hated me," he added. "There is passion in hatred. There is hope in it."

"You do not need to marry me," she said. "I have friends."

"*Damn* your friends," he said, and apologized again. "I suppose you are talking about those Survivor fellows rather than your neighbors here. I am beginning to dislike them intensely, you know, Imogen. Does any of them *love* you? There are a billion degrees of love, I know. But you know what I mean. Does any of them *love* you? The way I love you."

Her mouth was dry. Her knees felt weak. The struggle to stop herself from weeping made her throat feel raw with aching.

"To use your own word," she said, "we had *sex* together, Percy, and it was good. It ought not to have happened, but it did and it was good. It is over now, though. I am fond of you. I always will be. But it is over."

"You do not know how you tempt me," he said, "to unleash upon you the full arsenal of colorful vocabulary I normally reserve for male ears only and that only on rare occasions."

"Yes," she said sadly. "I believe I do know. But you will return to London and you will soon forget me."

"Well," he said, "that calls for the least offensive and most unsatisfactory item in that arsenal. Damn! *Double* damn! And don't expect an apology. Ah, I am sorry, my love. I truly am. I asked, you replied, and like a gentleman I should have started conversing politely about the weather. Forgive me?"

"Always," she said.

"I *will* ask again," he told her, "perhaps on the night of the ball. It would be a fittingly romantic setting, would you not agree, and we could make the announcement to our gathered guests. I believe you, you see, when you say that you are fond of me. However, I do not believe you have spoken the full truth and nothing but the truth. I shall ask again, but I shall try not to pester you. Which is precisely what I am doing now. Do you trust this weather? Or will we be made to suffer for it with storms and vicious cold for the rest of the spring? I never trust weather. It gives with one hand and then delivers a knockout blow with the other fist. If, of course, we pretend not to be enjoying the sunshine and warmth one little bit, then perhaps we can trick the weather fairy into giving us more of the same just to keep us miserable. Do you think? Are you a good actor? It is a dreadfully tiresome day, is it not? The sunshine forces one to *squint*."

And, incredibly, she ended up laughing. He went on and on, all on the topic of the weather, getting more absurd by the minute.

And he was laughing too.

It cut like a knife, the sound of their laughter and the feel of it bubbling up inside her. It hurt that he loved her, that he believed she loved him.

23

In less than a month, Percy thought several times over the next few days, he had made a thorough mess of his own life and countless other people's. And there had been no satisfactory conclusion to anything and very probably would not be.

Sir Matthew Quentin thought he was mad. He had not exactly said so, it was true. Indeed, he had even commended Percy for having the courage to speak out when no one else had for years past. But he still thought Percy was mad. And Quentin might have been a friend—well, still might, in fact. Percy liked him.

The customs officer was merely frustrated, but that, Percy concluded, was probably his natural state. Chasing down smugglers when they were shrouded by a conspiracy of silence was not the most enviable of jobs.

Everyone in the house and neighborhood had been stirred up, but to no purpose. It all seemed pointless, except that perhaps the whole organization might fall apart if the leaders had been shaken badly enough. *Might* was the key word, though. Perhaps Ratchett was *not* the kingpin or Mawgan his right-hand man. And even if they were, they may well be setting up somewhere else without having lost any of their control over their followers.

Perhaps Imogen was still in danger. And perhaps Percy's actions so far had merely made them more bent upon revenge. They knew very well that the worst thing they could do to him was to harm Imogen.

Devil take it, but he was desperate to get her away from here, preferably to London, where he knew a lot of people and perhaps she did too, where a gang of Cornish smugglers was unlikely to pursue her. And he was desperate to marry her so that he could keep her secure within his own home, surrounded by his own handpicked servants, and safe within his own arms both day and night.

He had thought she might agree. He really had. Oh, she had said she would never marry again, it was true, and he knew that a great deal more damage had been done her by the events of the past eight or nine years than she had admitted to him. He knew there was a gap in her story, and that knowing what was in that gap would explain everything. But ... could she never let it go? He had thought—damn it all, he had *known*—that their affair had been more than sex to her, more than just sensual gratification. He had had affairs before. He knew the difference between those and this.

And goddammit all to hell, he had told her he loved her, prize ass that he was. He had not known he was going to say it—that was the trouble with him. He had not even known he meant it until the words were out. He had realized he was *in love* with her, but that was just a euphoric sort of emotion relying heavily upon sex. He had not fully realized he *loved* her until he told her. And there was the trouble with language again. Whose idea had it been to invent a single word—*love*—to cover a thousand and two meanings?

She had refused him, and—the unkindest cut of all, to quote somebody or other—she had told him she was *fond* of him. It was almost enough to make a man want to blow his brains out from both directions at once.

Would she *ever* be safe here again?

And would he ever be able to live here again even if she was? If she would not marry him, he was going to have to stay away. This was her home.

But, hell and damnation, it was his too. The funny thing was that though he had grown up at Castleford House and had had a happy boyhood there, he never thought of it now as home. It was his father's home, and his mother's, even if he was the owner. Hardford Hall— perish the thought!—felt like home. It felt like his own.

And he had messed everything up. If all this had been a horse-jumping course, he would have left every single fence in tatters behind him.

These thoughts and emotions rattled about his brain while he divided his time between his social obligations and meetings and interviews. With only two days left before his belated birthday ball, his mother and the aunts became almost feverish with anxiety lest they had forgotten something essential, like sending out the invitations. At the same time, the house, which had appeared clean and tidy to him from the moment he had first stepped over the threshold and looked around him for cobwebs, took on a shine and a gleam that almost forced one to wear an eye shade. It was not only the ballroom that was being overhauled and cleaned from stem to stern, it seemed.

Cousin Lavinia took to the pianoforte bench in the

drawing room several times a day to play various dance tunes while the young cousins—and a few of the older ones too—practiced the steps. Cyril, whom Percy had sometimes accused of having two left feet, undertook to teach the steps of the waltz. That was an exercise that resulted in some progress and one spectacular crash to the floor when young Gregory got his feet hopelessly entangled with Eva's—or when she got hers entangled with his, depending upon which of them was telling the tale. No bones were broken.

Two days before the ball, there was finally progress in another area too. Someone broke the silence. Paul Knorr, who had taken up residence in the steward's office and disposed of most if not all of the dust and found homes for all but the current account books inside cupboards, sent Crutchley to the drawing room to request that his lordship come to see him.

"The room looks twice its size," Percy said when he got there. "Finally I will enjoy spending time here myself. I suppose that was deliberate, though—making the room look like a place one did not want to be."

"Bains," Knorr said to him after getting to his feet, "the stable hand with the bad legs, spoke with Mimms a little while ago, my lord."

"And?" Percy gestured for his steward to sit down again, and drew up a chair for himself on the other side of the desk.

"It was a very brief exchange," Knorr said. "He would not have wanted to be seen talking to your personal groom. He asked Mimms to give you a message—from Annie Prewett, the deaf-mute housemaid."

Percy leaned forward in his chair and raised his eyebrows. "A message from a *deaf-mute*?"

"I understand from Mimms," Knorr said, "that Bains has known her since they were children and has always been close to her. Somehow they learned to communicate. She helped nurse him after his legs were broken. They are still friends, perhaps even more than that."

"And?" Percy stared at him.

"She was cleaning Mawgan's house, one of her regular duties, apparently, when Ratchett came there soon after your meeting," Knorr said. "They made plans to run off to Meirion and to go into hiding."

"They planned it in her hearing?" Percy was frowning.

"In her *hearing*, my lord?" Knorr half smiled. "But she cannot hear, can she? Or talk. I think most people assume she is an imbecile, if they notice her at all. She is a bit invisible, actually, I would say."

"Why Meirion?" Percy was still frowning.

"Bains told Mimms to tell you there is a roofer there," Knorr said. "I believe he did repairs to the dower house roof a short while ago, though I can see no mention of the expense in the books. He is married to a sister of Henry Mawgan, James Mawgan's late father. And Mawgan sometimes stays with his uncle on his days off because he is stepping out with a girl from the village—or that is the reason he gives, anyway."

"Tidmouth?" Percy stared at him. And pieces somehow fell into place. Imogen away at her brother's house for several weeks over Christmas. Tidmouth delaying the repair work even though she had given the necessary instructions before she left and the job was likely to be a lucrative one. Continuing to delay after her return even though she was a titled lady and one might have expected that he would fall all over himself in his eagerness to serve her. Had the cellar of the dower house

been used again for the storage of contraband during those months, as being far more safe and convenient than the main house? Percy did not imagine a few locks and seals would have posed much problem, especially with the roof open to the elements and anyone who cared to climb through it.

He brought his hand down flat on the desk.

"I know the man's shop, with his home above it," he said. "Is that where they are hiding out, Paul? I want them. I want this ring smashed. It is no longer enough simply to drive them off my land. They will continue to terrorize everyone upon it and be a threat to Lady Barclay's safety for as long as they are allowed to settle in somewhere else and treat what has happened here as a mere minor setback."

"I took the liberty," Knorr said, "of sending Mimms to summon Sir Matthew Quentin, my lord, and the customs officer if he is still at the inn."

"Thank you," Percy said. "I do believe you are going to be worth your weight in gold, Paul."

"You had better not say that again," Knorr said. "I may demand a hefty raise."

Sir Matthew came within the hour, bringing the customs officer with him. And five hours after that a raid was made on the Tidmouth shop and house in Meirion. Both Ratchett and Mawgan were there. Both protested their innocence. Ratchett claimed to have made the decision to retire. Mawgan claimed to have resigned as a result of his insulting treatment at the hands of his lordship and the understeward. They had come for a short stay at a relative's home, they both said. And that might have been the end of the matter if a large number of dusty books had not been discovered inside two locked trunks in a far corner of Tidmouth's attic beneath piles of discarded junk of the sort that tends to fill attics everywhere.

Both men were taken into custody, as was Tidmouth, loudly protesting his innocence.

It was the following morning when Mawgan broke under the combined questioning of Sir Matthew and the customs officer while Percy stood in one corner of Quentin's study and listened. He could be charged with murder in connection with the drowning death of the late Henry Cooper, Viscount Barclay's valet, Sir Matthew informed Mawgan. Mawgan might be willing to take his chances on there not being enough evidence for a conviction, but he ought to be warned that the other two men who had been in the boat with his father and him and the valet had been identified and found. Their evidence would convict him—unless he could place absolute trust in their remaining silent. The choice was his—risk all on a murder trial with the certainty that he would hang if he was convicted, or be tried upon the lesser charge of smuggling if he admitted to the murder and told the whole story surrounding it, including his actions in Portugal.

Mawgan had blanched at the mention of hanging.

It seemed that he had indeed been sent to Portugal to make sure Lord Barclay never came home. He had waited patiently for the war to dispose of his lordship, which it had stubbornly refused to do for more than a year. Then, when they were in the hills one day, he was out looking for firewood—he really was, he swore to it— when he was surprised by a group of French soldiers, who were scouting behind enemy lines. They realized he was English, but before they could do anything to him he told them he could lead them to a far more valuable prize in the form of a British reconnaissance officer out of uniform and on his way to perform a top-secret mission behind French lines, his head full of secrets, his wife with him. He would lead them to the pair if they would let him go. They did, on a very loose rein, and he took them to Lord and Lady Barclay and then made his escape to raise the alarm.

"I had no choice," he said sullenly. "It was me or them, and why should it be me? I had put in more than a year of my time out there in that hell. I did not kill him for all that. You cannot put *that* murder on me."

Percy spoke up though he was there on sufferance, he knew, not being any sort of officer of the law himself.

"You might be advised to speak the whole truth, Mawgan," he said, "considering the high stakes for which you play."

They all turned surprised faces his way.

"You want us to believe," Percy said, "that foraging alone for firewood in hills that were potentially dangerous, you allowed yourself to be taken by surprise? And that your captors let you go free to lead them on what might well have been a wild goose chase?"

"May I remind you, Mawgan," Sir Matthew said, "of the possible consequences to you of being tried for the murder of Henry Cooper."

"I saw them," Mawgan blurted out after a short silence. "But they were going the wrong way. It was the only real chance I had had in more than a year, short of killing him myself. I took off my shirt and tied it to my musket and held it up and showed myself. It was a breezy day."

"You did have your musket with you, then?" Sir Matthew asked.

"Of course I did," Mawgan said scornfully. "I went in under a flag of truce and told them what treasure I could lead them to if they would swear to let me go. Luckily two of them spoke English. They asked me why, and I told them it was personal. The rest happened as I said. I did not kill him. Lady Barclay can vouch for that."

"Not directly," Sir Matthew agreed, "though it might be argued that you sold him into his death. But there may be others too, Mawgan. There have been a number of deaths and maimings with obvious connections to the smuggling trade. We may very well be able to get you for murder yet. At the very least I believe you will be spending many years behind bars and set to hard labor."

Percy let himself out of the room and closed the door behind him. He was not sure if he felt triumphant or not. Actually he felt a bit flat, he decided. He supposed he had imagined the climax as involving him in a fierce sword fight on the cliff path, himself against half a dozen cutthroat villains, and then a descent to fight off a dozen more in order to get inside the cave to rescue a trussed-up Imogen before the unusually high tide got to her first. And then a desperate climb up the cliff face, her fainting form over one shoulder, because the tide had cut off access to the path. Cheers and accolades from all and sundry. A weeping, grateful woman, himself all ardor down on one knee, proposing marriage—again—and bearing her off to the altar and happily-ever-after with church bells ringing and flowers cascading around their heads.

Sometimes, even in the privacy of his own mind, he could embarrass himself horribly. He ought to write the story and have it published by the Minerva Press—under his own name.

But there *was* something anticlimactic about this less

glorious end to the business, satisfactory though it was in all essential ways. They had undoubtedly got the leaders. Ratchett, when confronted again, would find himself unable to maintain any pretense of innocence in light of his great-nephew's confession and the evidence of the books that had been found. It did not necessarily mean that smuggling would stop in the area for all time, but it did mean he could control it on his own land, and it would be considerably weakened elsewhere if it did somehow survive.

Imogen was safe, though he would still not want her to be alone for a while yet. Not until the trials had taken place and the main players—including any who had not yet been apprehended—were behind bars for good and the sensation of it all had died down.

He felt sad that the murder of the valet, Cooper, had gone unavenged for so long and that now the decision had been made to offer Mawgan a conditional amnesty on that charge given his confession about everything else. But the decision had not been his to make. And it had worked. If Mawgan and Ratchett were not ultimately charged as accessories to the murder of Richard Hayes, Viscount Barclay, though, he would want to know why.

At the moment it was no longer his business.

And tomorrow there was a ball for which to prepare himself.

Life was an odd business.

Imogen was feeling as flat as a pancake, if that was a suitable image to describe the empty feeling inside she had not been able to shake since yesterday. Mr. Ratchett and James Mawgan were in custody, as well as Mr. Tidmouth, and both Percy and Sir Matthew were confident that the smuggling trade would collapse without them. There had been a few more arrests too of men high in the ranks of the gang whom James Mawgan had named, and there were others to be pursued for criminal actions that could not be ignored—the men who had broken Colin Bains's legs, for example. But beyond that there was to be no witch hunt for the rank and file, for those who had done the smuggling work either for a little extra money or because they had had no choice. Such men were unlikely to reorganize without their leaders.

She ought to be happy, Imogen told herself as she dressed for the ball. Everyone had been exuberant yesterday when Percy returned from the village with his news. There had been cheers and laughter and even champagne. All the ladies and female cousins as well as Tilly, who had been visiting at the time, had hugged Imogen and even kissed her. Two of the uncles had hugged her too.

And so had Percy.

She did not believe he had intended to do so, but his mother had just been hugging her and had turned to lay a hand on his arm. And somehow his arms came about Imogen and hers about him and they had held each other more tightly and for a little longer than they ought. He had not kissed her, but he had raised his head and gazed deeply into her eyes for a few moments before releasing her.

Everyone around them had been beaming. His mother had had her hands clasped to her bosom and tears in her eyes. Imogen had moved away to bend over Cousin Adelaide's chair and smile at her and kiss her cheek. Then she had patted the head of Bruce, who had exerted himself sufficiently to lumber to his feet and come sniffing at her skirts.

Everyone, without exception, had advised her for her own safety not to move back to the dower house until after she returned from Penderris Hall at the end of the month. She had, though, released Mrs. Hayes's maid last night to sleep in her own room again.

But the maid had returned this evening, on the strict instructions of Mrs. Hayes, to dress Imogen's hair for the ball. Smooth and elegant would simply not do, it seemed. There had to be at least *some* swirls and curls and a few wavy wisps to trail along her neck and over her temples.

She was wearing a high-waisted, low-bosomed gown of ivory satin overlaid with a tunic of dull gold netting, which she had bought in London a couple of years ago and worn only twice there. It had always seemed too grand for the country. But tonight was a special occasion. The house was almost unrecognizable what with all the gleaming surfaces and sparkling chandeliers and the banks of spring flowers everywhere. And, flat as Imogen's spirits were, she must rise to the occasion. It was Percy's thirtieth birthday party, for which an impressive number of his family and friends had traveled long distances and at which all the neighbors from a wider radius than just Porthmare and its environs were to assemble to welcome the Earl of Hardford home at last.

She looked well enough, she thought as the maid clasped her pearls about her neck and she looked at herself in the pier glass. The colors were a bit muted, perhaps, but with the addition of a smile . . .

She smiled.

"Thank you, Marie," she said. "You have done wonders."

"It is easy to do wonders with you, my lady," the maid said, curtsying before she withdrew.

Imogen celebrated with deliberate intent for the whole long evening—*almost* the whole of it. She smiled and danced with a different partner each time. She danced the first waltz with Mr. Alton, the second with an elegant gentleman she scarcely recognized since he lived twenty miles away and they agreed it must be two years since they last met. And at supper, for which meal she sat with Viscount Marwood and Mr. Welby and Beth, a betrothal announcement was made. It took everyone by surprise, except perhaps those most nearly concerned. Mrs. Meredith Wilkes, Mr. Wenzel announced, looking decidedly red in the face, had just made him the happiest of men.

After a two-week courtship! But Meredith, also blushing, looked as if *she* was the happiest of women.

The larger family celebrated in its usual way with exclamations of delight and general hugs and kisses.

"But Tilly," Imogen said, suddenly stricken as she hugged her friend, "what will happen to you?"

"Well," Tilly told her with a smile, "I do like Meredith very well indeed, even though I hoped not so long ago that perhaps it was *you* who would be my sister-in-law. You have brighter prospects, however, and Andrew is happier than I have ever seen him. I believe Meredith likes me too. But I am not without hopes of my own, Imogen. My aunt Armitage wants me to go to London for the Season to keep her company now that all her daughters have flown the nest. She claims to have a whole regiment—her word—of eligible gentlemen awaiting my inspection. Perhaps I will be spoiled for choice if I go, and I believe I will. Go, that is." Her eyes twinkled.

Tilly was twenty-eight years old. She had a trim figure

and an open, pleasing face, even if it was not ravishingly pretty. She also had a pleasant disposition and a tendency to see the humor in most situations.

And then Mrs. Hayes hugged Imogen.

"Well," she said, "I could not be more delighted by the announcement. Meredith lost her husband even before Geoffrey was born and before she turned twenty. She deserves happiness. But I must confess that I could be *as* happy with another such announcement. I suppose Percy has developed cold feet, the provoking man. But give him time. They will warm up, and it seems to me they are well on their way to doing so."

She laughed merrily as she turned to offer her congratulations to Mr. Wenzel.

And then, with supper over at last and everyone returned to the ballroom, Percy came to solicit Imogen's hand for what was to be an energetic set of country dances. He did not lead her onto the floor, however.

"Go and fetch your cloak," he said. "Please?"

She hesitated. She did not want to be alone with him. She did not even want to dance with him. She had been telling herself all day that there was just today to live through and tomorrow and then she would be on her way to Penderris. She would find out somehow before the end of the month if he was still here and make other plans for herself if he was.

Just today and tomorrow.

She went to fetch her cloak and gloves. She pulled on a bonnet even though it was likely to ruin her hairdo.

They strolled out across the lawn in the direction of the cliffs, not touching, not talking. The sky was clear and bright with moonlight and starlight. The sound of music and voices and laughter spilled from the house even though the ballroom was at the back. The sounds merely accentuated the quietness of the outdoors and the silence between them.

"You have become marble again," he said. "*Smiling* marble."

"I am grateful for all you had the courage to do," she told him. "Not just for me but for everyone here and in the neighborhood. And I am happy for you that so many of your family and friends and neighbors have come to celebrate with you tonight. It has been a lovely ball. It will be remembered for a long time."

He said that word again—quite distinctly and unapologetically. He came to an abrupt halt, and Imogen stopped a couple of paces ahead of him.

"I do not want your gratitude, Imogen," he said. "I want your *love*."

"I am fond of you," she said.

He spoke that word yet again.

"You see," he said, "I have been spoiled all my life. I have always been given just what I want. I become petulant when I do not get it. It is time I changed, is it not? And I *will* change. But why should I change on this? Help me. Look me in the eye and tell me you do not love me. But tell the truth. Only the truth. Tell me, Imogen, and I will go away and never return. You have my solemn promise on it."

She drew a slow breath and sighed it out. "I cannot marry you, Percy," she said.

"That is not what I asked you," he told her. "Tell me you do not love me."

"Love has nothing to do with it," she said.

"Should that not be *everything*?" he asked her. "Love has *everything* to do with it."

She said nothing.

"Tell me," he said softly. "Help me to understand. There is a gap, a huge yawning hole in the story you told me. It is a hole filled with horror and part of me does not want to know. But I must know if I am to understand. I will not be able to live with this unless I understand. Tell me."

And so she did.

But as she drew breath to speak, she lost control of her voice, and she yelled the words at him.

"I killed him!" she shouted at him. And then she stood panting for a minute before she could go on. "Do you understand now? *I killed my husband.* I took a gun and I shot him between the eyes. It was quite deliberate. My father taught me to shoot despite the disapproval of my mother. He taught my brother and me, and soon I could shoot better than either of them. And when I used to come here, I would shoot with Dicky—always at a target, of course, never at anything living. And more often than not, I could outshoot him." She paused for a great, heaving breath. "*I shot him. I killed him.*"

She was panting for breath. Her body pulsed with pins and needles from her head to her feet.

He was motionless and staring at her.

"Now ask me to marry you," she said. "Ask me to tell you that I love you. Do you understand now? I do not deserve to *live,* Percy. I am breathing and existing as a penance. It is my punishment, to go on year after year, knowing what I did. I expected to die with him, but it did not happen. So I have to be made to suffer, and I have accepted that." She paused a moment to calm her breathing. "I did a terrible thing almost two weeks ago. I decided to give myself a holiday for what I expected to be a brief sensual fling. I had no intention of involving your feelings and hurting you. That I did both is fitting for me. I deserve that extra burden of guilt and misery. But for you? Go away from here, Percy, and find someone worthy of your love. And then come back if you will, for this is your home now. I will go from here. You will never see me again."

He was still standing like a statue, his head slightly bent forward, hat low over his brow, hiding his face from her eyes.

"I killed Dicky," she said, her voice dull now. "I killed my husband, my dearest friend in the world."

And she walked away, back in the direction of the house.

"Imogen—" he called after her, his voice desolate, full of pain.

But she did not stop.

24

*P*ercy was convinced that going back to the ball-room—smiling, mingling, talking, dancing—was the hardest thing he had done in his life. And it was not made easier when his mother and then Lady Lavinia and Miss Wenzel and several other people asked what had happened to Imogen and he had to tell them that she was tired and had gone to bed. He was not sure if any of them believed him. Probably not. Doubtless not, in fact.

"Oh, *Percival!*" was all his mother said, but her facial expression spoke volumes of reproach. And she only ever called him by his full name when she was exasperated with him.

Getting up the next morning to be cheerful and hospitable all over again with his family and friends and the few neighbors from more distant parts who had stayed for the night was further torture, especially after a largely sleepless night. He had stood outside Imogen's room for perhaps fifteen minutes at some wee hour of the morning, his hand an inch from the knob of the door, which may or may not have been locked. He had returned to his own room without putting the matter to the test.

She did not come down for breakfast. He wondered if she would come down at all. Perhaps she was watching from her window, waiting for him to leave the house before putting in an appearance herself. He obliged her after he had seen all the overnight guests on their way. He went riding with Sidney and Arnold and a group of cousins. And no, he told Beth when she asked, he had not seen Cousin Imogen today. She was probably tired after last night.

It was only when luncheon was announced much later that Lady Lavinia decided she should go up and see if Imogen was perhaps indisposed. It was unlike her not to be up early in the morning even after a late night—and she had gone to bed before the end of the ball.

She was not there. A note was, however, pinned to her pillow and addressed to her aunt—who read it aloud when she returned to the dining room.

Do not be concerned about me, she had written after the opening greeting. *I have decided to leave early for Penderris Hall. I shall write when I arrive there. Please convey my apologies to Lord Hardford and his family for not taking a proper leave of them. It has been a pleasure to make their acquaintance.*

An hour later they were all—with the exception of Percy—still buzzing over the strangeness of Cousin Imogen's sudden departure, two days earlier than planned. A search of her room had convinced her aunt that she had taken almost nothing with her—only, perhaps, a small valise and whatever it would have held. All the carriages and horses were accounted for in the carriage house and stables. How had she left Hardford? On *foot*?

That was exactly how she had left, as it turned out. No sooner had they all finished luncheon than Wenzel and his sister were announced.

"We have just returned from a short journey," Wenzel explained after some opening greetings and a smile for his betrothed, "and thought it best to come straight here. Tilly and I arrived home from the ball last night to discover Lady Barclay sitting on our doorstep—she did not want to wake the servants by knocking on the door. She had hoped to wait at the inn for the stagecoach, but all the doors there were locked for the night. She asked if she might stay with us until the early coach was due. I did not think it appropriate for her to travel on the common stage, and Tilly backed me up when I told her so."

"We offered to take her to Penderris Hall," Miss Wenzel said, "or at least to send her in our carriage, but she would not hear of putting us to so much inconvenience. The best we could do was to persuade her to travel post and then take her to the posting house in Meirion. We did that this morning and have just returned from seeing her on her way. She will be quite safe, Lady Lavinia, though she flatly refused to take my maid with her. And she has only one small bag of belongings."

"I will see that a trunk is sent after her," Percy said, and found Miss Wenzel's eyes resting thoughtfully upon him.

"I daresay," she said, "*you* may know what this is all about, my lord. Imogen was not saying."

It was what everyone was thinking, of course, and had been thinking ever since he walked back into that infernal ballroom alone last night. Everyone's attention was suddenly riveted upon him. The air fairly pulsed with expectant silence.

But it was not the time for charm or easy social converse. Or lies. Or the truth.

Percy turned and left the room, shutting the door firmly behind him.

I killed him! Do you understand now? I killed my husband. I took a gun and I shot him between the eyes. It was quite deliberate.

And the devil of it was, he believed her.

And in doing so, he had plunged deep into the very heart of darkness with her—a place he had been at great pains all his life to avoid.

I killed him.

Imogen arrived two days early at Penderris, and she had come by post chaise, alone, with only one small bag. Nevertheless, George, Duke of Stanbrook, did not bat an eyelash. He must have seen the chaise coming and was out on the terrace waiting to hand her down.

"Imogen, my dear," he said. "How delightful!"

But then he took a penetrating look at her and drew her all the way into his arms and held her tightly.

She did not know how long they stood like that or what happened to the chaise. The tension gradually eased out of her body as she breathed in the scent of him and of home—or what had been a safe haven of a home for three years and was still her refuge and strength.

He took her hand on his arm when she finally stepped back and led her inside, talking easily to her just as if her early arrival and the manner of it were not quite untoward. He talked to her in a similar manner for the rest of the day and all of the next, until Hugo and Lady Trentham arrived halfway through the afternoon, also early. They had set off from home a day before they needed to, Gwen, Lady Trentham, explained, all smiles and cheerfulness, because they thought perhaps they would need to travel by easier stages than usual with the baby. They had been wrong, however, and here they were.

Hugo, large and imposing and as severe looking as ever with his close-cropped hair and tendency to frown, slapped George on the shoulder and pumped his hand while declaring that he was now the slave of *two* females. "A more than willing slave, though, I make haste to add," he said as he turned. "You have arrived even earlier than us, Imogen? That makes me feel better."

And he beamed at her and opened his arms and then stopped and frowned and tilted his head to one side. "Come and be hugged, then, lass," he said more gently, and once more she was enfolded in safety.

But there was Gwen to be hugged too and Baby Melody Emes to be admired—her nurse was just carrying her inside and Hugo was taking her between his huge hands, fairly bursting with pride.

The others arrived the following day. Ben and Samantha, Lady Harper, came first, from Wales. Ben walked into the house and up the stairs with his two canes, but he propelled himself about much of the time after that in a wheeled chair, having decided that it was not an admission of defeat but rather a moving forward into a new, differently active phase of his life.

Ralph arrived next with his very red-haired duchess, whom Imogen had not met before and who begged to be called Chloe. Imogen had not seen Ralph either since he inherited the dukedom on the death of his grandfather last year. His face was still badly scarred from a war wound, but there was a new serenity in his face.

Vincent came with Sophia, Lady Darleigh, and their son, and as usual it was hard to remember he could not see, he moved about so easily, especially with the help of his dog. Flavian came last with Agnes, Lady Ponsonby, and the announcement almost as soon as they stepped through the door that he was expecting to be a father within the next six or seven months and they must be very gentle with him because it was all a strain upon his nerves. And he spoke, Imogen was interested to note, with very little of the stammer that had stubbornly stayed with him even after he had recovered most of his faculties after his head injuries healed.

"In that case, Flave," Ralph said, "then I need gentle handling too. Never mind Chloe. She is made of sterner stuff."

And they exchanged shoulder slaps and grinned at each other in a male, self-satisfied, slightly sheepish way.

All of them—except Vincent—looked with narrow-eyed closeness at Imogen before hugging her. All of them hugged her more tightly than usual and looked into her eyes again before being caught up in the general hubbub of greetings. And even Vincent, after he had hugged her, gazed into her eyes—he had an uncanny knack of doing that—and spoke softly.

"Imogen?"

But she merely kissed his cheek and turned to hug Sophia and exclaim over how much Thomas, their one-year-old, had grown.

Two days passed and two nights, during which the seven of them sat up late, as they invariably did during these weeks, talking more deeply from the heart than they had all day.

On the first night Vincent reported that his panic attacks came far less frequently as time went on. Just sometimes it came over him, the realization that his blindness was not a temporary thing from which he would eventually recover, but a life sentence.

"I will never see again," he said. "I will never see my wife or Thomas. I will never see the new babe when it arrives—ah, I was not supposed to mention that there is another on the way because it is not quite certain yet. I shall have to confess to Sophie when I go up to bed. But why is it that though I accepted my condition long ago and have a marvelously blessed life and rarely even think about being blind, it can suddenly hit me like a giant club as though I were only just noticing?"

"The trouble is, Vince," Hugo said, reaching across Imogen on the sofa the three of them shared to pat his knee, "that most of the time *we* do not notice either."

"Vince is *blind*?" Flavian said. "Is *that* why he walks into d-doors from time to time?"

On the second night, George admitted that he still had the dreams in which he thought of just the right words to speak to his wife to stop her jumping off the cliff and was close enough to catch her hand in his and pull her back from the edge—but always the words and the hand were just too late. In reality, though he had seen it happen, he had been too far away to save her.

Imogen had hardly spoken since her arrival except in purely sociable platitudes. Indeed, she had talked more with the wives than with her friends. But on the third night no one had much to say. It happened that way sometimes. Their lives were not always brimming over with problems and difficulties. Indeed, five of them at least seemed remarkably contented with their lives, even happy. And three of them—oh, goodness, *three*—were expectant fathers. Their future reunions were going to be very different. Even this year there was Thomas toddling about and jabbering in a language even his mother and father did not understand, though Hugo offered some marvelous interpretations as he tickled his daughter under the chin to see her wide, toothless smile.

Now on the third night, Imogen drew an audible breath during a longish, companionable silence and closed her eyes. "I told him," she blurted out.

The silence took on an element of incomprehension.

But of course, they knew nothing. She had told them nothing. It seemed incredible to her that they did not *know* all that had been so central to her life for longer than a month.

"The Earl of Hardford," she explained. "He came to Hardford early last month. He— I— We—"

Hugo, seated next to her again, took her hand and drew it firmly through his arm before covering it with his own. Vincent on her other side patted her thigh and then gripped it.

"I told him my story," she said. "But he was not satisfied. He knew there was something missing and he asked again. It was the night before I came here. It was impossible not to tell him. So I did."

She tipped back her head, her eyes still closed—and the back of her head bumped against Flavian's chest. He had come up behind her, and his hands came to rest on her shoulders. Her free hand was suddenly in a strong grip. Ralph was down on his haunches in front of her.

And she realized she was wailing, a high, keening sound that did not seem to be issuing from her but must be.

George's voice was calm and soft—ah, what memories it evoked!

"*What* did you tell him, Imogen?" he asked.

"That I k-k-killed Dicky," she wailed.

"And what else?"

"What else is there to tell?" She hardly recognized her own voice. "There *is* nothing else. In the whole wide world, there is only that. I killed him."

"Imogen." It was Ben's voice this time. "There is a great deal more than just that."

"No, there is n-n-not," she said, shaking her head from side to side. "There is *only* that."

From behind her, Flavian cupped her jaw in his hands.

"One must ask," he said with his sighing, rather bored voice—it was deliberate, she thought, to try to soothe her with normality. "Does this Hardford fellow *love* you, perchance, Imogen? Or does he merely like to play heavy-handed lord of the manor?"

She opened her eyes and lifted her head. "It does not matter," she said. "Oh, but he is not heavy-handed or dictatorial or obnoxious, though I thought he was at first."

"And do you perchance love *him*?" Flavian asked.

"I cannot," she said, drawing her hands free of Ralph's and Hugo's arms and setting the heels of them against her eyes. "I *will* not. You all know that."

Ralph and Flavian resumed their seats. Hugo set an arm about her shoulders and drew her head down onto his shoulder.

"Why are you so upset?" he asked. "I mean, why are you *so* upset?"

"Someone else betrayed him," she said. "Dicky, I mean. He was never meant to come home alive from the Peninsula. Someone betrayed him to the French."

And she poured out the story of the smugglers and

Mr. Ratchett and James Mawgan and her husband's valet and how Percy had confronted them all when no one else would since Dicky's time and had pursued the matter recklessly and relentlessly until he had exposed the truth and the two men had been arrested and were awaiting trial. She had no idea if her story made sense.

Vincent was still patting her thigh when she had finished.

"I came here early," she said, lowering her hands to her lap. "I needed to feel safe. I needed to— I needed—"

"Us," Flavian said. "We all need us too, Imogen. You can rest here. We all can."

"Yes," she agreed. "But it must be horribly late. I should let you all go to bed. I am exhausted if you are not. Thank you. I do love you all."

George, smiling gently, was holding out a hand for hers.

"Come," he said. "I'll see you to your door. You know you can *always* come here, Imogen."

"I also know," she said, getting to her feet, "that I must live my own life. And I *will*. This is just a brief setback, like Vincent's panic attacks. Good night."

She squared her shoulders and looked at them each in turn. She did not even notice that none of them was making a move to follow her from the room.

Percy did not know why he was angry, but he was. No, not angry exactly. Disgruntled. All out of sorts. In as bad a mood as he could possibly be without actually snapping at everyone who came in his path.

Jealous.

But that was preposterous. Why would he be jealous of a collection of men he did not even know? Men who called themselves by the pretentious name of Survivors—with a capital *S*, if you please? Wasn't everyone a survivor? Wasn't he? What gave them exclusive right to the word? And how much could they love her when a number of them—he could not remember if it was all—had gone off and married other women.

But it was to them she had gone running—in the middle of the night without a word to him. Even her note had been addressed to her aunt.

And now he was playing messenger boy and deliveryman combined. In the carriage with him were letters from Lady Lavinia, Mrs. Ferby, his mother, Beth, Lady Quentin, and Miss Wenzel. It was ridiculous. If many more people had written, he would have needed a wagon to pull behind. And there was a large trunk of her belongings in the boot of the carriage, leaving hardly any room for his own luggage.

And here he was arriving at Penderris Hall, which was just as large and imposing as he had expected and considerably closer to the ever-present cliffs than Hardford Hall was, and he was having second—or was it forty-second—thoughts about the wisdom of coming here but it was too late to turn back because his arrival seemed to have been noticed and the main doors had opened and a tall man with elegantly graying hair—damn him!—was stepping outside to see who the devil was arriving when he had not been invited and Percy could see that he was the Duke of Stanbrook. He had seen the man a few times at the House of Lords.

He felt stupid and belligerent, and if the man stood in his way, he would first flatten his nose and then take him apart with his bare hands and maybe his teeth too. He was going to see her—he must see her—and that was that. She had had no business running off that night without giving him a chance to collect his thoughts and respond to what she had told him. He was going to talk to her—now. She owed him that much, by Jove.

Stanbrook was holding out his right hand as Percy stepped down from the carriage and closed the door on Hector.

"Hardford, I believe," Stanbrook said, and Percy shook his hand.

"I have brought Lady Barclay's trunk," he said, "and some letters for her. And I will see her."

The ducal eyebrows went up. "Come inside," he said, "and have some refreshments. Your man may proceed to the stables after unloading the trunk. Someone will see to him there." And he turned to lead the way inside.

There was an army lined up in the hall, of course. Well, there were only four of them in addition to Stanbrook, but they looked like an army. Or an impregnable fortress. But let them just try to stand in his way. Percy almost hoped they would. He was spoiling for a fight.

Stanbrook introduced him with perfectly mild courtesy—damn him again. The great big bruiser with the closely cropped hair was Trentham; the one with the nasty slash across his face was the Duke of Worthingham; the blond one who looked as though the whole world had been created for his amusement was Ponsonby; and the slight, blue-eyed boy was Darleigh. Percy looked at him, looked away, and then looked again. Was he not the blind one? And then he saw that the eyes that had appeared to be looking directly at him were actually missing his face by a few inches. It was a bit eerie.

Civil enough greetings were exchanged, and then another man appeared on the stairs, tottering slowly down them with the aid of two canes that encased his lower arms.

"Sir Benedict Harper," Stanbrook said.

Six of them. The seventh was missing.

"I will see Lady Barclay," Percy said curtly. Good manners might have served him better, but to hell with good manners. He was in a bad mood.

"There may be a slight problem," the blond one said on a sigh, as though even speaking those few words was a trial to him. "For you see, Hardford, Lady Barclay will perhaps not see you."

"And frankly," scar-face added, "I would not blame her."

The big tough one folded his arms and looked tougher.

"Then ask her," Percy said, "and find out. And tell her I am not budging from here until she does see me."

He felt as though he were standing back from himself and observing his bad behavior with a slightly incredulous shake of the head. Where had all his famed charm fled?

"Say please," he added, glaring at the lot of them.

"Perhaps you will step into the visitors' salon," Stanbrook suggested, "and have a drink while you wait. The others will go with you while I go talk to Lady Barclay. I warn you, though, that she may refuse to speak to you. She saw you come and was less than delighted."

Percy felt a bit like a hot air balloon that had sprung a leak.

"Let me go, George," Darleigh said. "Let me talk to her. And I will remember to say please, Hardford." He smiled with great sweetness. "Go and have some refreshments. You are upset."

And there went the rest of the hot air, leaving Percy feeling limp and deflated.

Good God and a thousand devils, what if she would not see him? He could hardly camp out beneath her window—even if he knew which one it was—forever and ever, could he? Not with the army on the prowl. He particularly did not like the look of the giant.

He turned in the direction of the room Stanbrook was indicating, while the blind Darleigh set off in the opposite direction, led by a dog Percy was just noticing for the first time. He remembered that he had left Hector in the carriage. The wretched hound had flatly refused to be left at home.

25

Imogen was in the conservatory, where she had taken refuge after seeing the familiar carriage approaching. She would not have had even that much warning if she had not been standing in the drawing room window at the time, rocking a sleeping Melody Emes in her arms and thinking that there could surely be no lovelier feeling in the world.

She was gazing out through the conservatory windows now at some daffodils blooming in the grass, though she was not really seeing them. She heard someone come—someone *with a dog*—but did not turn her head.

Vincent sat down beside her, first feeling for the seat. His dog settled by his knee.

"Imogen," he said, and he reached out and patted the back of her hand. "Does he always behave badly?"

"Oh." And strangely, bizarrely, she found herself smiling. "*Did* he behave badly?"

"There is a smile in your voice," he said, and that sobered her. "He was bursting with belligerence. It would not have taken much provocation for him to take us all on at once with his bare fists. I could not see him, of course, but I could hear him. Is he a large man?"

"Yes," she said. "Not huge, though."

"Then Hugo alone could have knocked him down with one punch," he said, "though I have the feeling he would had hopped right up again for more punishment. What does he look like?"

"Oh," she said, frowning, "tall, dark, handsome—all the old clichés."

"And is *he* a cliché?" he asked.

"No." She was still frowning. "I thought he was at first, Vincent. But not now that I know him better. No one is less of a cliché. He is . . . oh, no matter. Did he go quietly?"

She felt as though there were a leaden weight at the bottom of her stomach as she imagined his carriage driving away from Penderris. Actually, it had been there since the night of his birthday ball, that cold, heavy weight. Would it never go away?

"He is in the salon with the other men," he said. "He wants to see you. He demanded that one of us come and tell you so. But then he added a *please*."

Her lips quirked into a smile again, though she felt nearer to tears than laughter.

"Tell him no," she said. "And add *thank you,* if you will."

"We all expected him to come, you know," he said. "We were all agreed upon it the night before last after you went to bed. There was no point in laying wagers. We were all on the same side. And Sophie agreed with me, and the other ladies did too. We have *all* been expecting him to come."

There was nothing to say into the pause that followed.

"He is terribly upset," Vincent told her.

"I thought he was belligerent," she said.

"Precisely," he said. "But there was nothing to be belligerent about, you see, Imogen. George went outside to greet him like a courteous host, and we all behaved with the greatest civility."

She could just imagine them all lined up in the hall, not realizing how formidable they could look when they were standing between someone and what that someone wanted.

Poor Percy! He had done nothing to deserve any of this.

"I will send him away if you wish," Vincent said. "I believe he will go even though he told us he would not budge until he saw you. He is a gentleman and will not continue to pester you if your answer is no. But I think you ought to see him."

"It is hopeless, Vincent," she said.

"Then tell him so."

She drew a deep, audible breath and let it out. Vincent, she noticed irrelevantly, needed a haircut. His fair, wavy hair almost touched his shoulders. But when had he ever *not* needed a haircut? And why should it be cut? It made him look like an angel. His wide blue eyes only enhanced that impression.

"Send him here," she said.

He got to his feet, and his dog stood beside him. But he hesitated. "We never ever offer one another unsolicited advice, Imogen, do we?" he said.

"No, we do not," she said firmly, and he turned away. "But consider your advice solicited. What do you wish to say?"

He turned back. "I believe," he said gently, "we all

have a perfect right to make ourselves unhappy if that is what we freely choose. But I am not sure we have the right to allow our own unhappiness to cause someone else's. The trouble with life sometimes is that we are all in it together."

And he left without another word. That was *advice*? She was not even sure what he had been trying to say. Except that it made perfect sense while she waited and pondered his words. Are we not all responsible just for our own selves? she thought. Why should we be responsible for anyone else? Would that not be just meddling interference?

The trouble with life sometimes is that we are all in it together.

And she remembered her relatively minor decision to dance again at the village assemblies.

She heard more footsteps. Firm, booted feet this time. Belligerent feet, perhaps. Again she did not turn her head. He stopped a short distance away. He did not sit down.

"Imogen," he said softly.

She clasped her hands in her lap, lacing her fingers. She touched the tips of her thumbs together.

"You do not play fair," he said.

"I am not involved in any game with you, Percy," she said. "I cannot play either fairly or unfairly if I do not play at all."

"You told me a story," he said, "and left a hole in it so large and gaping that it would have made a crater in any highway wide enough to stretch right across the road. When I begged you to tell me the rest of it, you offered me a pebble with which to fill that great hole."

"What I told you was a *pebble*?" She looked at him

for the first time, anger sparking. She was shocked at what she saw. It was not quite a week since they'd last met, but his face looked drawn and pale with smudges beneath both eyes that suggested lack of sleep. The eyes themselves were fathomless.

The trouble with life sometimes is that we are all in it together.

"You shot him," he said, "between the eyes, deliberately. I believe you. But *why,* Imogen? How did you get to him? Where did the gun come from? Why did you use it to kill him? Maybe I have done nothing to deserve answers except dare to love you, but tell me for that reason if not for any other. Help me to understand. Tell me the whole of it."

She drew one breath and then another. "Over a number of days," she said, "they were unable to break him. I have no idea how many days that was. They all ran together for me. They must have thought he carried information inside his head that was essential to them. Perhaps they were right—I do not even know. Finally they took me to him—four of them, all officers. There were two other men there too. He was chained upright to one wall. I scarcely recognized him."

She lowered her head and touched the heels of her hands to her eyes for a moment.

"Oh, good God," she thought he muttered.

"They told him what they were going to do," she said. "They were going to take turns with me while he and the others watched. I have *no idea* why one of them set his pistol down on a table not far from where I stood. Contempt for a helpless woman, perhaps? Carelessness, perhaps? Or perhaps he was to go first and needed to divest himself of a few things. I picked it up and held them all at bay, their hands in the air. But the hopelessness of the situation was immediately apparent. If I shot one of them, the others would be upon me in an instant and nothing would have been accomplished. They would have raped me and he probably would have broken — maybe before it even started, maybe after one or two. He could not have lived with himself after, even if they had let him live, which is doubtful. If I forced one of them to free him, I could see that he would not be able to walk out of there. And even if I devised a way, there were dozens more soldiers in the building and hundreds, even thousands more outside. I do not believe it took me longer than a second to know what the only solution was. And Dicky knew it too. He was looking at me. Oh, God, he was *smiling* at me."

She had to pause for a few moments to steady her breathing.

"And I knew what he was thinking and he knew what I was thinking—we could always do that. *Yes, do it,* he told me without speaking a word. *Shoot me, Imogen. Do not waste your bullet on one of the French officers.* And just before I did what he bade me do, his eyes said, *Courage.* And I did it. I shot him. I expected—*he* had expected—that I too would be dead moments later. It did not happen. Those very courteous . . . *gentlemen*, furious though they were, knew how to punish a woman, and it was not with rape. They let me go, even escorted me back to my own people. They left me to a living hell."

She did not know how long the silence stretched.

"Leave now, Percy," she said. "I am a bottomless well of darkness. And you are full of light, even if you do feel that you have wasted the past ten years of your life. Go and forget about me. Go and be happy."

He muttered that word again. It really was getting to be a habit.

"He loved you, Imogen," he said. "If his eyes could have spoken to you for a little longer, if he had known that they would let you live, what would he have told you?"

"Oh." She gulped.

"Don't evade the question," he said. "What would he have told you to do?"

Somehow he compelled honesty—an honesty that penetrated the layer upon layer of guilt in which she had wrapped herself ever since that most dreadful of moments in that most dreadful of places.

"He would have t-t-told me to be h-h-happy," she said, her voice thin and high again, as it had been the night before last.

"If he could somehow be aware of the past eight or more years," he said, "and how you have lived them and how you intend to live the rest of your life, how would he *feel,* Imogen?"

She looked at him again. "Oh, this is unfair, Percy," she cried. "No one else has dared ask this of me—not the physician, not any of my fellow Survivors. No one."

"I am neither the physician nor any of those six men," he said. "And I dare ask the question. How would he feel? You know the answer. You knew him to the depths of his being. You loved him."

"He would have been dreadfully upset," she said. She drew her upper lip between her teeth and bit into it, but she could not prevent the hot tears from welling into her eyes and spilling over onto her cheeks. "But how can I let myself live on, Percy? To smile and laugh, to enjoy myself, to love again, to *make* love? I am afraid I will forget him. I am *terrified* that I will forget him."

"Imogen," he said, "someone would have to cut into your head and remove your brain and smash it to pieces. And even then your heart and your very bones would remember."

She fumbled for a handkerchief, but he took a few steps closer and pressed his own large one into her hand. She held it to her eyes.

He was on his knees in front of her then, she realized, his hands on the bench on either side of her.

"Imogen," he said, "I tremble at my presumption in trying to win your love for myself when you have loved such a man. But I do not expect to take his place. No one can ever take anyone else's place. Everyone must carve out his own. I want you to love me for my sorry self, which I will try very hard for the rest of my life to make worthy of you—and worthy of me. I can do it. We can always do anything as long as we are alive. We can always change, grow, evolve into a far better version of ourselves. It is surely what life is for. Give me a chance. Let me love you. Let yourself love me. I will give you time if you need it. Just give me hope. If you can. And if you cannot, then so be it. I will leave you in peace. But please—try to give me a definite maybe if you possibly can."

She lowered the handkerchief after drying her eyes. He looked like a poor, anxious schoolboy, hoping at least to avoid a caning. She reached out and cupped his face with her hands.

"I do not want to drain all your light, Percy," she said.

Something sparked in his eyes.

"But there is never an end to light, Imogen," he told her, "or to love. I'll fill you so full of light that you will glow in the dark, and then when I want to love you in a very physical way I will be able to find you."

Oh, absurd, *absurd* Percy. Yet so pale and anxious despite his ridiculous words.

"Do I dare?" she asked, but more of herself than of him.

He did not answer her. But someone else did, deep inside her in a voice she recognized—*Courage*. And for the first time in more than eight years her mind listened to the tone in which that silent word had been spoken. It was one of deep peace.

He had welcomed death—at her hands. It had released him from intolerable pain and the certain knowledge that there would be more of it before he died. And it had released her from the horrors of rape—he had believed that as he died, and he had been right, though not quite in the way he had expected.

He had been at peace when he died. She had been the instrument of his death, or of his release, depending upon how one looked at it.

She could live again. Surely she could. She owed it to him, and perhaps to herself. And perhaps to Percy. Oh, she could live again.

"I will wrap myself from head to toe in a thick blanket," she said, "and you will have to search for me. It will be more sporting and more fun that way."

She watched the smile grow in his eyes and gradually light up his whole tired face. And his arms closed about her like iron bands, and his forehead came to rest on her shoulder, and he wept.

It was the second week of May before Percy's wedding day finally dawned. He *thought* it was the same calendar year as that in which he had become betrothed to Imogen, but it could easily be anything up to five years after. It seemed like forever.

He had wanted to get up from his knees there in the conservatory at Penderris and dash off in pursuit of the nearest special license, dash her back to Hardford Hall, and then dash her off to the church in Porthmare for the nuptials—all within one day if it had been humanly possible.

Alas, sanity had prevailed, though not necessarily his own.

Those friends of hers had all assured her that if she must leave their reunion early, then they quite understood and would be delighted for her—or words to that effect. The wives had assented too with hugs and kisses and sentimental tears. But they had all somehow managed to look collectively forlorn at the same time, and it was Percy himself who had declared that there was no way on this earth he was going to come between his newly betrothed and the dear friends he hoped would also be *his* dearest friends in the future—or foolish words to that effect.

He had stayed for a few days, during which time he almost lost the affections of Hector to a one-year-old toddler who chased him and mauled him and giggled over him and fell asleep on his doggie stomach and generally enslaved him.

Percy had written a whole library of letters—perish the memory—while Imogen did the same beside him in Stanbrook's library, and sent them off. And then he had returned to London, where he saw to putting notices in the morning papers and arranging for banns to be read and—soon enough—being caught up in a ferocious tornado of wedding plans as his family gathered about him in force and his mother arrived from Derbyshire—*I came to London from Cornwall via the scenic route through Derbyshire* had become her joke of the moment.

Then the Penderris contingent had arrived in force, bringing Imogen with them—she was staying at Stanford House with the duke and had been joined there by her mother and the mother's sister, who were somehow related to Stanbrook.

Lady Lavinia and Mrs. Ferby, Imogen's brother and his wife, and numerous other people come for the wedding, had filled the Pulteney Hotel to the rafters.

There had been dinners and parties and soirees at the homes of various aunts and uncles of Percy's; a betrothal ball for Meredith and Wenzel at Uncle Roderick's, at which Percy's engagement had been celebrated too; a ball at the Duke of Worthingham's, at which there had been a betrothal cake in the center of the supper table; and another ball hosted jointly by Lady Trentham and her cousin, Viscountess Ravensberg, at which Percy found himself being congratulated by a rather large number of Bedwyns, including the formidable Duke of Bewcastle himself. Percy had heard him speak in the House of Lords a time or two, and for no apparent reason stood in awe of the man. Perhaps his intense light silver eyes had something to do with it, or his austere, haughty demeanor. It was something of a surprise to discover that he had a pretty though not ravishingly beautiful wife, whose smile seemed to light her up from the inside out and who seemed not one whit cowed by her husband.

It had all been enough, Percy decided as Watkins dressed him for his wedding all in silver and gray and white, to make him dashed sorry he had been forced to agree to marry the proper way—that had been Imogen's way of putting it, anyway.

"Oh, Percy," she had said with a sigh when he had still

been making hopeful noises about going off in search of a special license. "I do so wish we could marry that way. But a wedding is not just about the bride and groom, is it? It is about their family and friends too. It is one of those rare celebratory events that punctuate a happy life. Let's wait and marry in the proper way."

He had *not* asked if marrying the other way would be improper. He would have given her the sun if she had asked for it, or the moon, or a proper wedding.

A proper bridegroom went to church—St. George's on Hanover Square, of course—clad in silver, gray, and white, with yards of lace frothing at neck and cuffs and a diamond the size of a small egg winking in the linen and lace folds at his neck and rings and fobs and the Lord knew what other finery about his person.

And with unsteady knees. And two hands full of thumbs, any two or three of which were bound to drop the wedding ring at the key moment.

Cyril was no help, and Percy wondered if he should have chosen someone else to be his best man.

"What if I should drop the ring?" Cyril asked on the way to church.

Surely one of the functions of a best man—the *principal* function, in fact—was to calm the nerves of the bridegroom.

"Then you crawl around on the floor until you recover it," Percy said. "It will not happen."

"I have never done this before," Cyril added.

"Neither have I," Percy told him.

All the pews inside the church would surely have been filled just with family members and close friends. But of course, because this was a *proper wedding,* everyone who had a remote connection to the *ton* had been invited, and since the Season was just getting nicely launched and this was the very first fashionable wedding of the year—there would be others, since the Season was also the great marriage mart—everyone and his dog had accepted. Well, not dogs, actually. Hector's nose was severely out of joint. When he had tried to trot unobtrusively out to the carriage, Percy had put his foot down, not an easy thing to do with an animal that sometimes had difficulty with the master/creature distinction.

The church was packed. There might even be a few people sitting up on the roof. There should be a few rows of chairs up there.

Cyril's teeth were chattering almost audibly. Percy, seated with him at the front of the church, concentrated upon his ten thumbs and the necessity of converting eight of them back into fingers before they arrived at the ring part of the ceremony. He flexed them and did a mental check of his knees. He could not get married sitting down, could he?

And then it was starting—*really* starting. The clergyman, gorgeously vested, arrived at the front of the church, the buzz of conversation died to an expectant hush, the congregation got to its feet, and the organ struck up with something impressively proper.

Percy's knees worked, and he turned to watch his bride approach along the nave, on the arm of her brother.

Lord, dear Lord.

She was all ice blue simplicity and elegance. Not a frill or a flounce or even half a yard of lace in sight. Not a curl or a wavy tendril of hair escaping from her plain straw bonnet trimmed only with a wide ribbon to match her dress. Not a jewel, except for something sparkling in her ears.

She passed elaborate splendor in the pews on both sides of her as she came. They paled into insignificance. She looked like a Nordic goddess or a Viking princess or some such thing.

She was Imogen.

For a moment when she drew closer he thought she was the marble lady. Her face was pale and set, her eyes fixed upon him. And then—watch it, knees!—she smiled. And there was no need of candles or any other illumination in St. George's. The church was flooded with light. Or perhaps it was only his heart. Or his soul.

He did a mental check of his facial muscles and discovered that he was smiling back at her.

It was really a dashed shame, he thought later, for a fellow to miss his own wedding. But he effectively did just that, so dazzled was he by the light she brought with her and the warmth that reached out from her to envelop him too. He thought he remembered someone saying *Dearly beloved,* in the tone only a clergyman ever used, and he *did* remember a moment's anxiety as he saw Cyril's hand shaking like a leaf in a strong breeze while it held a gold ring, and he certainly remembered hearing that he and Imogen were now man and wife together and no man should even dream of putting them asunder and those other things that all meant simply that one was married right and tight for all eternity.

But he missed everything else.

He came back to himself only when he and his bride were in the vestry signing the register and Imogen was signing her old name for the last time.

"Though it remains the same," her brother remarked with a chuckle, "with the addition of Countess of Hardford."

"No," she said softly, "it changes. All of it. I am married to Percy now."

Percy could have bawled, but—fortunately—did not.

And then they were walking back along the nave together—he remembered to imitate the speed of a turtle—while the organ played an anthem that seemed designed to lift the top right off one's head so that one's soul could soar straight to heaven, and Imogen's mother and aunts *and* Mrs. Ferby and his own mother and assorted aunts wept shamelessly and everyone else smiled enough to cause wrinkles.

"For two pins," he murmured to his bride, "I would start skipping like a boy."

"For two pins," she murmured back, smiling to both right and left, "I would join you."

"But we are at a proper wedding," he said.

"Alas."

And then they were outside and the sun that had been at war with the clouds covering the sky earlier had won and a cheering multitude of gawkers and the merely curious greeted them as well as a small army of grinning Survivors and cousins and friends armed with the petals of a few thousand unfortunate flowers. The petals were soon raining down about them and quite ruining the lovely paleness of their wedding attire.

And Imogen was laughing.

He would never, *ever* grow tired of hearing—and seeing—her laugh. He was laughing too, of course, but that was less of a rarity. Indeed, perhaps she cherished the rare sight of him looking earnest.

"Oh, look," she wailed, though it was a happy wail. "Look, Percy."

He did not need to. He had fully expected it, having

been involved in his fair share of weddings over the past ten years or so. Their open carriage, bedecked nicely with flowers, was also all set to drag what appeared to be half of London's kitchen hardware behind it, and also an ancient boot or two, all the way to Stanbrook House, where the duke had insisted the wedding breakfast be held.

"After all," Percy said as he handed her into the carriage and the congregation began to spill out of the church behind them, "there may be one or two people in town who have not heard that we are getting married today. They must be made to hear."

"I think all the neighbors in *Cornwall* will hear too," she said as she settled herself on the seat and he took his place beside her. "It would not surprise me if Annie Prewett at Stanbrook House could hear the din."

Annie, the deaf-mute housemaid who had had the courage to pass on information about the whereabouts of Ratchett and Mawgan, had been promoted to the position of Imogen's personal maid after she had demonstrated that she had some skill in the performance of the necessary duties. And in front of them now, up on the box of the wedding carriage, waiting for the signal to move off, sat Percy's coachman and his new footman, Colin Bains, both of them resplendent in new livery.

"And since this is a proper wedding, Lady Hardford," Percy said in the precious remaining moments before the carriage moved and the unholy din of moving, jostling metal drowned out the joyful pealing of the church bells, "we must do what is now proper."

She turned a laughing face toward him as he set an arm about her shoulders and cupped her chin between the thumb and forefinger of his other hand.

"But of course we must," she said. "My love."

Cheers, laughter, the ringing bells, the snorting and stamping of the horses, the deafening din of hardware — none of it mattered as he kissed his bride and her hand came to his shoulder.

Percy was, at least for the moment, in another world. And Imogen was right there with him.

Read on for an excerpt from the first book
in Mary Balogh's Survivors' Club series . . .

THE PROPOSAL

Prologue

The Survivors' Club

The weather could have been better. Low clouds scudded across the sky, blown along by a brisk wind, and rain that had been threatening all day had started to fall. The sea was rough and metal gray. A chill dampness penetrated even to the interior of the carriage, making its sole occupant glad of his heavy greatcoat.

His spirits were not to be dampened, however, even though he would have preferred sunshine. He was on his way to Penderris Hall in Cornwall, country seat of George Crabbe, Duke of Stanbrook. His Grace was one of the six people he loved most in the world, a strange admission, perhaps, when five of those people were men. They were the six people he *trusted* most in the world, then, though *trust* seemed too impersonal a word and there was nothing impersonal about his feelings for these friends. They were all going to be at Penderris for the next three weeks or so.

They were a group of survivors of the Napoleonic Wars, five of them former military officers who had been incapacitated by various wounds and sent home to England to recuperate. All of them had come to the attention of the Duke of Stanbrook, who had borne them off to Penderris Hall for treatment, rest, and convalescence. The duke had been past the age of fighting in the wars himself, but his only son had not been. He had both fought and died in the Peninsula during the early years of the campaign there. The seventh member of the club was the widow of a surveillance officer who had been captured by the enemy in the Peninsula and died under torture, which had been conducted at least partially in her presence. The duke was a distant cousin of hers and had taken her in after her return to England.

They had formed a close bond, the seven of them, during the lengthy period of their healing and convalescence. And because for various reasons they would all bear the mark of their wounds and war experiences for the rest of their lives, they had agreed that when the time came for them to return to their own separate lives beyond the safe confines of Penderris, they would return for a few weeks each year in order to relax and renew their friendship, to discuss their progress, and to offer one another support in any difficulty that might have arisen.

They were all survivors and strong enough to live independent lives. But they were also all permanently scarred in one way or another, and they did not have to hide that fact when they were together.

One of their number had once dubbed them the Survivors' Club, and the name had stuck, even if only among themselves.

Hugo Emes, Lord Trentham, peered as best he could through the rain that was now pelting against the carriage window. He could see the edge of the high cliffs not too far distant and the sea beyond them, a line of foam-flecked gray darker than the sky. He was on Penderris land already. He would be at the house within minutes.

Leaving here three years ago had been one of the hardest things any of them had ever done. Hugo would have been happy to spend the rest of his life here. But of course, life was forever changing and it had been time to leave.

And now it was time for change again . . .

But he would not think of that yet.

This was the third reunion, though Hugo had been forced to miss last year's. He had not seen any of these friends for two years, then.

The carriage drew to a halt at the foot of the steps leading up to the massive front doors of Penderris Hall and rocked for a few moments on its springs. Hugo wondered if any of the others had arrived yet. He felt like a child arriving for a party, he thought in some disgust, all eager anticipation and nervously fluttering stomach.

The doors of the house opened and the duke himself stepped between them. He proceeded down the steps despite the rain and reached the foot of them as the coachman opened the carriage door and Hugo vaulted out without waiting for the steps to be put down.

"George," he said.

He was not the sort of man who normally hugged other people or even touched them unnecessarily. But it might very well have been he who initiated the tight hug in which they were both soon enveloped.

"Goodness me," the duke said, loosening his hold after a few moments and taking a step back in order to look Hugo over. "You have not shrunk in two years, Hugo, have you? In either height or breadth. You are one of the few people who can make me feel small. Come inside out of the rain and I shall check my ribs to discover how many you have crushed."

He was not the first to arrive, Hugo saw as soon as they were inside the great hall. Flavian was there to greet him—Flavian Arnott, Viscount Ponsonby. And Ralph was there too—Ralph Stockwood, Earl of Berwick.

"Hugo," Flavian said, raising a quizzing glass to his eye and affecting bored languor. "You big ugly bear. It is surprisingly g-good to see you."

"Flavian, you slight, beautiful boy," Hugo said, striding toward him, his boot heels ringing on the tiled floor, "it is good to see *you,* and I am not even surprised about it."

They wrapped their arms about each other and slapped each other's back.

"Hugo," Ralph said, "it feels like just yesterday that we saw you last. You look the same as ever. Even your hair still looks like a freshly shorn sheep."

"And that scar across your face still makes you look like someone I would not want to meet in a dark alley, Ralph," Hugo said as the two of them came together and hugged. "Are the others not here yet?"

But even as he spoke he could see over Ralph's shoulder that Imogen was coming downstairs—Imogen Hayes, Lady Barclay.

"Hugo," she said as she hurried toward him, both hands extended. "Oh, Hugo."

She was tall and slender and graceful. Her dark blond hair was dressed in a chignon at the back of her head, but the very severity of the style merely emphasized the perfect beauty of her rather long, Nordic face with its high cheekbones, wide, generous mouth, and large blue-green eyes. It also emphasized the almost marble impassivity of that face. *That* had not changed from two years ago.

"Imogen." He squeezed her hands and then drew her into a close embrace. He breathed in the familiar scent of her. He kissed one of her cheeks and looked down at her.

She raised one hand and traced a line between his eyebrows with the tip of her forefinger.

"You still frown," she said.

"He still *scowls*," Ralph said. "Dash it, but we missed you last year, Hugo. Flavian had no one to call ugly. He tried it on me once, but I persuaded him not to repeat the experiment."

"He had me mortally t-terrified, Hugo," Flavian said. "I wished you were here to hide behind. I hid behind Imogen instead."

"To answer your earlier question, Hugo," the duke said, clapping a hand on his shoulder, "you are the last to arrive and we have been all impatience. Ben would have come down to greet you, but it would have taken him rather too long to get down the stairs only to have to go up them again almost immediately. Vincent stayed in the drawing room with him. Come on up. You can go to your room later."

"I ordered the tea tray as soon as Vincent heard your carriage approaching," Imogen said, "but doubtless I will be the only one drinking from the pot. It is what I get for allying myself with a horde of barbarians."

"Actually," Hugo said, "a cup of hot tea sounds like just the thing, Imogen. I hope you have ordered better weather for tomorrow and the next few weeks, George."

"It is only March," the duke pointed out as they made their way upstairs. "But if you insist, Hugo, sunshine it will be for the rest of your stay here. Some people *look* rugged but are mere hothouse plants in reality."

Sir Benedict Harper was on his feet when they entered the drawing room. He was leaning on his canes, but his full weight was not on them. And he actually walked toward Hugo. So much for those experts who had called him fool for refusing to have his crushed legs amputated after his horse had been shot from under him. He had sworn he would walk again, and he was doing just that, after a fashion.

"Hugo," he said, "you are a sight for sore eyes. Have you doubled in size, or is it just the effect of the greatcoat?"

"He is a sight to *cause* sore eyes, certainly," Flavian said with a sigh. "And no one told Hugo that multiple capes on a greatcoat were designed for the benefit of those underendowed in the shoulder department."

"Ben," Hugo said and caught the other man carefully in his arms. "On your feet, are you? You have to be the most stubborn man I have ever known."

"I believe you could give me some stiff competition," Ben said.

Hugo turned to the seventh member of the Survivors' Club and the youngest. He was standing close to the window, his fair curls as overlong and unruly as ever, his face as open and good-humored, even angelic. He was smiling now.

"Vince," Hugo said as he advanced across the room.

Vincent Hunt, Lord Darleigh, looked directly at him with eyes as large and blue as Hugo remembered them—lady-killer eyes, Flavian had once called them in order to draw a laugh out

of the boy. Hugo always found his accurate gaze a little disconcerting.

For Vincent was blind.

"Hugo," he said as he was caught up in a hug. "How good it
is to hear your voice again. And to have you back with us this
year. If you had been here last year, you would not have allowed
everyone else to make fun of my violin playing, would you?
Well, everyone except Imogen, anyway."

There was a collective groan from behind them.

"You play the violin?" Hugo asked.

"I do, and of course you would not have allowed the ridicule,"
Vincent said, grinning. "They tell me you look like a large and
fierce warrior, Hugo, but if you do, then you are a fraud, for I can
always hear the gentleness beneath the gruffness of your voice.
You shall listen to me play this year, and you will not laugh."

"He may well weep, Vince," Ralph said.

"I have been known to have that effect upon my listeners,"
Vincent said, laughing.

Hugo removed his coat and tossed it over the back of a chair
before sitting down with everyone else. They all drank tea despite
the duke's offer of something stronger.

"We were very sorry not to see you last year, Hugo," he said
after they had chatted for a while. "We were even sorrier about
the reason for your absence."

"I was all ready to come here," Hugo said, "when word of my
father's heart seizure reached me. So I was prepared to leave almost immediately, and I arrived before he died. I was even able to
speak with him. I ought to have done it sooner. There was no real
need of the near estrangement between us, even though I broke
his heart after I insisted that he purchase a commission for me,
when all my life he had expected that I would follow him into the
family business. He loved me to the end, you know. I suppose I
will always be thankful that I arrived in time to tell him that I
loved him too, though it might have seemed that words came
cheap."

Imogen, who was seated beside him on a love seat, patted his hand.

"He would have understood," she said. "People *do* understand the language of the heart, you know, even if the head does not always comprehend it."

They all looked at her for a silent moment, including Vincent.

"He left a small fortune to Fiona, my stepmother," Hugo said, "and a large dowry to Constance, my half sister. But he left the bulk of his vast business and trading empire to me. I am indecently wealthy."

He frowned. The wealth sometimes felt like something of a millstone about his neck. But the obligation it had brought with it was worse.

"Poor, poor Hugo," Flavian said, pulling a linen handkerchief from a pocket and dabbing his eyes with it. "My heart bleeds for you."

"He expected me to take over the running of the businesses," Hugo said. "Not that he demanded it. He just *expected* that it was what I would want, and his face glowed with pleasure at the prospect even though he was dying. And he spoke of my passing it all on to *my* son when the time comes."

Imogen patted his hand again and poured him another cup of tea.

"The thing is," Hugo said, "that I have been happy with my quiet life in the country. I was happy in my cottage for two years, and I have been happy at Crosslands Park for the past year—though, of course, it was bought with some of my newfound wealth. I have been able to excuse my procrastination by telling myself that this is a year of mourning and it would be unseemly to rush into action as though all I ever wanted was his fortune. But the anniversary of his death is tomorrow. I have no further excuse."

"We have always told you, Hugo," Vincent said, "that being a recluse is not really suited to your nature."

"More specifically," Ben said, "we have compared you to an un-exploded firecracker, Hugo, just waiting for a spark to ignite it."

Hugo sighed.

"I like my life as it is," he said.

"So the fact that you were given your title as a reward for ex-traordinary valor is to mean nothing after all?" Ralph asked. "You are planning to return to your middle-class roots, Hugo?"

Hugo frowned again.

"I never left them," he said. "I have never *wanted* to be a member of the upper classes. I would despise them all collectively, as my father always did, if it were not for the six of you. Pur-chasing Crosslands might have seemed a bit pretentious, but I wanted my own little bit of the country in which to be at peace. That's all."

"And it will always be there for you," the duke said. "It will be a quiet retreat when the press of business is getting you down."

"It's the *son* part that is getting me down now," Hugo said. "He would have to be legitimate, wouldn't he? I would have to have a *wife* in order to produce him. That's what is facing me after I leave here. I have decided. I have to find a wife. Perish the thought. Pardon me, Imogen. I have nothing whatsoever against women. I just don't really want one permanently in my life. Or in my home."

"You are not looking for romance or romantic love, then, Hugo?" Flavian asked. "That is very wise of you, old chap. Love is the very d-devil and to be avoided as one would the plague."

The lady to whom Flavian had been betrothed when he went to war had broken off their engagement when she found herself unable to cope with the wounds he brought home from the Pen-insula. Within two months she had married someone else, a man he had once considered his best friend.

"Do you have anyone in mind, Hugo?" the duke asked.

"Not really." Hugo sighed. "I have an army of female cousins and aunts who would be only too delighted to present me with a parade of possibilities if I were to say the word, even though I have neglected them all shamefully for years. But I would feel out of control from the first moment. I would hate that. Actually, I was hoping someone here would have some advice for me. On how to go about finding a wife, that is."

That silenced them all.

"It is actually quite simple, Hugo," Ralph said at last. "You approach the first reasonably personable woman you see, tell her that you are a lord and indecently wealthy to boot, and ask her if she would fancy marrying you. Then you stand back and watch her trip all over her tongue in her eagerness to say yes."

The others laughed.

"It is that easy, is it?" Hugo said. "What a huge relief. I shall go down onto the beach tomorrow, then, weather permitting, and wait for reasonably personable women to hove by. My problem will be solved even before I leave Penderris."

"Oh, not *women,* Hugo," Ben said. "Not *plural.* They will be fighting over you, and there is much to fight over, even apart from your title and wealth. Go down to the beach and find *one* woman. We will make it easy for you and stay away from there all day. For me, of course, that will be simple, since I do not have a decent pair of legs with which to get down there anyway."

"Now that we have your future satisfactorily settled, Hugo," the duke said, getting to his feet, "we will allow you to go to your room to freshen up and change and perhaps rest before dinner. We will, however, discuss the matter more seriously during the coming days. Perhaps we will even be able to suggest some practical course of action. In the meanwhile, let me just say how very splendid it is to have the Survivors' Club all together again this year. I have longed for this moment."

Hugo gathered up his greatcoat and left the room with the duke, feeling all the seductive comfort and pleasure of being back at Penderris in company with the six people who meant most to him in the world.

Even the rain pattering against the windowpanes only served to add a feeling of coziness.